MW01092735

Copyright

This is a work of fiction. Names, characters, places, and incidents are either the product of the author's imagination or are used fictitiously, and any resemblance to actual persons living or dead, business establishments, events, or locales, is entirely coincidental.

Cover Art by Najla Qamber Designs
Cover Model: Justin Clynes
Editing by Leanne Rabesa
Proofreading by Virginia Tesi Carey

October 2019 Edition
Print ISBN: 9781697810165

Published in the United States of America

DREAMS OF 18

USA TODAY BESTSELLING AUTHOR
SAFFRON A. KENT

Other Books by Saffron

A War like Ours
(Dark enemies to lovers romance)

The Unrequited
(Sexy student-teacher romance)

Gods & Monsters
(Un-conventional coming of age romance)

Medicine Man
(Doctor-patient forbidden romance)

Bad Boy Blues
(Forbidden bully romance)

Blurb

Violet Moore is in love with a man who hates her.

Well, to be fair, she *kinda* deserves it.

On her eighteenth birthday, she got drunk and threw herself at him, causing a huge scandal in their sleepy suburban town.

Now everyone thinks she's a slut and he has disappeared. Rumor has it that he's been living up in the mountains of Colorado, all alone and in isolation.

But Violet is going to make it right.

She's going to find him and bring him back.

No matter how cruel and mean he is, how much he hurts her with his cold-hearted and abrasive ways, she won't give up.

And neither will she think about his tempting lips or his sculpted muscles or his strong hands. The hands that she wants on her body, touching her, feeling her skin…

The hands that make her want to forget everything and kiss Graham Edwards – Mr. Edwards, actually – again.

Because you don't go around kissing your best friend's dad, do you?

Even though that's all you ever dream about.

Dedication

To all the dreamers, the romantics, the outcasts, and
a man named Charles Bukowski...

And of course, the love of my life: my husband.

She was only 16...

I'm a lover of bad things.

Or so people say.

By people, I mean my mom.

My mom, Victoria Moore, says I love the things that are completely wrong for me. She's been saying that for as long as I can remember.

In fact, her favorite story to tell at her famous dinner parties is how when I was little, I'd steal strawberries from the kitchen and hide in my closet.

One by one, I'd eat them all and within thirty minutes of that, I'd start throwing up. So much so that my nanny would have to take me to the emergency room, because my mom *does not* look good under hospital lighting. Cue exaggerated laughter from her riveted audience, that reached me from where I'd hide under the stairs.

After a number of such trips, they found out that I was

allergic to a certain component in strawberries, and that was the reason for my nausea.

So one day my mom sat me down – my dad was away on a business trip or maybe he was getting drunk in his study; I can't remember that part – and told me that strawberries were wrong for me.

They are bad, she said. And if I didn't want to spend my days throwing up, I should stay away from them.

My answer was, "But I love strawberries, Mommy. And I'm not afraid to throw up because of them. It's kinda fun."

I was like five or something.

Mom sighed, took a sip of her chardonnay – she loved her alcohol as much as Dad – and looked away from me. To my nanny, she said, "Take her away, please. She's giving me a headache."

I give people headaches. That's my other thing.

But that's not the point.

The point is: I like bad things.

I like things that are wrong and harmful and maybe even toxic and deadly. Or almost deadly, like strawberries. Things that no one in their right mind would like.

Maybe I was born a little weird, a little off-beat.

Or maybe I'm too evolved to feel fear or caution. I don't know. All I know is that I want strawberries today. Like seriously. I've got a real craving for them.

I mean, if I can't have strawberries today, then when can I have them?

Today's my day.

Or at least, it should be. Not that anybody remembers it

but still.

Today's the day I was born, and well, there's a story for that, too.

Sixteen years ago, my mom gave birth to *moi* at Mount Sinai Hospital on the Upper East Side of New York City.

She didn't want to.

Not even a little bit.

I wasn't a part of her plan. Especially not after having my sister, Fiona, only a year before. Plus the fact that my father was out of town when I was conceived made it a little difficult for my mother to explain my existence inside her womb.

So she tried to get rid of me before I started to grow from fetus to an actual baby.

She went to a doctor to have her pregnancy terminated, thereby hiding all evidence of her infidelity. It wasn't as if no one knew of her extra-marital affairs. But before I accidentally got planted inside her, no one could've proved it.

Anyway, the doctor said that it was kind of not possible because she was too far along. So she had to keep me and less than nine months later, I was born.

Violet May Moore.

The living proof of my mother's exploits.

How do I know all this? Because my mom told me once.

She doesn't know that I know. She was totally wasted and in a very bad mood because she'd gotten a call from my school that I was flunking out of biology.

Again, that's not the point. My illegitimacy and the questionable circumstances surrounding my birth, nor that my own mother tried to kill me before I was born.

The point is that I want strawberries for my birthday and I know if I eat even one, I'm likely to spend my day throwing up my organs.

The question is: do I wanna commit to that? Do I want that kind of pain on the day that I was born?

I'm lounging in my bed and listening to a song about Brandy. She's a fine girl who serves whiskey and wine to all the lonely sailors. Apparently, she'd make a very good wife.

I chuckle to myself.

It's by Looking Glass, a pop/rock band from the early seventies.

I'm a lover of vintage music. Yet another thing of mine.

Wearing giant headphones, I'm nodding my head to the beat when my door bursts open. I don't even have the time to squeak with shock before a flash of pink and blonde streaks across my room and drops down in front of my window.

It's my sister, Fiona.

I tear the headphones off and jackknife into a sitting position. "What the…"

She's grabbing my windowsill and practically hanging out of the window, chanting, "Ohmigod, ohmigod, ohmigod."

I spring out of my bed in fright. "What the fuck are you doing?"

"Can you please not use that language?" she says, without taking her eyes away from whatever she's looking at.

I raise my eyebrows at her. "Is there a reason you're being so nice to me today?"

"I'm always nice."

"Not to me, you're not."

She rolls her eyes. "Can you shut up? I'm trying to concentrate."

I chuckle. "Besides, Mom's not here so you can drop the good girl act. What the fuck are you doing scaring me like that?"

"First, it's not an act. You just don't get it because your mind's always in the gutter. And second, don't you know what day it is today?"

At this, my heart starts beating erratically. Hope can do that to you. It can give you arrythmia.

Honestly, I'm not a fan of hope.

Especially when the giver of that hope is a member of my family. When it comes to my family, it's always better to expect the worst.

I narrow my eyes at her suspiciously. "I think I know."

"So you should also know what I'm doing here."

Okay, so I'm just gonna go ahead and think it: Is she here to wish me a happy birthday?

Because if she is, then it's unprecedented.

It's never happened before.

Last year on my birthday, I stole Mom's choice of poison, chardonnay, and gave myself the worst hangover in the history of mankind.

Which is okay. I mean, I deserved it for drinking that stuff like water, sitting up on the roof, singing happy birthday to myself and watching the moon. I would've gotten away with it too, if not for my lovely older sister, Fiona.

She saw me lurking around the house with the biggest pair of sunglasses, flinching at every loud sound, and immediately ratted me out to Mom.

When I told them it was my birthday the day before and I was just trying to have some fun, Mom's response was to avoid my eyes and plead a headache, while Fiona said, "Oh, I thought your birthday was in December. That's weird."

And then she walked away like I hadn't spoken at all.

So really, I should know better than to hope.

But what if?

What if Fiona remembers my birthday this year? I know Mom and Dad don't. They're not even home. Mom's at the country club and Dad's out of town.

However, it looks like I'm wrong about the birthday thing, and a sucker. Because Fiona hasn't looked away from the window ever since she came crashing through the door. Her eyes are glued to whatever is happening out there.

And there are things happening out there, for sure.

Now that my headphones are off, I can hear them – men talking, thuds of heavy things being dropped on the ground, a truck rolling in maybe.

Pushing my disappointment aside – because hello, this is my family, I *really* should know better – I walk to Fiona. I retrieve a lollipop from the pocket of my shorts and unwrap it, sticking it in my mouth.

Lollipops are another thing of mine.

Giving it a long suck, I ask, "What the hell is happening out there?"

The window in my bedroom overlooks the house next to us. It's been empty for the past couple of months because our neighbors moved away to go live on the west coast.

But it looks like someone's moving in today.

Twirling my lollipop on my tongue, I notice the front yard is overrun by boxes and random pieces of furniture. There's a couple of moving trucks parked out front. And there are people, lots of them. Moving guys from the looks of it.

They are all dressed in navy blue overalls with what's probably their company logo scribbled on their front pocket. A coffee table, a lamp, the thin rectangular box of a TV are emerging from the truck one by one and being carried to the house.

"Why are we spying on these people?" I ask Fiona.

"We're not spying. We're observing."

"Okay," I accept as I watch a few guys haul in a black leather couch. "Well, what are we observing?"

"Don't you ever listen to Mom?"

"Not particularly."

I hear Fiona sigh before she launches into a reply.

I would've listened to it, I promise. I'm not as horrible a listener as my sister thinks me to be. But as I look around, my gaze hooks onto something.

Or rather someone.

A man.

It's not my fault that my eyes won't move from him. Not really.

Because he sticks out. For more reasons than one, actually.

Firstly, he's the only one who isn't in blue overalls. He has a black and white plaid shirt on with a pair of black jeans and the biggest boots that I've ever seen. I think those boots are used for hiking.

I think he's just *come* from hiking, what with how worn and mud-streaked they are, making him look tough and manly.

With my lollipop stuck between my teeth and the side of my mouth, I look at his face and decide that I was wrong.

It isn't the streaks of dirt on his hiking boots that make him look masculine, it's his dark stubble.

Actually, can you even call it stubble if it's thick enough to bury your fingers in? A beard, then. Or the beginnings of one.

It covers his jaw, which is angular and square, broad even. He reaches up and scratches it, drawing my attention to his long fingers and his exposed forearm dusted with dark hair and the winding ridge of a vein.

Bones and muscles, that's what comes to mind when I see him do that, scratch his almost-beard, I mean. And strength.

The kind that I've never encountered before.

I take him in as a whole: his dark messy hair, his wide stance, his squinting-against-the-sun eyes.

Yeah, strength. And masculine beauty.

He can't be from around here. It's impossible.

We live in suburban Connecticut where men wear polo t-shirts, belong to the Yale Alumni Network and play golf in Italian loafers.

I'd shift my gaze and try to discern the logo of the moving company on the vans so I can figure out where he's from, but I just can't look away from him.

In fact, I track his movements.

His steps are long and sure as he comes to the rescue of a couple of moving men. They seem to be flagging under the weight of a giant coffee table. As soon as he lends a hand and grabs one end of it, the men stabilize. Their tense frames relax, and they resume moving toward the house.

Through it all, I notice that he isn't even breathing hard. There's hardly any strain on his body whatsoever, except maybe in his biceps. They swell up under his shirt, stretching the soft fabric.

I don't know why I think his shirt might feel soft to touch but I do. Maybe because everything else about him is so rough and coarse.

Something I know that my fingers have never encountered before.

I watch their progression across the yard, up the stairs, through the porch and into the house via the front door. Even though I knew he was going to disappear, I still feel a tiny bit shocked when he does. Like I just woke up from sleep and awareness is slowly seeping in.

My lollipop is stuck to the inside of my cheek and I tongue it free. My knees are digging into the hardwood floor and up until this second, I hardly felt it. Now, I shift to relieve the pressure on them.

But mostly, it's the awareness in my skin.

It's hot and flushed. And red.

I can see the goosebumps on my wrists, the hairs standing taut and my flesh colored scarlet. It's weird that my hands, clutching the windowsill like Fiona, are blushing, along with the rest of my body.

But they are.

Anyway, I don't have time to think about the whys and hows of it because a few moments later, he comes walking out the door.

He bounds down the front stairs, his thighs strong and powerful. I almost hear the thuds of his boots on the ground. He's stopped by a few moving guys, who reach up to his broad, thick shoulders.

As I watch them all talking, I realize that he might be the tallest man I've ever seen. Tallest man of all. Tallest man there ever was.

In fact, looking at him right now, at how tall and broad he is, I think that *maybe* I should see more people.

Maybe I should be more worldly. I should get out more and notice things around me, instead of keeping my nose stuck in Charles Bukowski and his wisdom, and my journals. Instead of keeping my face almost hidden behind my large headphones and my dull blonde hair that mostly just appears brown with slashes of gold in it.

For some reason, this man makes me feel younger than my sixteen years.

"Oh my God, he's hot," says Fiona.

It feels like she's talking after ages, although I know it's not true. While she was going on and on about something that I should've known already, I was watching this man.

But I do hear her this time. Probably because I've been thinking the same thing.

He *is* hot. And sexy and strong and commanding and just... capable of all the things.

"Yeah, he's hot," I breathe out, watching him run his fingers through his dark hair.

"I can't believe he's moving in next door," Fiona says in the same whispery tone as me.

"He is?"

My voice is squeaky and high. Flushed just like my body.

It makes sense though. That's why he isn't in the uniform. He's the one who's moving in.

Of course.

He's our new neighbor. I guess I just didn't think of it because he's so unlike the people who live here. All stuffy and pale and uptight.

"Didn't I just explain everything to you?" Fiona berates me. "I told you. Mom told us this last week. New people are moving in next door. And Brian Edwards is going to be in your grade. I looked him up online and oh my God, he's so cute. I've been waiting for this day. I wonder where his parents are. You know what? I'm going to ask Mom to invite them over for a welcome dinner or something. I need all the dirt on him. Everything." She squeals beside me. "Can you imagine, him living next door? So freaking cute and sexy. Ugh, I'm dying."

Fiona is a bit of a gossiper. Meaning she knows everything about everyone, and living in the same house as her means that I get to hear almost all of it.

I'm not usually a fan of gossip and rumors but right now I'm kind of thankful for Fiona's love for it. Because I know his name.

Brian Edwards.

That's his name.

Brian.

Bri. An.

And he's in my grade...

"What?"

Fiona's still watching the scene before us but at my sharply asked question, she faces me. "What?"

"Who's going to be in my grade?" I ask, belatedly realizing what she just said. My grade. Parents?

"I knew it. You don't listen at all."

I shake my head. "Can you just... Isn't he a little old to be in my grade and living with his parents?"

We both turn to look out the window.

He's still there but the moving guys are gone. He's with someone else, though. A guy who's wearing a yellow t-shirt – again, not the uniform – and they are talking. I think I saw him lurking in the background before, but I didn't pay much attention to him.

Anyway, this younger guy is cute, I'll give him that. He has dark blond hair and an easy smile. Plus the yellow makes him look cheerful and approachable, somehow.

Unlike the black and white plaid shirt and thick arms of the man I've been watching. They probably – *definitely* – say *approach with caution.*

"Isn't he a little older to be going to school at all?" I ask distractedly, watching the pair.

The yellow t-shirt guy's throwing around a ball and playing

one-man catch with it, as he grins and says something to the man. He answers the younger guy with a slow shake of his head and a slight stretch of his lips that can barely be called a smile.

I almost swallow my lollipop at the sight of it, though. Somehow, his non-smile is sexier than all the smiles I've ever seen.

"What are you talking about? He totally goes to our school," Fiona protests, then breathes out a dreamy sigh. "You know I'm not a fan of yellow but I'm willing to be a convert for him. Because that yellow looks amazing on him."

"He's not wearing…" I begin, but then I trail off because it finally occurs to me.

We're not talking about the same person.

Fiona's talking about the younger guy. The one who's wearing a yellow t-shirt. *He* is Brian Edwards.

Not the plaid shirt guy… man… whatever.

I feel Fiona looking at me and wrinkling her nose. Okay so, she's figured it out too. "Oh my God, are you… Eww!"

Looking away from the man who isn't Brian Edwards, I face Fiona. "What?"

"Have you been perving over that other guy?"

"No."

"Ugh. You totally were. You're so gross." Fiona shakes her head. "He's old, for God's sake."

I feel the need to come to his defense. "He's not old. He's…" I swallow, searching for a better word. "Mature."

And sexy.

Rolling her eyes, Fiona turns away and looks back out the window. "He's forty."

I do the same. "He's not forty."

I mean, yes, he's older. Like probably in his thirties.

It's in every line of his body.

It's in the way his shoulders stretch out his shirt and his strong thighs fill out his jeans. Those muscles, that bulk and hardness can only come from age. From years of work and toil.

From years of living.

Not to mention, his mannerisms and confidence. His authority and command. Again, that comes with age. With knowledge.

Something about that is so breath-stealing.

"I think he's like thirty," I say to Fiona.

I would've said more but right then, Brian Edwards throws the ball up in the air and the man we've been talking about reaches up and catches it before Brian can, in one fluid motion. Like, he just touched the ball and it slid into his big palm.

Talk about athleticism and reflexes.

Whoa.

"Thirty-seven," she counters.

"Thirty-three. Final offer."

She sighs. "Hmm. Okay. Thirty-three." Then, "But still. *Thirty-three*. That's like what? Seventeen years older than you."

"What does it matter how much older than me he is?"

"Um, because you were perving on him?"

"I was not."

I totally was.

"First of all, age is just a number. You're not what your age is. You are what you've gone through. Mark Twain said that age is just mind over matter."

Fiona makes a gagging sound; she hates it when I quote writers and philosophers. In her words, it's lame and weird.

Ignoring her, I keep going, "And secondly, he's handsome. Why wouldn't I look at him? Looking at a handsome man is not perving. Like when I pause the movie when Hugh Jackman takes his shirt off? That's not perving. That's observing. Same as you."

I probably shouldn't have made the Hugh Jackman comment because now I'm wondering the same thing about Not-Brian Edwards.

Him. Shirtless.

I'm wondering if he takes off his shirt and loses that little bit of softness that covers his hard body, will his muscles jut out like sharp and rough peaks.

"Well, I can see that he has a certain kind of appeal." Fiona drums her fingers on her chin. "He's tall. Rugged. Rough around the edges. Very masculine and tough-looking. I'd totally let him mow my lawn."

I grimace. "Okay. Now who's gross?"

"What? I'm just saying. He looks like a good worker. Like he can mow a lawn or carry furniture or whatever. They should probably tip him big. He totally saved the coffee table."

Fiona has her nose up in the air. Her shoulders are thrown back and her spine is straight. Condescension and superiority over mere mortals such as me. My mom has taught her well.

"I'm sure he'll be thrilled to hear that," I say sarcastically, strangely angry on his behalf.

Just because he's a moving guy doesn't mean he deserves to

be belittled. And just because he isn't the one who's moving in next door is no reason to be disappointed.

The latter is for me. Because I *am* disappointed.

More than I should be.

"Aww. Are you jealous?" She giggles.

I hate when my sister giggles. It's usually followed by a cutting remark.

"Why? Because you deem him worthy enough to mow your lawn?"

She outright laughs. "Oh, come on. I'm agreeing with you. He's hot. But you're right to be jealous." She continues in a singsongy voice, "Because you know that if I want him, I can have him."

I can't even say that she's wrong because she's not.

She's right. Very, *very* right.

If she wants him or Brian Edwards or any guy, for that matter, she'll have him. As evidenced by the trail of broken hearts she leaves behind. One of them belonged to our history teacher.

With her shiny blonde hair and blue eyes, Fiona is a complete copy of my mom and a phenomenon. Not only in our school but also on the internet.

My sister, Fiona Elizabeth Moore, is an Instagram celebrity. As in, she has about 50K followers, who moon over her beauty and make-up videos.

Sometimes I can't believe we're sisters, or half-sisters.

While Fiona thrives on attention, here I am, totally okay being invisible.

I always sit in the back of a class. I hardly ever talk to anyone or even if I do, the conversation lasts about two minutes. I always have my head down and my face covered by my hair to stay away from people's eyes.

Honestly though, it's not as if they're giving me any attention anyway, what with my colorless cheeks, great, big brown eyes and super full and weird stung-by-a-bee lips.

But it's fine. I have made my peace with it.

I mean, *someone* has to be lacking so people can appreciate beauty, right?

"Well, if you wanna get him, now is your chance," I say at last. "They're almost done moving in the furniture."

I get up and move away from the window. Suddenly, my lollipop has lost its taste and all thoughts of me sneaking into the kitchen to get strawberries seem stupid.

Suddenly, my birthday spirit has died.

Fiona gets up, too. "It's okay. I'll let you have him. You're the weird one in this family who's going to make all the wrong choices and send our parents to their early grave." She's almost to the door when she stops to face me. "Which reminds me. Don't mess this up for me."

I lie down on the bed, ready to put the music back on. "Mess what up for you?"

"The Brian thing," she explains. "He's in your grade. Which means you guys will be sharing classes. I don't want you to… weird him out, all right? I mean, we're neighbors now so there's no hiding that we're sisters but just stay away from him."

I put my headphones back on and salute her with two fingers. "Gotcha. No weirding out the new neighbor and ruining my sister's wedding plans."

She throws me another sharp look before sweeping her gaze around the room. "And clean your freaking room."

Then she leaves with a flourish, banging my door shut, and I throw a pillow at it. It slides down to the floor with a sad thud.

"Oh, by the way, Violet! Happy birthday! You're only sixteen once so enjoy it," I mutter to myself in Fiona's high voice.

God, I'm pathetic.

I'm so pathetic that as soon as my sister is out of my room, I rip my headphones off and dash back to the window to get a final look at him.

Why? I don't know. But I have to see him one last time before he disappears forever.

But apparently, he's already gone.

He's not there anymore. The front yard's almost cleared out and one of the moving vans is pulling off the curb.

I imagine him in it, his strong hands on the wheel and his long thighs sprawled on the leather seat. I imagine him driving with his window down and his elbow resting on the windowsill, all relaxed and loose, soaking in the summer breeze.

He just looked like that kind of a man. Outdoorsy.

Oh well.

I'm being silly. And slightly obsessive.

As usual, it's about the wrong thing: a man I've seen from afar for maybe a total of fifteen minutes. A man I'm going to forget about by tomorrow.

Shaking my head and sucking on my tasteless lollipop, I walk back to my bed.

But for some reason, I don't wanna forget him. So I bend down and fish out my journal from under my bed. I call it *The Diary of a Shrinking Violet.*

I open to an empty page and write about a tall man in a soft plaid shirt with big hiking boots and rough muscles.

A man I'm never going to see again.

Minutes shy of 18...

I call him the Strawberry Man.

In my head, I mean.

Because he makes me feel exactly how I feel when I'm craving the fruit I'm allergic to: restless and out of control, breaker of rules and avoider of common sense. I know I'm not supposed to want it but I do anyway.

But that's not his name, of course.

His name is Graham Edwards and he's not a moving guy. Which should've been kind of obvious in hindsight since he was the only one, other than Brian, who wasn't wearing a mover's uniform.

Anyway, two years ago on my birthday, he moved in next door with his son.

So really, he's Mr. Edwards – that's his correct nomenclature.

Or Coach.

Because he's the coach of the football team at our school. That explains his good reflexes and athleticism from that day long ago.

People say that he's abrasive. Tough and without mercy. He rides the players harder than any other coach before. They're all afraid of him.

Behind his back, everyone calls him The Beast.

People tend to scatter away and change direction when he walks down the hallway at school. Players tend to keep their heads down and come up for air only when he's passed.

Even a few teachers are afraid of him, but he's the best the school has ever seen.

Another fun fact: he's eighteen years older than me, not seventeen as me and my sister thought when we saw him for the first time.

Over the past two years, I've collected a lot of fun facts about him.

Like he drinks his coffee black.

He only has plaid shirts in his wardrobe, with a few thread-bare t-shirts that he wears over the weekends and which, indeed, seem very, *very* soft. I wouldn't know; never touched them myself.

Well, okay. I'm lying. They *are* soft and I *did* touch them once. After they came out of the dryer, freshly laundered. Long story.

Anyway, he goes running every morning at four. No exceptions. Even though he has trouble sleeping at night.

I found that out probably the first week of him being here. I can't sleep at night, either.

I'm the child of night and the moon. A moonchild.

I like the dark. I like being awake and alone when everyone else in the neighborhood is sleeping. I like climbing up to the roof with vintage music in my ears, a lollipop in my mouth and my journal. Under the flashlight, I write about my day. Sometimes I read Bukowski because he's the kind of a writer you read at night.

For the past two years though, I mostly watch him. I sit on the roof for hours, dangling my legs and sucking on a lollipop, wondering.

What keeps you up, Mr. Edwards?

Why can't you sleep?

Unlike me though, he's never watching back. He doesn't even know that I'm there. Instead, he does interesting things. He swims laps around his pool. He exercises. Or he works in the backyard on his passion project.

Oh man, his passion project.

I'm so in love with it. I love watching him work on it.

I'm not a stalker. Not at all. I know that all this knowledge that I have of him might seem stalker-ish. But it's not.

It's not as if I went looking for these facts about him. They just fell into my lap because his son, Brian? He's my best friend.

Incredible, right?

It's still as unbelievable to me as it was two years ago. In fact, I had no intention of being his friend and 'ruining' things for Fiona. But he was persistent. He wouldn't take no for an answer. He'd say hi to me whenever he saw me; sit beside me during lunch; talk to me in the hallways when no one ever did. Frankly, he kinda freaked me out a little bit in the beginning with his cheerfulness and interest. And then, we got paired up for a lab class and well, the rest is history. We became the best of friends.

And everything would be awesome, if not for this one little thing.

A thing called a crush.

I have it and because of that, when I close my eyes, I see him.

His dad.

Yeah, I have a crush – a massive, *massive* crush – on Mr. Edwards, my best friend's dad.

How wrong is that, right?

Right?

So, so wrong.

I'm probably breaking all the cardinal rules of friendship. In fact, I broke them even before Brian and I became friends because I inadvertently watched his dad the day they were moving in.

Ugh, why do I like the wrong things? *Why?*

But there's a silver lining.

You see, it's a crush – just a crush and not love.

Thank God, it's not love.

Thank. *God.*

There's no way it can be love. I don't know anything about love. It's not like I'm rolling in it. My dad hardly pays me any attention. I drive my mother to drink. My sister barely tolerates me. Before Brian, I had no friends.

But most of all, how can you fall in love with someone you haven't even talked to?

Mr. Edwards and I, we haven't had a single conversation

in the two years that he's lived next door. In fact, he's never even looked at me once.

Not once.

I'm not kidding. I don't think that Mr. Edwards knows that I exist, even though I'm his son's best friend.

Although, some of it is my doing.

After it became apparent that I had this massive crush on my best friend's dad, I stopped going over to Brian's house. I'd make excuses and avoid setting foot in a place that smelled so like Mr. Edwards: all spicy and musky. It got so bad that Brian would keep talking and I'd sniff the air just to smell more of his dad, completely tuning him out.

That's creepy, right?

So, I avoided going there and instead, started to have Brian over to my place. Which we've debated about quite a few times.

"Why can't we hang out at my place?" he asked me one time, while we were in my room, doing homework.

I pursed my lips, still keeping my eyes on the notebook. "We hang out at your place."

"No, we don't." Then he sat up straight, all blond and broad – not as broad as his dad though. "And I think I know why."

Thank goodness I was sitting at my desk and my head was bent over my homework so I could hide my face from him. My blushing, heated face.

"There's no reason," I said quickly.

"It's my dad, isn't it?"

"What?"

Oh God. Oh God. Oh God.

"You're scared of him."

At this, I had to look at him because… what?

"What?" I repeated my thought.

He had his arms crossed over his chest as he raised his eyebrows at me. "You are. It's because he's such a hardass, isn't it? You're scared of him."

"I'm not scared of your dad."

Quite the opposite, actually. I was afraid of the fact that I *wasn't* afraid of his dad at all. I was afraid that if his dad looked at me in front of Brian, I'd blush so badly that my secret would come out.

"Come on, Vi. You can tell me." He wiggled his eyebrows. "You can tell me anything. You can tell me all your secrets."

Um, I think not.

I threw a pencil at him and his goofy moves. "You're crazy."

He thumped a fist on his chest, going all macho on me. "What, you think I can't protect you? Come on, Vi, I can take my dad for you. You know I'll keep you safe. There's nothing to be afraid of."

I wrinkled my nose when he winked at me. "Yeah, why don't you save your flirting for the girls who're actually interested?"

"Well, if you gave me one indication that you are one of those girls, I'd leave everyone for you."

I rolled my eyes at him and his strangely grave voice before going back to my homework.

But then, that's Brian.

Completely crazy and goofy and oozing with boyish charm. Every girl at school wants him and every boy wants to be his friend.

So totally different than my weird, shy self and somehow we're friends.

Anyway, after a lot of avoidance and making myself scarce around Mr. Edwards, it's safe to say that I haven't exchanged a single word with him in two years.

So how can it be love?

How can it be that gravity-defying, soul-deep, bone-tingling, epic-as-fuck connection when we haven't done something as basic as have a conversation?

It can't be and it's not.

I don't even know the man. Not really.

All I have is a few scraps of useless information that I've either observed or heard from his son. That shirt-touching thing? It didn't happen because I broke into Mr. Edwards's room in the middle of the night to try to feel his clothes up. It happened because I was helping Brian with the laundry and I just… accidentally on purpose touched it a little.

Even so, how would Brian react if he knew that I was some kind of a creepy information-hoarder? That I watch his dad at night and that I love his plaid shirts?

He would flip out and dump me as his friend, that's what.

But more than that, he'd be hurt and I can't do that to him. I can't hurt the only friend I've got.

So I've decided to leave.

We've graduated from school now and I'll leave at the end of summer and go to a small college on the west coast. Brian is going to Columbia – his dream school. In fact, he's leaving early to start his new campus job there and even though we'll be apart, and I'll once again be friendless, I couldn't be happier for him. He deserves it for being such a hard worker.

But that's like, a month away.

Right now, it's a little before midnight. In only a few minutes, I'll be eighteen and I'm sneaking out the window of my bedroom on the second floor. But instead of climbing up to the roof, I'm making my way down using the branches of the tree that's been there for as long as I can remember.

My family went to sleep ages ago and like always, they're not going to remember my special day. Hence, I'm making my own arrangements.

It started with a little piña colada, the stuff for which I stole from my parents' liquor cabinet. I made myself one while listening to "The Piña Colada Song." Just seemed appropriate for the occasion.

Now on tipsy legs, I make my way across the driveway and step into Mr. Edwards's backyard. It's all dark and silvery and is visible in outlines, except for one thing.

This little garden toward the back – a rose garden.

It's laid out in a semi-circle at the far corner, adjacent to the wooden fence, and somehow the fat, buttery moon is directly up above it. I can see the roses, a mix of red and pink, their stems swaying slightly with the midnight-summer breeze.

As soon as I reach it, I kneel down on the ground. I'm in my shorts so the blades of dry grass tickle my bare knees and calves. Bending down carefully because, well, I *am* a little buzzed, I smell the nearest rose.

A rush goes through me as the scent hits my nostrils.

It slams the back of my mouth and fills up my lungs like smoke. Like a big drag of marijuana that makes you a little dizzy and lightheaded. A little euphoric. Brian insisted that I try it last year for the first time and we couldn't get the grins off our faces for hours.

Smelling these roses is sort of like that.

It makes me smile stupidly. I rub the tip of my nose against the velvet petals, feeling mellow and happy.

It's his garden, see.

Mr. Edwards's.

He's the one who grows these beautiful, fragile, colorful things. *This* is his passion project.

I've seen him kneel right where I'm kneeling. He bends the same way as me, curling his big, muscular body over these plants. He turns the soil, waters it, weeds out the dried leaves, the dying petals.

He takes care of them with his dusky and what I assume to be work-roughened hands. All in the darkness of the night, like he's doing something bad and criminal and can't bear for anyone to find out this little spot of softness in him.

It's hard to believe that someone so rugged and so harsh like him likes to grow these pretty, soft flowers. So hard to reconcile this with his silent, athletic, beastly personality, but there you go.

The beast likes the beauty of the roses.

Once I'm done smelling them, I focus on the ones that appear to be on the verge of dying.

There are a few of them and reaching over, I pluck them all off. I have four dying roses, all red once upon a time but now yellowed and curled over the edges.

I can't see them crumbling so I pick them off just when they are about to fall apart and put them in the pages of *The Diary of a Shrinking Violet*.

I bundle my roses together, careful of the thorns, and stand up. My legs are a little unsteady from the booze but I manage.

As soon as I turn around though, I almost come back down on my knees.

Because right in front of me, not even five feet away, is Mr. Edwards.

Mr. Edwards.

The man that I've just been thinking about. Although I'm always thinking about him, but still. He is here.

Here.

Like, right in front of me.

I blink.

Yup, still there.

How is that possible?

Am I dreaming?

I have to be.

He's not supposed to be here. He's not supposed to be home tonight.

"Should I be calling 911?"

His voice in the quiet of the night makes me flinch. It's a reaction suitable for voices that you haven't heard before.

It's not true in this case, though.

I've heard Mr. Edwards talk before. Either with Brian or with a student at school, with neighbors. He doesn't talk much.

But he does offer occasional dry, sarcastic, sometimes cutting comebacks.

"You do understand English, don't you?" he asks again, in a low, dusted-with-sand voice. A mix of a growl and a hum.

This time with a slight rise of his eyebrows and an arrogant, almost a superior look on his face that again, I've seen a number of times before.

"I…"

"You what?"

Okay, for the last time… is he *really* talking to me?

"I'm not sure." I answer my own question, which he obviously takes to be the answer to *his* question.

"You're not sure about what?"

"I'm not sure if…" I suppress the urge to glance back to see if there's someone else around, and continue, "If you're real."

What a stupid thing to say, Violet.

At this, he takes a moment to answer. His eyebrows have come down, but now there's a frown between them. Not dark and deep like when one of his players fails to circuit around the field within the specified time, but light and somewhat curious.

"Why, you do this a lot?"

"Do what a lot?"

"See things that are not there."

"No."

"You sure?"

"Yes."

He doesn't look convinced. So I try to get my act together.

"This is going horribly wrong." I lick my dry lips because

Jesus Christ, *I'm talking to him*. "I'm sorry. I, uh, you probably don't know who I am. I'm Violet. Violet Moore. I, uh, live next door. With my parents and my sister. Her name's Fiona. You've probably seen her around. She's in college right now but she's visiting."

Yikes.

What a moment to ramble.

"Oh, um, and I'm a friend of Brian's," I continue with a slight smile. "I go to school with him. In fact, I go to the same school you coach at. Go…" I squint, trying to get our mascot right. "I wanna say wolves. Go wolves?"

I pump a lazy fist up in the air for emphasis.

The truth is that I know nothing about sports and even less about football. Before the Edwardses came into my life, I hadn't even seen a single game played, either in real life or on TV.

But now, I see them.

Well, mostly I see Mr. Edwards, standing on the sidelines of the field, looking fierce and scary. But still.

"Lions," he murmurs, his gaze flicking to the fist for a second before coming back to me, his arms folded across his chest.

"I'm sorry?"

"Go Lions. Not wolves."

"Right. Go Lions." I lick my lips again – why the fuck am I running out of moisture when I'm sweating so much? "I don't know a lot about football, to be honest."

Mr. Edwards tips his chin at me. "So, a friend of Brian's, what are you doing sneaking into my backyard in the middle of the night, stealing my roses?"

Oh, fuck.

I'd completely forgotten about the flowers. Now, I feel them plastered to my rapidly breathing chest, my fingers wrapped around the stems in a death-grip.

Should I lie?

And say what? I *am* holding the flowers.

Besides, I don't wanna lie to Mr. Edwards. I lie to everyone now and then but I *never* wanna lie to him.

I tuck my hair behind my ears with my free hand and explain, "I only took the dying ones. Not the good ones."

Like that makes it any better. But I honestly don't know what else to say.

Mr. Edwards throws them a distracted glance like he couldn't care less about the flowers. "Yeah? Why not the good ones?"

At his question, I lower my eyes to them. I finger the yellowed edges lightly. Some of the petals are so loosened and dry that a puff of air could make them fall apart.

Poor babies.

"Because no one else wants the bad ones," I say.

"And you do."

I look up. "Yes. I always want the bad ones."

Bad things. Bad roses. Bad crushes.

His frown gets even deeper. I almost wonder if he's doing himself a permanent injury by frowning this much. "Why's that?"

"Because everyone wants something pretty," I blurt out, even though I have a feeling the answer won't matter to him. Nothing about me matters to anyone so why would something change now?

Even so, I keep going. "Something that's fresh and beautiful. Something that's perfect. But then, what about the things that are imperfect? Things that might not be as pretty or as conventional. Things that might be weird, outdated or outcast? They're not in much demand, are they? They're not wanted. But I do. I want them. So they don't feel rejected."

Wow, I don't think I've ever talked this much. Not to a person I've never spoken with before. I'm usually the non-talker but something about Mr. Edwards is making me wanna talk.

Something about him has sucked away all my shyness. Or maybe it's the buzz of piña colada.

Throughout my heartfelt speech, he kept his focus on my face, on my un-pretty, un-beautiful and imperfect face.

But now, his eyes have moved.

They're hazel, by the way. He's got hazel-colored, chameleon eyes. They change color. They go from green to brown to green again. I've never seen it happen in real life, though. I've only seen photos that Brian has showed me.

And his chameleon eyes are on my hands.

I look down and find that I'm moving my finger up and down the bumpy stems of the roses, grazing the thorns slightly. Not only that. My thumb is flicking the fragile petals, very slowly and carefully, lovingly even.

At his continued stare, my hands blush.

"Do your parents know you're here?"

I focus back on him and catch the end of his eyes flicking up and coming back to me. Although I do witness the complete clench of his jaw. His almost bearded jaw.

He's annoyed, I think.

"No," I reply on a whisper that comes out strangled. "I mean, they won't care."

"They won't care you're talking to a strange man in the middle of the night."

"You're not a stranger. You're my neighbor."

He leans toward me, even though we're still a few feet apart. And I swear to God, I feel the air around me grow hotter because he moved a micro-inch toward me.

"That's how little girls like you end up getting kidnapped. Because they think talking to their neighbor when everyone else is sleeping is a great fucking idea."

God, he's so stern.

I mean, I knew that. But I didn't know the effect it would have on me if he got stern with me, specifically.

All the wrong effects. The quickening of my breaths and the urge to smile.

Seriously, how am I not shy in front of him?

Not to mention, I didn't know how it would feel when someone called me little.

I know I'm little.

I'm 5'2" on my best day and he's at least 6'5" on all of his. I was right the first day I saw him. He is the tallest, broadest man, at least in Cherryville, Connecticut. He towers over everyone that I know and now that he called me little, I should be embarrassed by my size.

Shouldn't I?

But again, I'm not. No embarrassment. No shyness.

All I can think about is how he can pick me up with one hand and how I can perch on his thigh like it was a log from a tree.

"Are you going to kidnap me?" I ask with amusement in my voice.

"No, I don't want the hassle. I'm more of a serial killer type."

Oh man, he's funny.

"You can't murder me, Mr. Edwards. You'll end up in jail."

He takes a few moments to answer. "Strangely, I don't care about that right now."

I look down at my red sneakers for a second, trying to control my smile. "I –"

"Leave."

A muscle jumps on his cheek and everything slows down inside of me. I have to part my lips to drag in a breath because, well, I'm not afraid at all.

I'm not afraid of that lash of a sound that came out of him.

But I saw something. When I was looking down at my sneakers, I saw his shoes.

They aren't his usual hiking boots – he's had the same pair since he moved in. He isn't wearing his usual jeans, either. Also, not his plaid shirt.

I can't believe I didn't notice before.

He's in fancy clothes.

Being single, every once in a while, Mr. Edwards puts on fancy clothes – dress shirt, neatly pressed pants and dress shoes – and goes out on a date.

I knew he was going to go out tonight; Brian told me. But

I didn't know that he was going to go *out* out.

He hasn't been on very many dates but he does go out sometimes. And every time he does, I picture him with a sophisti-cated, pink-champagne drinking, lobster-eating woman and it feels like someone's sticking me with needles or peeling off my skin or making me eat strawberries when I don't want to.

My nod is jerky, as all my smiles and euphoria go out of me. "Yeah. I'm sorry. I didn't mean to disturb you."

I take a couple of steps toward my house. But my feet prove to be drunk and uncooperative, making me flounder.

Even before my world tips, I know I'm going to fall.

Miraculously though, I don't.

Instead, I'm plastered against something solid and heated. Something expansive and breathing.

I'm plastered against Mr. Edwards.

"You're drunk," he bites out as his fingers dig into the sleeves of my t-shirt.

"I'm not," I say automatically, staring up at him, my hand catching hold of his shirt at his chest.

Soft, *soft* fabric hiding hard, sculpted pecs that I've seen on summer days when he takes his shirt off and mows the lawn.

"I can smell it on you," he growls.

"I could be a little tipsy though," I reply quickly.

His eyes – those *gorgeous* eyes – narrow.

"But only because it's my birthday," I add.

"So you thought taking it out on your liver was a good idea."

"No. I was just… listening to this song and it made me

want a piña colada."

"Unless it's your twenty-first birthday, which I don't think it is, you should've made it a virgin."

"I'm eighteen."

At my blurted-out reply, the muscle on his cheek lunges. It's not a jump; it's a tight lunge. His fingers jerk around my arm.

"Definitely a virgin, then," he says and his voice goes harsh as well.

My teeth find my lower lip and bite it hard.

Virgin.

Yeah, I'm definitely that.

Of course, he didn't mean it that way. It's my own dirty, twisted mind.

"And you're eighteen years older than me. So that makes you thirty-six," I say needlessly.

"If you're trying to impress me with your math skills, you should know that it's useless. Try Mr. Gunderson."

Mr. Gunderson is our math teacher and one of the few who's afraid of him. He'd be happy to see me take an interest in the subject but fuck that right now.

Right now, all I care about is him. Mr. Edwards, the football coach, my neighbor and my best friend's dad.

My crush.

Who just came back from a date.

"What's useful then?" I ask him. "If I'm trying to impress you?"

What?

What am I saying?

His stomach hollows out on a breath and despite myself, I fight not to close my eyes at how intimate it feels, him breathing against me. His tight, hard abdomen moving against my delicate ribs.

Everything about me feels delicate pressed up against his body, more delicate than the dying roses that are trapped between us.

"Stepping away from me would be a good start," he grits out in an abraded voice.

He's right.

I should step away, but I can't. Not yet.

"I don't... I don't make it a habit to sneak into your backyard. I swear to God. And you weren't supposed to catch me, anyway."

"What was I supposed to do, then?"

"Not be here. You were supposed to be on a date, right?"

God.

Did I really just ask that?

Did I *really* just ask that like I have a right to know?

What's wrong with me? What's happening to me tonight?

Apparently he's thinking the same thing, because he draws closer to me; his sharp face, with jutting-out cheekbones and angled jaw and heavy brows, blocks out the stars and his fingers around my arm are probably in the process of leaving marks.

"Who said I was on a date?"

Your clothes. And shoes.

"Because, uh, Brian told me."

"Brian told you."

"Uh-huh." Not a lie technically; he did tell me, but he didn't mention his dad was going on a date. "Plus, it's Friday, right? People go on dates on Fridays."

My explanation isn't making any difference as far as Mr. Edwards's anger is concerned. If anything, his features are turning even angrier and harder.

So obviously, I keep talking, "Not that you do. Go on dates, I mean. I don't mean to imply that you're a serial dater or a player or anything. Just so I'm clear. In fact, all I've ever seen you do is coach football and take care of Brian. Which is amazing, you know. It's not…" I swallow. "Not every parent takes care of their kid. Brian's very lucky. You're a good dad. You really are."

I totally wasn't expecting my ramblings to take this turn but now that they have, I can't deny it. It's the truth.

He *is* a good dad.

Brian told me that his mom, Cynthia, left him when he was just a baby. Only a few days old. It was a one-night stand and his mom didn't want the responsibility so she left Brian with Mr. Edwards and never looked back.

He also told me that Mr. Edwards had a scholarship from a college to play ball but he gave that up when Brian came into the world.

Mr. Edwards has always been very upfront about it with his son. Brian says that his dad thinks he should have all the information because him getting abandoned by his mother is not his fault and is not something to be ashamed of.

In fact, the night we were smoking pot, Brian got really emotional – he's super emotional and passionate, actually – and said, "I lucked out, you know? My dad's probably the best man I know. Like, he's given up so much for me. I wish I could do the same for him some day."

It makes me feel warm, how caring and protective and responsible Mr. Edwards is. So unlike anyone I've ever known.

"Go home."

His words, spoken with finality, break my thoughts. He even lets go of my arm and straightens up.

Even though it's night, the world suddenly seems too bright as his shadowy, looming presence goes away.

But I'm still holding onto him, his shirt.

I'm addicted, it feels like.

To talking to him. To being looked upon by him. To not feeling shy with him.

"Violet."

The way he says my name for the first time ever – low and rough like a secret – makes me think that he means someone else. Someone pretty and sexy.

Someone who has a right to say his name back.

"Graham."

"Who said you could call me that?"

His words are almost a snarl and I wince. "But you just –"

"That's Mr. Edwards to you."

"Right. Okay. M-Mr. Edwards."

His gaze dips to my parted mouth before he jerks it away. "You don't want to spend your birthday behind bars, do you?"

"No."

He looks down at the roses I stole, still crushed and trapped, before gazing up. "Then step away from me and go home."

I should.

He's right.

If all the information I've collected over the years is right, then I know he'll make good on his threat. He'll call the cops on me.

But if I moved away and went home, then this would be over. This whole surreal, moonlight encounter will disappear.

It took me two years, *two fucking years*, to be this close to him. To have him *see* me.

To finally find out that I come up to his chest when we stand like this. That when I take a breath my breasts brush against his ribs and that if I were to lean forward and put my forehead on him, I'll barely touch his collarbone.

Two years.

I can't move away.

I look at his lips. "Mr. Edwards?"

"Step. The fuck. Away."

There's a warning in his tone. An urgency, even. Or maybe it's me. I'm the one filled with all the urgency that this is my only chance.

The only chance to know how it feels.

I keep watching his mouth. "It's my birthday."

"Go. Home."

For two years, I've been good.

I never wanted anything from him. I never expected anything. I never even tried anything with him. I've kept my distance, knowing he's my best friend's dad.

But for one second, I wanna forget.

"I can't."

And then, I step up on his date-shoes.

I'm probably ruining them but this is the only way. This is the only way I'll reach his mouth.

This is the only way I'll get what I want.

A kiss.

"Violet."

This time, it feels like he's smashing my name between his teeth but I'm so far gone that it doesn't make me stop.

Just a brush of my mouth over his. Just one taste before I go to the west coast and leave him behind.

This could be my goodbye.

Besides, no one is here. It's dark. No one is going to know. No one is going to see. It's safe. I can kiss him and run away.

"Step away from me before I make you," he threatens.

I should probably heed it.

But I know I'm not going to.

Bukowski said to let the thing that you love kill you. Not that this is love but it's okay if he kills me for this.

"I just wanna know how it feels. Just once. Please."

Without another word, I reach up and put my mouth on his.

I feel the roses getting completely crushed between our bodies. I even feel the prick of thorns in my chest.

But nothing compares to the softness and heat of his mouth.

It's a dry kiss. A hard pressing of mouths. I feel him breathing against me and that makes me so hungry for him. Hungrier than I've ever been for anything.

Even strawberries.

Just when I peek out my tongue and go to taste him, everything falls apart.

"Dad?"

It's Brian's voice.

And then, "Violet?"

Holy fuck. That's Fiona.

I jerk away from Mr. Edwards and spin around to find a shocked Brian and an open-mouthed Fiona.

"It's not... I didn't..."

I don't know what to say in the face of their horrified, grossed-out, betrayed, you name it, emotions.

"We didn't..."

I look at Mr. Edwards, only to find that he never moved from his spot.

He's standing there, turned away from them, his jaw gritted and his dark, angry eyes on me.

Just me.

And my dying roses are lying crushed and scattered at his feet.

Part I

1

On the day I turned sixteen,
I saw a man
who reminded me of deadly
pink strawberries and
great breezy outdoors

-The Diary of a Shrinking Violet, Age 16

Ten months later...

He's staring at me.

Like, really.

At first, I didn't notice. I had my head down and my head-phones on, listening to "Surrender" by Cheap Trick. But then, I felt a little prickling in my scalp and I looked up.

This guy is sitting right across from me and his eyes are glued to mine.

I'm not sure why.

Does this guy know who I am? Does he know what I've

done?

But that's impossible, right?

I mean, look at where I am.

I am at a coffee shop in the city, miles and miles away from Cherryville, Connecticut. No one knows who I am in New York City.

In fact, no one knows anyone in New York City. That's the beauty of it. Anonymity.

But why the hell is he staring at me? Why?

Why?

If he knows me – *if* – then doesn't he also know that it freaks me out? I've never been good with people's attention anyway. So if he knows me, doesn't he know what happened to me and how I lost it when people wouldn't stop staring at me and harassing me?

I hate it, okay.

I do.

My doomsday brain has started ticking. I'm already going flush around the throat. My heart is swelling and swelling in my chest and I know it's going to burst.

Not to mention, I'm starting to lose my breath. I'm sweating. My body is itching to curve itself into a ball.

I'm losing it. I'm losing it.

I knew it.

I knew going out of the house was a bad idea. I don't even know why people go out and walk on streets and talk to other people when being alone is just so damn wonderful.

When you're alone, no one's staring at you. No one's pointing fingers at you. No one's snickering or stopping you on the street and asking you questions.

Did you really do it?

Is it really you? From the photo?

Did you really kiss the coach at your school?

But!

But…

Everything is going to be fine. It's going to be okay.

Everything is going to be fucking perfect.

Because I can stop it. I can.

With trembling hands that almost knock my coffee cup down, I reach across the table to get to my baseball cap and my Audrey Hepburn sunglasses.

I put them on. I lower the rim of my magenta cap and inch upon my huge sunglasses and bring my dull blonde/brown hair forward.

Now, I'm covered.

I'm protected against the dark rays of people's eyes.

I fold my arms across my chest and try to breathe.

In and out.

Out and in.

I do it. I keep doing it. I keep breathing. I keep breathing like they taught me back at Heartstone.

"Hey."

The voice makes me flinch and look up. It's my friend, Willow. She's standing by the table and immediately, a rush of warmth flows through my body.

She's blocking me from that guy's eyes.

Everything is fine.

See?

I blow out a breath. "Hey. When'd you get here?"

"Like a second ago." She turns to look at the guy before taking a seat opposite me, appearing concerned. "You okay?"

I sit up and wipe my clammy hands on my shorts. "Of course. Why wouldn't I be?"

Her concern grows. "Because when I came in, I thought I saw you having an almost panic attack?"

I wave my hand. "Oh. That. It's nothing. It's, uh..." I wave my hand some more and clear my throat. "I was just trying to, uh, breathe. That's it."

Sighing, Willow cocks her head to the side. "And you have your disguise on because there's a lot of sunlight in here? And not because that guy was staring at you?"

My heart jumps.

She sounds exactly like my therapist, Nelson.

If he knew that I put on the cap and the glasses to ward off – for argument's sake, let's call it a panic attack – he wouldn't like it.

He'd say, "Violet, you're using these as a crutch."

When in fact, crutches are not so bad. They help me. It *helped* when I colored my hair pink for a while so no one would recognize me. But it was too much maintenance, so I stopped and got myself a disguise.

So what? Shouldn't I be helped?

Besides, I'm fine.

Everything is *fine.*

I smile, or at least, I try to. I'm still recovering from what she calls an almost panic attack brought on by some random guy's eyes on me.

"It doesn't matter. I'm fine. And look, I can even take these off."

I make a big show of taking off my disguise and putting it on the table.

Willow smiles back. "Oh yeah, you definitely can. Definitely. You're *definitely* not denying anything."

At this, my heart doesn't jump. It leaps off my chest and gets jammed up in my throat.

Deny.

I don't like that word.

I'm not denying anything.

I'm not.

So yeah, I can't handle when people stare at me. I can't handle talking to strangers so I never go out of my house, and yes, I use a crutch from time to time.

And okay, fine. I do get panic attacks sometimes.

But can anyone blame me?

I'm used to being invisible.

Ten months ago, the world didn't care about me. They didn't know who I was. They didn't care if I sat in the back of a room or walked down the street with my headphones on or sang along to a song tunelessly in my backyard or climbed up to the roof at night or read books on a park bench.

No one cared that I could disappear into my own world.

But there's no disappearing now. There's no *my own world* when the entire world seems to be watching me.

When my own friend is watching me like I'm about to

blow.

My eyes sting but I blink and take a deep breath.

Everything is fine, Violet.

"Can we please not talk about it?" I almost beg.

Willow stares at me a beat before nodding. "Absolutely. We totally don't have to." Then, she beams. "Let's talk about how awesome my husband is."

I breathe in a sigh of relief and sit back. "Oh yeah?"

"Uh-huh. He bought me this set of all the Harry Potters. Brand new covers. With illustrations. He says it's a wedding present. Can you believe it?"

Willow is a Harry Potter fiend. Like, you can't be her friend if you don't know what Quidditch is and where to find the train that will take you to Hogwarts School of Witchcraft and Wizardry. Oh, and she makes you take a test to determine which house is yours.

I'm a Hufflepuff.

"*That's* your wedding present?" I cup my chin in my palm. "What about other things? Like, you know, stuff that requires a bed and a bedroom."

"Oh, there's that." A dreamy smile. "There's so much of that. But for the record, it does not require a bed and a bedroom. A table, a couch, a floor. A wall. All of that works too."

I wrinkle my nose. "Let's not talk about that. I can't think of Dr. Blackwood in those terms."

So I met Willow while I was at Heartstone.

Okay, so last summer and a little bit of fall, I spent some time at Heartstone Psychiatric Hospital because of how things blew up on the night of my eighteenth birthday.

Actually, that was the only bright spot in all the misery that followed: spending time at Heartstone. I liked it there. I liked how invisible I was. How people didn't pay me any attention. It was peaceful unlike how crappy my life had become.

Oh and I made some friends while on the Inside too.

"Fine. Although I love thinking about Dr. Blackwood in those terms. That's how I got through all those sessions back at Heartstone."

I cover my ears with my hands. "No more!"

She laughs, her face and her signature silver hair glowing.

It's love. Love can do that to you.

No matter how unconventional it is. And Willow Taylor and Dr. Simon Blackwood's love story is unconventional, to say the least.

They are the two people who never should've fallen in love. In fact, there are rules against it.

Things like that don't happen in real life. You don't fall in love with your psychiatrist and you certainly don't marry him over your Christmas break from college.

But somehow all of that happened to Willow and I couldn't be happier for her.

A second later, the coffee shop door opens and the other two members of our little gang step inside: Penny and Renn.

And as usual, they're bickering. That's what they always do.

"I can't believe you did that. I still can't believe you did that," Penny says, disbelief evident in her voice.

Renn shrugs. "Well, why can't you? It's me. What else do

you expect from me?"

Penny shakes her head as they approach our table. "You're gross."

"You're just jealous because you didn't come up with it yourself."

They both drop down in their chairs at the same time. Penny turns to us. "She stole my phone and texted my objectionable photo to Cooper."

Cooper is Penny's lab partner. We all think there's something there but Penny denies it. Renn, who recently gained Penny as a roommate after Willow moved out to live with Dr. Blackwood, is on a mission to find out.

"Like how objectionable?" I ask Renn.

She grins, looking super pleased with herself. "In lingerie."

Penny stabs her finger at Renn. "Which she forced me to wear and then took pictures of, even when I said I didn't want to."

"Oh please. Forced?" Renn addresses us. "She was happy to pose."

"I was not."

"Um, you were. And then, her phone was just sitting there. And this Cooper guy texted. Something like, 'Hey, wanna meet up before the anatomy class to prep for the test?'" Renn shrugs. "Meet up. *Before* the class? Duh. What else could it mean? It was a booty call."

Willow chuckles. "Not necessarily. It could mean exactly what he said: to prep for the test."

Renn frowns at her. "You know, ever since you got married, you're no fun."

Penny acknowledges Willow's statement with a nod. "Thank you, Willow." Then she narrows her eyes at Renn. "And now he thinks I'm a perv who sends nude photos to my classmates."

Willow and I laugh. Renn throws Penny an air-kiss.

"You disgust me," Penny says, turning her nose up.

"I amuse you. You love me."

So, this is our gang: Me, Willow, Renn and Penny.

I call us The Heartstone Sisters because we all met at Heartstone.

All of us were in there for different reasons: Willow for her severe depression, Renn for an eating disorder, Penny for her anxiety, and me?

Well, I was there because I kissed my best friend's dad and ruined everything. And being a ruiner of lives comes with the consequences of a mental breakdown.

I'm calling us sisters now, but it took me a while to become a real member of the gang. In fact, for months I didn't even acknowledge them. Not really.

After what happened last summer, I wanted to be completely left alone. I didn't want to be friends with anyone. I didn't want to talk to anyone. In fact, I didn't want to utter another word for the rest of my life.

But I didn't stick to the plan. These girls didn't let me, and now, we're friends. The ones who make a point to meet every two weeks.

Those are the only times I ever go out, to see the girls.

Our next meeting wasn't until the coming week, but I called it early. It was an emergency.

It *is* an emergency.

I have news and a plan.

"Now, are we done chit-chatting about inconsequential things?" Willow chimes in.

"Yeah. What's the emergency?" Penny asks, focusing on me.

I take a deep breath and sit up in my chair.

They're all staring at me and even though they're my friends and their stares are the ones that I can tolerate, it still makes me squirm in my seat.

Their stares and the fact that I'm about to tell them.

I'm finally going to tell someone about my plan. I've been sitting on it for the past week, trying to gather courage.

It hasn't helped. I'm still as afraid as I was when I thought of the plan a few days ago. But if I can tell this to anyone, it's them.

All right.

"I'm going to Colorado," I say, just coming out with it.

There's a minute of confusion where there's more staring.

"What?" Willow frowns.

"Why Colorado?" Penny frowns too.

"Yeah. Like, for vacation?" Renn asks.

I can't look at them so I stare down at the table, brown and polished and perfect, unlike me. And I just blurt out, "To see him."

Him.

My best friend's dad.

The man I kissed on my eighteenth birthday. The man I haven't seen since.

"You mean... Mr. Edwards?" Willow breaks the silence after a few seconds, guessing correctly.

"Really?" Penny goes in an awed voice.

"You know where Mr. Edwards is?" Renn's eyes are wide.

I nod, still looking at the table.

Again, there's a few moments of quiet while they absorb the news. I expected as much but it doesn't make it easier.

Their silence. The things I know they are thinking. That I can't do this. That I'm too weak, too ill, too fragile for this.

"How'd you find out?" Willow asks.

I sigh and look up. "Facebook."

Renn screeches, "You used Facebook?"

Her voice is high and disbelieving, and I can't blame her for it. I never had any social media accounts, not even when I was in high school. I never saw any point.

I didn't have friends, except Brian who lived next door. There was no one I wanted to keep in touch with or anyone who wanted to keep in touch with me.

So I was practically non-existent.

I shrug. "Yeah. I made an account last month."

"And you never told me?" She's hurt.

"I'm sorry, but it's not under my real name. That would cause mayhem. Can you imagine? Violet Moore, The Slut of Cherryville, Connecticut, is on social media. Hate emails were enough. That's all I can deal with in this lifetime." They all seem to agree. "It's just a dummy account I made to... well, spy on people."

"People like Mr. Edwards?" Penny asks.

"I can't believe Mr. Edwards is on Facebook though," Willow muses.

"Yeah, Mr. Edwards does not seem the type," Renn agrees.

This is not a laughing matter but I can't help but want to at least chuckle.

Like me, they all call him Mr. Edwards. Religiously. Without the pronoun.

He is this great, unknown entity that they're all afraid of and fascinated with and can't call by his first name. In fact, I specifically asked them not to when I finally told them the real story as to why I was at Heartstone and what put me there.

That's Mr. Edwards to you, he said.

It's silly to remember what he said and to actually follow through on his command. Especially when he won't even know if I broke the rules or not.

He's not here.

But that's exactly why I can't say it. *Because* he's not here.

"He's not. I looked. He doesn't have any social media accounts whatsoever." I shrug. "But Brian does and he posted something about doing a cross-country trip with his friends instead of going home to Colorado this summer."

Colorado.

The only thing I know about that place is that it's full of mountains. Also, that it follows Mountain Standard Time, which I didn't know existed until I looked it up. They are two hours behind us.

Now whenever I look for the time, I think about Mr. Edwards and the time he's keeping. And then, my heart starts to beat really fast. It starts to pound, not in the panic attack sort of way, but like I'm still infatuated with him.

Like I still dream about him.

I don't.

Not anymore.

Last summer, I was this naïve little girl who thought that she could take something for herself. She thought that for once, she could dare to touch her dream – something she only saw from afar but never reached for – and no one would get hurt.

But I was wrong.

So I don't dream anymore. I don't even write in my journals. I don't read Bukowski, the miserable bastard whose advice I took and ruined everything.

"Mr. Edwards is in Colorado, then?" Willow's voice brings me back into the moment.

"Yeah. I think he's living in the town he grew up in. Brian used to talk about it, the town, the cabin. I think I know exactly where Mr. Edwards is."

"And you wanna go there?" Renn asks, looking so grave, which happens only rarely.

"Yes."

"What about…" Renn pauses for a second. "What about Nelson? And your sessions?"

"Yeah, you sure you want to put yourself through such stress? I don't mean to sound blunt or anything, but, Vi, look at the coffee shop you chose," says Penny.

I knew it.

I knew they were thinking I'm not ready.

"What about it?" I ask, defensively.

"It's a hole in the wall," she answers. "You can't even see it from the street. There's no one in here except that weird guy who keeps looking over. And it has a back door and it's quite possibly the farthest away from your house with all the above-mentioned qualities."

Okay, so everyone knows how weird I am.

Everyone knows about my front-door phobia – I can't get in through the front door; too much attention. I like backdoors and sneaking in. Not to mention, they know about my disguise and the fact that I'm not well.

But I *am* well.

I am. I am handling things my way.

I narrow my eyes at her.

I narrow my eyes at all of them. "I'm fine. Everything is fine, okay? I'm handling everything."

They don't believe me.

It's okay. They don't have to. Only *I* have to believe that I'm fine.

Positive thinking, right?

I take in a deep breath – probably my eight-hundredth – and unclench my hands in my lap and bring them up to the table. "And I have to do this. I owe it to him to do this."

Finally, Willow asks, "Do what, exactly?"

"Apologize. For what I did to him. For everything that happened."

"For kissing him, you mean?"

"Yes."

"So you're going to go say sorry?"

I open my mouth to answer, then close it. I don't know

how to explain it to them. I don't know how to explain it to myself, even.

I don't know how to put into words what I feel.

Every time I close my eyes, I see him. Not in the way that I used to, through the eyes of an infatuated teenager, but through the eyes of this grown-up girl who has done him harm.

I see his anger.

I see his fury just when they – Brian and Fiona – had caught us. I feel it burning hot even through time and space.

Like it's happening right now. Right this second.

His dark eyes are glaring at me. His chest is heaving under that dress shirt he wore. I see his date-shoes that I ruined by stepping on them to reach his lips. I see the scattered, dead roses.

He looked like I'd ruined his life in that moment, and guess what, I did ruin his life.

He had to disappear because of me.

Finally, I manage a few words. "Sorry. Yeah, that's something to start with. I'm not sure what I'll do next though."

"Vi, you made a mistake," Willow says.

"Yeah. It was a mistake," Renn confirms.

"A mistake that cost everything," I say angrily.

On his behalf.

I'm so fucking mad, not for myself but for what he went through because of me.

"You didn't know what was going to happen," Penny argues. "You didn't know someone was going to see it."

"And take a photo of it," Renn goes on.

"*And* put it on social media for everyone to see," Willow

finishes.

That was done by my sister, Fiona.

Yup, I kissed the wrong man and the whole world found out about it through my sister's Instagram feed. She never liked me after I became friends with Brian so that was her way of taking revenge, I think.

It started with Brian and Fiona, who were coming to surprise me with a cake at midnight and they were meeting up in the driveway before going up to my room.

But then, they saw me.

My sister has never remembered my birthday. And the one time she remembers, I'm out kissing my best friend's dad.

By the next morning, the whole neighborhood knew.

Slowly, the news reached farther because that photo – as blurry as it might be – got passed around and shared and commented on hundreds, if not thousands of times.

When one person called me a slut for kissing my neighbor, the coach of our football team, a man eighteen years older than me, ten different people cropped up and called me the same. People would send me hate emails, proposition emails. I got inundated with *so many emails* from creepy old guys that I had to shut down my email account.

I couldn't go out without being recognized. Everyone in our town knew who I was. They'd stop on the streets and ask me if I was really her, the girl who kissed the coach at her school.

I stopped going out. I stopped even leaving my room. I'd keep my curtains closed, hide myself inside the comforter.

I'd only come out at night when no one could see me and

I could see no one.

And God, the rumors; I'm sure Fiona was the source of them.

The rumors that went around. The theories, all the different versions of what happened.

In one version they said that I'd cheated on Brian who had been my boyfriend of two years. While my *supposed boyfriend* was about to surprise me with a proposal on my birthday, no less.

In a different version, he'd already proposed to me and we were keeping it a secret from everyone and pretending to be best friends. But then, he broke off the engagement – obviously – because I was cheating on my *fiancé* with his father.

In yet another, very twisted version that came a few weeks later, I killed my fiancé. He was so distraught at seeing me with his father that he smashed his car into a tree and died on the spot.

Seriously?

He's alive, people. He has social media accounts where he posts regularly.

This last one stuck with me the most, though, as preposterous as that sounded. It stuck with me so much that this is what I told Renn when I first went to Heartstone.

She kept asking me and asking me and I got fed up. So to scare her away I said, "My fiancé died. I killed him."

That sounded so much worse and more tragic than *I kissed my best friend's dad.*

And sure enough, that stopped her. That stopped everyone from asking the questions. Questions about why I don't talk or why I pull out a chair next to mine: I guess, for Brian; my mind broke down for a while and I missed him so much that I'd pretend he was still my friend.

Anyway, things got so bad for me on the Outside that one night I got super drunk on piña coladas and tried to run away from the town in my car. Only I lost control of it a few miles down and almost hit a tree.

That's when they put me in the hospital.

They called it a mental breakdown before they gave me a proper diagnosis. It's a thing. Mostly, celebrities go through it when people won't leave them alone.

So, I'm a celebrity now: The Slut of Cherryville, Connecticut and I suffer from Panic Disorder, a type of anxiety disorder.

I'm not sure how long the silence has gone on but I break it. "No one told me to go kiss him, you know. *He* definitely didn't. In fact, do you guys know what he said to me? He told me to go home. Repeatedly. Over and over. He told me, '*Violet, go home. Violet, step away from me.*' He kept saying it and I didn't listen. I didn't care.

"You know what I was thinking when I went in to kiss him like a crazy person? I was thinking that it was going to be this one kiss in the middle of the night and that's it. I thought I'd kiss him on the lips and then I'd go home. I thought he wouldn't even remember it in a few days. Or even if he did, I thought he'd consider it a silly, drunken mistake by a teenage girl next door. The worst-case scenario in my head was he might glare at me the next day or say something mean to me or even tell my parents, who wouldn't have cared anyway. So yeah. That's what I was thinking would happen. And through it all, I thought I could just… steal a piece of him for myself. Something that once belonged to this man whom I was crazy about. Something that I could tell my children, even. Something I could laugh about later. I didn't wanna hurt anyone. I was going to move away and forget all about him. It was just my goodbye. A gift for my eighteenth birthday, along with those roses. That's all it was supposed to be."

I sniffle and wipe off my tears. "But it turned out to be this huge disaster that doesn't seem to end."

"Oh, Vi." Willow squeezes my hands on the table. "You have to move on. You have to forgive yourself."

Renn and Penny are looking at me with concern as well.

"I can't. Not until I know that he has. I have to go see him. I have to make sure that he's okay. That... *he's* moved on," I insist. "I keep thinking about him all the time. Everything he went through because of me. All the stigma and rumors. I can't let this go. I-I just have to see if he's doing fine."

Willow nods, although I can still see she's troubled. They all are. But I know that they'll support me anyway.

"Okay, if this is what you want, go apologize. Go do whatever you have to do so you can focus on yourself."

Penny nods too, as she warns me, "I don't think it's going to be easy, though."

Willow agrees. "Yeah, Mr. Edwards does not sound like a guy who forgets *or* forgives easily."

"Yup." It's Renn's turns to nod. "Mr. Edwards sounds like a tough cookie."

I know. I'm aware of that.

I know he's not going to make it easy for me. He probably

won't even see me if I gather enough courage to go knock at his front door, but I'm doing it.

I'm going to Colorado and I'm going to find him.

I'm going to somehow make up for everything that happened.

Because what he went through was worse than everything I endured.

2

I stole a rose today but only to
save it. I couldn't bear the
thought of it lying on the
ground, dead and scattered.
It's his.

-The Diary of a Shrinking Violet, Age 16

The P word.

There are a lot of words that start with P: pizza – I like pizza; prickles – the start of my anxiety; perv – the guy who was staring at me at the coffee shop a couple of days ago.

There are a thousand words with P as the first letter. But there's this particular word that I despise the most.

I hate to think about it. I especially hate to think about the fact that people used it in relation to him.

First of all, it's not accurate. He is not *that*. He can't be that. I was eighteen when I kissed him, and he didn't even kiss me back.

He didn't seduce me. He didn't violate me. He didn't lead me astray.

It was a ten-second kiss, for God's sake. It wasn't supposed to mean anything. It wasn't supposed to be life-changing.

It was a stupid drunken mistake. Mistake like my crush on him was.

It wasn't supposed to turn me into a slut and him into this vile, defiling, sexual predator.

That's what people have been calling him. That and the other P word: pedophile.

If I was crucified in the dark corners of social media, Mr. Edwards was in the local paper, along with the kiss, the photo and an article that I want to set fire to.

The headline read: *"The celebrated coach of Cherryville High caught after-hours and on camera."*

The article blasted his reputation. They called him an alleged sex offender. They said that I was a teenage student and that the best coach that high school had ever seen was taking advantage of me. They knew he was my neighbor so there were speculations. They said that maybe he'd had his eye on me long before he made the move.

The article went on to list all the other places Mr. Edwards had worked at, mostly in Denver, and that even though there was no indication of any misconduct on his part, the board should have a formal inquiry. The truth should come out. Because really, how safe were the kids if we had a teacher like that?

It was a tabloid piece. I don't even think anyone reads the Cherryville Chronicle but that week, they sure did.

The article painted me as innocent, though. An innocent, naïve high school student caught in the clutches of a lecherous coach, eighteen years her senior.

If anyone's lecherous in this scenario, it's me. I'm lecherous. *Moi.*

I tried to fix it, too. I called the newspaper people and demanded that they print a retraction. I told them the whole story. I even went to Principal Jacobs, and told him everything.

He thanked me for coming forward with the information, but he said that I should let the adults handle it.

Yeah, those were his exact words – *let the adults handle it, Violet.*

I wanted to punch him in the face and tell him, check your facts, moron. I am an adult. I'm fucking eighteen.

None of that seemed to matter anyway because a week later Mr. Edwards was fired. He packed up everything and left town.

I've never seen anyone disappear so fast. Like he wasn't even there. Like he never came into my life and everything was a dream.

An elaborate, two-year-long dream that my fevered, lonely brain came up with.

But I'm glad that he left when he did.

I'm glad he wasn't there for the worst of it. When the rumors started to catch fire and more and more people started to know.

So, it's a good thing that he left town.

Only I never saw him after that night.

Mr. Edwards was always so good at making himself scarce and I was so good at avoiding him myself that I hardly ever saw him except in the night. I didn't see him after the kiss, either.

Not even when I went to their house, banged on their door

so Brian would let me in.

Sometimes when I focus on all the bad stuff that happened, especially with Mr. Edwards, I almost forget what Brian went through.

Almost.

He was my best friend. He wanted to surprise me on my birthday and look what happened. I broke his trust. I hurt him so much.

After witnessing my crime, he got into his car and left for the night.

He didn't come back until the early hours of the following morning. I went over to his house to try to explain. He didn't give me a chance. He wouldn't listen to me, no matter how much I groveled.

I decided to try again the next day and the day after that and then yet another day after that. Either he wouldn't open the door or he'd make an excuse and walk away from me. Calls, emails, everything went unanswered, which was so surprising because no matter how much we fought, he'd always say something.

Brian always had something to say. He was always so open and talkative even when he was upset.

And then, he left early for college a week later.

I haven't heard from him since, either.

But I do hear *about* him. I do hear about all the things that he does. Although, I never – not in my wildest, *wildest* dream – could have ever imagined the source of my information.

I shouldn't be surprised though. She does seem to know everything about everything.

Fiona. My sister.

And of course, she knows everything about Brian too because he is dating her now.

Yeah, they're dating.

They started dating last fall. Actually, that's when I snapped. Fiona called me to brag about it and I lost my shit.

That's when I got drunk and lost control of my car.

When they put me in Heartstone, I had a lot of time to think about why Brian would do such a thing when he hated Fiona more than me. She would deliberately try to make my life difficult back in school and Brian never liked her. So it was a shock.

But I think I know the answer.

He did to me what I did to him. I hurt him. I betrayed his trust. So he did the same.

I just hope he doesn't get hurt in the process because according to Fiona's Instagram, they're still going strong.

The only consolation is that when I asked Fiona to never mention my breakdown to Brian, she agreed. Her exact words were, "If you think I'm going to mention Heartstone to my boyfriend, Brian, you really *are* crazy. You're not taking this away from me, not again. For some reason, he chose to become friends with you and your weirdness. I'm not adding fuel to the fire by painting you as this poor, crazy little Violet who ended up at a psych ward and risk being sympathetic to you. So yeah, I'll personally make sure that Brian never finds out."

For once, I was happy to be on the same page with my sister.

I don't want anyone to find out. Ever. Besides, it's in the

past now. I'm on the Outside and I'm handling things.

And I've got bigger fish to fry. That's why I'm here.

In Colorado. In the middle of nowhere, it looks like.

It's a small town called Pike's Peak and Mr. Edwards lives a little over an hour outside of it.

The first thing that I notice when I reach my destination and park my car by the side of the road is that this *road* is endless.

It stretches on and on, flanked by dense trees.

In the midst of all the green and the open skies is a winding dirt path that cuts through the woods and on the cusp of it is a little red mailbox. Or rather it used to be red once upon a time, I think. Now, it looks more rusted than anything.

I should really get out of my car right now.

I've been sitting here, staring at that mailbox and that dirt path for about thirty minutes.

"It's gonna be okay," I tell myself, gripping the wheel tightly. "You can do it. You can face him."

Then, I chuckle nervously. "Really? Can I?"

They told me not to go, my friends.

They did.

They told me that it was a bad idea.

Why did I not listen to them again?

Oh yeah, because I'm crazy.

Puffing out a breath, I sit up and straighten my shoulders. From behind my Audrey Hepburn glasses, I squint at the endless road, the mailbox and the trees.

"Just do it. Don't think."

I jump out of the car before I can change my mind and

start jogging.

A second later, I'm standing at the mailbox. It has the house number on it, along with *Edwards*.

Edwards.

It sends a jolt through my body. So much so that my hand raises itself and my fingers grab hold of the rim of my glasses so I can pull them off and read the letters that make up his last name in technicolor.

But I stop myself.

For some reason, it feels too intimate to see them without the lenses. And I have no plans of feeling any kind of intimacy toward Mr. Edwards whatsoever.

So I move on.

I walk past the mailbox, putting one foot in front of the other. It's hard. But I do it.

The dirt road is littered with leaves, some green and some crunchy yellow. My red sneakers chomp on them as I walk through them and toward what I'm hoping is going to be his house.

Right now, I can't even see it.

Just when I think that I'm going to be walking forever, lost in the thick woods, I reach a clearing.

And in that clearing sits a house that kind of dries out my throat.

Mostly because it's not what I expected but at the same time, it's exactly where I expected Mr. Edwards to live.

On one hand, everything about his cabin is very masculine and woodsy and outdoorsy and tough. It's exactly what I felt when I saw Mr. Edwards on my sixteenth birthday, hauling that coffee table.

But on the other hand, it doesn't look like anyone lives here.

Or anyone can live here.

Because it seems inhabitable. Take the front yard, for example. It's overrun by brambles and wild grass and shrubs that haven't been trimmed in years. There's a snaking stone pathway through them that leads to the stairs, which in turn lead to the porch of the cabin.

Now the stairs and the porch.

Wow. They're made of wood but they seem to be sagging.

In fact, through all the savage flora, I can see that one of the stairs is cracked and a piece of wood is simply hanging there. Like someone's foot just went through it.

And don't get me started on the front door, man.

Like the mailbox, it used to be a different color but now it's all discolored and dull.

Oh and let's not forget the roof.

The roof is pointed toward the sky but that's the only detail I can tell. Because all of it is covered by ivy and something else that I don't even know the name of.

How does anyone live here?

How does *he*?

Because I know he lives here.

It has an air of loneliness to it. If I focused harder, I could smell it. I could smell the old wood, the mothballs, the musty scent of dust. The neglect and disarray and even hate.

Forgotten and lonely.

Just like him. So far away from civilization and aloof.

I shake my head to dispel all these silly thoughts.

I need to walk farther, go to the front door of his house and knock. But I'm not moving. I'm not even looking at the front door anymore.

I'm looking around.

There's a garage on the far right with an old-fashioned barn door, which is padlocked closed. It must hold the truck he used to drive, all black and big and so different from the BMWs of our neighborhood.

The truck I so wanted to ride in but never got the chance.

According to Brian, Mr. Edwards was possessive of his truck. He wouldn't even let Brian drive it. It used to frustrate my best friend to no end.

But I used to find it cute – Mr. Edwards's possessiveness – among other things. Other less appropriate things that I don't want to think about.

The only thing I should be thinking about is apologizing. That's why I'm here.

To apologize. To make up for what I did.

How am I going to do that? I'm still as clueless as I was when the girls asked me about it.

But I have to start somewhere, right? I have to take the first step and go knock on his front door.

God, front doors freak me out.

But it's fine.

I'm fine.

I skip on the spot as if getting ready to go into the boxing ring or something, instead of knocking on a door.

But suddenly, I realize that I might not get an answer, even if I did knock.

Because no one seems to be home. The house sits in darkness.

I take a few steps toward the house, and through the big dust-stained window on the porch, I see the silhouettes of furniture. Maybe a couch and a coffee table. Even a lamp.

But there are no lights on and the sky's getting darker by the second.

I bite my lip and stand there, trying to think about what to do next. Before I know it, my legs are moving forward.

I go around the cabin and look through other windows to confirm my suspicion. No signs of any light or movements. There's no sound except for my own choppy breathing and a slight rustle of the breeze.

He's not home.

I'm relieved.

I'm also disappointed. As afraid as I am to face him, I don't like it that he isn't here.

For a few moments, I thought he was close. He was right here. A knock – as impossible as it is for me to make it – and he'd open the door and I'd look at him after ten long months.

Now I don't know what to do. Where to find him. When I'll get to see him.

If I'll get to see him.

Maybe I should go and regroup, come up with a different plan. And I'm all set to do that but I stop.

Because my gaze falls on something.

Something that makes my heart squeeze in my chest. So much so that I feel like someone is strangling it, suffocating it to the point where I can't breathe.

It takes all my strength, but I move. I get my legs working, and then I'm running toward it.

His garden.

His rose garden.

I almost scrape my bare knees dropping to the ground. I snatch my glasses off and stare at the dead flowers.

The shrubs are bare and thorny, with hardly any leaves hanging on. The red and pink petals are scattered on the ground, warped into themselves.

As soon as I touch a curled-up bloom still attached to the stem, it crumples.

"Oh, poor babies," I whimper.

No one has been taking care of them.

He is not taking care of them. They are forgotten and neglected, thrust into a little corner in his backyard.

Just like this house and him.

Mr. Edwards has always been so meticulous about his roses. So careful and religious about looking after them.

Once Brian told me that Mr. Edwards drove two counties over to get the right brand of peat moss for them because the one they had at our local store wouldn't let the moisture seep through the way that he wanted.

God.

My heart is breaking in a million ways right now and I have

to find him.

Not tomorrow. Not an hour later. But right now.

I have to find him *right this second*.

I have to see him with my own eyes. I have to look at him, ask him about his roses. I have to ask him so many things. I have to *say* so many things to him.

The next thing I know I'm in my car and I'm driving away. I'm flooring it.

I've never driven this fast in my life. Not even on the night I was running away. I go back to the town that I'd only passed through on my drive in.

I literally have no idea what I'm going to do once I get there. But I can't not do anything. Not after what I've seen.

Oh God, the roses.

I'm aware that I'm losing my mind over a bunch of plants. But they're not just plants. They are... *his* plants.

I still have the petals from all the dying roses I stole from him over those two years. I kept them safe between the pages of my journals. The old ones, the ones with my dreams: *The Diary of a Shrinking Violet*.

Forty-five minutes later, I reach the main part of the town. It's kind of a tiny place with a few stores, office buildings and restaurants probably covering about four to five blocks in total. I find a parking spot on one of the streets and jump out of the car with my large hobo bag – that I literally can't go anywhere without – and my disguise on.

I don't even know if he's here. Maybe he's out of town. Maybe he'll come back next week.

But I can ask.

Yes, I'm aware that talking to strangers isn't my forte anymore but it's going to be okay. I'll do anything to find Mr. Edwards.

I will.

And my weird hang-ups won't stop me.

It's a small town. I bet someone will know where to find him. My plan is to go to the bars first and ask about him and –

"Holy shit," I breathe out and halt in my tracks.

Someone bumps into me from behind but I don't move or pay attention to their mumbled apology and my anxious heartbeats.

Because I've found him.

I've found Mr. Edwards.

Or at least, his truck. His black truck is parked across the street, and like a lunatic, I run toward it.

It's definitely his truck.

There's the Connecticut plates – which apparently, he hasn't changed – and that's his plate number that I could recite even in my dreams.

It's parked right in front of a bar. There's a window to the side, a big window, and without thinking about it, I approach it.

The interior is neon-y and dark. The walls are made of dark wood and there are leather booths to the side, along with a few free-standing tables in the back.

The place is somewhat crowded, and I scope through it, looking for him. For that one man for whom I drove thousands of miles and crossed multiple state lines.

And in a rush of breath, I find him.

My legs stagger a bit when I see him sitting in one of the leather booths close to the window.

"Holy fucking shit," I whisper. "Mr. Edwards."

He's here.

I found him.

And God, he's glowing.

Something is illuminating the contours of his body. Even through the tint of my sunglasses, I can tell its sparkly and bright.

It's something out of a dream.

Thousands and thousands of dreams that I've had. Some drunk, some electric. Some psychedelic and stoned. Some lonely and horny.

But all of them about him.

I press my hand even more aggressively on the glass window, probably leaving the print of my fingers and palms.

In fact, I give my entire weight to the thick glass as I watch Mr. Edwards.

He's sitting alone, all shiny and magnificent and I'm finally basking in his light after ten months.

Ten *fucking* months.

Right now, his head is bent and except for the dark mess of his hair, I can't see anything else of his face. His elbows rest on the wood, his strong, veiny forearms exposed.

He caught me with those hands when I stumbled the night I kissed him, my feet tipsy and my body drunk.

I bite my lip as a great big shiver runs down my spine.

I know I'm flushed; I can feel the heat spreading all over my skin. It's the kind of heat I haven't felt in a long time. It has nothing to do with the prickling.

It's different.

It's from the olden days, thick and edgy.

I'm itching to go to him and I don't even care about the logistics of it all, the front door, approaching him through the crowd and all that.

But then, I become glued to my spot like I'll never move again. Because he's not alone anymore.

A woman approaches him.

She's tall, made taller by the heels she has on. She moves toward him slowly and with swaying hips, which look very rounded and soft in the tight dress that she has on.

I can't tell the color of it through the lens of my glasses but I think it's dark and appealing. Mostly because Mr. Edwards lifts his eyes, finally.

So far he's been staring down at the bottle like he doesn't care for the world, like nothing is interesting or worthy of his attention. But now something has suddenly appeared.

As soon as his spiky lashes flutter up and his eyes come into view, I breathe on to the glass, fogging it up.

Those eyes.

Hazel, chameleon, unpredictable.

So unpredictable that I used to make up silly guessing games about them. I used to wonder about the nuances and shades of brown and green when he was unhappy with one of his players.

On the night of the kiss, his eyes appeared black.

I wonder what color they are now, as he's flicking his gaze up the body of the woman, both emotionlessly and with such laziness that I can't help but bite my lip again as I feel every fucking inch of it.

The woman is smiling in what I think is a seductive way, so I guess she can feel it too. The intensity of his eyes.

For some reason, it makes me want to claw through the glass and run to them. It makes me want to stop them.

Should they really be looking at each other that... sexily in a public place? There are people here. There needs to be some decorum.

Then, I forget everything when he deigns to lift his face.

At last, I can see his features. I can see the sharp jut of his cheekbones and that hard jaw. God, he has a beard now.

A beard. Thick and dark. Almost wild like the front yard of his cabin.

At the discovery, I really go and claw my fingers on the glass, digging in my nails.

While the woman who's now bending over him, exposing her fantastic cleavage, buries her fingers in that beard of his.

Mr. Edwards turns to the side and opens his powerful thighs and she steps into them. When she does, he smiles.

Jesus Christ, he's smiling.

Not the full-blown smile. No, he's too serious and too stern for that. It's half a smile. Maybe even less than that: a quarter of a smile. And since he doesn't do it often, or at least I haven't seen him do it a lot, pull up his strawberry lips like that, it has an effect similar to a thunderstorm.

At least, in my heart. Which is pounding in my chest.

He says something to her – I can't hear what obviously

but the shape of his lips and the way they move and stretch makes me think that his words were low and rough. She laughs at them, which in turn makes him smirk.

Oh God.

He's smirking.

Mr. Edwards is *smirking*. Has he ever smirked before?

I press my entire body into the glass like I'm really about to burst through it as I realize this is the way he is with women. This is the way he acts – smirking and lazy and all intense and sexy – when he's turned on.

Is that what he did on that night, as well? He was coming back from a date and I can definitely imagine he went out with someone like her, like this woman, all sexy and mature.

I think I'm having a heart attack.

Can eighteen-year-olds have a heart attack?

I have a pain, *severe* pain, in my chest and my left arm. It has to be a heart attack. What else could it be?

My heart is being attacked.

And then, it dies – my heart dies – when Mr. Edwards grabs the back of her neck in a possessive hold and brings her close before kissing her.

He's kissing her, out in the open, in front of all these people. I can't see the finer details of it, but I can at least see that his mouth is moving. His mouth is moving in a very dominating way.

So dominating that even I can feel it.

I feel it so much that I *have* to put my lips on the fogged-up-by-my-rapid-breaths glass. I have to press my lips on it the same way as I did on the night of my eighteenth birthday.

Yes, I'm kissing glass – a non-living thing with no warmth or breath – because the man I kissed ten months ago is kissing someone else.

He is kissing another woman and she's going wild in his arms and here I am, going crazy.

This is what happens when he kisses back. *This.*

You go wild.

You forget where you are. You forget the people around you, and you become this thing. This sexual thing and you put your hands on his broad shoulders. That's what this woman is doing.

They're perfect together.

So perfect and beautiful that it makes me sick.

It makes me think that I'm spying on a king and his queen, in the hopes that the king will look up and catch me. He'll catch me staring at them with this feverish, turned-on look in my eyes and he'll leave the queen.

For me.

Instead of the sophisticated, experienced queen, the king will want me: the plain, bedraggled princess who can't control herself.

God, I so, *so* want that.

I'm so weak in the moment that I can't even pretend to deny it.

I want him to look up. I want him to see me.

"Please, Mr. Edwards," I whisper like he can hear me.

Just like that he does, though.

He rips his mouth away from her, his fingers now fisted in

her loose, wavy hair. His chest is heaving, panting. The woman's confused and she wants him to come back to her. She even tries to put her mouth on his but Mr. Edwards turns his face and his eyes somehow, miraculously, land on me.

On me?

I actually stumble back with the force of it. The force of his gaze and the sheer absurdity of what just happened.

It was like he heard me or read my mind or just *knew* that I was there.

And I know the moment he figures out it's me. The girl who kissed him that night.

His jaw tightens. A frown emerges between his heavy brows and his eyes begin to narrow.

I don't wait around for his eyes to become slits because I'm running away.

Without really thinking about it, I pick a random direction and start walking really, really fast. The sidewalk is packed with the dressed-up evening crowd.

I'm bumping into them, hitting them either with my hunched shoulders or my fat hobo and my anxiety is jacking up.

Finally, finally I find a secluded spot where I can stop.

It's a narrow alley wedged between two buildings and I get in and lean against the wall, almost falling into it, breathing hard.

The bricks at my back are damp and hot but they feel good against my bare thighs and the nape of my neck.

My entire body is burning, and I know it has very little to do with my speed-walking or even my anxiety.

It has everything to do with that kiss I witnessed. That kiss and his stare.

My hobo slides down and off my shoulder, dropping to the ground, and I look at the sky, exposing my flushed throat to the night air.

I sigh when the breeze flutters over my skin. But my relief doesn't last long because someone appears at the mouth of the alley.

Him.

Mr. Edwards.

He's standing by the opposite wall, staring at me.

My feet kinda slip on the ground, even though it's dry as the desert, when I try to stand up straight. My breaths are coming in short bursts like bombs exploding in my chest. Too much air one second and the next, not enough.

"You f-followed me?" I whisper hesitantly and also unnecessarily.

Of course he did.

He's here, isn't he?

At my question, he comes off the wall and moves toward me.

His eyes are deep and unfathomable, and it seems like he hasn't unclenched his jaw since the moment he saw me minutes ago.

"I didn't mean to run," I say when he doesn't utter a word. "It was a reflex. Absolutely no thought involved. You shouldn't have followed me though."

In fact, I came to the bar to find him. But I don't say that.

Words are falling out of my brain with every step he takes toward me. Slow and fraught with some underlying meaning.

I can figure it out though, the underlying meaning. His clenched jaw and furious eyes are super clear about that.

He's angry.

As soon as he reaches me, I blurt out the only words I seem to remember in the moment.

"I'm sorry."

3

His eyes change color.
I wonder what color they'd be,
if he ever
lo●ked at me.

-The Diary of a Shrinking Violet, Age 16

"You are?"

His voice is the same, low and rumbly.

It makes me jump the same way it did that night. In fact, it makes me jump *and* it makes me arch up against the wall. Like the gravel in his voice controls the curvature of my spine.

"Yes."

He cocks his head to the side, studying me. "For what?"

The eye-sweep he gives me is completely different than what he gave her, the queen-like woman. With her, he was slow, and he was deliberate.

With me, he's dismissive. He takes one look up and down my body, my t-shirt and shorts, and that's it.

I bet he's already forgotten what I look like even though he's staring at me directly.

Fisting my hands at my sides, I lick my lips. "For running and, uh, for ruining…" *Your life.* "Your evening."

That's the least of my crimes but it's the only thing I can think of to say right now, especially after his careless look.

Not to mention, that's the only thing I've got the courage to say.

"Ruining my evening," he murmurs, scratching his jaw, and I swear I hear the rustle of his thumb and his beard and it steals away my breath. "Yeah, you did that. You ruined my evening."

"Maybe you can still save it," I whisper, feeling foolish and breathless at the same time.

"What do you suggest?"

I swallow, wanting to look away from him.

I mean, I should. I really, *really* should. I'm staring at him a little too much.

Even though he's doing the same to me, I highly doubt he's harboring the same thoughts as me.

Thoughts like how tall he is and how his shoulders are massive. Massive enough to block out the street beyond him and all the people and buildings. How the open collar of his plaid shirt gives me a peek of the triangle of his throat along with a smidge of his chest hair.

"You should…" Looking down, I fight the urge to stick my tongue out and gag at the words I'm about to speak. "You should go back to her and uh, finish what you started."

"What was it? That I started."

I whip my eyes up at his question. I do it so fast, I nearly bump my head against the wall.

Is he really asking me that?

Looks like he is. His jaw is dipped, and his eyes are on me, intense and watchful, like he's waiting for my answer.

"I... Well, you know, you were kissing her, so," I say lamely, childishly. Like I can't understand the concept of kissing and things that happen because of it.

He squints his eyes a little as if he really can't figure it out. "So?"

I swallow.

I wait for a few seconds, debating what to say, and then go for it.

"So, I'm sure you wanted to do more." And just because I can't help myself, "She definitely wanted you to do more."

It's a muttered add-on. I completely had no right to say that and no right to let my teeny-tiny bit of bitterness show.

I mean, why am I even bitter? What am I bitter about?

Why wouldn't he kiss that woman? Why wouldn't he make out with her and do other things with her?

Mr. Edwards's lips pull up again like they did back at the bar, in one direction and only slightly. Again, it's nothing like the smile he gave her. This one's cold and mean, but still, I respond to it.

I respond to it by going breathless again. By putting my left foot over my right and clenching my thighs.

"What do you think she wanted me to do to her?" he asks.

With every question that he asks me, the answers become

more and more difficult. I should really put a stop to it.

Mostly because it's none of my business. But also because I don't wanna talk about her. I don't wanna talk about what that woman wanted from him and what he wanted from her.

And yet, I can't help it when my lips part and my answer slips out. "Keep kissing her and never stop."

His eyes flick back and forth over my face and I think this is it. He'll stop now. He has to. I don't even know what I'm saying.

But he doesn't.

His face dips even more, like he's trying to gouge the answers out of me. "What else?"

As it turns out, he doesn't have to gouge anything out. I'll give him the answer anyway. I'll keep talking and talking like an idiot.

"Touch her, maybe."

"Where?"

"Everywhere. All the places you could reach."

Stop. Stop. Stop.

What am I saying? Why does he keep asking these questions?

Why am I gauging the distance between us? Why am I trying to see the places he can reach on *my* body?

"Her hair, maybe?" he asks curiously, as if I'm telling him something he never could've figured out for himself.

I become hyper-aware of my own loose hair, brushing against my arm, my shoulders, going down to the small of my back. "Yeah."

"What about her neck? Does she want me to touch her

neck?"

My neck tingles. "Yes."

"Her waist. Maybe slide down a little?"

I nod, feeling the brick wall brushing against my ass. "To her ass."

"What if I bring my hand forward, slide it down her stomach? Would she like that?"

My eyes go down to his hands. They're clenched into fists by his sides, mimicking my own.

His stance is wide, and his body sprung tight, completely in conflict with his low, lazy, almost sleepy voice. And I realize that maybe this is how he looks when he's aroused.

Oh Jesus, is he aroused? Did she get him going that much?

It makes me wanna sob.

Instead, I whisper, "Yeah. Yeah, she'd like that. Very much."

"What if I don't stop there? What if I keep going and going until my hand is somewhere else?"

"On her thighs?"

I say that but I'm not really thinking that. I'm thinking of something else.

Something that I'm currently clenching and pressing between my thighs as I watch his tight fists. As I try to make my fists as tight as his, as tight as the knot in my lower belly.

"Yeah. But that's not what my hand's after. You know that, don't you? It's after something else. My hand's after her p —"

"Okay!" I almost scream, trying to get him to stop talking. "I get the picture. She wanted you to touch her everywhere."

Jesus Christ, he has to stop now.

He has to.

I can't take it anymore. I can't take him saying the P word, and I'm not referring to all the P words he's been called.

He was gonna say something else, something like *pussy*, and no.

Just no. I can't.

I can't take that he can make me aware of my own body while he's talking about touching someone else's.

Mr. Edwards's smile goes even meaner, even colder. "You look a little flushed. Are you okay? A little turned on, maybe?"

"I'm…"

"Does watching people get you off?"

My eyes go wide; I'm sure he can see it through the tinted lenses. "What?"

"You watch people, Violet?"

He just said my name.

He said it the same way as he did that night. Like he's murdering it between his teeth.

I shake my head, scraping the back of it against the brick wall. "No. Of course not. I don't… don't watch people."

"No?"

"No."

"So why were you watching me?"

"I didn't mean to watch you. I was just… I just happened to be there. A-and you were, you know. And then, I couldn't stop watching. It was kinda hypnotic and I'm so so–"

"Maybe next time when two grown-ups are kissing, look the fuck away."

I'm so freaked out that I don't even take offense at his *grown-ups*. "Yeah, okay."

"Or try some porn in your free time. For educational purposes, you understand, so you don't get *hypnotized* again."

I grimace; I knew that would somehow come to bite me in the ass, the hypnotized comment. "Okay. Porn, yeah. I'll try that."

Then I see his lips twitch. Only once, but I catch it and for such a small, minuscule action, it has an avalanche of an effect.

My heart skips a beat before jackhammering inside my rib cage.

Was that his way of… smiling?

"Jailbait," he murmurs out of the blue, and my heart that's been flying inside my chest slows down.

I flinch, as if reality smacked me across the face. I loosen my fists and my shoulders go limp.

In a very small voice, I say, "I'm not. I'm eighteen."

Like I was when I kissed him.

Like I told people over and over after that.

And then, I jump in and add, "And ten months. I'm eighteen and ten months."

It's important.

If I could somehow make myself age faster, I would. But I can't. So I'm going to count every single day toward my pathetic, inappropriate age.

"You shouldn't be wearing that, then." He jerks his chin up, pointing at something. "If you don't want people to get the wrong impression."

I frown for a moment, then comprehension dawns.

Oh.

Fuck.

Reaching up, I snatch off my baseball cap. It's magenta with 'Jailbait' written in black. God, I'm an idiot.

"It was a stupid gift from one of my friends. Don't worry, I'm gonna set this and *her* on fire tomorrow."

"Yeah? For your birthday?"

It's a taunting voice, aimed to sting. It does and my embarrassment grows.

"New Year's," I still tell him.

If he wants to mock me for it, I won't take away the opportunity. He has every right.

Besides, it *was* a New Year's gift from the one and only Renn. By then, I'd told them all the truth and she bought me this present as a joke. Surprisingly, it made me chuckle at the time.

I'm not chuckling now.

I'm doused in shame.

"Take 'em off," he orders instead of acknowledging what I just said, gesturing toward my sunglasses.

"Uh, I'm not sure that it's such a good idea," I offer truthfully.

It's not as if I don't want to take them off. In fact, I've been itching to take them off ever since I saw him through the glass back at the bar.

But what if I take them off and my anxiety comes back? What if his eyes, like so many others', make my skin crawl?

I won't be able to bear it.

For years, I wanted him to see me, just see me. Even though

I avoided him myself, I harbored this little dream where he'd see me and his heart would start beating faster. But now I'm not sure if I'll be able to take it, his eyes, and it scares me.

He's not taking no for an answer though.

"Just do it," he clips.

As if he's the boss of me, I do it. I reach up and take them off and wait for my doomsday brain to start ticking.

I wait for the familiar flush to rise up around my throat and familiar prickling and itching and hyperventilation, to come back.

The flush happens.

I *do* feel the flush but it's the same kind that I felt back at the bar, when I saw him. The edgy kind. The kind where the heat spreads out from my stomach and covers every part of my body, making me red.

Making me bloom like a rose for him.

Oh God. Thank God.

Thank fucking God.

I can stand his eyes on me. I can.

I *can* take it when his eyes move from one spot of my face to another. And they move thoroughly, almost frantically.

He goes from the top of my hair to my stubby eyelashes. From the side of my rounded cheeks to my small chin. From my little, slightly freckled nose to my parted, bee-stung lips.

I can take it all.

Maybe it's the shy thing again. I'm shy to the world but not to him.

With that happy thought, I do my own taking in of his face.

Or rather his hair.

His hair has grown in the past ten months – that's the very first thing I think of. It's longer now, flicking against the collar of his blue plaid shirt.

Not to mention his cheekbones. Strangely, they've grown too.

They have sharpened, giving him somewhat of a gaunt look. And God, his eyes. The pupils are dark, blown-up, almost black but they are rimmed with red.

He looks… wild.

Messy and even untamed.

My Strawberry Man.

"You have a beard," I say in awe.

Like he's the only man in this world with facial hair.

For me, he might as well be.

In fact, that beard makes him look sexier. More masculine and dominating. Kind of older in that bone-tingling sort of way. It makes his strawberry like mouth even pinker and thicker.

"And you're really here," he muses.

He squints too as if he can't believe that I'm here.

As if he's seeing things and all this conversation was part of a dream.

"Unless you…"

I trail off, realizing what I was about to say. I was about to repeat what he said to me that night.

"Unless I what?"

His eyes are glinting in the dark. Glinting with knowledge. I think he knows what I was about to say.

"Unless you do this a lot," I whisper to him. "See things that are not there."

I thought he'd get angry. Get agitated, but he doesn't. All he does is shake his head and mutter almost to himself, "Seeing things. Yeah, you have no idea."

"I'm sorry?"

That seems to piss him off though. My non-apology apology.

"How the fuck are you here?" he asks, drawing out the *fuck*. This is it.

I need to tell him. I need to say sorry. I need to ask him what I can do to make it up to him.

"I came for y-you."

The reply blurts out of me without thought or any effort.

He flinches.

But it's the truth. I did come here for him. I came here to face him and his anger. I came here to fix what I broke.

"For me," he says woodenly.

"Yes."

"Why?"

"Because of what happened. What I did. I hurt you and –"

Suddenly, a squeak escapes me because his fingers are on my bicep.

Before I can comprehend what's happening, he jerks me forward by the sleeve of my t-shirt.

And knocks the breath out of me.

4

I had a dream that I was a child
of the eighties. Like him.
And he was giving me a ride in
his truck, taking me somewhere
secluded so he could suck
on my lollipop lips...

-The Diary of a Shrinking Violet, Age 17

At his yank, my spine snaps off the wall and my feet stumble.

Then he turns around and begins walking, dragging me behind him.

I only have the time and presence of mind to pick up my enormous hobo and sling it over my shoulder.

"What... What are you doing?" I ask his broad back.

The ripple of his muscles is the only answer I get.

"Where are we going?" I ask again, trying not to look around at the pedestrians.

Who are all watching us as we pass them by.

I can feel their stares. Most of them are jerking to a halt at the sight of us. At the sight of a large man dragging a tiny girl by the sleeve of her t-shirt.

That's the part that I find more horrifying than the stares, him pulling me forward with the sleeve of my top.

The part where he isn't touching me.

Not even through my clothes.

He has made a fist out of my t-shirt and he's pulling on that.

Is it because he can't stand to touch me? Is that why he won't put his hand anywhere on my body, not even to manhandle me?

Maybe I make his skin crawl the same way the world does mine when it stares at me.

I look up at his profile. It's stony and cold and frankly, super terrifying.

"Mr. Edwards –"

He cuts off whatever I was going to say by delivering his harshest jerk yet. His fist tightens, making my t-shirt stretch and distort against my body, making me think that he's going to tear off the fabric.

"Mr. Edwards, you're hurting me."

He comes to a stop then, at my blurted-out warning.

Spinning around once more and facing me, he pushes me back, his knuckles digging into my flesh. My spine hits something – something metallic – and I gasp at how cold it is against my heated body.

He studies my face, my frown, my parted and panting lips with a menacing look. "Trust me, I haven't even begun hurting you."

His growled-out words sink into my skin, sink into the exact spot he's clutching me at, the exact spot where his knuckles are almost gouging a hole on my arm.

This is it, then.

I wanted this, didn't I? I came here to face his anger and here it is.

Be careful what you wish for.

Be careful because you just might get it. You might just get burned by the dark, *dark* eyes of a beast.

"Mr. Edwards —"

I try again, and again he cuts me off. "Get in."

"What?"

"Get in the truck."

I look back and realize that the something metallic that I'd hit a few seconds ago was his truck. We're back to where we started — at the bar where I found him.

Where I watched him kiss another woman.

"You want me to get in your truck?" I ask inanely.

No answer. But he does clench his teeth and I notice that when he does it, the bones of his face look even more chiseled and blade-like.

Like if I accidentally touched his face, I might cut myself.

"But I've never been in your truck before. I thought it wasn't allowed."

Yikes.

Could I sound any younger than I did just now?

Allowed?

He leans toward me, looking me in the eyes, like he really wants me to concentrate on his next statement. "Get in or I'll put you in. And you're not going to like the way I do it."

"P-put me in?"

He straightens up, and letting go of the sleeve of my shirt, he grabs me by the waist.

In a flash, I'm in the air. My feet leave the ground and my eyes go wide but I don't even get the chance to gasp before I'm being dumped on the seat of his truck.

I have no idea how he did that so fast. How he got the door of his truck open while still holding me and how he deposited me inside like I'm a bag of feathers, all in the space of three seconds.

All I know is that I caught a grimace on his face when he put his hands on me to do the deed.

Man, he really hates me, doesn't he?

The sight of that grimace is so jarring, so saddening – even though I should've expected it – that I don't even let out a tiny *ow* when my butt hits the leather and my glasses and cap fall away from me. I still manage to hold onto my hobo though.

Mr. Edwards is about to shut the door when I put my hand on his chest and stop him.

I think along with stopping him, I stopped time, as well.

Or at least, it feels like it.

It feels like I stopped time, froze it and froze the world around us, by putting my small hand on his massive chest.

His grip on the door goes really tight. So tight that I can see the tendons in his wrist stand taut. As taut as his pecs.

Which I'm touching right this second.

"Get your hand off me," he orders.

Immediately, I do.

I glance at his razor-sharp features. "My glasses. I-I need them."

"What?"

"My sunglasses. They fell. On the ground."

He gives me a deadpan look like he didn't hear me.

But then, a muscle jumps on his cheek and I think that maybe he'll run over my sunglasses with his truck just to spite me.

In my head, I'm already thinking about getting a new pair, probably a few more as a backup, when he bends down and grabs them. He returns them to me with a jerky motion of his hand and I accept them quickly, before he changes his mind and throws them away.

Clutching them to my chest, I say, "Thanks."

Again, he goes to snap the door shut but I stop him.

"My cap. It fell too." His chest rises and falls on a long breath and I can't help but add, "B-but it's okay. I didn't love it that much. We can just –"

He steps back and slams the door in my face, in the middle of my sentence. I flinch and my eyes fall shut as the strands blow over my cheeks.

I'm going to buy a new cap tomorrow. I'll order it online like I've been doing since I got out of Heartstone and it'll be fine.

It's okay. Everything's okay.

I'll buy several new caps and sunglasses, in fact. I'm actually surprised at myself that I haven't yet since my entire life depends on them now.

Lesson learned.

A few seconds later, he opens the door to the driver's side and slides in. He has my cap in his hands that he throws over at me and I catch it, letting go of my glasses.

It's like he threw me air and I caught it, breathing again.

Swallowing, I peek at his harsh profile. "Thanks."

His reply is snapping his seat belt around himself, which reminds me that I have to do it too. Before he can get even more pissed, I fasten the seat belt around me.

And then we're off.

To parts unknown.

"Where are we going?" I ask hesitantly, watching the play of lights on his broad frame as we pass by restaurants and stores and various buildings in downtown.

Silence.

"I'm assuming it's somewhere to talk?"

Nothing.

I squeeze my hobo with my legs. "Actually, I have a car. Uh, it was parked right there, a little bit farther. If you'd told me where we were going, I could've just followed you."

I throw him another glance to check if he's listening. But I can see no outward signs of that. I might as well be not here.

Inside his truck.

I'm inside *his truck*.

Whoa.

I've imagined it so many, many times before. I always thought it would be a dream unfulfilled, like all my other dreams when it comes to him.

"It's spacious," I murmur, looking at the roof, the dashboard, his old-fashioned CD player.

Then I notice the smell.

I sniff.

It kinda smells… boozy. Not too much but slightly. There's a hint of it.

Now that I'm thinking about it, Mr. Edwards smells that way too. Musky and tangy like liquor.

I clear my throat and continue to dispel the awkward silence. "The truck, I mean. It's spacious. So it's not like I don't like it. But I guess, if I had my own vehicle, I could just drive myself back. You know, when we're done talking. But now, you'll have to drop me off and…"

At this, I get several ticks on his jaw.

"But it's okay. I can just call a cab." Then, "You guys have cabs here, right? I didn't see a single one on my way over."

Still nothing.

"Of course there are cabs here." I chuckle nervously. "Stupid question. But if you could just give me like, a number? Like, where I can call, that'd be great. Oh!" I throw my hands in the air. "I can Uber. You guys definitely have Uber, right?"

Oh God, this is not helping. I'm getting more and more nervous. Why won't he say anything?

Just say something, anything.

I don't like this silence-before-the-storm type situation. I swear I'm about to hyperventilate.

"Mr. –"

"How'd you know I was here?"

Fucking *finally*.

I tuck my hair behind my ears and answer, "Uh, I saw it on Facebook."

"Facebook."

"Yes. I saw that you were living here."

I know how that might sound. That I was stalking him or something. But I don't wanna lie to him.

"How'd you see it?" he asks.

"Brian... He, uh, posted about it."

At the mention of his son, his fingers tighten on the wheel. In addition to that, his nostrils flare and I have absolutely no idea what to make of it.

"So what, you thought you could drop by to say hi?"

I squirm in my seat. "Not hi, exactly. I told you I came –"

"Why aren't you in college?" he grits out, staring at the road.

Whoa, okay.

The correct answer is, I'm not in college because I lost my shit last summer and spent some time in a psych ward. And now, going to a crowded place like college terrifies me so I'm taking it easy.

That's the correct answer.

But the other correct answer is, I'm fine now. I'm handling things. It's all in the past. So what's the point of telling him?

I feel the leather of my hobo with my legs as I tell him, "Because it's summer vacation. College is usually out."

Lies. Lies. Lies.

I'm lying to him and I wanna throw up. But again, what's

the point of telling him when it's all done and over with?

He accepts my answer by clenching his jaw and white-knuckling the wheel.

A few seconds pass until he asks another question. "Your parents know you're *vacationing* here?"

No.

They think I'm at a yoga retreat with the girls for my anxiety issues; they helped with the convincing. Nelson recommended it a long time ago and last week, I fake-agreed to go.

"Yes," I lie the second time in the space of a minute, and the bile is so high up my throat that I feel it on the tip of my tongue.

"Is that right?"

I can see why this is a little harder to believe for him but I keep at it. "Yes. That's right."

"Your parents know that their innocent little schoolgirl daughter's here. With the alleged sexual predator. Is that what you're trying to tell me?"

He's quoting that article from the Cherryville Chronicle and as soon as he's said it, the tic in his jaw doesn't stop.

My heart follows its lead and begins to tic as well, slowly gaining speed.

"First of all, I'm not a schoolgirl. I'm an adult. I can make my own decisions," I tell him fiercely. "Second of all, my parents don't care. My mom's busy with her new affair. And my dad's out of the country for the rest of the month."

After my accident, my dad remained the same but my mom changed.

She started to kinda *care* for me. Not a lot, of course. I'm still the living proof of her exploits. But she had a talk with Fiona about the photo and the social media disaster; not that my sister listened but still. Mom even started to ask about my health, my treatment, my therapy and all that.

More than that though, she gets pretty worked up whenever Mr. Edwards is mentioned. Especially when I'm the one mentioning him, insisting on his innocence and my culpability.

In her eyes, it was Mr. Edwards's fault.

He somehow made me kiss him and I'm the innocent one, and I'll never understand why. She's always been so sure that I am Satan's re-incarnation.

Sometimes I think she's the one who had that article printed in the paper, making me out to be this damsel and him the villain.

In any case, we're not a happy family and since I never step foot out of the house, it's really, really tough. So as soon as I told her that I was going with the girls for the summer long yoga camp, she booked my tickets in a flash – *great idea, Violet,* she said – and then, I overheard her talking to her new boyfriend on the phone, making plans to meet with him the following day.

"And most of all, you're *not* an alleged anything," I finish just as fiercely, turning so I'm facing him.

"Yeah? It was in the paper. It must be true," he says sarcastically, eyes on the road.

And that just totally blows me up.

I get so angry on his behalf. So rage-y that I can't stop from raising my voice and fisting my hands on the seat.

"Fuck the paper, okay? Fuck everyone. Fuck every single

person who says that about you. It was my fault. Mine. All of it. I made a stupid drunken mistake and you had to pay the price for it. It's not –"

I almost bite my tongue when the truck comes to a violently abrupt stop. Despite wearing the seat belt, my body shoots forward and jerks against the strap.

The pain's so sharp that all I can do is gasp, without being able to make a sound.

"Get out."

Still gasping painfully and rubbing my chest, I look at him. "What?"

He clicks off his seat belt; the rustle of it snapping back is loud, louder than anything I've heard tonight, before facing me.

He not only faces me, he comes closer to me. But not by sliding toward me on the seat – that would've been less scary for some reason.

He comes closer by leaning, looming, *hanging* over me.

He tips his head softly, pointing at something, but his eyes are on me. "You see that?"

His intimate voice makes me tremble. The interior of the cab is barely lit up by the overhead light, turning the air thick and cozy.

It's hard to look away from him. But still, I do it.

It's a sign, neon green, on the side of the road, announcing our arrival at his town, Pike's Peak. I passed it on my way over.

I'm confused.

Why are we here?

It's a deserted area, miles away from the downtown we were

in. How long have we been driving for?

I shift my gaze back to him. "Yes?"

"I want you to get out of the truck and walk up to it," he says, again in that intimate tone of his.

"Why?" I ask, warily.

"And when you reach it, I want you to keep walking." He pauses but he's not finished; I can feel it. "I want you to walk until you get out of this town, this county. This state." Another pause. "I want you to walk until you get back to where you came from. Do you understand?"

"B-but I –"

"I want you to walk."

Everything he's said, he's done it in a calm way. So, so calm that it's deadly and chilling. And so opposite of what I'm feeling right now.

Frantic.

That's what I am. That's how I'm doing things.

Frantically, I look at the sign. *Frantically*, I'm dragging in breaths and looking back at him.

"Mr. Edwards, I know you're mad. I know that. T-that's why I came. I wanted to apologize and –"

"I know why you came," he interrupts – again calmly. "You came because of your *stupid drunken mistake*, isn't it?"

I'm this close to wheezing, this close to passing the fuck out with how fast my heart's beating. But somehow, I manage to nod.

"You came because I paid for it. For *your* mistake."

I give him another nod.

"So you think I want your apology, isn't that it? You think

that?"

"Yes."

"Now, let me tell you what I think, yeah? You want to know what I think when I look at you?"

God, why's he asking me?

It makes everything doubly dangerous and scary. Like I have a choice. I can tell him no and he won't tell me.

But I'm never going to do that. I'm never going to tell him no.

I'm going to take whatever he gives me.

I smother my Audrey Hepburn sunglasses between my hands and nod. "What?"

At my small voice, his calm breaks. The hand he has on the wheel flexes and I prepare myself.

"When I look at you, Violet, I think about the night that changed my life. Everyone has that moment. When things change. The moment that you remember for the rest of your life. The moment you *think about* for the rest of your life. *You* are that moment for me."

He takes another pause here like he's digging out words from somewhere deep inside his soul. Words that he probably wanted to say for a long time but never got the chance to.

Words that I know are going to break apart what little heart I have left.

And then, he proves me right.

"You. A teenage girl who stunk of a thousand-dollar rum. You are my moment. A girl who ruined my life. That's what I think about. I think about my lost peace of mind. The peace that you took from me. I think about the shitshow my life has become. I think about how the fuck to forget you. And I think about how no matter what I do, I never will. Because you're a nightmare that's goddamn unforgettable."

I scrunch my eyes closed as his stare, his anger, his words burn me.

"So I don't want your apology. I don't want you to be here for me, understand? I want you to leave. I want you to get the fuck out of this town and never come back."

He looks like a towering mountain right now, his shoulders stretched out in front of the window, his chest heaving, his thighs sprawled.

Or maybe a volcano that seems to be on the verge of exploding.

Because of me.

His nightmare.

"Okay," I whisper, nodding.

I grab my bag, open the door and hop down, all in one breath, and I do what he says.

Shutting the door behind me, I walk to the sign and dump my hobo by it. With my back turned, I squat down and open the zipper.

I root around the hobo for a while, not sure what I'm looking for. Not sure what the fuck I'm even doing.

A few minutes later, I hear the rev of his truck, the screech of his tires as he probably backs up, turns around and leaves me.

All alone on the side of the road.

I wanna cry. I wanna cover my face with my hands and sob

into them until I don't have any tears left in me.

But I'm not gonna do that.

I'm not gonna cry over something I already knew in my heart of hearts.

I knew he hated me.

I knew he was angry and furious and seething.

I expected it.

What I didn't expect was the fact that I'd become his nightmare.

In all the dreams I've had about Mr. Edwards, I never once thought that. I never thought I'd ruin his life and steal his peace.

But it's okay.

I'm here to fix it. I'm here to make everything right. To pay for my crimes, and I'm not going to be defeated so easily.

I get up and I put on my disguise.

Cap, headphones and sunglasses. I also whip out some lollipops.

I stand up and heave the fat hobo over my shoulders. Turning around, I look at the dark, endless road made even darker by the tint of my shades.

At least he chose to leave me in a deserted area where there are no people around.

Unwrapping my candy, I shove it in my mouth and begin walking.

Not away from his town or him.

But toward him.

Because I'm not going anywhere.

Mr. Edwards

Hallucinations.

Delusions. Illusions. Figments of the imagination.

All of the above are symptoms of a diseased mind. A broken mind. A sick mind. Maybe even a sick heart.

I never liked them, the hallucinations.

Definitely not the ones that are brought on by a sober brain.

Up until tonight, I wanted them to go away. I wanted them to leave me alone and fuck off.

In fact, I'd drink and drink until I made *sure* they left me alone. I made sure that my brain was shut off and my heart was numb.

I'm doing the same thing right now. I'm sitting here, in my darkened truck, gulping down Jack Daniels like water.

Right now, I'd give anything, anything at all, for this to be a bad dream.

A nightmare, like I told her.

I'd give anything for her to not be here.

I'd give anything for me to be seeing things. To be imagining, hallucinating, daydreaming like I've been doing for the past ten months.

Hallucinating her pale face. Imagining her smell, her voice. Her red as fuck lips.

But it's not a dream.

If it were, my truck wouldn't be hiding in the woods by the road that I abandoned her on like the goddamn asshole that I am, waiting for her to walk by like some criminal.

Just to make sure that… no one is kidnapping her. Apparently, I have a conscience when it comes to her.

Jesus Fucking Christ.

What the fuck is she doing here? Why the hell won't she leave me alone?

It was a stupid drunken mistake…

So it was a mistake.

She made a fucking mistake. Because she was drunk. Because she thought she could do whatever the hell she wanted.

Because she's this terrible thing that I can't seem to forget.

The most terrible thing that's ever happened to me.

I strangle the bottle with my fingers and take a deep, deep pull and bark out a harsh laugh.

Fucking teenager.

I lied.

I told her that my life changed that night, the night she kissed me, the night of her *stupid drunken mistake.*

My life changed the moment I moved into that house over two years ago.

I never should've done that. I never should've moved to Connecticut in the first place. It was a mistake.

The only reason I did it was for Brian.

It was a good school for him. When they contacted me out of the blue and offered me a job, I was hesitant. We were happy in Denver. We were settled. I had a good job. We lived in a good neighborhood. Brian had life-long friends.

But then, they told me that kids from Cherryville High usually end up at Yale or Columbia or something similar, and I knew Brian wanted that.

Unlike me, he's always been a straight-A student. He's always been excellent at everything according to his teachers. Not only that but he's one of those rare kids who are good at sports too.

Sometimes I can't believe he's my kid. My son.

I raised him. Me. An aimless, angry kid from a small town who never thought he'd get anywhere. Whose only goal at eighteen was to get out of this shitty place and maybe use that scholarship they accidentally gave him for playing some ball to go to college.

How the hell did *my* son get so talented?

So smart that my chest hurts with pride for him.

If only I hadn't moved cross-country.

I should've known that Brian would end up at an Ivy League school anyway. All I wanted to do was make it easier for him. All I wanted was for him to have his best shot, to be able to give him all the help I could so he could go wherever he wanted.

Isn't that what parents do?

They try to make it easy for their kids. They try to give them all the opportunities that they can so their kids can be whoever they want to be.

I've never been very confident in my parenting abilities. I never had a very good example from which to learn – my dad was a drunk and my mother left when I was five or so – but goddamn it, I thought I was doing the right thing.

I should've stayed put, however. I should've refused their offer.

We were *happy* in Denver.

In Denver, I could sleep.

In Denver, there were no brown-eyed girls with long, thick hair that doesn't stop for miles and milky-white skin that shines under the moonlight.

The first time I saw her, she was climbing out of a window at night.

I was in my bedroom, trying to fall asleep in the new bed, in a new house that I didn't like very much. I noticed a movement from the corner of my eye: someone jumping onto a tree branch, outside of a window next door.

By the time I'd sprung out of the bed, thinking there was an intruder, the climber had scaled that branch so fast that all I could do was stand there.

All I could do was stare.

At her long, thick hair, wondering how I missed seeing it in the first place.

Because that hair appeared alive. The strands were blowing and winding and fluttering in the breeze and I wasn't even sure that the wind was so strong that night.

Then, the 'intruder' looked up at the sky and opened her arms wide.

I was too far away to notice anything minuscule about her but I could've sworn, the way she was staring up at the sky, she had just sighed. And smiled.

A second later, she sat down on the slanting roof and reached behind her to get at something. That's when I noticed she had a small backpack slung across her back. One by one, she fished out a notebook, a flashlight, and a giant pair of headphones, along with a lollipop.

Popping that lollipop in her mouth and putting those headphones on, she lit up the flashlight and began writing.

It was clear by then that it wasn't a break-in. She wasn't an intruder.

She was the girl next door who was probably a little crazy and in some serious need of parental guidance.

The following day I saw her again.

After coming back from a late run, I was in the kitchen, trying to find our coffee machine in one of the unopened boxes.

And there she was.

Out in her backyard, sitting at the edge of the pool, her arms behind her propping her up and her feet dangling in the water. Again, she had those headphones on and a lollipop in her mouth and her eyes were closed.

Her hair appeared dark but had streaks of gold in it or something similar. Something I'd never seen before.

Just then a blonde came rushing out the door and started

shouting at her, gesturing wildly with her hands. I couldn't hear what she was saying but I could hear her high-pitched, whiny voice. The golden-haired girl opened her eyes, squinted at her and in the midst of all the obnoxious wild gesturing, she pointed at something behind the blonde's shoulder.

The blonde looked and I knew what a mistake it was as soon as she'd done it. Because now, the blonde was going to end up being thrown in the water.

In a flash, I was proven correct.

The girl from last night grabbed hold of the blonde's ankle and pushed her in. I would've done the same thing just to make her shut up.

Only the blonde's shouts turned into shrieks and the other girl began laughing. Loud and fresh, and I wondered if there was something wrong with their parents that they weren't immediately out there, putting out the fight.

The golden-haired girl tugged on her ears, probably saying sorry to the blonde, before she jumped into the pool too.

It was a shock to me, her antics. I'd never seen anyone act so... brazenly and crazily. But then, in the coming days, I saw her dancing in her backyard, singing by the pool, running out of the house, sticking her tongue out just to feel the snow.

So I realized that this was the norm for her: doing her own thing when no one was watching or at least, she thought no one was watching. When people were around, she'd keep her head down and cover her face by those brown/blonde hair of hers.

Maybe because those people back in Connecticut looked at her like there was something wrong with her.

Stupid fuckers.

There was something wrong with them. They were all dead and dull and boring and she was a burst of life in their world.

Two days after the pool incident, I found out her name from Brian – Violet.

Two years after that she told me herself when I caught her stealing my roses.

I'm Violet. Violet Moore. I live next door...

I wanted to laugh and tell her: *I know.*

I fucking *know.*

I wish I didn't. I wish I didn't know the name of the teenage girl next door, the girl half my age, but I did. I wish I didn't know that she liked to climb up to the roof at night or that her skin shines when the light of the moon falls on her.

That night I could've stopped her from unnecessarily intro-ducing herself. I could've stopped a lot of things. But I didn't want to, for some reason.

If I had, then none of this would've happened.

The scandal at school, that article.

Fight with Brian. I wouldn't have hurt him the way I did.

We had a great summer together.

He'd just graduated and he was going away for college in the fall. In fact, he was going to leave early so he could start his new campus job. So we spent as much time together as we could.

But then just before he was set to leave, everything blew up.

Everything went to fucking hell.

I came here, to this isolated, abandoned cabin I grew up in because I wanted to get away, be alone or maybe to punish myself for everything. Because it is punishment, isn't it, to live in a place that never held any good memories for me.

And Brian went to go live with one of his friends in the city before he could move into his dorm room. Again, unlike me, Brian had a lot of friends in school.

He's open and adventurous and friendly. He's always been popular and well-adjusted with regular teenage concerns. It makes me feel that maybe I did do something right after all, giving him a normal environment to grow up in when I had no idea myself as to what a normal environment consisted of.

After that night, when he left to go live with one of his friends, I didn't stop him. I figured he needed some time alone. I figured he needed some time away from me.

But it's been almost a year and we still don't talk. He still hates me. We barely keep in touch. Our form of communication is either texts or two-minute phone calls.

It's okay, though. I deserve it all.

I deserve his hatred. His anger, his disgust.

For watching a girl half my age. For watching my son's best friend, a teenage girl when I had no business to.

But more than that, I deserve it for watching a girl my son, my blood, my kid watched as well.

"You know how creepy this is? How perverted? Have you been watching her or something? She's my age, Dad. You have a son her age. And you like her? You like Violet. Fantastic. Guess what, Dad, I like her too. She was special. She was fucking special. I was going to... I was going to ask her out before she moved away for college. I was finally gonna take a chance but you fucked it up. You ruined everything. So

fuck you, Dad. Fuck. You."

I take a long pull of whiskey when I hear my son's words from ten months ago. When for the first time in my life, he looked at me with disgust, with horror, with fury.

I take another swallow of Jack Daniels and it goes down my throat burning, scorching me as my guilt does.

And now, she's here.

I came here for you...

Goddamn it. Her soft voice makes me crazy.

She needs to leave. She needs to fucking leave. I'm going to *make* her leave.

No matter what.

5

Today I saw him make a guy on his
team cry. He was so cold. So
mean. I came home and tapped my
chest with a pen, and
asked my heart: Why him?
My heart smiled and shrugged
and kept beating for him.

-The Diary of a Shrinking Violet, Age 16

I'm back to where I started.

At my car.

I walked for miles and miles and for hours and hours and I'm almost dead now. Almost but not quite.

I'll die as soon as I open the door to my car and hit the seat though. I'll die of exhaustion and hunger and cold.

Jesus Christ, it's cold.

A second later, I practically fall on the seat, my legs giving out. I get rid of my disguise, my hobo, my headphones. I empty my pockets of the lollipop wrappers, littering them all on the floor.

I promise to clean it tomorrow.

But I can't figure out if it's tomorrow already and I should get on with the cleaning.

I'm in a daze and it's still dark outside. So maybe not.

Maybe I can just rest my head on the wheel for a while. *Just* for a little while and then, I'll go and find a motel, and figure out how to book a room without freaking out about talking to the receptionist.

"Okay… just… five seconds. Just five and then I'll go…" I whisper and hug the wheel before closing my eyes.

The next thing I remember is a tap and it wakes me up with a jolt. Shrieking, I jump and bang my head against the headrest.

That's when I realize it couldn't have been a tap. It had to have been a bang because the face staring at me through the window belongs to a very angry, impatient man.

It belongs to the man who left me on the side of the road.

"Get out," he clips when he knows he has my attention.

I frown at him, unable to understand how he got here and what he's even saying.

Then I hear a bang on the roof. It's not a huge bang but it's enough to clear off my sleepy cobwebs, making me think that he just kinda smashed his fist on the roof of my car.

Yikes.

How can he make my car feel – a piece of heavy machinery – all puny and little, I'll never know.

"Get out now."

I don't even wait to obey him. I get out.

"W-what are you doing here?"

He stares at me blank-faced. "You got luggage?"

"Yes."

"In the trunk?"

"Yeah…"

"Open it."

"Huh?"

He shoots me a look. "Just do it."

He doesn't wait to see if I've obeyed. He simply turns around and makes it to the back of my car in two steps. When I still haven't popped the trunk, he throws me another impatient glance and I dive into my car to do his bidding.

It's the sleep, I tell myself.

I'm sleepy and that's why I'm acting like his slave girl. *That's* the only reason.

Yeah, right.

Mr. Edwards grabs my luggage – a red suitcase – from my trunk and strides back to me. "Let's go."

"What?"

Again, he doesn't explain, nor does he wait for me to see if I'm following him. He keeps walking, carrying my suitcase in his hand. He doesn't even wheel it and I know it's kinda heavy. Needless to say, it makes my entire body tingle that he's carrying my heavy luggage like it contains air.

He's at the end of the block when I wake up and lunging back into my car, I grab my disguise and my fat hobo – can't forget my hobo – before following after him.

My entire body is stiff and my legs are going to abandon me any second but I keep walking. I have a feeling that he's going to throw my luggage in the trash or something just to make it clear how much he doesn't want me here. So I need to be there to fish it out of the dumpster.

But shockingly, he doesn't.

He keeps walking and walking, and then enters the same bar I found him at. The sign says closed, but still he pushes the door open and gets inside.

What the hell is he doing?

I reach the threshold of the bar and my feet come to a stop. I literally can't move them and make them take the last step.

God, sometimes I think I'm a vampire or something. Or one of my ancestors was a vampire. I love the night. I'm pale as fuck. I can't enter through front doors.

The only thing left is sucking blood.

So maybe I'm like, seventy percent vampire.

And Mr. Edwards doesn't like that.

Of course.

By the time I make it to the bar, he is already in conversation with a guy behind the counter. A heavy-set, bearded rocker guy that I caught a brief glimpse of before darting my gaze away. Now, Mr. Edwards looks at me and glares when he realizes I'm not moving.

"What's the problem?" he asks impatiently.

I wince. "I… What are we… What's happening?"

"Get in here."

I lick my lips and look at the doorjamb. Thank God, I had enough presence of mind to put on my disguise because the guy behind the counter is staring at me with amusement.

"I don't think that I can."

At this, Mr. Edwards really glares. Like, really. This is the glare to end all glares. Then he addresses the man and excuses himself and marches over to me.

I take a step back as soon as he reaches me. He studies me for a second and I'm already cringing at the lie I'm gonna have to tell him when he asks about my fear of the front doors.

But then, he grabs my arm – over the t-shirt, mind you – and drags me inside.

Reaching the man at the counter, he clips, "Key."

The man throws it to him and he catches it with his usual, familiar athleticism before getting on with the dragging.

We go through the back of the bar, take the hallway and climb up the stairs until we come upon a room, the door to which he opens with a jerk.

Dumping my suitcase, he faces me. "Since there are no drunks passed out up here, Billy will let you stay here for the night. But only one night. Tomorrow, you leave."

And just like that, he spins around and begins to climb down the stairs.

Did he just… kinda book me a room?

I look back at the room and yes, there's a bed, a dresser, a small chair even and an ajar door that opens into the bathroom.

He did find me a room. The very thing I was dreading.

Not to mention, he forced me to enter through the front door and he did it so fast that all I felt was this great jolt and nothing else.

Nothing. Else.

I mean, he did leave me on the side of the road. But then, he didn't have to do any of this. The man hates me. He could've left me there and I would've slept in the car. Because let's face it, I was not going to do something that involves talking to a stranger to book a room for the night.

But because of him and his twisted ways, I get to sleep in a bed.

I take a step forward, toward him to thank him maybe, but he's disappeared from view. And I have absolutely no idea what to feel in this moment except a big surge of relief.

***

I hear his voice.

It's coming from downstairs. A little dull and diluted and mixed in with another voice. This one belongs to Billy, the amused man I saw last night in passing, I think.

So, he's downstairs.

Mr. Edwards.

What is he doing here?

He's probably here to see if I've left or not. Because he said that he wanted me to leave today.

He did say that, right?

So much of what happened last night feels surreal. It feels like the dreams that I don't see anymore.

But no, it happened.

He did find me a room and I did sleep in a bed like the dead. Then I woke up, took a shower, and as soon as I got out, I heard his voice.

And now, I'm out the door before I've thought my game

plan through.

I'm not sure what I'm going to say to him or how I'm going to break the bad news that I'm not leaving yet, but I have to see him.

I climb down the stairs, walk down the hallway and reach its mouth to find that Mr. Edwards is alone, leaning against the bar, and that Billy has left.

Maybe he's heard my clumsy, rapid footsteps because he turns around and faces me.

He has a plaid shirt on today as well, the sleeves folded up to his elbows, one of which is propped on the wooden bar. His fingers are clutched around a bottle. A bottle of Jack Daniels, and I'm reminded of the boozy smell of his truck.

Is he drinking first thing in the morning?

As if to answer my unspoken question, he picks up the bottle and takes a huge gulp of it, without breaking our stare.

"What's with the cap and sunglasses?" he asks, as if we're just chatting, as if he's not intent on kicking me out of his town and as if I don't plan on foiling his attempts, at least for a little while.

I put my disguise on when I heard Billy's voice but as it turns out, I don't need it. Even so, I don't take it off as I approach him and the bar. Reaching it, I prop my own elbow on it and lean a few feet away from him.

"It's my new look," I answer.

At least that much is the truth.

"Yeah? Being a gigantic pain in the ass stopped working for you?"

I swallow, looking away from his searching eyes and at the

bottle he's currently strangling with his fingers.

"Yes. As a matter-of-fact, it did. I needed a change."

"So what are you supposed to be now? A hungover teenage princess?"

No. It's my crutch against the world.

But it's okay if he thinks something else entirely.

It's okay.

I lift my chin, even though I'm dying a little inside because I'm hiding things from him, lying to him. "I prefer diva, but princess works too."

His eyes narrow for a second before he takes another gulp of his whiskey, studying me.

"Uh, thanks for... booking the room for me. I would've thanked you last night but you just left," I begin. "Although, I'm not very sure how you even knew where I was going to be."

Which is only occurring to me right now.

It's a mystery, right?

How *did* he know where I was going to be? How did he know that I'd fall asleep in my car?

Thoughts flick through my brain one by one for about five more seconds, when abruptly, he moves and they run away.

He takes another sip of his Jack Daniels, this one the biggest, and I hear the glug of the liquid going down and his Adam's apple sliding down with it. Then he thumps the bottle on the counter, wipes his mouth with the back of his hand and takes a step toward me.

"So you found your way back," he murmurs, completely ignoring my question.

Although even I don't remember what I was wondering about in the face of this giant, bearded man advancing on me.

Automatically, I start moving back. "It wasn't hard. I had my phone. GPS is a wonderful thing."

All the while, I'm feeling this reluctant thrill go through my body. A stupid thrill.

A thick thrill that we're alone. The bar is closed. The windows are barred and draped. I don't hear anything other than our moving steps and our breaths.

"Next time I'll take away your phone," he whispers.

"Next time I won't get in your truck."

All the while, I'm wondering why I'm not afraid of being alone with him. I never was actually; not that night either when he himself warned me about little girls getting kidnapped. This little girl was hardly afraid or even shy.

Although now I have all the reasons to be afraid and shy and cautious.

The man hates me. *Hates* me.

He left me on the side of the road last night and now he's trying to run me over with his body.

Yes, I'm moving back as he walks toward me but it's not with fear.

I'm dancing to his tune. I'm matching him step for step. I'm keeping the rhythm of his feet like his prowl is a dark music of some kind.

"And next time too, you won't have a choice. Like you didn't last night."

I swallow.

I lick my lips.

I breathe heavily.

It feels like I've been trudging through desert. The driest and hottest desert on the planet, so scorched by the sun that my skin is cracked and my tongue is parched.

"Take 'em off," he orders, referring to my disguise, like he did yesterday.

And I realize I didn't take it off because I wanted him to say it. I wanted him to command me first, make me feel all tiny and dominated. So like last night, I do it in a flash.

God, I'm crazy.

I do it so fast and I do it in a way that says I can't *wait* to be fragile and vulnerable in front of him, that I feed him the bullshit line, "You can't tell me what to do."

We both know it's the lie of the century. His eyes even go to the disguise that's dangling from my sweaty fingers.

He humors me with a twitch of his lips. "I'll keep that in mind."

"You do that," I say, keeping up the charade.

Then my back hits the wall and settles into it and I forget how to make words.

He comes to a stop a few feet away from me, his shoulders blocking the measly light trickling through the windows, completely throwing us into shadow, turning day into night.

I notice his eyes are brown, dark brown, rapidly going darker. Will I ever get over how gorgeous his eyes are, and how chameleon-like and unpredictable?

He roams them over my face, rattling me a little more before carelessly murmuring, "Tell me something. What do you do when someone leaves you on the side of the road?"

"What?"

When he leans toward me and puts his hand, splayed wide on the wall, up above my head, I know I'm not going to like what he has to say.

But that doesn't matter, not at all, because he's just inched closer to me.

I can smell his spicy scent mixed in with whiskey, and I can feel his heat on my skin.

"It's late at night. The road's deserted and you know fuck-all about the town. What do you do, Violet?"

My hands are fisting and un-fisting the same way my mouth is opening and closing, trying to come up with an answer.

I mean, what is he even asking me? It's not as if I get abandoned all the time.

"Well, I'm not sure what the right answer is. Seeing as it had never happened to me before last night. But I opted to walk back to civilization."

That gets me flaring nostrils.

"You walk back to civilization. But let's say that you had your phone and you could've called for a cab. You could've called for an Uber. Do you do that? Or do you walk for miles? Not only that but you walk like you own the highway. Like you have no cares in the world. You've got your giant, ridiculous headphones on and you're dancing to the music. Is that what you do?"

He's talking a lot.

He never talks this much and he's saying a lot of things that he should have no knowledge about.

I mean, how does he know I was dancing? I was sad and I knew if I didn't do anything to distract myself, I'd lie down on the road and cry until dawn.

"How do you –"

"And then, when you've walked for miles like an idiot, what do you do? Do you sleep in the car? Instead of finding a decent, secure place to spend the night in? Come on. Enlighten me, Violet."

I try again when he pauses, his chest swelling, pushing his plaid shirt to its limits. "How do you know what I did after you left me?"

I swear I hear something.

A growl, maybe, originating somewhere deep in him. Or the fabric finally being pushed to its limits and tearing with how large his breath is.

"Answer me. Is that what you do when you've been left on the side of a motherfucking deserted road?"

His tone is thick and coated with sand. Every word he's uttered, every curse he's spewed, is seething with heat.

They hit me like darts, sharp and cutting. But I'm not cringing with the sting of them. I'm not wincing or hissing in pain.

I like them.

I like the burn of his razor-sharp words. I like how electric they are.

Because I get what's happening here.

He's mad at me for surviving his wrath, isn't he? He's mad that he did something horrible to me and yet, I came back. I didn't run away, crying.

I'm still here.

He's mad that he hasn't been able to scare me.

I unclench my hand and my disguise falls down to the floor. "You came back for me, didn't you? That's how you know what I was doing. That I walked for miles. That's... That's how you knew where to find me."

His frown is thundering but I don't get deterred. That's agreement enough.

He did think I'd be scared of him. He thought I'd be like one of his players or something.

Oh, Mr. Edwards.

I'm not normal. Typical things like angry beasts don't scare me. I'm scared of other tiny things like front doors or getting stopped on a street by a stranger.

"What I don't get is, why didn't I see you?"

"Because as I said, you were too busy to notice anything. Too busy and too fucking reckless."

"So you came back and then what? You followed me?"

He's silent and still frowning, and again I know I'm right.

I also know I shouldn't get too excited.

But I can't help it. He not only saved me the whole anxiety of talking to a stranger and finding a room for the night, he followed me home.

God.

I feel... all charged up and bubbly and light. "Where was your truck? I mean, I'm not *that* blind. I would've seen the headlights."

"Yeah, that's debatable." Then, "I left it in the woods. I

wanted to see how far you'd walk before you smartened up and called a cab. But apparently, you were too stupid to do that. Apparently walking all alone, in the dark, was preferable to calling for help. I almost wish I'd left you sleeping in your car just to teach you a lesson."

I shake my head at him, kind of amused and a whole lot of tingly. "You not only came back for me and found me a place to stay for the night, you walked all the way back into town, on foot too."

My voice sounds more fluttery and full of air than I'd intended for it to be. And Mr. Edwards hears it, as well.

His brows snap together, and he bends lower for this. "Let's get this really fucking straight – the only reason I did any of that was because you looked miserable when I kicked you out of my truck. So I took pity on you. It was an act of pity, understand? Call off the teenage hormones because you're leaving now."

He removes his hand from the wall and gets up to his full height, towering over me like a pillar, and folds his arms across his chest, completely expecting me to nod and walk away.

Teenage hormones.

Right.

Of course, I'm a teenager so I'm bursting with hormones and I don't know what I'm doing.

He really knows how to piss me off, doesn't he?

I wasn't going to be, but now I am.

I glare up at him, fisting my hands. "No."

"Excuse me?"

"You heard me. First of all, I don't need your pity. I don't need any favors from you. And second of all, I'm not going any-where. It's a free country. I can stay here as long as I want. You can't stop me."

He goes all still and dangerous. As if I just challenged him, his inner beast. "Is that really something you want to say to me?"

Oh, man.

He doesn't know what he's done.

Challenge accepted.

"Yes. You can't stop me. Boom. There. I said it. It's out there now." I make jazz hands and widen my eyes. "You wanna leave me on the side of the road, fine. Do it. I'll walk back every time and I won't call a cab just to spite you. That's why I didn't call it the first time. Because I knew you'd want me to give up. And you know what else? I'll fall asleep in my car, every night. Again, just to spite you. I'm a teenager, right? Teenagers do crazy things. So yeah. I'm not one of your players and you can't control me."

I'm panting, watching him through this fog that seems to have settled over me, making me kind of numb and the world kind of blurry.

The only problem with the world being smudged is that now, he burns bright. Brighter than before. He appears sharper to me, clearer than ever, more in focus with his cold face and savage beard.

"Free country, huh?"

"Yup."

"So you can do whatever you want."

"Yes, I can."

His smile is slow and lazy and one-sided, colder than ice.

I haven't touched it, his smile, with my hands but my fingertips are going blue anyway.

His dark eyes drop to my mouth for a second. "So you do this a lot? Make a lot of drunken mistakes?"

I part my lips because holy shit, I can't breathe. He's staring at my lips.

Also, what?

"What?" I say it out loud.

He unfolds his arms and closes the distance between us again. This time there's no dance, there's no keeping rhythm with his feet. He comes at me in a flash.

"Drunken mistakes," he says. "Like the one you made that night. Have you made them a lot? Since it's a free country and all that. And you can do whatever the hell you want."

I would've answered. I would've said something in response to his statement.

If he hadn't dropped his gaze even lower.

If he hadn't started staring at my chest.

Which in itself is so surreal that he's doing that. That he finds something on my body interesting enough to do what he's doing.

Staring. Very, very lazily. Like he has all the time in the world to look at it, to study it, memorize it.

And after a moment or two of his staring, I feel something on that exact spot where his eyes are.

I feel wet.

I whip my eyes down and realize that my wet-from-the-shower hair is draped over my shoulder and hangs over my right breast. The water from it has seeped into my t-shirt, making it damp and translucent. Making it so that the outline of my breast is visible along with my red bra, and my hard, puckered nipples.

Oh God.

He's looking at my nipples.

Mr. Edwards is looking at my nipples.

"Have you, Violet?" he repeats the question hoarsely, lifting his eyes.

"I-I don't understand the question," I say weakly, in the face of the fact that his hot stare is making me want to clench my thighs. Curl my toes and bite my lips and move my body in ways that are super inappropriate.

Super.

"I think I know the answer," he tells me as he arranges his body in the same position as before, hand on the wall up above my head so he can loom.

"What's the answer?"

"I think you do go around kissing whoever you want to. Isn't that right?"

"What?"

He jerks his chin up. "Yeah, I think that's right. I think that's what you do. You get drunk and you throw yourself on men. Those teenage hormones, yeah? They make you, don't they? Maybe you even let them go further."

"Further?"

"Yeah, maybe you let them put their hands on your tiny, little body. Maybe they touch you in ways I wanted to touch that woman last night. Before you showed up and ruined it for me."

"I –"

"Because it all starts with a kiss, doesn't it? Because none of it means anything to you. It's all one stupid drunken mistake that you won't even remember the next day."

He finishes his sentence with clenched teeth and I think he's done.

It's over.

But no, he has more to give me. He has more gasoline to pour over the fire his words have started in my veins so that it burns down my whole body.

"Were you going to remember it the next day? The kiss? Or were you just playing a game? It was all a game, wasn't it? You did it all for shits and giggles. It could've been anyone. It could've been the whole neighborhood. For all I know, it *was* the whole neighborhood. Maybe you made rounds through every man in the area before you came to me. Isn't that right? Because let's face it, it was a mistake, wasn't it?"

My chest is heaving. It's shaking, almost vibrating with the violence in my breaths.

I'm angry.

God, I'm so, so angry.

But I can't make myself move. I can't make myself escape the flames that are licking my skin, tonguing my nipples, turning them into these hard little points, making them ache.

How dare he?

How dare he say that? How *dare* he?

How dare he stand there, all outraged and tightened up like a fist, glaring at me like he wants to kill me for kissing other men when I've never kissed anyone in my entire life?

But you know what, fuck him. I'm too far gone now. Too far gone in my anger.

I'm not gonna correct him.

If he wants to be an asshole, he can be one. But I'm not going down.

Challenge accepted, Mr. Edwards.

"Well, now you know. Now you know that this is what I do."

As soon as the words are out of my mouth, all fight leaves me. All fire, all anger.

I know I shouldn't have said it. He's right to be angry and I should've taken it. I should've taken his wrath.

A second later, I hear a smack, a slap that he delivers to the wall, sharp and powerful that practically shakes the whole building.

"Don't play games with me, you got that?" he growls. "If I tell you to do something, you do it. If I tell you to leave, you fucking leave. You walk away. You don't mess with me. You *never* mess with me. I eat girls like you for breakfast. Do you understand? And you? I'll eat you up so slow that you'll feel every painful bite. I'll *make* you feel every painful bite. Every sharp stab of my teeth. Every vicious pull of my mouth. And trust me, you're not going to like it, not one bit. So smarten the fuck up and leave. This is the last time I'll ask nicely."

With that, he whirls around and marches out the door.

6

Dear Heart, seriously.
Why him?

-The Diary of a Shrinking Violet, Age 17

I'm at his place.

Or rather outside of his place, where his dead rose garden is, surrounded by thick woods on all sides and crunchy, leaf-filled, untamed ground, all against the backdrop of mountains.

Seriously, *how* does anyone live here?

It's practically impossible to live in this falling-apart cabin in the middle of the woods where even the sun doesn't shine.

But whatever.

I am here because *he* lives here.

I'm not sure if it's the right move. In fact, I should've left the moment he marched out of the bar after saying all those wonderful things to me and I'm being totally sarcastic here.

But I didn't leave.

I wrote a note to Billy, the amused man, and told him that I'd be staying up in his room for a few more days. And then I left him some cash – which my mom generously gave me before I left – telling him that if he needed more, he could just slide the bill in through the door.

After that, I went up to the room and cried the day away.

Once I was done, I pulled out my phone and looked up gardening stores in the area and if they delivered. Turns out, there is a gardening store in Pike's Peak that does deliver, and they had everything I needed. So I had them deliver some stuff to the bar, which I told Billy about with another note that I quickly left at the same place before the bar opened for the day.

A day later, here I am.

In his dead garden with all the supplies I need to grow him the roses. Once I'm done planting the new flowers for him, *then* I'll leave.

I know, I know I said I wouldn't be mad at him but screw him.

He's not the boss of me.

If I want to learn how to grow roses on the internet, I'll do it. If I want to use my newly-acquired knowledge and clear out the dead bushes, turn the freaking soil, dig a twelve-inch hole and add peat moss to it, I will fucking do that too.

I stab the shovel in the ground with a grunt. "Stupid, freaking jerk."

Another stab. "Asshole."

Stab number three and a kick, and I lower my voice and

imitate his tone. "'Were you going to remember it the next day? It was a game, wasn't it? It could've been anyone.' Yes. It could've been anyone, Mr. Edwards. It could've been the whole fucking neighborhood. What, you thought you were special? You're not special. You were never special. Never."

I kick at the ground again and the dirt goes flying. "Do you see how special you are, now? Do you?"

I raise the shovel high up and smash it back into the earth. "'I eat girls like you for breakfast.' Oh please. As if."

"Are you trying to murder the ground?"

His groggy voice pierces through my anger and I whirl around.

I shouldn't have.

Or maybe I should've taken a little time to control my raging emotions and *then* turned around and looked at him.

Because he's not wearing a shirt.

Oh my God, he's not wearing a shirt.

The only thing he has on is a pair of plaid pajama bottoms that look old and worn and so comfy. The hem of them is grazing his bare feet.

Such a non-threatening picture. Old pajamas, bare feet, sleepy voice.

Such a freaking lie.

"Only because I can't get to my actual target right now," I reply.

"And who's your actual target?"

I flex my grip on the shovel. "People call him The Beast."

"Yeah? Sounds dangerous."

"He used to make students cry back at my school. Everyone hated him."

"Everyone's smart."

"Oh, and he eats girls like me for breakfast."

"You should probably stay away, then."

"I should." I raise the shovel and kind of wave it. "But I have this, remember? And I know how to use it."

"Clearly."

When all the words run out between us and silence descends, I can't ignore the elephant in the space.

Or The Beast.

The Beast who's not wearing a shirt.

I can see every ridge and groove of his upper body. The tight slabs of his pecs and rigid slopes of his sides.

Not to mention, I can see the hair on his chest, a light smattering at first, but then thickening and darkening as it goes down and becomes a furry trail around his belly button, that disappears under the waistband of his pajamas.

It kills me. It literally kills me how sexy it is, his chest hair. How appealing.

More appealing than the veins going up and down on his arms and that bulge in his bicep when he raises that arm and glugs something down from a bottle.

He does it all with his eyes on me and...

Hold on a second.

He's drinking from a bottle? Again?

"Is that..." I squint. "Is that whiskey?"

"Scotch," he corrects me, taking another sip of it, like that's what's important.

"But it's like, first thing in the morning."

"So?"

I stick the shovel into the ground and rest my elbow on it. "So, people drink coffee in the morning. Or juice."

"I don't like juice."

"Well, there's always coffee."

"Don't like coffee either."

"That's such a lie. You like coffee."

"Really?"

"Uh-huh. You like it black."

"I'll take your word for it."

I narrow my eyes at him. "You also wake up really early in the morning."

"Do I?"

"Yes. I used to live next door to you, remember? So I know. You used to wake up at four or something. It's not four now."

Nope, it's not.

It's like, after eleven, and I've never seen him sleep this late.

"So you *do* know how to tell the time. Your babysitter will be pleased."

I scoff. "Of course. How did we go so long without you making a crack about my age? But I guess it helps you sleep at night. So sure, let's call my imaginary babysitter and tell her the good news. But only after you tell me why you're drinking when you've just woken up? Late, no less."

Leaving the shovel in the ground, I fold my arms across my chest and wait for his answer.

"I like this now," he says after a few seconds, and as if to emphasize it, he wraps his lips around the rim and chugs down another shot of it.

It's fast and so sudden that even I feel the burn of whiskey going down. I can feel it settling in my stomach like it does in his and I don't like it one bit.

I don't like that he's drinking like this.

"You want some?" he dares, tipping the bottle toward me.

"Absolutely not."

"Afraid you might do something stupid?"

I grit my teeth. "No."

"Come on. We both know how much you like it."

I think I broke my jaw just a little, with how hard I'm grinding it. I might have even pierced the skin of my palms with my nails if I wasn't wearing my newly-acquired work gloves.

"I don't drink anymore," I tell him.

At this, he laughs.

It's a rusty sound. Gravelly and loud, coming from a place deep inside of him, it feels like.

"You don't drink anymore," he says in a voice laced with amusement.

"Nope."

"Since when?"

"Since I kissed an asshole."

It's true.

I don't touch liquor or any of the addictive substances. Well, except for this one time when I baked funny brownies for the girls just after we got out of Heartstone. But I only ate one and decided to never touch them again.

And Mr. Edwards believes that, I think.

He sees the truth of it on my face.

The face that's exposed and unhindered by the cap and my Audrey Hepburn sunglasses. For some reason, I don't need them when it's just me and him.

"Well then, you'll be disappointed because this is all I've got."

Sighing, I step away from the shovel, which stays standing, buried in the soil that I haven't finished prepping for the roses but I will, just not now.

Looking him in the eyes, I take off my gloves, pick up my fat hobo and begin to walk toward him.

I stop at the rickety stairs and tilt my neck up. "You do have water, don't you?"

His answer is to keep staring at me with a dipped, neutral face.

His eyes are dark, but I can see little flecks of green shining through, as if light is breaking through thick clouds. As if there's a softness in him and it's seeping through the cracks of all that is hard in him.

"I'm thirsty," I continue. "And I need to wash up."

His eyelids drop low and take in my state.

I'm wearing a red t-shirt with a black rose printed on the chest along with jean shorts and red sneakers. My knees and calves are caked with mud. I somehow got a little bit of it on my clothes too.

He's looking at all of that.

And I'm trying to stay calm and breathe normally. And not think about the glory that is his chest.

Man, I wanna touch it, like bury my fingers in that curling hair and…

"Yeah, you're dirty," he says in a tone as low and hooded as his eyes, breaking my quite frankly dirty thoughts.

But at the same time, I have to do something at his low words.

I have to make my body move or I'll die. So I curl my toes inside my sneakers and bite my lip.

"There's a lake right behind you. Through the woods. It should take care of both your problems."

I shake my head at him and get a hold of myself. "I know you think you can make me do things but I'm not jumping in the lake for you."

"Not today."

I roll my eyes. "Not ever."

Then, something happens that I thought was a myth.

I see the lines on the corner of his eyes. Three deep ones. They twitch just as his strawberry mouth pulls up on one side.

It's not a smile. Not per se. It's amusement – pure amusement – in its very thin and basic state. But it's there and I feel myself flushing.

With pride, no less.

"Are you going to let me in?" I ask, hopping on my spot impatiently. "I'm dirty, as you said. And I need a little break before I go back to the roses."

Frankly, I'm dying to see the inside of his cabin. Like, what am I going to find when the outside is so neglected and falling apart.

He doesn't move, of course.

In fact, he leans against the doorjamb, crosses his ankles and folds his arms, his bottle getting tucked at his side.

"When did I hire you as my gardener?"

"You didn't. I'm doing this for free and out of the goodness of my heart."

"And what did I do to deserve that?"

"Absolutely nothing." I raise my eyebrows. "I'm doing it because I'm awesome and fabulous and a hundred other words that you probably never use for me."

He hums, as if really thinking about it. "Yeah, those are not the words that I use for you."

I give him a sweet smile. "I was right. So…" I gesture toward the hallway. "Can I get some water?"

"Are you stupid?"

I draw back at his question. "What?"

"How is it that the entire world is afraid of me and knows to leave me alone but you don't seem to care?" He nods, as if coming to a conclusion. "You have to be stupid. That's the only explanation."

I climb up another step so now we're even closer. In fact, we're the same height. I look into his dark brown eyes as I whisper, "I'm going to tell you a secret about me." His frown is curious. "You know what's my favorite fruit?"

"Is that the secret?"

"It's strawberry. And you know what else?"

"What?"

I smile. "I'm allergic to it."

"You're allergic to your favorite fruit."

"Uh-huh. But I still eat it if I'm in the mood to throw up. You know what that means?"

"Why don't you tell me?"

He looks lazy and relaxed and so freaking delicious that I have to stop a second and gather my wits before answering. "It means I'm a masochist, Mr. Edwards. I like the pain. The pain doesn't scare me. *You* don't scare me. And let me tell you another secret – masochists like me? We have really tasty skin. You can eat me up all you want. You can eat me up a hundred different ways. I'm gonna like your teeth and your tongue and I'm gonna fall in love with the sting of it all. You're my Strawberry Man. At least, that's what I call you in my head."

There's a certain heat radiating off his sleepy, bare skin. Thick like molasses, and I'm reveling in it.

Reveling in the treacle that's sliding down my bones and his smell and his nearness.

He flicks his eyes down to the side of my neck and I feel him there. I feel the sting of his teeth that he hasn't given me. The wetness of his tongue that I'll never know.

"I'll keep that in mind, Jailbait."

Jailbait.

It's supposed to be this stigma-filled word. It should horrify me and it would, if he hadn't said it with… a fondness, almost. Or at least, with some lightness injected into it and if I hadn't felt it in my belly.

"You do that, Strawberry Man."

Then, he puts a period in the conversation with another glug of his whiskey.

"You know you really shouldn't drink first thing in the morning."

"You know you should really mind your own business."

I laugh.

I don't know why but I do, and something changes in him for a second.

Something goes both soft and intense on his face. He swallows like his throat is dry when I know it isn't; he just took a huge swallow of that dreaded whiskey.

He drops his eyes to my mouth, as if willing me to laugh again. Willing me to stretch my lips, and it's such a crazy thought that he wants me to smile for him that I speak. "Mr. Edwards?"

He jerks up his eyes and almost glares at me. He takes a violent pull of his liquor before growling, "I don't like loud sounds first thing in the morning. So keep your laughter to a minimum."

I'm so confused as to what just happened that it takes me a few seconds to realize that someone has knocked at his front door.

Someone is at his door.

Someone is *at his door*.

Oh Jesus Christ.

I'm not equipped for that. I'm not equipped to handle knocks at the door.

Okay so, along with not being able to enter through the front door, I kinda get spooked when someone knocks at the door as well. Back in Connecticut, as soon as I heard the bell, I'd lock my room, dive into my bed, put my headphones on so I wouldn't hear why someone was there. Or if someone was there for me, gossiping about me downstairs in the living room. It has happened during the initial days when the story had just broken.

And now someone is here and I don't know what I'm going to do because I'm this close to losing my shit.

Right in front of Mr. Edwards's eyes.

7

I saw him in a leather jacket
yesterday. Winter is officially my
favorite month now. On second
thought, how can I forget last
summer? I saw him bare-chested
and forgot other seasons existed.

-The Diary of a Shrinking Violet, Age 17

Oh God.

No.

No, no, no.

I can't have my doomsday brain ticking up right now.

I try to breathe normally. I try to purse my lips, press them together lest my heart jump out of my mouth and smack Mr. Edwards in the chest. I even try to control the flush that's rapidly covering my throat.

Oh God, please. No. Please, please, please.

I'm usually fine. Why is this happening right now? Why in front of him?

Not to mention, he is frowning.

He also takes a step back and I think it's because he knows I'm losing it by the second. He's finally realizing what a basket case I am.

Which is so not true.

I'm fine.

Fiiiiine.

But no, that's not it. He hasn't realized it yet.

Oh God, he hasn't.

Because he's not paying attention to me. His thoughts are far away, probably on that someone at the door, and to prove it, he whirls around and leaves. He strides down the hallway of his cabin and goes to the front door.

Just when he turns the knob, I flip around and plaster myself on the wall, hiding away from sight.

I hear the door open, followed by Mr. Edwards's voice. "Richard." He sounds bored. "What do you want?"

"I'm surprised to see you're up so early," the man, Richard, says.

"When you knew there was a possibility of me sleeping, why did you come?"

Richard chuckles. "To wake you up."

"Well, as you can see, I'm up and about. So you can go back now."

"Not so fast."

A few seconds of silence and creaking of the floor as if someone is shifting legs on the spot. And then, "Please don't tell me that's what I think it is."

"I won't," Mr. Edwards says.

"Have you been drinking?" Richard's voice has grown louder. "Never mind. Don't answer me. I already know."

"Why are you here?"

"Whose car is out front?"

I freeze at that.

That and gasp. Or almost gasp because I have the presence of mind to whip a hand over my mouth and catch it.

I swear I hear an imaginary clock ticking as I wait for Mr. Edwards's answer.

"No one's."

"You've got company?"

My heart jumps in my throat and I press my hand on my mouth harder. Will Mr. Edwards tell him yes? Would he bring Richard out back to see me?

Oh God, I can't see people without my disguise.

I can't.

I can't talk to them. I can't look at them.

Richard will know who I am. He'll know what I did, how I ruined things for Mr. Edwards.

He will. He will. He will.

As irrational as the thought is, I can't shake it; then, I hear a sigh, followed by the words that bring me sweet relief.

"What do you want, Richard?"

A few beats of silence again before Richard answers, "The football camp starts next week, Graham. I'm here to make sure you know that."

"I know."

Richard makes a non-committal sound. "It's surprising given that you've hardly been to any of the meetings."

"I'm handling everything remotely."

"So maybe your assistant forgot to mention that to me. When I had my chat with him this morning."

"How do I know what my assistant forgot to tell you?"

"I'm not here to fight with you, all right? My daughter's in town. I'm taking her and my wife out for a nice lunch. I don't want to ruin my day."

"Then don't."

"Good. I'm glad we're on the same page. I want you to come in to school tomorrow so we can bring you up to speed, all right? I'd like my coach to get with the program. The one he's supposed to have come up with himself."

There's a thread of sarcasm in there and it's so thick that even I'm cringing.

I hear a sigh, a long one. I have a feeling it's from Mr. Edwards.

"All right, look. The camp doesn't start until next week. Which means I've got time. Just email me the program and I'll go over it in my own time."

"Do you think I'm stupid?"

Nothing except shuffling of feet and I can very well imagine that Mr. Edwards is either clenching his jaw at Richard or scratching his beard in a way that makes other people *feel* stupid.

"Yeah, I do. Why, haven't I been clear enough about it in the past?"

"Graham, I'm going to level with you. I've known you a long time. You're my friend, okay? I'm glad to have you back in town. Even though I don't know how you live in this miserable house or how you're still alive when you're such a giant asshole that I want to kill you on a daily basis, I'm happy. But we're not in high school anymore. Or at least, we're not the ones *going* to high school anymore."

"Yeah, I value our friendship too."

"Now you listen to me, I'm not going to stand for any more of your bullshit. You show up for the camp, on time, fucking sober, okay?"

"Or what?"

"Or you're fired. I'm not kidding around. I've tried to be nice. I've tried to be patient. I've overlooked your drinking on the job, your unprofessional conduct and the fact that you don't show up or if you do, you show up late. And I don't want to remind you but I've even overlooked what happened back in Connecticut. You were accused of having an affair with a student. A minor, Graham. I know it's not true. I know that. But it doesn't matter. It does not look good period. But despite it all, I gave you a fucking job at my school. I risked my reputation for you. Because you're my friend and I wanted to help you. But it's time for you to pay me back for that. It's time for you to pay me back for the favor I did you. Because it was a favor, understand? Don't make me regret having your back."

The silence is slashed with heavy breaths.

A second later, I hear rapidly moving footsteps, followed by the loud bang of the door closing.

I'm glad it was loud. Otherwise I would've given myself away. My broken, loud sob would've told everyone that I was here.

Listening and hiding.

The girl who ruined Mr. Edwards's life. The girl with poison lips and stupid teenage dreams.

He was right the other night. I took away his peace. I am a nightmare. A nightmare he can't forget or outrun or out-sleep.

Not when he's reminded of it at every turn. Not when he has to live with it.

Tears are streaming down my face, too quick for me to wipe them off. But I do. I do wipe them off because I didn't come here to cry.

I came here to face him. To face his wrath, to face what I did to him.

I came here for him.

And he needs me now. I have to go to him.

In a daze, I come away from the wall I've been hiding behind. I climb up the steps in a trance. I walk down the creaking hallway that he took not ten minutes ago.

I reach the living room just as I hear another sound. Louder than the bang of the door. Shriller, higher. It's the sound of something being smashed and wrecked into countless pieces.

It's the sound of Mr. Edwards throwing his liquor bottle on the floor.

He's standing at the kitchen island. The island that's buried under tens and tens of liquor bottles. They are littered almost everywhere. On the counters, by the trashcan. The smell of alcohol hangs thick and heavy in the air.

When I look back at Mr. Edwards, I see he's watching me. His chest is heaving and that burly body of his has somehow grown in a matter of minutes.

"Are you an alcoholic?" I ask in a small voice, knowing the answer already.

Each time I've seen him, he's been with a bottle. He drank so much whiskey just now but hardly anything happened to him.

He looks sober. Except for the tangy, addictive smell and the dilation of his pupils, I can't see any more effects.

Actually, no.

I'm wrong.

There are effects. He's lost weight. That's why his cheekbones look sharper now. There are even little pits under his eyes.

Now that I understand this, I can see him clearly.

I can see how he's let himself go. How long his hair is, messy and dark. How untamed his beard is. How angular his jaw looks. How his collarbone juts out, how his entire body has been reduced to sharp bones and muscles. No room for any softness.

He looks savage. Beautiful but uncivilized.

My hobo slides down my shoulder and thuds down on the floor, beside the broken glass. "I heard everything."

At this, he widens his stance, his mouth parting as he drags in a charged-up breath.

"You are an alcoholic, aren't you? I mean, ever since everything happened. I gave up drinking and you've taken it up. And you hate schools too, don't you? That's why you don't show up."

I have to take a pause because I see his chest vibrating.

"I hate schools too," I continue because I want him to know that he's not alone. "I hate corridors and students and teachers. Everyone with their judgement and their gossiping. I went there once after… everything happened, to see the principal, and I hated every second of it. I hated the smell, the air, the lockers. Everything."

I went back to school to tell Principal Jacobs that it was me who did the wrong thing. The building was empty, save for a few people. I didn't meet anyone on my way to the principal's office, but I could still feel my skin crawling. As if they were all watching me.

"That's not it, though, is it? You don't only hate schools, you hate everything. You hate your roses too. Is it because I was trying to steal them that night? Is that why you don't take care of them anymore?"

I wipe my mouth with the back of my hand, feeling so small and so vulnerable.

"They remind me of you," he rasps at last, jolting the breath out of me.

"Your roses?"

"Yeah."

It's a hoarse sound, his *yeah*. It's both sad and angry. It's tortured. Anguished.

It squeezes my heart so much that I think it will explode. The veins will burst. The chambers will collapse. My heart will self-destruct.

"And that's why you hate them now, because you hate me," I conclude on a whisper, wondering how many girls dream of being someone's rose and how many of them cry when they really become it.

He flinches; it's a big flinch.

As if I slapped him. As if I smacked his chest or kicked him in the gut.

As if I sliced his skin by uttering those words and I don't understand.

Isn't that the truth?

He does hate me, doesn't he?

His features rearrange themselves in a flash and I don't have time to wonder about inconsequential things. They morph into what they always are when I'm around.

Cold and sharp.

"Yes, I'm an alcoholic now. Yes, I hate schools. Yes, I don't take care of roses. Are you going to say sorry now?" he lashes out. "That's why you came. You told me that, right? To apologize. So are you going to get down on your knees and beg for my forgiveness?"

"I…"

"Is that your plan? To get down on your knees and beg me to forgive you? To do my bidding, plant me new roses, sacrifice yourself? What if I ask you to crawl around on your knees? Are you going to do that too? Are you going to follow me around like a lost little puppy? Are you going to take every cruel thing I do to you before it gets through your head that this whole thing is not worth it? It's not worth it, okay? So leave."

Somehow, his rapid-fire questions, his callous words fill me with more determination. A new, solid kind of determination.

He's hurting.

It's plain to see. He's in pain and he's lashing out and it's my doing.

So yeah, that's my plan.

To beg for his forgiveness. To take every cruel thing he does to me. Because even if he doesn't believe it, this whole thing is more than worth it.

It's so worth it and I so feel it in my bones that I get down on my knees. I don't even think about it. I do it just because it was something that fell out of his mouth.

And when I do get down on my knees, he frowns.

He almost stumbles back as if this time I shot him with a gun and the bullet went straight through his heart.

"What the fuck are you doing?" he growls.

"Whatever you said," I whisper, looking up at him, my knees on the squeaking, ancient hardwood floor.

Then I go ahead and put my hands on the floor too, going down on all fours. My hands are a few inches shy of where the shards of glass start. They are scattered around, between him and me, and I don't care if I have to crawl through glass to get to him.

I glance up at him again and find his frown the thickest I've ever seen. It's so deep, it's almost like a hole in the ground.

"You told me not to play games with you. Not to mess with you. To do as you say. So if you want me to kneel, then I'll kneel." I put my hand forward and take a step toward him. "I'll crawl and beg and sacrifice myself until you move on. Until you don't hate or feel angry. I'll do anything and everything. Because that's all I can do. I can't change the past. I can't take back my kiss, Mr. Edwards, but I can make you forget and move on."

And then, I lift my hand and walk it forward.

I'm about to bring it down on the first broken piece of bottle and cut myself on it so I bleed and seal the oath that I've made him in blood when a hand grasps my wrist.

Before I can even process this strange turn of events, I'm snatched up and pulled off my knees.

The sudden change makes me dizzy and a furious Mr. Edwards swims in front of my eyes. The bones of his cheek and jaw are hard. As hard as his grip on my wrist, my bare wrist.

He's touching my skin.

I'm so confused and distracted by his fingers on my naked skin for the first time that I wince when I hear his voice again. "Don't. *Ever*. Do that again. Not for me."

That's when I make sense of it all.

He pulled me up at the last second.

Not only that but he pulled me up by walking through the glass himself, on bare feet.

In horror, I look down and find those feet of his, all bloody, but before I can say anything, he pushes me away like he burnt himself on my skin, so that I stumble back.

And he stalks out of the room, leaving bloody footprints in his wake.

8

I cut my finger on a thorn
of one of his roses tonight. The
pain was so sharp and brilliant.
I smiled, thinking he left
a mark on my skin.

-The Diary of a Shrinking Violet, Age 16

He asked me what my plan was and I do have a plan.

I'm at his cabin again and with me, I brought stuff for that plan too.

Stuff like my suitcase, which I'm going to leave in my car for now; I don't wanna spook him this early in the morning by showing that I'm here to stay with him for a little bit. Other than that, I left a note for my new pen pal, Billy, and asked him to do me a favor and buy stuff on the list I attached with the note.

He did. He even left it at my door with a note of his own, saying that if I need anything else, all I have to do is ask. I left him another note and thanked him and told him that I was going to go away for a while.

I wish I was strong enough to see Billy face to face. I wish I could at least say hi.

But that's not important right now.

My entire energy needs to be focused on Mr. Edwards and the plan that I have for him. It's going to be hard but he can do it.

Okay, first order of business is to get these new roses planted.

So I go out back to his rose garden that I worked on yesterday. I let my hobo slide down to the ground and squat to fish out my headphones and lollipops. Popping one in my mouth and putting on "The Chain" by Fleetwood Mac, I get to work.

The air is quiet and the breeze barely exists. It's like even the wind doesn't blow in this part of the world. Everything, even the trees, the ground, the grass is abandoned and on its own.

Something about that, about the silence and the loneliness of the place tugs at my heart as I'm digging holes and planting the overnight-soaked-in-water roses.

I'm on the ground, bent over, my knees mashed into the dirt and my hands pressing the soil around the last rose bush when I hear the backdoor open even through the song in my ears, and I stop.

Hastily, I straighten up, take off my work gloves and my headphones before turning around.

Mr. Edwards is up.

Like yesterday, he's standing at the threshold, leaning against the doorjamb with his arms crossed over his chest. He's just woken up; sleep is evident in every line of his sharp face and the stuck-up strands of his thick hair.

There's one difference though. He's wearing a t-shirt: white over his plaid pajamas, and he doesn't have a liquor bottle in his hands.

So I guess there are two differences.

Swallowing, I leave my stuff on the ground and stand up, all dirty and mud-caked. My eyes instantly drop to his bare feet. The hem of his pajamas flutters around them, making them seem as vulnerable as yesterday.

I still can't get over how he walked on broken glass to prevent me from doing it myself. I was supposed to bleed for him, seal my promise in blood.

But he bled for me, instead.

Gosh, he *bled* for me. And he touched my bare skin.

Biting my lip, I ask, "How're your feet?"

His gaze drops to my mouth, making it tingle. "I'll live."

"You should really put bandages on them."

"How are my roses?" he asks, ignoring my advice.

They remind me of you...

His words flash through my head and every part of me blushes. I remind him of delicate flowers he used to grow and care for. The flowers with pink, velvet petals. The color I'm sure my skin is turning into.

If only that was a good thing.

"Well, at the risk of pissing you off, I think they should be good. Unless you remember that you hate them now and forget to water them on purpose, they'll live too."

A glint shines in his eyes. If I didn't know better, I'd think it's a glint of light amusement that somehow cuts through the tension.

"By the way, they're Peace, the roses. Since you know, I took away your peace and all that. So I'm giving it back."

"You are, huh?"

"Yup. They're supposed to have lemony –"

"Lemony yellow petals with pale pink edges, I know."

Damn it.

Why is it so sexy that he knows these things? Someone like him, someone so rough knows so much about something so tiny and fragile. Before I can ask him how he knows so much about the roses, he tells me, "I'm not paying you for all the yard work. In case this is how you plan to finance your college education."

A churning happens in my stomach.

Liar.

I'm a liar.

But I still try to tell the truth. "I don't want your money."

"You want water?"

"Are you going to tell me to jump in the lake again?"

"I'm going to go back to the kitchen, open my fridge and bring you a bottle of water."

I blink.

Then I blink some more.

Did he really just say he was going to bring me water?

I narrow my eyes at him. "Are you going to poison it? The water?"

"Hadn't thought of that."

"Seriously?"

"Yeah." He scratches his beard. "Actually, I was thinking it's the least I could do for all the free yard work you insist on doing around here. But if you want to jump in the lake instead, you're more than welcome to."

And just like that, he straightens up from the doorjamb and leaves.

I stare at the door, now empty of his presence, wondering what just happened? Is this somehow... a truce?

I can't keep the smile off my face as I dash up to the rickety stairs and enter his house.

I was so distracted yesterday that I didn't notice a single thing about this cabin. But I do now.

The hallway is short and narrow and as I walk down it, the floor squeaks. The walls are beige in color and bare. Once upon a time, I think this hallway was clean and free of dusty cobwebs that hang in the corners of the ceiling. The wooden walls didn't have cracks in them, either.

I come upon the living room and the state of disarray is even more pronounced.

The dusty, marked-up windows. In fact, one of them is broken even. A jagged hole in the glass, with cracks running up and down in all directions.

The furniture is all old, reminding me of those abandoned mansions where everything is covered by white sheets for years and years, until someone comes along and takes the sheets off and lets the couch and the coffee table breathe.

Only here, nothing is breathing.

Everything is suspended and alone. Almost dead and life-less.

And in the midst of all this is Mr. Edwards. He stands in the kitchen – tall and aloof – at the island where he was yesterday when I wanted to crawl up to him, as he watches me watch where he lives.

"Nice place," I tell him.

He accepts the fake compliment with a dip of his chin. "Thanks. I decorated it myself."

I shake my head at him. "You do know that I'm going to clean it all up, don't you?"

"Why? Are you my maid now?"

"No. I'm your fairy godmother."

He studies me, runs his eyes up and down my disheveled body. Like yesterday, I'm mud-caked and dirty. The tendrils of my hair hang around my pale face in a sweaty mess, and I think I left muddy footprints on his floor when I walked inside.

He's not looking at the muddy footprints though. He's looking at the state of me and I'm not sure if I pass muster.

I so wanna, though.

So, so wanna.

Finally, he looks me in the eyes, nothing on his expression to suggest what he's thinking as he says, "My godmother is dead. And I'm allergic to fairy dust."

Slowly, I smile.

Then I chuckle and he watches it all like he can't stop.

I know it's not true but I'm liking the delusion in this moment. So much so that I tell him, "It's okay. If you faint from your allergies, I'll stab you in the heart with a very sharp needle and bring you back to life, Mr. Edwards."

Mr. Edwards looks at my chest for a flicker of a second before murmuring, "Yeah, I'd rather you don't. I'm not sure being alive is on my agenda."

Then he walks away from the island and goes to the cabinet above the sink. Out comes his precious: Jack Daniels.

But before he can take a sip, I blurt out, "I wouldn't do that if I were you."

His eyes flick to me, bottle clutched in his hand. "Yeah? Why? Is it poisoned? Like the water I'm going to give you in about two minutes."

I roll my eyes at his sarcasm.

"Yeah, that's funny." I go to the island and lean against it. "What I mean is that the precious Jack Daniels of yours is not doing you any favors."

He narrows his eyes. "Noted."

"You know, every alcoholic thinks that he's just so smart, doesn't he? But he's not. For example, did you know that drinking has both short-term and long-term effects? Like, long-term, you could lose your memory. You could get alcoholic hepatitis. Cardiomyopathy, liver fibrosis, high blood pressure including erectile dysfunction." I pause so the information can sink in. "Yeah, I'm not kidding. I mean, it's all over the internet, the news, the TV. Everyone knows how alcohol is bad and —"

"What was the last one?" he interrupts.

"What?"

"The last thing you said. After high blood pressure."

I squint, thinking about it. And just as I figure out what I did say, I notice that his eyebrows go up in challenge.

"What, you don't think I can say it?" I fold my arms across my chest.

He shrugs. "If I thought that, I wouldn't have asked."

"Erectile dysfunction, okay? You'll get erectile dysfunction if you keep drinking."

He sets his bottle down and folds his arms across his chest too, leaning against the counter. Now it looks like we're having a face off of some kind.

"What's erectile dysfunction?"

"Really?"

"Yeah. Enlighten me."

I tap my foot for a few seconds before I round the island, causing a ruckus on the sagging hardwood floor, and stand directly in front of him.

I crane my neck up to look at him – God, he's tall – and he bows his head, looking down at me. We're so close that I can feel his minty breath on my lips. So close that my feet recklessly think that it's okay to close that inch of distance between us and get up on *his* feet.

So close that they recklessly think that they are in love with his feet.

"Fine. You want me to enlighten you? Your dick, Mr. Edwards, your dick won't work, if you keep drinking. That's what erectile dysfunction is. Now, are you happy? Did you think I wouldn't say it? Do you think I'm some kind of a delicate flower who can't say dick?"

He unfolds his arms and comes away from the counter.

His bare feet touch my sneakers and I'm forced to make

space for him. Well, not forced exactly.

I move back and keep moving back because I want to. Because I can't help myself.

His eyes are trained on me and he's so big that he overtakes and hijacks all my willpower. I *want* him to hijack all my willpower and pin me down like a butterfly.

Which happens exactly five seconds later when my butt hits the island. "What are you doing?"

"I'm trying to tell you something."

"Tell me what?"

"That I don't have a dick."

"Wh-what?"

He nods, staring me in the eyes, making me squirm. "Boys have dicks. Dicks that sometimes don't work. I'm not a boy. Do I look like a boy to you?"

"No."

"What do I look like then?"

Does he really have to ask?

I mean, just look at him. Look at that beard of his. All thick and dark and lending him a dangerous quality. Not to mention those lines around his gorgeous eyes. His high, sculpted cheekbones. That brawny body of his.

He leans down toward me, bringing that body closer as he puts both his hands on the island, caging me in. "So?"

"You're a man," I whisper, thinking that if he puts a little more pressure on the island, if he throws in a little bit of his strength, he can rip it out. So very easily.

As easily as he can carry me and throw my tiny body

around.

I should really stop having that thought. *Really.*

"Right." He nods. "So, I don't have a dick. I have a cock."

Jesus Christ.

He said cock.

Cock.

So much filthier. Dirtier and more illicit. Like, you can only say cock when it's the middle of the night and all the lights are turned off.

I grab the island as well when I feel something tickle in the back of my knees, making them weak. "Okay."

"What do I have, Violet?"

I'm not sure if he's growing bigger with every second that passes or if I'm growing smaller. More feminine and submissive and pliant.

"You have a cock," I whisper like the slave I am.

And then, I focus really, really hard so I don't look down and check out the area where his cock is supposed to be.

"Good." He straightens up and moves away. "So I guess erectile dysfunction is off the table then."

After that, he makes for the counter and picks up his bottle again. I wake up from my daze as well and blurt out, "Don't do this."

He gives me a blank look and takes a sip of whiskey.

"Please, Mr. Edwards." I step toward him, feeling a little disoriented from the fog he just put me in.

"I think you should get your water and go."

He goes to take another sip but I make it to him in time

and put my hand over his.

I can't even cover it, his hand. My fingers are so tiny and so pale against his bronzed ones. I could look at them forever, his big fingers and my moon-colored, small ones.

I squeeze his hand not only to stop him but to feel his strength, and his entire body goes tight. As if I somehow squeezed his heart, that beating, vital thing inside his chest.

"Let it go," he warns.

I glance up at him and find those cheekbones of his darkened and flushed probably with anger and hate for me. "I know you don't like me. I know you hate me." His jaw clenches and his knuckles tighten up under my palm. "But I can't let you do this. I'm not going to stand aside while you ruin the rest of your life. Alcohol is bad for you. It's unhealthy. It's destructive. You can't waste your life like this. You can't drink your life away because I kissed you and your whole world exploded because of it. You can't do this to yourself. *Or* to Brian. I know he hates me too. I've betrayed his trust. You probably already know that we aren't even friends anymore. He won't talk to me. He won't pick up my calls and I... know that's my fault. But I'm not going to watch while you hurt yourself and him more, okay? I can't."

I squeeze his heated fingers again. "I can't watch you hurt yourself. You have to stop because I don't have the strength to take on more blame, Mr. Edwards. You can blame me for all your problems. You can be cruel to me. You can be mean, but you can't do this to me. I won't be able to bear it. I won't. So please, stop. For your sake, for your son's sake *and* for mine."

Something hot trickles down my cheek and I realize it's a

tear. A lonely trail of salt water, burning my skin.

I actually wouldn't have noticed it or noticed the burn even, if it wasn't for him.

I noticed it because he's watching it.

He's watching that lone tear trailing down my cheek, followed by another one. And another.

He's watching me cry and I'm not sure I like it. I promised myself that I wouldn't cry in front of him. I wouldn't show him any weakness.

But I failed. I failed because I can take everything he wants to throw at me but I can't take him destroying his life like this.

I can't take it.

I expect him to be disgusted like he used to be when one of his players cried. Or even unmoved.

I never expected him to look like this.

This stricken.

This... affected. There's a groove running down the center of his forehead and he has made himself so rigid that he's almost vibrating with the effort.

If I didn't know better, I'd think...

I'd think he can't see me cry. That it's painful for him, my crying.

That in itself makes me stop crying. That in itself makes me more worried about him and I can't help but ask, "Mr. Edwards, are you okay?"

My question jolts him and he lets the bottle go. He almost jerks his hand off of it and steps back.

And then he practically runs out of the cabin, leaving me a

mess of confusion.

Mr. Edwards

Two years and ten months ago when I moved to Connecticut, someone stabbed me in the chest with a knife.

Or at least, it feels like it.

It feels like someone stabbed me in the chest, right where my heart is, and now I'm stuck with it. That knife for the rest of my life.

And sometimes, that knife twists.

It twists and it digs into the wound and everything is so fucking painful that I can't see straight.

I can't breathe. I can't think.

All I can do is feel.

I feel and feel and feel until it becomes a living thing that presses into my very skin from the inside out.

It used to happen every time I saw her.

Every time she'd walk down the street, the knife would twist and I'd have to bite down on my teeth to stave off the pain.

Or every time she climbed up to her roof to watch the moon, or when I saw her around the school, bobbing her head to the music or smiling at something she'd read. Every time I heard her voice, her laughter…

I hated it.

I hated the effect she had on me – something unprecedented, something that never happened before and something completely inappropriate – so much so that countless times I imagined going up to her parents and telling them to fucking lock her up in a room or something.

She's a menace. A terrible thing.

But that's not the worst part. The worst part is that my pain reaches catastrophic levels when she cries. The knife twists and twists and doesn't stop at her tears.

I've treated her badly, yes. I've tried to scare her but it messes with me when she cries.

I saw her one day, crying in her backyard, by the pool. I'd just gotten home from work and there she was. She isn't a crier. So that sight was doubly shocking. I saw her through my windshield and even though I was too far away to tell, I knew she wasn't making any noise. I knew her tears were thick and silent.

And I felt this pain in my chest, all of a sudden. The tremendous pain of that knife twisting.

I would've jumped out of my truck and gone to her. I would've talked to her that day, asked her who the fuck hurt her, who made her cry.

But then, I was saved.

I was saved from rushing over to the teenage girl next door

whom I shouldn't have been watching in the first place. I shouldn't have been looking at or thinking about.

So when Brian walked out of our house, I remained stuck to my seat. I saw him crossing over to her and sitting beside her. He wiped her tears and made her stop crying.

He even made her laugh.

That eased some of the pressure. That laughter.

And then, I sped off in my truck. Because why the fuck did I care if she laughed or cried?

Why the fuck do I even care now?

Tears don't mean anything to me. I've made students cry. I won't deny it. I won't even make excuses for it. If it gets results on the field, then I'm all for it.

Yes, my son, when he was little, used to cry and it would pain me. But he's my son, I'm supposed to protect him.

I'm not supposed to think about her tears though. Her tears shouldn't have this strange effect on me.

A few drops of them from her eyes and I haven't touched my bottle all day. A few drops of them and I'm sitting here in my truck, staring down at the black screen of my phone, all ready to call my son.

I'm ready to call Brian when I haven't talked to him in months.

But I need to call him. I need to ask him what the hell is he doing? What is he thinking punishing her like this?

I thought he was punishing me – for good reason – but I didn't know that he was punishing her, as well. They've always been inseparable and I thought nothing, not even this, would come between them.

Apparently, I was wrong.

Apparently, I need to do what I haven't done in months. I need to call my son and have a talk with him.

It's making me antsy, however. It's making me shake and sweat, as if my bones are running dry and they're rattling against each other.

My throat's on fire, begging for one drop of alcohol, just one.

I even tell myself that no one is going to know. I beg myself to take a sip and when I almost throw away my phone and my good intentions and reach for that secret bottle I keep in the glove box, I hit dial.

I'm not sure if he'll pick up. In fact, I'm pretty sure he won't, but tonight, I'm not going to stop until he does.

I'm not going to stop until he does what I want him to do.

I'm ready to leave him a voicemail when I hear a click and his voice. "Hello?"

I grip the wheel tightly when I hear him. He sounds hesitant, unsure.

It throws me back in time, reminding me of when he was a kid. He'd come to my room in the middle of the night because he heard a noise or had a nightmare. And he'd tell me with this small, anxious voice, *Dad, there's someone in my closet.*

He'd look at me with those big hazel eyes similar to mine and I could see complete trust in them. Trust that now that I've told my dad, everything is going to be fine. He'll take care of everything.

"Dad?" he says again when I remain silent.

I unclench my jaw and make it move. "Brian, hey, kiddo."

I close my eyes at *kiddo*.

It's been ages since I called him that. He hates it so I'd use it to piss him off when he was being a smartass or to embarrass him in front of his friends.

"Hey," he greets me.

I don't know what to say after this. I'm completely drawing a blank.

"How are you, Dad?"

Apparently, he's more articulate than me. Good thing.

I've always failed at this emotional crap.

"I…" I clear my throat and loosen my grip on the wheel. "I'm good. Yeah. How are you?"

"I'm fine, too."

"Do you need anything?" I ask, slipping into the role that I know: of a provider. "Any money or something… something like that?"

"No, Dad. I'm okay. Yeah."

"Okay. Good." I swallow. "Good."

I'm parked on the side of the road, thinking about how we got here. How we got to this fucked up place where we can't talk to each other?

We've always been able to do that before. He'd always tell me everything and I'd listen. Of course, I knew he had his secrets; he's a teenage boy. He's going to have secrets from me but I knew what was going on in his life.

It's always been us against the world.

How did I become my own father? Drunk and absent.

After growing up with him, I never even wanted a relationship, let alone a kid.

But I had one.

And when I held Brian in my arms for the first time, every little bit of softness and vulnerability inside me in the shape of a tiny human being, I made him a promise.

I promised that I'd always be there for him. That even though Cynthia – his mother – had left him, I'd always put him first.

So what happened?

"Where are you right now?" I ask after a few beats.

"Uh, California. We're gonna stay here for a few weeks and then head back east."

I nod, staring into the darkening sky. "How..." I scratch my forehead. "How has it been so far?"

"Good, yeah. It's been a ton of fun."

"I'm glad."

"I actually have some photos on Facebook. I wanted to, uh, send them to you but..."

I chuckle, feeling an ache in my chest. "Yeah, I guess I better get on Facebook like the rest of the world, huh."

This ache is different than the knife.

The knife is vicious, edgy, deadly even.

This is the ache for my child. My son.

He chuckles back; it's awkward like everything between us now. "Yeah. You're several decades behind, Dad."

"Yeah, I am."

"So what's up, Dad?" he asks abruptly.

You can't do this to Brian. I'm not going to watch while you hurt yourself and him more...

Her voice echoes in the dark of the cab and I push the words out, "Listen, Bri, I know we haven't talked in a while. But I want you to do something for me, all right?"

I can sense him getting serious, paying his entire attention to me. "Okay."

I pinch the bridge of my nose. "I want you to call her."

"What?"

"I want you to call her and I want you to talk to her."

"Are you... Are you talking about... Vi?"

Brian calls her that.

In fact, everyone around her calls her Vi.

But she's never been Vi to me. To me, she's always been Violet. The bright color with a dominant wavelength at the end of the spectrum.

The color I never paid attention to until I saw her.

The knife is twisting in my chest again, gaping the wound open. "Yeah. Yeah, I am. You need to call her. I know you haven't in a while. But I want you to do this for me, okay? Just call her."

"Why?"

I grit my teeth. "Because it's the right thing to do. Because... whatever happened shouldn't come between you two."

"Oh, you mean the fact that she kissed my dad?"

It hits me right in the gut, his words, and I flinch. "It doesn't matter now. It's over. You need to talk to her. You..."

"Me what, Dad?"

I rub my forehead. "You need to stop punishing her, okay? She made a mistake. It was a mistake."

Those words sound bitter, fucked-up on my tongue and I curse myself in my head for feeling this way.

Stupid, drunken mistake.

His breathing has gone heavy. Agitated.

"How do you know?" he asks. "How do you know it was a mistake? She tell you that?"

I go silent, words clamming up in my throat.

But Brian breaks the tense silence. "How is it that you call me after months, Dad, and you ask me to talk to her?"

I bump my head against the headrest. I haven't been keeping in touch. That's true. Initially, that's what he wanted. We'd occasionally text but that was all. I offered to visit him once, but he refused.

And I'm ashamed to say that I was relieved.

I didn't know how to talk to him. Every time I thought about picking up the phone and calling him, his words from that night would run through my mind. All of them true, all of them making me even more ashamed and guilty. Disgusted with myself.

So I drank and drank until I forgot them. Until I forgot her.

But I should've tried harder.

I should've gotten my shit together and behaved like a responsible parent. At the very least, I would've known what he's been doing to her.

How he's been punishing her all this time and I've been so checked out from the world that I had zero clue about it.

"I know I haven't been the best of dads. I haven't been keeping in touch and –"

"But have you been keeping in touch with *her*, Dad?" His voice sounds angry now.

Just like that, I get a flashback from ten months ago.

Do you like her, Dad? Is that what's going on? You want her? You want *my best friend? Answer me.*

Maybe I should've given him the answer he wanted.

Fisting my hand, I say, "Just fucking call her."

"You have, haven't you?" He scoffs again. "Is that how you know that she made a mistake? What, do you call her? Do you talk to her on the phone? Text with her? She tells you things?"

I say in a stern voice, sterner than I want it to be, "Brian, do the right thing. I thought you guys were okay. I thought you'd talked things out and everything was fine now. But it isn't. And not to mention, you're dating her sister. Fucking do the right thing, Bri, all right? Call her and talk to her. The rest doesn't matter."

His laughter is scathing, laced with anger. "Like you could talk, Dad. You could talk about doing the right thing. You betray me. You want the girl that I wanted, and now you're asking me to patch things up. Just like that. What does that mean?"

I grit my teeth again. I clench my eyes shut and dig my fist on my thigh. "It means you call her. That's what it means. Period. You wanted to ask her out, right? She was your best friend. Is this how you treat her? I told you she made a mistake. It's time to move on, okay? You want to hate me, go right ahead. I should've been a better father. I should've known your feelings about her but I didn't. I fucked up. You can hate me all you want but you're calling her. You're calling her and you're apologizing. I didn't say anything about Fiona before because I knew you were angry. I knew you were hurting. I knew you needed your space but this has gone on long enough, you understand? You punishing her and not talking to her has gone on long enough. I'm not going to ask you again. You know you've hurt her. You know that. So just make this right."

"You know what, Dad, I gotta go. I can't do this right now."

He hangs up then, and I throw my phone across the seat.

I bury my hands in my hair and make a fist and pull. Then, I smack the wheel over and over.

Do you like her, Dad? You want her?

I wish I had lied.

I wish I had said no to that question ten months ago.

I wish I didn't want my son's best friend – the girl he secretly liked.

9

Sometimes I think it's a good thing
that he doesn't see me.
One look at me and he'll know my
secret. He'll know all the dreams
I have about him, in the
dark of the night, with a hungry
heart and horny fingers.

-The Diary of a Shrinking Violet, Age 17

Detoxing is so not fun.

I know.

I've gone through it myself. When they put me in Heart-stone, they gave me all kinds of medications, cocktails of medications. They all had side effects. Some worked, some didn't. So they'd wean me off and I'd go through withdrawals. I'd go through the shaking, the shivering, the night sweats, night chills, vomiting and all the fun stuff.

Four days ago, I cried in front of him for the first time and he left. Hours later, he came back from wherever he'd gone. The entire time I'd been alone in the cabin waiting for him, I'd cleaned up a little. I threw away the trash, did the dishes, wiped down the kitchen counters. The basic stuff.

He took it in with a blank face and a silence that I had to break.

"I just, uh, tried to make it better…" I trailed off when he shifted his eyes over to me before adding on a whisper, "For you."

He stared at me with an intensity that burned my skin and made it bloom a pretty red color. An intensity that I'm still feeling four days later.

I thought he'd say something, something rude or scathing or something about where he went and what he did. Why he practically ran away when he saw my tears.

Because I still think he ran away. I still have this feeling that he couldn't see me cry.

Which has to be the most ridiculous thing in this whole world, right?

Why would he care? He hates me.

Anyway, all he did was walk toward me with a purpose until I became breathless and he handed me a bottle of Jack Daniels.

That's it. That's all. A bottle of Jack Daniels and nothing else.

But I knew.

I knew he'd agreed to my plans. He'd agreed to quit.

I smiled that day.

But I'm not smiling now. It has not been pretty.

I knew that, though.

I knew it wasn't going to be pretty and I thought I was prepared for it. But you're never prepared when it comes to seeing someone else live through the pain of detox. Someone you care about so deeply that their every discomfort makes you feel useless.

First of all, there are the headaches.

God, his headaches.

It's like I can feel them myself. I can feel his temples pounding. I can feel the heat and the pulse of his pain at the base of my own skull. His eyes water when it gets too bad. They get red-rimmed, bright in a way that I know comes from exhaustion.

It would've been okay if he just got the headaches, though.

But it's never just the one thing, is it? It's never just the headaches. It comes with waves of nausea.

Yeah, nausea is even worse.

It burns your gut and your chest and your throat. It makes you sweat and shake and sometimes, with all your gagging and retching, nothing comes out. Because you've already expelled everything.

I've been through this. But Jesus Christ, did I sound so agonized? Did I sound like someone was torturing me, strangling my windpipe and I was hoping and praying that I'd die?

I don't think so. I don't think I was as tortured as he is.

Through the bathroom door, I keep telling him that it's going to be okay. That it's going to pass and he's going to be fine.

But he never utters a word. He never complains about any of it.

Although he does ask me this one thing, when I tell him to drink more fluids and count out the multi-vitamins that I had my pen pal, Billy, buy for him so he can keep up his strength.

He trains his eyes on me, his hazel-colored, chameleon eyes, as he gulps down the pills with the juice. "How do you know so much about this?"

"You mean, alcohol and all this?"

"All of this. Yeah."

Now *I* feel like throwing up. I feel my stomach churn.

"Google." My heart starts to hammer when he doesn't buy it. I can see it in his speculative gaze. "And because I come from a family of closet alcoholics."

That seems to satisfy him. "Your mom."

Phew.

Good.

"Yeah."

He scoffs. Like he doesn't approve of it. Like he doesn't approve of my mom drinking and I feel so guilty about lying to him.

I mean, of course my mom drinks. But all this knowledge I have comes from something else. Something else that I can't tell him about.

I don't want to tell him about.

But it's getting harder and harder to lie to him.

It's fine, Violet. You're fine. There's nothing to tell. It's all in the past.

Just focus on him.

So that's what I do. I focus on him.

I don't understand how he can be so calm and tight-lipped and un-mean to me when I know – I *know* – he's suffering. I can see it in those eyes of his.

Like for example, take the bathroom incident.

I was taking a shower and when I was done I wrapped myself in a towel. But as soon as I walked out to go to the room I was currently occupying – which was like, three steps away from the bathroom – I came to an abrupt halt.

Mr. Edwards was standing at the mouth of the hallway, his eyes on me. It looked like he was walking but had come to a stop, as abruptly as I had, at the sight of me.

There was a huge frown on his forehead like he was having a headache. And his jaw was clenched so tight, like it usually does when he's trying to stave off the pain, that I thought he was grinding his teeth into dust.

I wanted to ask him if he was okay. If his head was bothering him again, but I couldn't speak. Because man, he was staring at me.

Staring and staring and burning me with it.

My hand was on the knot of my red towel and my fingers tightened. They kept tightening as he moved his eyes. With every inch of skin he gazed at – my throat, my collarbone, my bare shoulders – my fingers tightened a little more. My pulse fluttered so much that I was sure he could see it.

His stare, heated and slow, became too much, so that I had to clench my thighs and stop my thoughts from going to inappropriate places.

I had to blurt out, "I-I thought you were sleeping. Or you were in your room."

His eyes came back to mine and I could've sworn they were green-ish when he started looking at me but now they were all dark and brown. And I could've sworn that his sharp cheeks were tanned but now they were colored in a dark flush.

There were even a few drops of sweat beading his forehead,

as if just standing there was too painful for him.

Too much suffering.

With a tic of his jaw, he raised his hand and showed me that he was holding a bottle. "I was thirsty," he said in a raspy way.

"Oh, I –"

He didn't wait to see what I was going to say. He whirled around and walked out of the cabin, closing the door violently.

See? Detox is not pretty at all. The man is not doing well.

But on day five, things change.

He starts to look better.

His skin glows. The dark circles under his eyes have almost disappeared. Even though it looks like he's lost some more weight, he's healthier.

More awake and present.

Most of all, he's interested.

Or at least, that's what it feels like when I see him making repairs around the cabin. He starts with the front yard. He opens that padlocked garage and gets all the tools out before getting down to business.

I watch him through the dirty living room window before walking out on the porch. I have been cleaning up around the house in my spare time. See, I had to do something while he was suffering and I couldn't make it better for him.

So I tried to do other things that might make his life easier. I threw out all his liquor bottles while he was throwing up in the bathroom and I did his laundry while he was shaking in his bed with the cravings.

Oh, and I've been baking up a storm.

I love to bake. A love I discovered when the Edwardses moved in next door and Brian told me that his dad sucked at baking. He could cook but he couldn't bake. I thought it was adorable. But then, I find every little thing about Mr. Edwards adorable.

Found. I *found* every little thing about Mr. Edwards adorable. Not find.

So yeah, I took up baking because the man I used to dream about couldn't bake. And I haven't looked back since. Not to mention, being a hermit and living indoors 24/7 becomes a lot easier if you've got things to bake and things to clean up and launder around the house. I actually gave our housekeeper back in Connecticut a tough competition.

Long story short, I've been doing things around the cabin to keep myself busy and not think too much about how Mr. Edwards is suffering, but this is the first time in days that he seems interested in these things.

"What are you doing?" I ask him from the sagging top step.

He stops in his cutting, more like hacking, the shrubs that seem to have grown to almost my height. "Making things better."

His voice is so low that even the wind could carry it away. But there's no wind in this part of the world. Everything is quiet and lonely so I hear him.

I hear him and I bite my lip, giving him a smile.

Mr. Edwards though? His eyes go to my mouth for a second before he turns away almost violently and gets back to work.

Oh well.

He's still grumpy, but at least he's not throwing up. So for the next couple of days, we make things better. Together.

We fix things, clean things. He clears out the entire back-yard, front yard. He fixes the porch steps and I dust the furniture, mop up the floors, wipe up the dirty windows.

And because I'm the stupidest person ever, I cut my finger on the one that was cracked and squeal like someone's trying to kill me. It doesn't even hurt that much but for some reason, I chant *ow, ow, ow* until he's right next to me.

Not only that, he's holding my hand.

Yup.

I don't even know how he got here so fast because he was out back, standing on a ladder, pulling out ivy and things from the roof. But now, he's here, right next to me, clutching my wrist with his long, dirty and smudged fingers, staring down at the cut on the pad of my thumb.

"What the fuck happened?" he asks with a frown.

I try to ease it, that frown, I mean. "It's nothing. Really. I was just being a drama queen."

He lifts his eyes, his fingers flex and move, almost caressing the delicate skin of my wrist. "You're bleeding."

I swallow.

I so want to look down where he's holding my hand and see if those fingers of his are leaving dirty prints on my pale skin. God, I hope they are.

Instead, I do the appropriate thing.

I wave my other hand and tell him, "It's…"

And then, I trail off.

Because man, he's close to me. So close that I just got the whiff of his thick smell: musky and outdoorsy. The scent I've been living with for the past few days. I get a waft of it here and there. I smell it in the hallway, the living room, the kitchen, the room that I sleep in, which is right next to his.

But this is the first time that it's so strong that I'm drowning in it.

I don't want to come up for air.

"It's what?" he asks when I don't complete my sentence.

But then, I complete it and I wonder what the fuck I'm thinking.

"It hurts," I breathe out.

He frowns and tugs on my wrist. "Come on."

But I resist moving. "I, uh, it's..."

I leave my thought hanging again because it doesn't make sense. Nothing about this is making sense. I'm not supposed to act this way. I'm not supposed to lie to him when it's not hurting at all. Or at least, not very much.

"Violet," he warns.

I raise my hand – the one he's holding – between us and almost whisper, "Will you make it better?"

"What?"

Oh God, I'm crazy but whatever. He's close to me and I can't breathe without breathing him into my lungs and he's touching me – only the second time he's touched my skin – and I want more.

A little bit more.

"I... I read it somewhere that when you're bleeding from a cut and it hurts a lot, it's always good to suck off that blood with your mouth. It stops the pain and the blood right away."

By the end of my stupid, transparent lie, I'm all heated. I bet I'm red and the pulse at my neck is jittering so much that he can see it.

He can see everything.

He can see that I'm lying and I'm making things up. It's in his eyes that are curious and narrowed and that are circling over my features.

Circling and circling until I'm convinced that he can decipher all my thoughts and my emotions. The entire history of them. The entire history of my crush and obsession.

"Is that what you read?" he rumbles, at last.

I glance at his lips, the ones I got to kiss for about ten seconds, ten months ago. So soft looking against the backdrop of the beard. The beard I've never even gotten a chance to touch. Probably never will.

That somehow helps me keep up with the charade. The fact that everything is so complicated and impossible between us. Not that I want things to be possible – I don't have a crush on him anymore.

Right?

Right. But still.

"I did, yeah." I nod as I stare at him, pretending to be innocent. "So, uh, will you make it better?"

"You want me to make it better?"

"Uh-huh."

"Because it hurts."

"It does. So much."

My heart's booming in my chest, thundering as I stare at

him. As I dare to imagine… As I dare to imagine those lips wrapped around my slightly bleeding thumb and sucking the hurt away.

It probably won't happen, of course. He's not crazy. He's not buying this but what if?

What if he puts it in his mouth and I feel the heat of it? I feel the flick of his tongue.

Slowly, he raises my arm further. He brings it close to his mouth and I stop breathing. He looks at the blood, a tiny drop oozing out of the cut, and grazes his thumb over the pulse on my wrist.

My own mouth parts as if I'm the one who's going to suck on my wounded digit.

Turns out though, I am.

Because his eyelids flicker up and he murmurs, "I think you're better at sucking, don't you?"

He pushes the thumb in my mouth then, and my lips close over it.

"Suck."

As soon as he says it, I do. I suck on my thumb because he asked me to. The metallic taste of blood spreads over my tongue and I almost close my eyes. I bet it wouldn't feel this erotic, that taste, if he wasn't watching me like he is.

If he wasn't so focused on my mouth and the little sucks I'm taking. This wasn't what I wanted, my own mouth on me. But somehow, this is beyond anything I could've imagined.

His eyes, all dark and dilated. My mouth.

His rough fingers on my wrist that he's still clutching on to.

The flutters in my belly. The clenching of my thighs. The

throbbing that I feel between them.

This is surreal, isn't it? The way he's watching me.

I think I'll explode. His eyes will make me fall apart and break open my body because I'm swelling and swelling with feelings when he rasps, "I think you got all of it."

Only then, he steps away and lets go of my wrist, before leaving me there, all crazy and horny still drowning in his scent and wondering about his eyes.

I wonder about them the next day too.

I wonder about them and debate what to do about groceries. We're running out and I've been thinking if I should have them delivered to the cabin or if I should don my disguise, drive into town, wait for the bar to close so I can slip in the list for my pen pal, Billy.

At some point, I might have to ask him for his phone number though. I can't keep slipping him notes like we're in middle school.

I need to be more mature about this.

I'm debating it and mixing the wet ingredients for the muffins I'm baking, while listening to "You Give Love a Bad Name" by Bon Jovi and singing along, when I hear a noise from behind me.

I whip off my headphones and turn around to find Mr. Edwards standing at the island, his eyes glued to me.

Man, his eyes.

"Oh, hey." I press a hand to my chest. "You scared me."

He looks at my hand. "I can see that."

"I didn't hear you come in."

He looks to the headphones I haphazardly took off and

threw on the counter. "I'm not surprised."

I tuck my hair behind my ears and duck my head down, and mutter uselessly, "I was listening to my kickass playlist."

"Kickass playlist."

I nod. "Yeah. It's all my favorite songs from like, forever. And of course, they're kickass so I just can't stop singing along."

"Of course."

The way he says it with such sarcasm, I have to kinda take offense. "Why, you don't think "You Give Love a Bad Name" is kickass?"

His gaze flicks back and forth between mine. "You know the lake behind the cabin? Through the woods?"

"Yeah?"

He scratches his beard with his thumb, momentarily distracting me with his sexy gesture. "Kickass or not, I think you should stop singing if you don't want the fish in that lake to drown themselves."

Fish? Drown themselves?

My mouth gapes open. "Are you saying that I'm a bad singer?"

Amusement flickers through his eyes. Damn him. Why does it have to be so sexy, sexier than his beard scratching?

"I'm saying that you're killing the fish."

Before I can retort, he sets something down on the island. "Here."

And then, he walks out.

It's a brown grocery bag. I dash to it and see it has everything from the list I was going to give to Billy. But it has something else too. It's sitting right at the top and I fish it out, running after him.

"You went grocery shopping?" I ask his back; he's in the hallway.

"Looks like it."

"You bought me lollipops?" I say, breathily but whatever.

He bought me lollipops. *No one* has ever bought me lollipops that I can remember. Maybe my nanny when I was a kid and didn't know how to buy things for myself.

He stops at his bedroom door and looks at me. "I bought everything on the list. So call off your teenage hormones."

I laugh. "Oh yeah?"

"Yes."

I shrug, tearing open the packet of lollipops, unwrapping one and popping it into my mouth. "No can do, sorry. You're stuck with my teenage hormones. I'm actually oozing them right now."

His eyelids flicker as he watches me suck on my candy like he watched me suck on my thumb yesterday. "Yeah, I can smell it."

With that, he enters his room and closes the door. And I beam.

Because see, lollipops weren't on the list.

Nope.

They weren't. So that means he bought me them himself.

Not only lollipops though. He bought me tons of other things that I never put on my list. I didn't even think to put them on there.

Oh wow, the things he bought me.

He bought me my favorite juice: watermelon. He bought

me packs of my favorite chips: barbecue sauce. The favorite candy bar that I eat, other than the lollipops: almond and chocolate. My second favorite fruit: again watermelon. Chocolate-covered pretzels, normal pretzels, veggie sticks, all the stuff I used to survive on back in Connecticut. In fact, I'd carry around their packets at school. It used to be my lunch.

But how does he *know* that?

He doesn't know anything about me. He didn't even know who I was until the night I stupidly kissed him.

I'm the one who knows things about him. Me.

I'm the one who was a creepy information hoarder.

But why does he appear to be the information hoarder instead?

I can't get over it. I think about it and think about it and think about it until I'm compelled to ask him.

It's night and we've just had dinner. After going grocery shopping, he finished clearing out the roof and started to work on the broken porch steps. Honestly, I was a little disappointed.

I thought he'd go to his roses next.

I thought he'd work on them, water them, or at least look at them.

But he hasn't and it hurts me more than I want to admit.

So I'm distracting myself with the question I'm going to ask. We're sitting on the old, musty couch, which is surprisingly super comfortable – him on one side and me on the other – and watching a movie on TV. I told him to stop at a channel and he did, and now we're watching something that I'm not even paying attention to.

I give up all pretense of watching and turn toward him.

Propping my back against the arm of the couch and bringing my knees to my chest, I ask, "How do you know so much about me?"

10

Things I dream of doing before I die:
learn to play guitar,
write a song that I can
then play on that guitar,
watch them make lollipops,
watch the moon from the highest
mountain in the world
and sleep in his arms...

-The Diary of a Shrinking Violet, Age 17

He stiffens as soon as I ask the question.

Which makes me cringe.

Yikes.

Did I have to be so blunt? Maybe I should've eased him into it. I just made him feel like a criminal or something.

Or did I?

Because he glances toward me, his eyes sharp. "What?"

He asks the question in such a lashing voice that I'm cringing for different reasons now. I'm cringing for jumping to God-knows-what conclusion.

I wiggle my toes on the couch and he notices the gesture. "I mean... I just, was wondering that you bought all that stuff? You know, all the juices and fruits and things? I was wondering how you knew that I liked them?"

He flicks his gaze up and thank God for that, my toes were starting to blush. "How do you think I know?"

His words make me feel like a fool. They also fill me with all those teenage hormones he keeps talking about.

I fight them, those hormones. I fight them because they want to fly me away in a dreamland. They want me to think that he knows all this about me because he watched me like I watched him.

But that's not true, is it?

So I take a guess. I make the rational, smart choice. "Uh, Brian? Maybe. He told you."

The source of my information could be the source of his, too.

He confirms it a second later with a tight nod and by glancing away from me to the TV. "Yeah. Brian."

I bite my lip in disappointment, which is ridiculous.

First of all, I already knew the answer. I don't even know why I asked him the question.

Second of all, it doesn't matter to me. It doesn't. It shouldn't. I'm over him. I'm smarter now. Ten months older in age and ten years older in experience.

I hug my knees to my chest and rest my chin on them. "It was just surprising, that's all. Besides, the first time you saw me was that night. The night I, you know…"

"The night you attacked me, you mean," he deadpans, still looking at the screen.

"I didn't… I didn't attack. There was no attacking."

He glances back at me, his eyes alight with something similar to humor. "You wouldn't let go of my shirt. You got up on my shoes, Jailbait. There was definitely attacking."

I gasp even though I'm barely outraged; his humor-filled eyes are making it a little hard to take offense. Even so, I should at least pretend.

"I got up on your stupid shoes because you're... monstrously tall, okay? You're a giant."

I gesture at his sprawled form with my waving hand. He *is* a giant.

He's sitting on one end of the couch but somehow, he's taking up half of the space. His thighs are spread wide and they look so powerful and brawny. It makes me think once again, that I can crawl over to him and perch my entire tiny self on just one of those limbs. He probably wouldn't even notice I was there.

While I'm staring at him, he takes in my curled form. He takes in my bare legs, folded up at the knees, and my puny arms wrapped around them.

"Maybe to you," he says.

I narrow my eyes at him. "It's not normal. You being this tall. And big."

Okay, I shouldn't have sounded this... fluttery, but I did and I'm not happy about it. But it's true. His size is intimidating.

Or should be.

He half-smiles. "Again, maybe to you."

I have this strong urge to be a brat and stick my tongue out at him. But all I do is mumble, "Whatever. It was a mistake, anyway. The kiss."

"A stupid, drunken one, I know."

My eyes fall to his lips then.

It's been ten months – ten freaking months – since I touched them for the first time and obviously, the last.

But I remember everything about them.

I remember that his lower lip is plusher and meatier than his upper lip. There's even a groove there, right in the middle of it, that you can see and that I wanted to lick. I wanted to dig my tongue in there. I wanted to dig my tongue inside his mouth and see what he tasted like.

On the outside, he tasted like those strawberries that I love so much but am allergic to. Which is so stupid and irrational because I know for a fact that he doesn't even eat strawberries.

"Yeah," I whisper, nodding.

But the problem is that it doesn't feel like a mistake, that kiss. Not right now.

In this moment, it feels like destiny.

Like I was meant to kiss him. I was meant to throw myself at him, clutch onto his shirt, step onto his shoes and put my mouth on his.

Because if I hadn't, I wouldn't be here tonight.

Yeah, maybe I was meant to wreck it all, destroy everything. So I could finally do what I'm doing right now: talking to him.

"Who was she?" I ask all of a sudden, glancing up to his eyes.

He snaps his eyes up as well, and I could swear that they were on my lips. Although he looked away so quickly that I can't say for sure.

"Who?"

"The woman you were kissing that night?"

That blonde and busty and queen-like woman. The one he was kissing back.

His chest expands with his breath in a way that makes me think he doesn't like the question. Even so, he answers. "No one. Someone I picked up at the bar."

"Do you pick up a lot of women at the bar?"

He frowns. "Shouldn't you be going to sleep? I'm pretty sure it's past your bedtime."

"It's okay. I can stay. We just won't tell my babysitter that I'm breaking the rules," I sass with a false sweet smile.

He watches that smile with a dangerous glint in his eyes. "Babysitter, huh?"

"Yup. I have two." I show him the fingers. "You know, since I'm such a hormonal teenager and a bad girl and all that."

His lips twitch slightly before he tips his chin up, still keeping his eyes on me. "I can believe that."

"So?"

"So what?"

"Let's chat."

"You want to chat?"

I nod enthusiastically. "Yeah. I'll tell you something and then you tell me something back, you know. That kind of stuff."

Like the night of my eighteenth birthday, I'm filled with this urgency. A need to keep this going, whatever this is.

I wanna talk and talk and keep talking until I've got no words left or he gets bored of me. Until he stops looking at me like he doesn't hate me. Because in this moment, it seems like he doesn't.

In fact, I haven't felt his hatred in days. For days, all I've felt is a peaceful, domestic, happy truce.

So I wanna talk and talk until this goes away because I feel like I can talk to him.

"Are we going to paint our toenails too?" he asks, sarcastically.

I shrug. "Maybe. I could do your nails, if you want."

His eyes – dark and bottomless – sweep all over my face before he replies in a gravelly voice, "You don't give up, do you?"

I shake my head. "Nope. So is that a yes on toenail painting?"

"That's a *maybe* on chatting."

I fist pump and he does the most extraordinary thing ever. He smiles. Not only that, he chuckles.

Oh man, he chuckles. His chest shakes and his head pitches back a little and those three lines around his eyes, the ones that I thought were a myth but weren't really, appear and I forget to draw in a breath.

I swear the sound of it – rusty and delicious and thick – hits me in the chest. No, scratch that. It hits me in my tummy, making it suck in a breath.

Making something flap inside of me. Wings and petals and flames.

I dig my toes into the leather couch and tighten my arms around my knees to stop my body from going haywire over something so simple.

And come out with the first question. "So, do you?"

He shifts, turning his magnificent body toward me and propping his back against the arm like me, as if he's committed to this whole chatting thing. "Do I what?"

At this, I can tighten my entire body until the world burns down around me, but I still won't be able to stop the flapping and fluttering and clenching of my stomach. "Pick up women at bars a lot?"

He narrows his eyes. "Next question."

I raise my eyebrows and rock in my spot. "I'll take that as a yes."

Actually, I knew this already. Mr. Edwards doesn't date or does it very rarely. Brian told me that his dad just fucks and doesn't do relationships because he doesn't want to bring that kind of complication into his son's life. I actually coughed out the watermelon juice I was drinking at the time but that's beside the point.

"What's your favorite color? Mine is pink."

Again, I know the answer. It's not a mystery why my sneakers are red, my suitcase is a mix of red and maroon and my fat hobo is red leather.

He gazes at my lips for a second before answering, "Red."

I smile. "Tell me a dream of yours."

He looks... confused. "What?"

"Yeah."

More confusion and it's silent and frowning.

"Uh, okay. So let me break it down for you a little," I explain. "Tell me a dream. Like somewhere you want to go or something you want to do. Or oh! Something you want to have."

My eyes are wide and excited for him.

He watches my enthusiasm with both a blank expression and an expression that indicates that I'm crazy. "I think I'm a little too old for dreams."

"No, you're not. You're never too old for dreams."

They could be toxic though. Like my dreams were. But I don't wanna think about that right now.

"Sure."

"What, you think people in their thirties can't dream?"

"Next question."

"Fine. Tell me a dream you had when you were a kid, then."

"I didn't dream," he says.

"You didn't?"

"No."

Now, it's my turn to watch him, watch his impassive face. How is it possible that he didn't dream? Everyone dreams. Everyone has wishes.

Right?

"But that's... not right." I shake my head. "I mean, you must've wanted something, right? Maybe you wanted to be a big football star or something like that."

"Yeah, that."

The way he says it, the way he jumps at my suggestion makes me think that he's lying. He's making it up.

And gosh, that's so sad.

So fucking gloomy that I don't know what to do. I don't know what to think other than the very melancholic fact that Mr. Edwards – the man I dreamed about for two years – is dreamless.

This beautiful, isolated man doesn't have any dreams.

It makes my eyes water and since I don't want to cry in front of him and turn this into a depressing chat session, I ask him an easy question. "How do you know so much about roses?"

He keeps looking at me intensely as he replies, "My dad."

Okay, good.

That was an easy answer.

It brings back the smile on my face. I didn't expect his answer at all, actually. I thought he learnt it off the internet or something but this makes everything so personal, so intimate and meaningful.

"Was he like, into gardening and stuff like that?"

At this though, his features ripple, going all tight and strained.

Shit.

How do I keep doing that? Maybe I should've stuck with superficial questions.

But the truth is that even though I know so many things about him, there's so much that I don't know and tonight, I'm hungry.

My heart is ravenous, my stomach starving.

I'm all famished for him, for all the things that I don't know about him.

So I plead with him, mutely. I bite my lip and look at him with all the need that I'm feeling, every tiny bit of it.

I do it even though I know he doesn't care. He doesn't care what I want or what I need.

Even so, through some miracle, some divine intervention,

he gives it to me.

He looks into my eyes, takes in my need and says, "No. Not gardening and stuff. My dad was just into my mom." When I frown, he explains, "Her name was Rose and he grew roses for her. When she left him for another man, he continued doing that in her memory. And no, he didn't teach me. Not that I can remember. He was too drunk to teach anyone anything. I just took care of them when he got sick. He didn't care. All the while I was growing up, he never cared about anything except getting drunk and talking about my mother. I don't know why I did it. I just did."

My eyes sting again but I manage to hold back my tears. I manage to hold myself back even.

Because I want to lunge across the couch and wrap my arms around him. I want to wrap my arms around his neck and tuck my face under his chin and hug him to me.

Hug this dreamless, lonely, forlorn looking man.

He is sitting there, all rigid in the shoulders and straight in the spine and with an impassive face.

But I know it's affecting him. It's in the way his jaw is locked tight and his fist is pressing on his thigh.

So I tell him, "You know, when I was like five or so, I had a ton of imaginary friends. I'd talk to them all day. I'd read with them. I'd listen to music with them. Because no one would play with me and everyone would play with Fiona. But then I realized I didn't want imaginary friends. What I wanted was imaginary parents. I mean, I did have parents but they weren't really... around, you know. Like, my mom's always boozed up and my dad – who isn't my real dad, by the way; my mom had an affair – is never home. Anyway, I invented these fabulous imaginary parents who always remembered my birthday. They gave me gifts and hugs and all the regular shit they gave to Fiona. My imaginary mom baked me a cake and my imaginary dad took me to amusement parks. So that's why."

"That's why what?"

I give him a sad smile. "That's why you took care of those roses. The same reason I invented imaginary parents. You wanted to be less lonely. You wanted to be closer to your dad like I wanted to be closer to my parents."

A pulse runs between him and me. A pulse so thick and so full of voltage that I'm surprised that we aren't electrocuted by it.

This is it, isn't it?

This is why I felt something that day, when I saw him on my sixteenth birthday. I recognized him, something in him.

He's made of the same lonely fabric as me. Lonely and abandoned and alone.

God, he could be my soul mate, couldn't he?

The one person who electrifies the very being of me. The one person who could set it all, my soul, my heart, my body on fire.

How is it that we aren't meant to be together?

How is it that I drunkenly kissed him and ruined things and he hates me now?

"You don't want them," he says, breaking the silence with a low growl that vibrates this pulse around us. "You don't want your boozed-up, clueless mother and your dumb as fuck father who doesn't realize what he's got. They're not worth your time, you understand?"

I'm so taken aback at the sternness of his tone that I don't know what to say except, "Okay."

"You don't want anyone who's stupid enough not to realize what they've got. Yeah?"

He looks like he's waiting for my answer, so again I go with, "Okay."

"And that includes Brian. That includes all those kids who wouldn't play with you. All those dull, boring people who have ever looked at you like you didn't matter. Fuck those people. People are motherfuckers, okay? They lie. They cheat. They gossip. Most of all, they leave. Because they're selfish. No matter who they are. So don't waste your time on them. Don't waste your time on those fuckers who don't know what you are."

"And what am I?"

That's the logical question, right? That's what I was supposed to ask because I'm not really sure.

I'm not sure if I'm even breathing. Or forming the right words or putting them in the right order.

I'm not sure of anything except this man in front of me.

This man who just defended me to the entire world.

And he's staring at me with a burning gaze as he rasps, "Something made of moon and magic."

After this, he looks away at the TV. Meanwhile, his hoarse words settle in my bones like warm honey.

They settle and settle and make everything sticky and slippery as I blurt out, "No one's ever said that to me before."

I notice his hands.

They are curling and uncurling, fisting and unfisting on his thighs. Until they decide to remain fisted and tight as he replies, without looking at me, "Someone will. You go to college, don't you? Some guy will say that to you. He'll say it better. He'll even write you poetry or something. Or whatever the fuck kids are doing these days."

I don't want someone to say that to me.

I want him.

I want his words. His poetry. His growls and his hands.

I want his hands on me. The ones that are still fisted and digging into his thighs like the words he just uttered about college were some of the most painful ones he ever had.

But they're all a lie, right?

They're a lie because I'm lying to him. *I* am a liar.

I don't go to college.

The truth is that I don't even know if I'll ever go to college. I can't even imagine setting foot in one of those crowded establishments when I can't even go grocery shopping.

And it didn't bother me up until a few days ago.

It doesn't even bother me right now. It doesn't.

I'm fine.

Fiiiiiine.

I'm handling things my way.

It's just that… I hate lying to him. I absolutely *loathe* that I'm lying to him.

"No one will ever say that to me," I mumble that without really thinking things through.

Because I don't go to college.

"What?"

Oh fuck.

He's back to looking at me and I'm not sure how I'm going to lie my way out of this. How the fuck do I make something up to get out of this when I've got all his attention?

Damn it.

Why is it so hard to lie to him?

Then I decide to tell him a different truth. I tuck my hair behind my ear and shrug. "Because guys don't notice me and that's okay. I'm pretty invisible, Mr. Edwards."

I chuckle.

Because chuckling is so much more preferable to crying over the fact that I'm lying to him. That no one forced me to do it but I'm doing it anyway.

But then, I notice something that makes my chuckle die down.

He's staring at me so hard that I'm pretty sure that he's drilling holes in my body.

"What?" I ask.

"You're kidding, right?"

The way he says it makes me think that he wants me to be kidding. That I better be kidding.

"I'm kidding?" I dart my eyes around the room and sit up straight, lifting my chin from my knees, going alert. "Okay. About what though?"

He doesn't answer me as he takes long seconds to analyze my face. I'm analyzing *his* face, in turn. For the first time ever, I can read him. There's a touch of disbelief on his features. His frown is one of incredulity and his eyes are inquisitive.

"You don't know," he concludes finally, whatever he was trying to conclude. "Yeah, it makes sense. It's the highway all over again. You don't notice anything. How could you? You with your giant headphones and your nose stuck in a book. You'd sit under that tree, the one by the chemistry lab window and you'd write whatever the fuck you write in those goddamn journals. Of course, you don't have a clue."

"What?"

He shakes his head and scoffs. "Tell me something. In a class, how many times has a teacher singled you out to answer a question?"

That is a very weird, out-of-the-blue query. I was not expecting it at all. On top of that, there's another concern.

How does he know this about me? About the tree and the journal and...

I swallow when I see that he's impatiently waiting for my answer so I reply, "I... um, I don't know. Almost every day, I think."

"Every day."

"Almost. And that's because teachers liked to pick on me in school. They thought I wasn't paying attention in class."

Which is the truth.

Students would ignore me, which was fine by me. But I was somehow really visible to the teachers. I think it was because I'd stare out the window or doodle in my journal while they were teaching us important life lessons or something.

"And how many of those teachers who picked on you were men?"

This is getting weirder by the second. But still, I indulge

him. "I don't know, most of them?"

"How about all of them?"

"Um, okay. So all of them. What does that matter? Men are assholes and they like to show it off."

"Fuck yeah, men are assholes."

"What's happening? What are we even talking about?"

His jaw goes really hard at this. So hard and tense that it makes me think that he'll never utter another word. He'll never tell me what's going on and what he's trying to get at.

But then, he goes and says, "We're talking about how blind you are. How you have no idea what men think and why they do the things they do."

When I still appear somewhat confused to him, he goes on, "Let me explain it to you, all right? Because I'm pretty sure your boozed-up mommy never explained anything to you. They single you out not because they want to pick on you, it's because they want you to look at them. They want your attention. They want your big, brown, innocent eyes on them. They want to hear your voice. They want to look at your pretty, schoolgirl face. They want to look at your hair, your milky white skin and they want to imagine things."

"Imagine th-things?"

That's the only thing that I could think of to say and still remember to breathe.

"Fuck yeah, imagine things. When they ask you to talk, they want to stare at your lollipop-sucking lips and imagine what else you can suck on. When they ask you to stand up, they want to stare at your teenage body and imagine how they can put their hands on it. Can they pass you by in the hallway and walk a little closer so they accidentally brush against your arm? Can they pat your back when you leave the class and feel the delicate lines of your shoulders? Can they ask you to fucking bend over and help with the papers they let slip on the floor on purpose so they can stare at your tight ass?"

I can't seem to catch my breath.

I can't.

I can't seem to form a single coherent thought. So again, I come up with something completely stupid and inane. "I-I don't... I don't think that's true."

Only, all those things kinda did happen.

I mean, not everything but some of the things. The patting, the brushing of arms. But I didn't think they meant anything.

He runs a savage hand through his hair. "Do they stop you after class? Do they tell you they want to help you with your grades? That they have a special project for you?"

My nails dig into my calves as I try to think, which is proving to be impossible right now. But I still do it.

"A few times. But I never... I never did them," I whisper, thinking about how Mr. Gunderson, our math teacher, would tell me that he had ideas for extra credit since I was failing that class.

Is *that* what he meant?

"Yeah, that's because somewhere deep down in your naïve little brain you knew what they wanted from you. That the special project they want you to do has nothing to do with books and papers and everything to do with how fast they can get you to *do* things to them. How fast can they get you to sit on their desk and spread your legs, while they try to catch a peek of what's between your thighs. And how fast they can get you to sit on their laps so they can rub up against that ass they can't stop thinking about."

Every nerve ending in my body is standing taut and feels raw and exposed. His words are like the air, brushing against the very tips of them, making me all hot and bothered.

On the verge of melting away.

But before I go, before I become a puddle on his couch, I ask, "Are you saying that I'm... visible?"

"No, Violet, I'm not saying that you're visible. I'm saying that you're the only thing that a man sees. I'm saying that you're a thing that drives a man to distraction. You make him forget what's right and what's wrong. You're a thing so terrible and beautiful and fucking breathtaking that he can't escape you. He can't think of anything else, not about his job, his responsibilities, his promises, his family, nothing but you. You undo him. You make him helpless. You turn him into an animal who wants to rut. You're a girl who makes a man go bad."

***

I walk to my room or rather the room I'm currently occupying in a daze. He's already gone to his. He left right after he said those things to me.

Those things that are running in my veins instead of blood and life.

I'm so charged up with them, his words, that when I lie down on the bed, the sheets and the blankets scrape against my skin.

They scratch and scrape so much that I have to writhe and toss and turn in the bed.

I have to rock my hips and press my thighs together. I have to creep my hand down. I have to get it inside my panties and cup my naked core because it's aching now.

And I have to do all of that with his words in my ears. With his face behind my closed eyelids.

I imagine him doing all those things to me, the things he talked about.

I imagine him stopping me in the school hallway and asking me to bend over and I do it. I do it with all the eagerness. Then, I imagine him calling me into his office and shutting the door.

He tells me to take a seat and I do. I sit in the chair and he stares at me from across his desk. He's frowning, rubbing his thumb over his beard, unhappily.

I ask him *what's wrong, Mr. Edwards?*

And he growls, *get over here.*

I go over there and he motions toward the desk. I look at him all confused and he gets impatient and angry.

He snaps, *sit the fuck down.*

I obey.

And then, he puts his hands on me. He grabs my thighs, the juicy part, the part high up, so close to my pussy that I'm touching right now.

He spreads my legs and my spine arches up.

He keeps his face lowered but lifts his eyes up to me and says, *You don't pay attention in class, do you? You think you're special,*

Violet? Better than the rest of the students?

"No, Mr. Edwards," I whisper out loud, in the real world as my fingers work my slippery clit.

I think you do. And I think I'll teach you how to behave. And you'll thank me for it, won't you?

In the real world, my back bows at his stern tone and I get super close to coming. "I will, yes."

What will you say?

I think about it. Again, in the real world. I think about it as I move my hips and play with my pussy. I think about what to say to him for all the things he said to me, back on the couch. All the things about how beautiful I am.

How visible and breathtaking.

You make a man go bad...

Just as I reach that line of his whole spectacular speech, I come and I know what to say to him. To my fantasy Mr. Edwards and the one who called me beautiful tonight.

"Thank you, Mr. Edwards."

11

Last night I imagined his
soil-caked, callused,
rose-growing hands on my body.
He was stroking my flesh,
caressing it with his dirty fingers,
leaving streaks
and globs of mud on my skin.

-The Diary of a Shrinking Violet, Age 17

He called me beautiful.

Beautiful.

Me?

No, actually he called me beyond beautiful. He said that I have the power to distract a man, make him forget things. Things that are important to him.

I feel like a butterfly this morning. Pretty and beautiful. Made and metamorphosed just by his words.

Made into a dreamer, even.

Because I dreamed about him last night. Not only that, I played with myself. Something that I hadn't done in months.

Oh God, it was so good though. So good to come like that,

come on his sheets and I'm still riding the high of it that I don't even feel embarrassed about it.

Not at all.

Maybe once I wake up and see him, I'll be shy but not right now.

Right now, I wanna dream more and I would if not for the horrible ringing of the phone.

Jesus Christ, who's calling me?

I'm not even sure what time it is as I fumble around the bed, looking for my stupid phone. Keeping my eyes shut, I hit accept; I get it right on my third try and mumble, "Hello?"

The voice on the other side makes me pop my eyes open. Not only that, it makes me spring up on the bed and pinch myself to make sure I'm not dreaming.

Because the voice belongs to my best friend.

It belongs to Brian.

Oh my God.

"Brian?"

"Hey, yeah. Did I... Did I wake you?"

Oh my God, I'm hearing my best friend's voice after ten long months. "I... Yes, you did. But it doesn't matter. It doesn't..."

I'm trying to breathe. I'm trying to calm my heartbeats. I can't believe what's happening. I even take the phone away from my ear to read the display and it does say Brian.

"Vi?"

I put the phone back on my ear and clutch it with both hands. "You're calling me."

I hear a rush of breath and it makes me almost double over

with nostalgia. It means he's either smiling or shaking his head while smiling.

"Yeah. I am," he says.

"How are you calling me?"

I think the last thing he said to me was two days after the kiss, after multiple attempts of me trying to talk to him: *Please, Vi. Just leave me alone, okay? Stop calling me. Stop coming over to my house.*

That's all.

That's all he said to me before he went away and never said anything up until today.

He sighs then. "I, uh, I should've called way earlier than this."

He sounds guilty. He sounds as if it's his fault that he didn't call, that he didn't want to talk to me. When I was the one responsible for everything.

"Brian, it's… okay. It's okay. I know why you didn't call. I know why you never picked up my calls, either. I know. I fucked up and –"

"Vi, stop. Stop, okay? Just stop."

I do. I go silent.

He's breathing hard; I can hear it. He's preparing to say something and I can only hope that I can bear it.

God, please let me bear it.

"Vi, I'm sorry."

He tells me that and I think I've heard it wrong.

I think I'm hearing things.

"What?"

"I'm sorry, Vi. I'm so fucking sorry." His voice sounds clear and low, as if he somehow moved closer to the mouthpiece and wanted me to hear it clearly.

"For what?"

"Fiona," he replies and I clench my eyes shut.

Up until he said it, I didn't realize how much it had hurt me. How betrayed I'd felt when I found out. Brian always used to jump to my defense whenever Fiona would say something cutting to me. He used to be my champion, but overnight everything changed.

But then again, it's not as if I'm very innocent in all of this. I pushed him toward her.

"You don't have to apologize. I know why you did it. I hurt you and betrayed you, Brian, and I can't tell you how sorry I am for all of that."

"God, no, Vi. Listen, I've been a punk, all right? I've been a fucking asshole to you. I got so mad and Jesus, I acted out in the worst possible way. But I broke up with her. I broke up with Fiona. Not that it changes anything but yeah."

"You broke up with her?"

"Yeah. It was long overdue. I was with her for all the wrong reasons."

I can't deny the ease that spreads through me at this. "I'm sorry. Did she take it okay?"

"Nah. She was shrieking. I cut the call in the middle of it."

Despite everything, I chuckle. "Oh my God, she's not gonna like that."

"Yeah, I'll pay for that later."

I chuckle again.

He's right. Fiona is spending her summer in Paris this year and yeah, he's gonna pay for it when she gets back.

A few moments later, he says, "I wanted to call you, Vi. I've been wanting to contact you for ages now but I didn't know what to say after the way I behaved. I didn't know if you wanted to talk to me or what. And when my dad asked me to call you, I freaked out on him too. And I've already been acting like such an asshole to him –"

"Wait, wait, wait," I stop him, all kinds of confused.

We're both breathing hard now and even though I don't want to, I still take a few seconds to calm down before launching into questions.

"Your dad asked you to call me?"

I hear him swallow. "Yeah, he did. He said I was punishing you and that I shouldn't."

"When was that?"

"About a week ago."

As soon as he says it, I know. I know exactly when. It was the day I came over to ask him to quit drinking. It was the day I cried in front of him and it felt like I shouldn't have.

Because it felt like he couldn't see that.

He couldn't see me cry and this is what he did. He called up his son and told him to talk to me. To not punish me anymore.

Gosh.

I feel a tear roll down my cheek, hot and thick. "He never told me."

He never said anything. Not one thing.

Why didn't he say anything?

Why didn't he tell me after he did the nicest thing anyone'd ever done for me? A thing that I never even dreamed of someone doing for me. Let alone a man who hates me.

He does, doesn't he?

Why am I getting more and more convinced that he doesn't?

"Do you guys... talk?"

Brian's question brings me out of my thoughts, and I fist the sheet covering my body. I fist it so hard that I'm almost sure I'm this close to tearing it apart.

"Yeah." I scrunch my eyes shut. "Brian, I... I looked you up on Facebook and I saw your posts about traveling and not going home this summer and I... I came to Colorado. I came to see your dad, Bri. I'm here."

Although, his dad is not. Today was supposed to be his first day of summer camp and from the looks of it, he's already left while I was sleeping.

How strange that I could never sleep back in Connecticut but here I don't realize what's happening around me while my eyes are closed.

"Do you know where I am right now?" he asks, breaking the tense silence.

I swallow. "Yeah. California."

He chuckles.

Although there's no happiness in it. It sounds broken and I feel so guilty for doing this to him again.

Why do I keep hurting him?

"Bri, I'm sorry. I came to apologize to your dad. I swear to you. There's nothing between your dad and me. I –"

"You knew where I was but instead, you went to him."

"What?"

I don't understand what he means. I really don't and before I can ask him, he speaks. "I like you, Vi."

I still don't understand and maybe my silence alerts him of that because he explains, "I wanted to ask you out that night. On the night of your birthday."

"You wanted to ask me out?" I ask in a squeaky voice.

"Yeah, I did."

He wanted to ask me out.

Like, on a date?

"You mean, on a date?" I ask him, out loud.

"Yeah. On a date."

"But... How's that..." I lick my lips. "How's that possible? I thought you were always dating someone and... I... We were... We were friends."

"Yeah, we were. But I wanted more. I wanted to ask you out a million times but I never had the courage. You were always so busy in your own world and... When I saw you with my dad, I fucking lost it." He sighs. "I just wanted you to see me, you know."

He wanted me to see him. *See* him.

God, isn't that what I used to think myself? Despite all my avoidance of him, I used to think that I wanted Mr. Edwards to see me.

And Brian, his son, wanted the same thing from me?

He wanted me to see him the way I wanted *his dad* to see

me.

Oh God.

God.

All the while I was waiting for his dad to see me, he was waiting for me to see *him*?

I think I'm gonna… I think I'm gonna throw up.

"I didn't… I had no… idea."

He chuckles again but it's rueful this time. "I know. I know that."

I press a hand to my chest, trying to smother the pain in there.

"Brian, I'm so sorry."

"Hey, it's okay. Believe me, it is," he tries to calm me down.

"It is?" I ask in a tear-thickened voice.

"I don't feel that way about you anymore, Vi."

"You don't?"

"Nope. I don't, sorry. I think it was the whole moving away thing, you know. You were going somewhere else and I was going somewhere else and I just felt sad about that, I think."

"Really?"

"Yeah, trust me. I'm over it. I'm not in the same place."

I grab it as a lifeline. I *grab* it with both hands and breathe out a sigh of relief. It's big, huge. I almost dissolve in the bed. "Oh, thank God. Thank. God. You have no idea how relieved I am. Gosh. I got so scared for a second."

He laughs. "Yeah, I heard that."

I go to smile but then I remember something. Something he said before I got all sidetracked.

"Did you just say that you've been acting like an asshole to your dad? Why'd you say that?"

He goes all silent and I don't know what to think.

All I know is that something bad is coming. Even worse than when he said he wanted to ask me out. Although, for the life of me I can't imagine what it could be.

"Bri? Why did you say that?"

"Because he likes you too."

I've never been shot before. I don't know what it feels like to have a tiny bullet, traveling at the speed of sound, hit your body.

I imagine it's jarring, to say the least.

I imagine it's painful. It's shocking. It makes your bones rattle and it makes your breaths fall out of your lungs. It makes a hole in your body.

That's what it feels like right now.

Like I've been shot and I don't know how it happened and I don't know what to do next.

"What?"

I've barely said it; my voice is thin as paper, thinner, even. But my best friend hears it.

"Yeah, he does. He wants you. I asked him point blank that night and I could read it on his face. I could see it. He didn't say anything. He didn't have to. It was all there. He looked so guilty. So fucking tormented over it."

He wants me.

Mr. Edwards wants me.

The man who hates me, the man whose life I ruined. The man I've had feelings for ever since I was sixteen wants me.

"He wants me?" I breathe out.

"Yeah. And the things I said to him for that. The things I put him through."

He utters those words on a sigh, a regretful sigh.

"W-what did you say?"

"I told him he ruined my life. I told him that he betrayed me for wanting the girl I want. That I hated him. That he's a fucking pervert for wanting a girl his son's age. When he lost his job, I told him he deserved it. When the article came out and they called him all those names, I… I did too. I called him sick, a pedophile. Fuck…"

He pauses to draw a breath before starting up again. "He never said a word, Vi. Not once. He took it all. All my tantrums and hatred and disgust. God, I don't even know what to say to him now. I feel so *wrecked* over it. We were always so close and now we haven't seen each other in almost a year. We don't talk. I don't know how to talk to him. I don't know what to say and how to make it go away and…"

Brian says a lot of things, but I don't hear any of them because I finally understand. I get it now. I get Mr. Edwards's anger, his hatred, all the drinking.

His roses.

I even understand about the roses. The flowers he grew to cure his loneliness when his dad was sick.

I understand why it doesn't feel like he hates me anymore.

Because he doesn't. He doesn't hate me.

If he did, he wouldn't have asked Brian to talk to me. He wouldn't have asked his son to stop punishing me.

No, he doesn't hate me. He hates himself. He's punishing himself.

Because he thinks he's betrayed his son.

He thinks he's betrayed his son for wanting me. He hates himself for wanting what his son wanted.

Oh God, he hates himself.

I grip the phone so tightly and press it so hard against my ear that it should be painful and maybe it is, but I don't feel anything right now except this urge to make Brian understand.

"Brian, you need to talk to him," I cut him off. "You need to talk to your dad. He's not… He's not in a good place, Bri. He's not doing okay. He lives out here, in this cabin, all alone. He used to drink up until a week ago, did you know that?"

"What?"

"Yeah. You need to fix it. You need to tell him that you don't hate him. You don't even like me anymore. You need to tell him that. He's heartbroken, Brian. God, he's so… he's heartbroken. He's in pain. He hates himself. Do you realize that? How could you do that to him? He's your father. How could you call him all those names? You're his son. You guys were best friends. You were supposed to stand beside him when everything happened. He doesn't deserve your condemnation. He doesn't deserve your hatred, you got that? Promise me you'll fix it. Promise me, Brian."

"You love him, don't you?" Brian responds. "You're in love with my dad. You've always been."

All the fight goes out of me at his abrupt question.

I sag under my own weight. I sag under the weight of my feelings.

All this time, I thought Mr. Edwards hated me. All this time, I thought if he poured out all his anger on me, he'd be free.

Most of all, I thought I came here just to apologize.

None of that is true, is it?

He doesn't hate me. He's not angry with me, either. And I didn't come here just to apologize.

I came here because I'm not over him. I was never over him.

In fact, what I feel for him is bigger. So much bigger than I gave myself permission to even think about. It's always been bigger.

It's been that way since the day I saw him through the window of my bedroom.

"Yeah. I do. I love your dad, Brian. I've always loved him. Ever since I was sixteen."

And he wants me.

Part II

Mr. Edwards

I found out about Brian just after my father had died.

I was alone, sad, angry, all ready to leave for college in the fall when Cynthia – the girl I'd hooked up with weeks ago – called me out of the blue and told me about him.

If I was scared and feeling alone before, I was fucking terrified after that. I didn't know how to take care of a kid. I didn't *want* to take care of a kid. I'd just finished taking care of my drunk father. I didn't want another responsibility.

I wanted to get out of this town. I wanted to forget my life and do something… different. Than what I'd been doing up until then – cleaning up after my dad and playing ball.

But then, I saw him.

As soon as Cynthia put him in my arms, he began wailing and I forgot the things I wanted. I only knew I had to take care of him.

He was my kid. I had to be whatever he needed me to be.

A protector, a cook, a storyteller, a soother.

I had to be there for him, my son. My blood.

I wasn't going to let him down.

Until I did.

Actually, it was better when I was drunk. Things didn't have an edge. Guilt didn't pierce me this deeply, this excruciatingly.

I'm starting my truck to get back to the cabin after a long fucking day at the camp when my phone buzzes. It's Brian.

I hit accept so fast that I almost smash the screen. "Hello?"

"Hey, Dad."

"Hey, you okay?" I ask, hoarsely, thinking that maybe he's calling because something is wrong and he needs me.

Because why the fuck would he call me after how we left things last time?

"Yeah, Dad, I'm fine. Everything is fine."

I whoosh out a breath. "Okay, that's good. Great."

After a few moments of tense silence, he says, hesitantly, "Dad, I... I broke up with Fiona."

"Yeah?"

"Yeah. You were right. I had to do the right thing. I was doing it all for the wrong reasons. I was doing it to hurt people."

A rock lodges itself in my throat and I somehow push it down to speak. "That's... That's good. How do you feel, though?"

"I'm okay. It wouldn't have lasted long anyway." Then, "Dad, I also realized something else."

"Yeah? What?"

"I talked to her."

The knife in my chest starts twisting at a mere mention of

her and a throb starts up just under my rib cage.

"You did," I almost choke out with relief.

"Yeah, I did," he replies. "I talked to Vi and she forgave me for Fiona so easily. So fucking easily that it made me realize how much of a douchebag I've been. I let my ego rule. I got so pissed that I hurt the two most important people in my life. And the truth is that I didn't know how to reach out to you, Dad, after everything I said. After the way I behaved, I didn't know what to say to you..."

That rock tries to crawl up but I force it down again, even though it's infinity times harder to do it this time. "Hey, it's over now. It's done. I'm proud of you."

I am.

He did the right thing and besides, I didn't know what to say to him, either. So it's water under the bridge.

I'm glad we're talking now.

"She deserves better, Dad. Vi deserves better. She deserves someone who doesn't hurt her like I did. She deserves someone who puts her first."

Now the pain in my chest is so tremendous that it radiates out to my whole body. I remember her words from last night.

Are you saying I'm... visible?

Jesus Christ.

I wanted to break something then. Punch something. Maybe even her parents.

"She does," I say, at last.

"She deserves someone like you, Dad."

"What?"

"There's no excuse for how I behaved. I'm so fucking

ashamed. There's no way I can ever make up for it, for all the things I did to you over the past year, the way I froze you out, the things I said just to hurt you because I was angry. But Dad, I want you to know this. I want you to know that she deserves someone like you in her life. Someone good and noble. Someone who won't hurt her. I claimed to have feelings for her and look at what I did. I got so lost in my ego. I was like, how does she not like me when every other girl does. How the fuck does she not like me, you know? And I stepped on everything that made our relationship special. She deserves someone who –"

The pain becomes so unbearable, so intense that I clench my teeth and cut him off. "We're not talking about this."

"Why not? Dad, please. You gotta believe me."

"Brian," I warn.

"Please, just give me one good reason why we shouldn't talk about this. I know you like her, Dad. I know that."

"I don't," I clip.

"Stop lying, Dad. If you didn't, you never would've called me and asked me to patch things up. I know how difficult I've made things for you. I know how hard it was for you to reach out to me after the way I acted. So I know. What I don't know is why you're resisting this. I know she's there with you. She told me. Do this for me, Dad. You asked me to do something for you and I'm asking the same now."

"Let it go, Brian."

"I will," Brian says urgently. "Just tell me why you dating her is such a bad idea. Just give me a reason."

"Because she's half my age," I bite out. "Do you realize

what that means? Because I've got a son her age. Because she's still naïve and innocent and full of life. She talks about dreams and wishes and…"

And she saved me.

She fucking saved me from drinking when she had no reason to.

After the way I grew up with my drunk father, I've hated drinking. I've always considered it a liability, something I wouldn't do. Something I promised myself that I wouldn't ever put my son through.

But then, it became necessary. It became imperative to drown out everything that happened past summer. The guilt, the fact that my son hated me.

She saved me, though.

She came in and she saved me.

She *saves* people. She makes the world a better place. She dreams.

I don't even remember the last time that I had a dream. I don't remember my wishes or things that I wanted while I was growing up.

All I know is that my mother left when I was five and my dad was an alcoholic. All I know is that I took care of him and when I couldn't and I needed a distraction, I played.

I played not because I wanted to or I loved it but because it took me out of the house.

It exhausted me so I didn't feel lonely. I didn't feel aimless or angry at having a father who drank and a mother who didn't care enough to stay.

"Dad?"

Brian brings me out of my thoughts. "She deserves someone who's good. You're right. Someone who won't hurt her. Someone who'll give her whatever her romantic heart wants. I'm not that person. I've never been that person, all right. And I'm not starting now. She probably never even had a heartbreak and I have no interest in being her first. So drop it."

I have no interest in making her cry and leaving her like the people in my life have left me. I've no interest in breaking her heart and making her a cynic like me.

I have no interest in taking on that burden. That blame.

I've got enough blame to deal with. I've committed enough crimes.

Brian says that he doesn't mean any of the things he said. That he was angry, he wanted to hurt me.

The reason those things hurt me was because they were true. Every single one of them. Even that article was true.

They called me a pervert, a sick, twisted individual. A danger to society.

I am all of that.

Because two years and ten months ago, I saw a sixteen-year-old girl climbing out of her window and I couldn't look away. I didn't *want* to look away.

It felt like someone had stabbed me in the chest.

Someone infected me and I lost my mind over her.

12

Graham.
Just Graham...

-The Diary Of a Blooming Violet, Age 18 years and 10 months

I've got a red dress on tonight.

And make-up.

It's not much, really. Just some mascara and lipstick.

I'm not a dress girl or a make-up girl at all. In fact, I don't even own a lot of dresses.

But I own this.

It's red with flimsy spaghetti straps. It has frills along the hem that stops midthigh and along the neck that goes down to show a little bit of my cleavage.

I got it on my seventeenth birthday, a little present to myself. A dress in his favorite color.

I've hardly ever worn it, except for in the privacy of my

room back in Connecticut.

When I was coming here, I didn't know why I packed it. Or why I packed this little cherry-red lipstick and mascara.

You know what, scratch that.

I do know why.

I know why I packed these things.

I packed them because I love him. Because I was thinking about him and I was going to see him and even though I thought he hated me, I wanted to have this dress with me.

God, it's so freeing to admit this.

To admit that I'm in love with him.

I've always, *always* been in love with him. Since the beginning. Since the very first moment. The very first sight.

Maybe it's naïve and romantic. But fuck it.

I am a romantic. I'm a dreamer. And I accept that now.

Acceptance is wonderful, isn't it?

The most wonderful thing.

I've always felt ashamed of my feelings for him. Even before everything went down. I felt ashamed that I wanted my best friend's dad. I wanted to move away so I could forget him. So I didn't break any rules. So I could bury my dreams. I even thought that I'd find someone else, maybe. I'd find an appropriate guy to crush on.

Instead, I should've believed in my dreams, my desires. I should've believed in my heart.

It's okay, though. It ends tonight.

All of this. This guilt, this shame, this anger. This whole fucked-up mess that started on my eighteenth birthday, that started with my poison kiss.

Only it wasn't poison.

It was just that: a kiss. A lonely, filled with longing and overflowing with dreams kiss.

Besides, the timing wasn't right then. I was too young, barely eighteen, but I'm not too young now. There's no one in the world who can stop us.

No human, no law, not even God.

After I made Brian promise that he'd call his dad and fix things, we talked for hours. I told him not to tell his dad about my feelings and he agreed. He asked me if his dad was the reason why I wouldn't come over to his house and I said yes. I told him how it all started and how guilty I felt for crushing on his dad.

He told me that he'd cut ties with everyone back in Connecticut. He'd blocked all the people on social media who'd message him about me and the kiss.

In fact, there were several people who messaged him about my breakdown too and for a second, I really got freaked out. I thought he knew, but as it turns out, he doesn't. Because when he shared those things with Fiona, she wrote them off as rumors.

Thank God for her.

We even talked about all the stupid, nasty rumors about him and me. And for the first time ever, I laughed about them. It felt okay to laugh about him being my alleged fiancé.

It felt like old times.

Then, I did something important.

Something that has been missing in my life for months now. I got out a new diary from my fat hobo and I gave it a different name: *The Diary of a Blooming Violet.*

I wrote it with a red glitter pen, even.

To honor my new dreams and a certain someone who said I was beautiful.

The certain someone who came back from work a little while ago.

He took one look at me, my red dress, clenched his jaw in anger, shot me an almost accusing glare and disappeared down the hall like I set him on fire.

He's in the bathroom now, taking a shower. I can hear the water as I walk toward him.

With every step that I take, my heart grows bigger. Bigger and bigger until it's like a balloon in my chest, so swollen that it's painful to cage it in my ribs.

I reach the bathroom door after what seems like ages. I'm expecting it to be locked but it's not. In fact, it's not even closed the whole way. Like he just wanted to get out of my presence as fast as possible and didn't care about locking doors or where he went.

The steam flows out of the ajar door like water, like something from a dream.

I know a normal, sane girl wouldn't go in there and intrude on his privacy, but I'm not a normal girl.

I'm not sane either.

I'm crazy for him. Crazy, crazy, crazy.

And in love.

I'm in love with the man on the other side of the door and I'm going in. I push at it with my trembling fingers and it opens without a sound.

As soon as I enter, I'm hit by the misty quality of the air. Everything is foggy and thick and barely visible. Even so, I still make him out.

Just like I thought when I was sixteen, he still looks like the tallest and the broadest thing I've ever seen.

So tall that I have to stand on his feet to reach up to his mouth. So broad that when I hug him, I don't think my arms will meet.

And he's naked.

Oh God, he's naked.

He is partially hidden by the shower curtain –stupid shower curtain –so I can only see the back of his body but gosh, do I see it.

His shoulders are corded. So corded. They are like heavy slabs of stone that slope down to his back. The back with all the grooves and the great plains and terrains that the water is sluicing down from.

But that's not the shocking part.

I've seen his bare upper body before, back in Connecticut when he'd work in his yard during the summer. What I haven't seen ever in my entire life is his… bare ass.

My breath hiccups when I see it. When I see how round it is. How tight and honey-colored like the rest of him. There's a curve to it that I wanna run my hands over.

And then there are his thighs.

His heavy, powerful thighs, and just the sight of them makes me wanna clench mine. Because they are so muscular and big, dusted with dark, springy hair.

I was right about them.

They are so big that I can easily perch my tiny self on them.

I can straddle my little body over one of his mighty thighs and I can rock against it. I can rock and undulate and rub my needy core against his flesh until I become so wet that I'll glide. I'll sail over his limb and his coarse hair will rub against my oh-so-swollen clit and I'll come.

I'll cream all over his tree trunk of a limb.

God, I so wanna do that. I so wanna ride his thigh that I'm dying with the need.

I'm so dying with it that I almost miss something important. In fact, it's the most important thing.

I miss the fact that his hand is holding something. Something big and thick and hard.

Oh my God, his hand is holding his dick.

Although, it's not a dick, nope.

He was right. It's a cock. For some reason, dick makes me think of something narrow and something pale and thin.

So unlike this.

So unlike his cock.

Somewhere in the past few seconds I've been staring at him, he's moved and now I can see the front of his body too. I can see his cock.

It's wide and big and his fingers are wrapped around the base of it. Not only that, they are moving. They are moving up and down and for a second I think, I've caught him washing his shaft.

But that's not true.

I've actually caught him masturbating, I think. Because his

hand is not moving, it's pumping. It's stroking and going up and down so fast that it makes me think that he's angry at his cock.

Mr. Edwards is mad at his erection and so he's beating at it and beating at it. And all the muscles on his body are standing taught and beautiful. I can even hear the slick sounds of his frantic movements, which is crazy because the shower is loud.

My breaths are louder. Louder than his hand jerking off his cock.

God, he's jacking off and I don't know what to do.

How to simply stand here and not go to him.

I'm salivating for it. My mouth is full of saliva and I'm biting my lip and licking it.

I'm gasping and probably rolling my hips in the air and that's how he knows I'm here.

He catches me perving over him while I'm making noises.

Yikes.

As soon as his eyes hit me, his face goes from flushed to furious in a split second and he whips around, his shaft hard and pointing toward me. "What... What the... What the fuck?"

I don't flinch. I don't act ashamed or afraid.

My shyness as always is a thing of the past when it comes to him.

"Were you thinking about me?"

His expression scrunches up and he snaps at the shower curtain and covers his lower half. "What the fuck are you doing here?"

"The door was open."

"And you thought you could just walk in?"

"I wanted to talk to you."

"You couldn't have waited until I was done?"

I shrug, watching water rivering down his chest, slicking his dark hair against his flesh. "I could've but the thing is, I didn't want to."

"Get out. Out. Right now."

He's angry, understandably so. I intruded on him.

But I'm not going anywhere.

I won't.

Until he accepts it too. Until he's free and at peace.

Until he admits he wants me too and it's okay to do that.

"You never say you hate me."

"What?"

I swallow and fist my hands. "You called me a nightmare. You said my face took away your peace. But you never say that you hate me. Not once have you said that."

All day today, I replayed his words over and over. I thought of everything he said to me. Every little detail. I analyzed it to death and I realized that he never said it.

He never said the word *hate* ever.

I've said it but he hasn't. Not once.

Shutting off the shower, he scrubs a hand over his face. "Violet. Get the fuck out right now."

I take a few steps in. "It's because you don't hate me, do you?"

"I'm not going to ask you again."

My legs are overcome with a strange current and I can't stop myself from walking in further and further, until my bare toes bump with the ceramic bathtub and he actually has to take a step back to get away from me.

He doesn't go easily though. His chest heaves; his fists clench; his jaw grinds; and he glares at me like I'm torturing him.

"You don't say it because you don't hate me. If you did, you never would've asked Brian to call me and talk to me. You did it because you *don't* hate me. You just want me to *think* that you do so I'll go away. And I did think that. I did and you never corrected me. You never told me the truth. Why didn't you tell me the truth? Why do you want me to go away?"

His mouth twitches and curls and he takes such a long, deep breath that the wayward strands of hair around my face flutter.

"I don't have time for your teenage hormones right now, okay? I need you to back off and leave me alone."

"You know, you call me a teenager a lot," I whisper, studying his features.

He cleaned up today for the camp, I realize. He trimmed his beard. It isn't as savage and untamed anymore. It reminds me of the beard he had back in Connecticut, polished and civilized.

Although there's no way after seeing him make repairs around the yard and living in this woody cabin that I can ever think him civilized.

He's a man of nature to me. All big and flowing with strength.

"That's what you are, aren't you?"

"I am, yes." I reach up with my hand, wanting to caress his jaw, touch that neatly trimmed beard but he stops me.

He grabs my wrist with his wet fingers, the only place he's touched me so far, and squeezes. "Don't be dumb enough to touch me right now."

I didn't expect anything less from him. I didn't expect anything less than threats and a cruel grip.

"You saying it over and over won't make me grow up any faster," I tell him, ignoring his warning.

"And I care about that? You growing up faster."

I nod, letting my hand, my entire body go limp and lax. Like clay. He can mold me and press and push into me as much as he wants. He can shape me however he wants.

I'm his.

"You do. Because if you didn't, you would've kissed me back that night."

I think I dropped a bomb on him or something.

Or at least, that's what it feels like when he shudders and jerks back. He steps away from me and lets go of my wrist.

Then he snaps the shower curtain open and climbs out, reaching for his jeans and whipping them off the hook. In a flash, he has them on, covering his gorgeous nakedness.

"Brian told me everything."

He pauses, going still.

I watch the planes of his back shift up and down with his breaths, as I say, "How he wanted to ask me out that night."

"So you have your answer now, don't you? I'd like you to go away because my son wants you."

He's not getting off that easily.

"But he doesn't. He doesn't want me anymore."

At this, he turns around, his face a blank mask and his eyes arrogant and slitted. "So what? Am I supposed to pounce on you now? Because my son doesn't want you and my path is clear."

"No."

"Good. Because I'm not going to."

"You're supposed to tell me the truth though."

He folds his arms across his misty, wet chest. "Truth about what?"

"Would you have kissed me back that night if we hadn't gotten interrupted and I was older?"

His response is to grit his teeth.

"Because see, I've been thinking about this too. That's what I did today. I thought and analyzed. You know all these things about me. You know where I liked to sit in school while I wrote in my journal. You know my favorite things to eat. So that means you watched me, right? You knew who I was that night. The night I kissed you. But still, you pretended not to know me. You let me think that you hadn't seen me before then. You kept saying go home. You wanted me to go away then too but you didn't know about Brian's crush."

"And that's supposed to mean something?"

"Yes. It means that you were ashamed of watching me, weren't you?"

A growl escapes him then.

It's very low, barely audible, and I wouldn't have heard it if I wasn't so attuned to every little detail about him in this moment. His breathing pattern. The tick-tock of the vein on the side of his neck. The flare of his nostrils.

"You were. You were ashamed maybe because I was too young and you were too old." I swallow. "And I know this because I was too. Not because of those reasons. But because I was watching my best friend's dad. In fact, I used to avoid you. I mean, I'd only go over to your house when you weren't there and the rest of the time, I'd have Brian over to mine."

I realized this much, much later in the day.

When Brian's words really sunk in.

He likes you too…

He likes me. That means he knew who I was on my eighteenth birthday. Not only that, he kept asking me to leave. I was throwing myself at him but he kept saying go home.

Go home, Violet…

And then, I realized the only reason he did all of that was because he was ashamed.

Just like me, he was ashamed of his desires, his wants. Long before everything went to hell. Long before he found out about Brian's crush. Long before he started to hate himself for wanting what his son wanted.

His eyes narrow at my declaration. There's a genuine curiosity, disbelief, shock in them. "You watched me?"

I could've laughed. I could've cried.

Jesus Christ.

Have there ever been any other two people so fucking similar to each other?

All the while I was dreaming in my bed, he was across that driveway, dreaming in his. All the while I was writhing, he might have been longing for me too.

I nod, smiling slightly. "Yes. I did. I watched you like there was no one else in the world."

"Why?"

"Because I had this massive, gigantic, epic crush on you."

"You had a crush on me?"

"Yeah. It wasn't a stupid, drunken mistake, Mr. Edwards. I would've kissed you regardless. I would've kissed you because I wanted to kiss you. I've wanted to kiss you since I was sixteen."

He breathes out after I finish.

A tight but long breath as his eyes sweep all over my face. They sweep and swirl until I think he's touching me with his gaze.

Touching me and holding me up, keeping my feet on the ground because I wanna fly right now. It feels so, so good to finally tell him that.

To admit my truth to him.

But then, he speaks and his voice is tight and angry. "You know what happens when a thirty-four-year-old man watches a sixteen-year-old girl?"

"But I'm not... I'm not sixteen anymore."

"Tell me what happens."

I swallow, my heart hammering in the chest. "He goes to jail."

He nods. "Now tell me what happens if he kisses her."

I take a step toward him. "It doesn't matter. Because you didn't. Nothing happened."

He scoffs, running a hand through his drenched hair. "Yeah, nothing happened. So that makes all of it okay, doesn't it? It makes everything okay. I'm off the hook for all the things I thought about a sixteen-year-old girl."

Fuck it.

I'm going to him.

I don't care if he doesn't let me touch him, I'm going to try regardless.

Thankfully though, he lets me touch him and I make contact with his bare skin for the first time ever.

I put my hands on the globes of his shoulders, touch my bare toes to his and crane my neck up to look him in his tormented eyes. "Yes. You are. You're off the hook for everything."

His shoulders shudder when he barks out a rusty laugh. "Yeah? I'm off the hook for watching a girl half my age? Watching her like I couldn't take my eyes off her. Watching her like I had this... this compulsion. This need to look at her. To look at her pale skin and her gorgeous as fuck smile."

I dig my nails in his hot flesh as I'm overcome with a swell of emotions. "Y-you think my smile is gorgeous?"

He looks at me like I'm crazy. "Fuck yeah, it's gorgeous. Every night, you'd climb up to your roof and you'd just open your arms like you were soaking in the moon and you'd smile and Jesus Christ, I'd lose my mind. And I'd tell myself over and over I wouldn't do it, that I wouldn't go out but I did anyway. I'd still go out there and watch you while pretending to work on my roses. I'd still wander around the house, chasing after your strawberry smell like a disgusting creep."

So years later, I get my answer.

I get the answer for the question I always wanted to ask him: *What's keeping you up, Mr. Edwards?*

Turns out, it was me.

I was keeping him up. My smile was keeping him up.

My hands snake up to his drenched hair. "Is t-that why you were never there? At the house? I mean, I'd make sure you weren't but sometimes you'd just run away. Disappear."

"Yeah. I couldn't bear it. I couldn't bear to be in the same room as you and not..."

"Not what?"

"Not go to you. Not touch you."

"But it's okay now, isn't it? I'm eighteen. It doesn't matter. You don't have to suffer like this."

I swear his flesh turns up in temperature. "You don't get it, do you? It's not about the fact that my son doesn't want you anymore or that you're fucking eighteen now. It's about the fact that whatever they said was true."

"What?"

His eyes are glowing now, brimming with everything he's been feeling and thinking for the past years. Everything that's torturing him, giving him pain, and I can't see that.

I can't see him like this.

"You want the truth, don't you?" he rasps. "Here's the truth: you didn't ruin anything for me. You didn't take away my job. I quit. You didn't make me move halfway across the country, I did it myself. I did it because everything they say about me is correct. I wanted you to think that I hated you, I wanted you to go away because whatever they think I am is true. I am dangerous. I am diseased. I belong on the fringes of society. I belong in fucking jail. They can't trust me around their kids. No one can trust me.

I'm sick, you understand? I am everything that they say I am. Every filthy, vile, criminal thing."

My fingers fist his hair. They clench and flex. They tug and pull at his strands.

It's like they're going into shock. They're spasming.

How can he say that about himself? How can he not see that he's different, this fucking amazing?

Instead of giving in to his desires, he chose to ignore them. He chose to hate himself, torture himself, *remove* himself from my presence.

If he'd given me one hint, one sliver of a clue that he wanted me, I would've done anything for him. Anything at all.

If he'd wanted it to be a secret, I would've been his dirty little secret.

If he'd wanted everyone to know, I would've screamed it from the rooftops.

How does he not see any of this?

I'll make him see, though. I will.

So I blurt out the only thing I can think of. "They called me a slut."

He pauses.

His heavy, noisy breathing stops and his eyes, brimming with hot emotions, go cold. "What?"

"There were rumors and gossip and…" I swallow, trying to gather my thoughts. "They'd make up stories about me. People would recognize me on the street and stop me and talk to me and say things to me. I'd get all these emails and they were, like, really bad and they all called me names. They called me a slut for throwing myself on you. They said that that's what I do, I go for older guys and all of that. And…"

I lower my eyes and look at his throat. It's flushed around his collarbone, droplets of his shower still sticking to the skin.

I'm not sure where I'm going with this story because I'm not going down the anxiety route. Because, hello? I'm fine. So I'm not telling that but I'm telling him something.

I *have* to tell him something; I can't let him think the worst of himself.

I have to make it better. I have to.

"Tell me what happened," he says in a low, pulsating voice. "Tell me what they did."

With stuttered breaths, I look up at him and see all this anger on his face.

On my behalf.

It makes my stomach clench in that achy way that I used to feel whenever I thought about him in my bed. Achy and heavy that I felt last night, and I whisper, divulging my illicit secrets. "I had this pillow and when everyone would go to sleep, I'd put it between my legs. I'd press down on it. Really hard. And after a while, when I'd get really restless, I'd begin to rock. I'd rock against it and I'd bite my lip. Because I'd want to moan and call out your name. But I'd be afraid that someone might hear me. So I'd keep quiet and I'd keep going. I'd keep rocking against the pillow because I wanted you so much."

I can't believe I'm telling him this.

I watch a crimson flush overcome his cheeks. I watch the dilation of his pupils, his breaths going low and heavy, as if he's sleeping, but I don't think he's ever been more awake.

More aware.

Because I'm the same way and I can tell.

"A-and we had this maid, she'd do our laundry and every-thing. And she'd come to my room to change the sheets and she'd always give me this look. Because I think she could... she could smell me on them. She could see the wet spots and then, when everything happened, I heard her talking to Fiona downstairs and she was calling me a slut. Like everyone else."

I've been breathing really hard through this. Panting, al-most. But then he puts his hands on me and my lungs forget to draw in a breath.

My heart forgets to beat.

My eyes go wide and I have to look down.

I have to see his hands on me. They are wrapped around my waist. His bronzed fingers over my red dress. They are so long, his hands, that he can span my entire waist with them.

His thumbs meet in the middle where my belly button is, and they dig into my flesh, press into it, and my thighs clench.

But not only my thighs; my core clenches too.

My pussy.

That I used to rub on the pillow because I wanted him so much.

"You're not a slut," he growls, and I look back at him.

His face is made of furious lines. His brows snap together angrily as he continues, "Not for that kiss. And definitely not for what you felt. Never for what you felt. Whoever said it, I'm going to take them apart with my bare hands, you understand? And that maid of yours, if you waste a single thought on her, on that pathetic excuse of a human being, I'll hunt her down and make her wish she was dead."

By the time he finishes, his hands are squeezing my waist so tightly, massaging the flesh almost that I have to go up on my tiptoes. But it's okay. I don't mind.

I've got him to lean on.

My arms have wrapped themselves around his neck and I'm leaning into him.

I'm leaning into him the way I was on my eighteenth birthday. The way I'm beginning to think that I was always meant to do. "Y-you will?"

He nods slowly. "Yeah."

I take a moment to process this. To process the sheer enormity of what just happened.

He not only absolved me of all the crimes I thought I committed against him, he single-handedly destroyed all the voices that belonged to those people.

The voices that called me names.

And the truth is that I believed them. I've always been so ashamed of my desires for him that I believed that I deserved to be called a slut for kissing him, for wanting him, for crushing on him.

I didn't think I'd feel any freer than I did a minute ago, but this is barely keeping my feet on the ground.

Now it's his turn.

"But then, if you do those things, you'll end up in jail," I whisper, my nipples going really, really hard against his chest as I give him more of my weight.

A second later, he makes me give him all of it.

He brings me forward, tugging on my waist, and crashing our torsos together. It's all very sudden and violent and glorious and I gasp as my soft, melting body clings to the hard planes of his.

"You think I'm afraid of that? I'm afraid of going to jail for you?" he rasps.

I lick my dry lips and shake my head rapidly.

I shake it like my heart is shaking inside my chest. With thrills and excitement and a dark sort of pleasure. "No, I don't think so."

"No, I'm not. For some very strange reason, I'm not. Not for you," he says like he doesn't understand it. But then, his tone becomes firm as he promises, "Anyone who hurts you goes through me, you got that?"

"Why?" I ask, melting and melting, drop by drop. The only reason I'm standing on my two feet is because he has a grip on me.

At my question, he brings one hand up and cups my cheek and I think that even his grip on my waist won't save me now.

I can't be saved from melting away because he's holding my cheek with his rough, callused fingers and it's so tender and scrape-y that I could almost be his rose.

"Because you're my Jailbait." He presses the pads of his fingers on the apple of my cheek as he continues, "And I'll destroy anyone who dares to hurt you. All the people who made you feel less and called you names for that kiss. Everyone. You're not a slut, all right? I won't let you think you are."

I grab his wrist and whisper, my heart so full of him and his words and his dark promises, "Okay, I won't think that. But only if you don't think you are what they say you are."

Going still, he watches me a beat. "Is that right?"

Swallowing, I nod. "Yeah. I don't want us to be ashamed anymore. I don't want all the guilt and anger and pain. I don't want us to be what they said we were. I don't want other people defining us. I just want us to be... us. Just you and me."

"You and me, huh."

I nod before whispering, "Besides, I don't wanna be their slut, anyway."

"What?"

I close the last inch.

Our bodies were already touching. My breasts were already at his ribs and my stomach was already pressing against his pelvis and now, I get up on his feet to reach his mouth.

"I'm tired of being their slut, Graham. I wanna be yours."

A current goes through his body that transfers from his flesh to mine, and I feel it right in my gut. In my pussy.

His eyes go blazing as his fingers jerk on my face and I know it's going to happen before it does.

I know he's going to kiss me now.

And he does.

He puts his mouth on mine.

13

I think we're lovers from a past
life, trapped in ages deemed
inappropriate by this century.
I think when we break free
and kiss,
there will be fireworks.

-The Diary of a Blooming Violet, Age 18 years and 10 months

His mouth is on me.

His mouth. Is. On me.

His mouth is on my mouth.

People call this a kiss.

I have to tell these things to myself. I have to run them in a loop inside my head because I can't believe it.

I can't believe it's finally happening.

I can't believe he's finally kissing me. And it's not like the kiss that I gave him on my eighteenth birthday, when he was an unwilling participant. When he was a big mountain that wouldn't be moved.

He's big still but he's moving.

God, is he moving.

In fact, he has this intensity rolling just under his skin, this heat, this passion, that I can feel in his touch.

His touch.

He's *touching* me. I could just smile about that till the end of my days. The fact that I thought he didn't wanna touch me, and now he can't stop.

His hands are all over my body.

They grab my waist and squeeze, making me arch up against him, making me rub my hard nipples against the lines of his pecs. Making me drag my trembling, shaking stomach against the grooves of his abdomen.

And when I feel the hair on his chest rub against my cleavage, I go crazy. I grab him back. I dig my fingers in his long, untamed hair and push back against him.

That just makes him even more frantic. It makes him roam his hands even more.

They leave my waist but they seem to be reluctant. They fist and bunch in my dress as if he doesn't wanna let go of my hips yet.

They drag my pretty red dress up and down my legs as he rubs his hands in circles and sweeps. He goes down to my thighs and then comes back up to my waist. He's making me feel his fingers through the fabric of my dress and it's creating this hollow inside my stomach.

This hollow that is rapidly filling up with need and lust and everything sweaty and sticky.

So much so that I clench my thighs. I clench my stomach and my pussy.

My wet, *wet* pussy just because he's playing with my dress. Just because he doesn't wanna let go of it like it's a toy of some sort and he hates to be parted from it.

But then, he does.

He does part with it and goes up to my neck. He grabs the back of it, covers the entire width of it with one of his hands while the other makes a fist out of my hair. Out of my thick and straight hair that never seems to curl even though I've tried to a million times before. Now, the strands give so easily beneath his fingers. They twist and curl and get wrapped around his grip like they are his slave.

Like every other part of my body is.

Like my lips.

They open and close and go loose and pliant under his and I wasn't even paying attention to that. I've been so distracted by all these new sensations that I forgot about the kiss itself.

I forgot about his mouth. That's moving on mine and making me do things for him.

It's more than moving, actually.

It's sliding and slipping and almost groping.

He sucks on my lower lip, makes it all slippery and swollen and achy before nipping it with his teeth and making me jerk.

And he likes that.

He likes me jerking for him so he makes me do it again. He tugs on my string like I'm his puppet, a doll, and bites my lip again and I jerk and twist in his arms.

I rub my needy breasts against his bare chest. I rub my nipples and I swear I can feel the coarse hair of his chest on them, even through the fabric.

He lets go of my lip and pants over my mouth. "You like that, huh? You like me biting your lip."

Oh God, his voice.

I've never heard it before. I've never heard this rough, low, raspy tone from him before and it makes me twist again, roll my hips against his body.

"Yes," I whisper with a tingling mouth.

His lips, those beautiful, gorgeous lips that were just wreaking havoc on mine, stretch on one side and he gives me such a sexy smirk that I almost melt away.

"Yeah, my baby likes it."

Okay, so there's no almost about it. I am melting away. I *have* melted.

"You called me y-your baby," I say uselessly as my arms go limp and leave his hair, almost falling down to the globes of his shoulders.

"And you called me Graham."

"I've wanted to call you that forever."

He tugs at my lower lip with his thumb. "Yeah, me too."

My eyes go wide and I blurt out, "For me to call you Graham?"

"Yeah, that as well."

And then, he goes for my lips again and I realize what he meant.

I realize that he wanted to call me his baby like I wanted to call him Graham. We probably wanted this for ages.

We probably wanted it ever since we saw each other. Ever

since we first laid eyes on each other and got stung by this obsession. This need, this craving, this fever that made us outcasts and different. But most of all, it made us *bad.*

You're the girl who makes a man go bad.

I made him go bad, didn't I? My need for him was contagious and he caught it too.

And me? I always liked bad things anyway.

Things like this.

Things that he's doing to me right now.

Things like feeding.

He's feeding on my mouth now and I love it. It isn't even a kiss, anymore. It can't be.

My entire mouth is inside his and he's sucking on it. He's sucking on it like I'm his candy. Like my bee-stung, cherry red lips are made of sugar and he can't get enough. He wants me to melt in his mouth; he wants to pierce me with his teeth, lap me up with his tongue.

And like a good little candy girl, I let him. I moan to urge him on. I stretch my calves so much that they burn but it's such a small price to pay when I get to be closer to him. When I get to give him all the access to me. To my open mouth.

Which he takes in a flash.

In a flash, his tongue is inside and he's tasting me, the thing I'm made of.

And I moan again.

I moan into his kiss and suck on his tongue like he was sucking on mine. I moan because it's glorious to be fed on. It's glorious to feel the sting of his feeding and his tasting.

I'm a masochist, aren't I?

I fall in love with the sting. I fall in love with his kiss.

I fall in love with him as I kiss him back messily and sloppily.

His hands start to roam once again but this time they do something that I never even dreamed of.

My innocent, schoolgirl dreams weren't made of this stuff.

The stuff his hands do and completely ruin me in the process.

In response to my shameless kissing, he moves his hands away from my hair and my neck. He moves them down feverishly and gets them under the straps of my dress.

And then, he pulls.

He pulls it so much and with such force that I gasp mid-kiss and scrape my nails over his biceps.

Our lips part and I look into his eyes, his dark, beastly eyes, and groan when I feel his fingers tugging on those straps.

My breath halts when the fabric digs into my shoulders like a rope and I have this silly thought that it's going to snap. That he's going to tear off the straps of my dress.

And just like that, he does it.

The straps give way under the unrelenting pressure of his fingers and I jerk again. I gasp when it happens. My hands fall away from his biceps and grip his sides.

He actually tore off my dress.

He *actually* did it.

"You tore off my straps," I whisper uselessly, like he doesn't know. Like he didn't do it with his bare hands.

One hand, actually. One hand for each strap.

That's all it took to lay waste to my dress.

"I did," he pants, watching me like before when he promised he'd go to jail for me. Like he can't believe he did that, tore off my straps, but he likes it. He wants to do it over and over again.

"I bought it for you."

"You did?"

I nod, my chest moving up and down, grazing *his* up and down moving chest. I'm not wearing a bra and the dress is still tight enough that it clings to the curves of my breasts but I don't know how long he'll let me be covered up. I don't know how long *I'll* wanna be covered up.

"I-I knew red was your favorite color and I bought it for my seventeenth birthday. Kinda like my gift from you."

He searches my features, which I'm sure must be as red as my dress. "But you never wore it."

I bite my tingling, wet-from-his-kisses lips and shift on my feet, which are still up on his bigger ones. "Because I thought I'd look... stupid. I mean, I'm not a dress kinda girl, you know? So I just bought it and wore it in my room. I'd look at myself in the mirror and I'd wonder what you'd think. If you saw me."

Now that he's done tearing my dress off, his hands move away from my shoulders and go back down to my waist.

In fact, they grab onto my waist and pick me up. It's so sudden that all I can do is feel the air beneath my feet as they leave the floor and obey his command when he growls, "Put your legs around me."

I do that.

I practically grapple him with my thighs that go around his slim strong hips and my hands that go around his neck.

When I'm eye-level to him and all wrapped around him, he splays his palm on the back of my head and whispers, "You know why my favorite color is red?"

I shake my head.

"It's because it's the color of your lips. It's the color of your smile."

The said lips part and I breathe out, "No way."

"I didn't have a favorite color before you."

My mouth falls open. "Seriously?"

His nostrils flare. "I didn't notice colors before I met you."

My heart squeezes. It squeezes and squeezes because it's so sad, as sad as him being dreamless. So sad that I wanna hug him. I wanna touch his face. Caress it. Trace it with my fingers.

Suddenly, I realize that I can.

I can now.

I *can* touch his beard, and as if I needed that reminder to be able to feel the marks on my skin, they come alive.

I feel the sting of his beard, all over my chin, my jaw, around my lips. I feel the belated scraping, the rustling of it over my face when he was kissing me.

How did I miss that? How? Those marks are burning now, burning so deliciously.

My hands move up and I finally, *finally* touch it.

I touch his beard. I feel it with my fingers, all rough and soft, silk and sand, as I whisper, "God, I wanted to touch your beard for so long."

He rubs his jaw against my palm and I almost moan. "Yeah?"

"Uh-huh. I had dreams about it."

"What dreams?"

"Of rubbing it with my hands. Rubbing it all over my body. It'll make me all red, won't it?"

He rubs his jaw harder against my palm, as if trying to make it red, trying to make my dream come true. "Red as a rose. Red as my favorite color."

I shake my head at him. "You know, for an asshole, you say the nicest things."

His eyes go heavy at that. Heavy and hooded as he boosts me up higher with his arm under my butt and again, it makes me feel like a bag of feathers that he can lift and throw around just like that.

"Do I?

I kiss his beard, then. I lick it, feeling the scrape and rustle that I missed before right on my tongue. "I think if you tried you could write all the poetry for me that I'll ever need."

He fists my hair, tugging my lips away and stares down at me. "I can't do poetry, Jailbait. But I'm going to do other things for you."

"Like what?"

He bounces me in his lap again and I bite my lip to keep from moaning. "I'm going to buy you a hundred dresses. A *thousand* dresses. And you're going to wear them all. You're going to wear them all for me. And I'm going to tear them all off with my bare hands. You know why?"

"Why?"

"Because I'll buy them all in red. They'll be as red as your pretty lips. And I'm going to lose my mind over it. That color will call to me, call to my blood like I'm this bull of a man who just has to get to you. Get to your red as fuck mouth."

I'm breathing against his lips – I know that – but my body is going into a state where I don't know if I'm alive or dead or simply burning in lust.

"O-okay," I whisper and rock against him.

"And I'm going to grow all the roses for you," he promises like all the other promises he's made tonight weren't enough, like I needed to be slain some more. "All the roses that you'll ever want so you don't have to pick off the dying ones for your gift. That's what you were doing that night, wasn't it? You wanted your gift from me."

I swallow. More like I hiccup and go all limp in his arms. Limp and breathy and a panting mess as I nod haltingly. "Y-yeah."

He looks over my entire face, soaks in my features, and I love that.

I love so, so much that he's seeing me.

Not only that but he's been seeing me, watching me for ages. I thought I was invisible but I wasn't.

I was visible to him.

To my Graham.

"And I'm going to do one other thing."

"What?"

In reply, he presses a hard kiss on my mouth and I kiss him back. This time around, I feel his beard rubbing against my skin. I feel the sting as it happens and it makes me even hornier.

It makes me messier and sloppier, both my kiss that I can't stop giving him and my pussy.

My pussy is running like a river. It's clenching and releasing and I'm gushing cream and soaking my panties. I'm probably getting it all on my thighs too. Thighs that are wrapped around him and I bet he can feel my wetness.

I'm smearing it all over him as well. All over his stomach where my pussy is at. It doesn't even cross my mind to stop. Not even for a second.

It just makes me more shameless and lusty.

It just makes me moan into his mouth continuously.

I feel him walking then, going through the bathroom door, striding down the hallway and entering a room – his room, most likely. But through all this, I don't stop kissing him or moaning and rubbing my hands all over his face and rubbing my pussy over his stomach.

But then, I have to stop.

Because he breaks the kiss and launches me in the air.

I fall on the bed a split second later and scramble up on my elbows. I look up at him, at his harsh, panting form, and a pulse goes through my core.

He stands tall at the foot of his bed. His chest is flushed a dark hue and his entire body is heaving, juddering up and down, all bathed in sweat.

While I'm running my eyes over his body, he has his glued to my chest. By some miracle, my dress is still up and around my breasts – it's the zipper around the back, I think – but it's sagging.

The straps lie limply around my arms and I have a feeling that it won't take much to bare my heaving breasts to him.

"Graham?" I call out his name when it looks like he's not going to say anything.

Actually, it looks like he'll never say anything because he's just so lost in his staring.

He looks up now, though and inhales a heavy breath.

Then he gets on the bed. And he does it in a way that the whole frame shakes. The mattress dips under his weight, sags and submits like my dress did, back in the bathroom.

"I'm going to do one other thing to you, Violet," he repeats, kneeling in front of me but still towering.

"What?" I ask, looking up at him with wide eyes.

He licks his lips as he bends down. Down and down, as if descending on me, until our foreheads are almost touching. Until I can't see anything of his room, not the walls, not the ceiling, nothing at all except him and his darkly flushed face.

Clamping his jaw tight, he grabs hold of my dress.

My spine arches with the force of it. He pulls at my dress with both hands, bent over me like a beast from the mountains.

"I'm going to make you my slut," he growls, tugging the dress down and it goes easily.

In a second, I'm bared to him and his gaze drops to my breasts.

I've always thought they were average. They were small and nothing to go crazy over.

But he's going crazy over them. I can see that.

He likes the shape of them, the size, the paleness of them.

And I know he likes my nipples. They're cherry-red too. Hard and tight and rude, sticking up like that. Sticking up for him.

He swallows tightly and looks up. "You want to be my slut, don't you?"

I nod and fist the sheets. "Yes."

"I'll make you my slut, Violet," he whispers, coming even closer to me, his hands on my ribs now, spread wide, just under my breasts. "I'll make you scream like a slut. You know how I'm going to do that?"

I'm breathing so hard that I'm actually shaking with it. I'm rolling my hips already, undulating my spine, making my breasts jiggle.

"How?"

"I'm going to give you your birthday kiss." He licks his lower lip again like he's imagining it. "The kiss I wanted to give you as soon as you turned eighteen. The kiss I couldn't stop thinking about while I was on that useless date."

I'm pretty sure he can feel my heart right now. He can feel it bouncing around in my rib cage, pounding against the bones and muscles, probably pounding against the palm of his hands.

"The date you were on?"

"Yeah."

"Is that why... you came back early?"

"I came home early because I wanted to see you. Up on the roof. At midnight. But you weren't on the roof, were you?"

"No."

"Where were you?"

He digs the pads of his fingers into my ribs and my heart

shifts there, where his hands are. Banging inside my body. "I was stealing your roses."

"Yeah, you were. Because you wanted your gift from me."

I nod. "Uh-huh."

"So I'm going to give it to you now. I'm going to give you your special birthday gift." He presses down on my body and I realize he wants me to lie down, so I do.

"And you're going to scream, isn't that right?"

I lie down on his bed and put my head on his pillow and almost drown in his scent, his musky, outdoorsy scent. "I will."

"Yeah." He hovers over me now, his hand on my stomach. "You'll scream so loud that everyone will hear you. They'll hear you screaming for me. Everyone back in Connecticut will hear you, won't they? Everyone who made you cry and called you names. The ones I keep wanting to destroy every five seconds. They'll hear it and they'll know. They'll know what I'm doing to you. You'll *make* them hear it, won't you?"

Oh God.

I'm so turned on right now. So fucking turned on.

I'm nodding to everything he's saying, to his every question. To every demand he's making of me and I'm nodding not only with my head but with my entire body.

I'm sliding my legs up and down his sheets. I'm rocking my hips, and all the while he has this one hand on my stomach, keeping me pinned on his bed.

"I will. I will. I will scream. I promise."

"Good. I want them to hear it. I don't want you biting your lip. I want them to hear you scream and moan when I give you your kiss, Violet. I want them to know that I make it so good for you, that I make it so fucking fantastic that you can't help but scream. You scream because you're mine and I want them to know that. I want them to know that you're in my bed. That you're my slut and if someone dares to call you that again, I'll fucking destroy them."

I arch up at his tone, at the finality of it, at his determination to make things right for me. To make all those people pay and to make me feel cherished.

I do feel cherished. In a way that I've never felt before. Cherished and protected and so completely dominated as he moves down and spreads my legs and at last, I get the presence of mind to ask him, "W-what's my birthday kiss?"

Like, how did I not ask him this before?

How was I not curious?

But whatever, I'm asking now. I'm looking up at him with needy eyes and in reply, he inches up my dress, exposing my damp panties.

He shifts it up and reduces it to a red sash around my stomach, exposing my breasts and that place between my thighs.

It makes my heart skip a beat. It makes my heart skip several beats, actually. It makes my heart beat in my stomach. In my pussy, which he's looking at right now, for the first time ever.

Or rather, he's looking at my panties – red ones – and they're wet, getting wetter under his scrutiny.

And instead of feeling shy, I think they're a nuisance, my panties. They're hiding what I really wanna show him.

I wanna show him my pussy.

My wet and deep pink and pulsing core that's been dying for him. That I especially prepared for him. I shaved and primped not because I expected this to happen but because I just wanted to be pretty for him even though he'd never know it.

But he'll know it now, I think.

Because he has the same idea of my panties being a nuisance and so, he goes for them.

He goes for my panties.

He hooks his fingers in my waistband and yanks them down. He keeps yanking until they are off and somewhere on the floor where he throws them before coming back to me.

Before coming back and lying down on his stomach, as sprawled as I am on the bed.

My legs are all open now, almost in a split and his shoulders are jammed between them. His face is at my open, bare core that he's breathing over, fanning my steamy folds with the air within his lungs.

He stares at it, burning my most intimate flesh with his eyes, as his thumbs run in circles at the juncture where my thighs meet my hips.

He stares at it and stares at it, getting lost for a second like he did when he looked at my breasts, and I have to call his name again. "Graham?"

He looks up, then.

"What's my special kiss?"

Finally, he growls, "This."

With that, he licks me.

He licks me right there. With the flat of his tongue, going

from bottom to top, and he does it so lazily that it makes me think he's lapping up the juices of a fruit.

A fruit that is me.

And then, he goes and finishes that shameless and open and direct lick with a groan. As if it really was juicy. My pussy really is a fruit, his favorite fruit.

In fact, it's such a favorite that he does it again. And again and again. He licks and licks and licks, using the flat of his tongue, so that my hands snap off the sheet and go to his hair.

I arch up on the bed, thrusting my core into his mouth. Not only thrusting, I rub my core over his mouth, his jaw.

His bearded jaw.

And God, *God*, that makes me moan like the slut I am.

His beard on my pussy makes me moan like a whore. I moan so loudly that I swear I hear the rattle of the bedroom window. I hear the glass crack, almost. I hear my moan reverberating and echoing through the woods.

So it's really a surprise when amidst my screaming and moaning, I hear him groan.

Which only makes me moan some more. His sounds of satisfaction, his approval and of course, his tongue.

He's swirling it around now, I think. He's up at my clit and he's flicking it with his tongue. He's going in circles up there, lashing it, slapping it and I'm writhing because of it.

It's like that hand on my stomach that he had a little bit ago. He was keeping me pinned to the bed with it.

Now, it's his mouth at my pussy.

He's keeping me glued to the sheets, he's keeping my ass

glued to the bed while my entire body jerks and twists under his ministrations.

It twists and twists so much that he has to bring his hands in to the mix.

He puts both of them on my thighs and grabs me there. He nails my legs to the bed and now my lower body is really at his mercy.

Who am I kidding? My entire body is at his mercy.

My heart, my soul, everything about me is in the palm of his hands and the flat of his tongue and hooked on his heavy, panting breaths.

His wild breaths.

As if he's really this beast who found me somewhere wandering in the woods. He came upon me and he wanted me.

So he dragged me back to his cave and now has me trapped in his clutches, the girl in the red dress. And he's making her scream as he takes juicy bites out of her, out of her pussy like he's so hungry.

So hungry that it's in every beat of his tongue and pull of his lips. At one point, he does what he did on my lips. He takes my core into his mouth, my wet, silky folds, and sucks on them.

He feeds on them and my knees jerk up and fold. My ankles go around his neck and I'm thumping my heels on his upper back. I'm jerking my hips to the rhythm of his feeding, rubbing his beard with my thighs, feeling the scrape, the sting, and I'm moaning.

I throw my head back into the pillow as I do that. As I make sounds and needy noises.

I'm so close. So fucking close.

My pussy is clenching and I bet he can feel it because that's where he is. He's moved down from my clit, so he can be at my hole.

He can be at my needy, horny hole that's rippling and he circles it with his tongue.

He goes round and round, his fingers spasming on my thighs.

It makes me think that he'll enter me with that tongue. He'll enter my body and taste the walls of my pussy, the messy, sloppy walls. It makes me think he'll dig out my juices. He'll curl his tongue inside of me and make me cream for him.

Make me gush all over his jaw and beard and just the thought of that makes me do it.

The thought of him entering my body makes me come.

I draw my knees up to my stomach, fist his hair and press my core in his mouth and I come.

I come in great, rolling waves. They take me away with them, make me move up and down. Make me shake the bed with the violence of his kiss.

His special kiss for my eighteenth birthday.

And it's not over yet.

As I'm coming down from my high, my body going lax and sated, I feel him moving up. I feel his lips pressing small kisses on my stomach and my chest. He takes a nipple in his mouth and pulls at it hard and I go up, I arch up at his mouth and my core jerks.

"Graham," I whimper, my hands going to his chest, my

fingers burying in his chest hair.

He lets go of my nipple and moves further up. He kisses my pulse and I bend my neck to the side to give him more access. Then, he's at my lips. But he doesn't stop there. He goes up and up and finds my forehead.

Closing my sleepy eyes, I nuzzle my nose at his stubbled throat as I feel him kiss me there, at my sweaty forehead, and whisper, "Happy birthday, baby."

Graham

I had a dream.

I was a kid, probably four or five and I was with my father.

We were in his rose garden out back and we were picking out flowers for my mother. Then, the scene changed and we were inside the cabin.

I was the one offering her the bouquet of roses and she took it with a smile. She appeared happy and I was filled with pride. I was filled with this boyish accomplishment that I made my mother smile and then, I woke up.

I'm not sure if it was a memory that I'd forgotten or if I made it up in my head. I'm not even sure why I dreamed it in the first place when I haven't had a dream in so long. Probably, never.

I think it's her.

I think she gave me some of her magic.

Or at least I'd think that if I didn't know better. If I believed in things like magic.

If I believed that simply because I tasted her on my tongue – both sweet and salty with a hint of strawberries – I'm a changed man.

I'm a man with dreams.

I take in a long breath then and smell her scent. She's sleeping right next to me.

She went to sleep as soon as she came. She sighed, said my name and curled up on her side and went to sleep.

Like she hadn't slept in ages.

Instead of leaving her alone and giving her privacy, I put her head in my arm and spooned her with my body.

Her back is stuck to my chest now, her dress is all rumpled up and those straps that I destroyed snake down her delicate arms like red ribbons.

Jesus Christ. What the fuck came over me?

Why would I do something so... savage and untamed? Something so criminal and crazy. Something I've never done before.

But the moment I kissed her, something happened to me. It was beyond the mere knife in my chest. The pain, the need, the craving was more like a phenomenon. An earthquake that destroys towns and cities and apparently, my self-control.

She affects me in ways I don't understand.

I don't understand why I want to consume her. Why I want to ruin her and keep her safe all at the same time.

Why am I such a fucking asshole that I haven't even straightened up her clothes? I haven't even pulled down her dress to cover her tight ass that's currently glued to my very hard cock or covered her perky tits. All I've done is shield her against the cool air with a blanket and my body heat.

Maybe it's because I like to look at her. Because I could look at her for hours and hours.

So that's what I'm doing.

I'm staring at the slope of her shoulders and the line of her fragile neck. I'm smelling her hair that's in my face, rubbing my jaw in it. While my hand is tucked in the nook of her waist and my palm is open wide on her stomach.

Every now and then, I press on it.

On her soft flesh, and she sighs and wiggles around my cock, making it hurt like a motherfucker.

Making *me* hurt.

But it's too little punishment for me and what I want to do to her.

For how selfish and bad I want to be. How goddamn possessive and dominating.

Even if I forget the fact that I had an unhealthy obsession with a barely legal girl, what I said to Brian still stands true.

She deserves better.

So much better than me. Better than a middle-aged man who has no interest in a relationship. I'm not going to date her. I've never dated anyone before. I don't even know how.

I'm not a teenage kid who's going to change his ways for the girl he wants.

I can't.

I'm too hard, too severe for her. I've seen too much roughness in life, too much reality, too much abandonment to ever be foolish enough to hope for anything else.

And she's too young to know anything else but hearts and dreams.

As much as I love my son and admire how he did the right thing, he has hurt her. I'm not going to do the same. She has known too much hurt already.

I refuse to do that to her.

Besides, she's going to college, isn't she?

This is her vacation. Come fall, she'll leave. She'll find someone who'll suit her better.

I have to do what I told Brian to do the other day, then.

I have to do the right thing.

I have to give her a chance to leave. One last chance to back out before I lose all semblance of decency and goodness and keep her here selfishly, for myself. And take and take and take from her.

Without promises. Without hearts and dreams and all the bullshit I've never had the time for.

That she deserves, anyway.

Because she's made of moon and magic.

14

I've counted hours and I've counted
minutes. It's been eighteen hours
since I woke up and found
him gone. It's been one thousand
and eighty minutes since I've
opened my eyes to nothing.

~The Diary of a Blooming Violet, Age 18 years and 10 months

He left me a note.

A note.

It said: *I want you to leave before I come back from work tonight.*

That's what he said to me. In a *note*.

The man didn't even have the decency to say it to my face. After everything we talked about, after everything we did last night, he left me a note on his freaking side table.

Asshole.

I've been seething since then. Seething and stewing with every second that passes. Oh, and I snooped around in his room.

I did.

He lost all his rights to privacy when he told me to leave on a fucking piece of paper. Not that I found anything. His room is almost bare.

Just a king-sized bed in the center with dark sheets and wooden slats for the headboard and a tiny side table with a lamp on it. A dresser with his clothes that are neatly folded like they used to be back in Connecticut, and a small closet full of his plaid shirts.

Although I did find a stack of gardening books in a corner, left all abandoned and forgotten. So I pulled them out and read them one by one.

That's how I spent my day.

Reading his books on roses and seething and seething until my anger turned into sadness and I started crying.

How could he do this to me? I thought we'd crossed a hurdle. I thought we became closer last night and he turns around and pulls this shit.

It's midnight now and I'm hugging his pillow.

It was dry once but now it has wet splotches all over it.

Good.

He should sleep in my tears and realize for once how much of an asshole he is. How much he's hurting me. How he's breaking my heart.

A second later it looks like I can tell him, myself.

I can show him my tears and make him realize his cruel and mean ways.

Because he's here. He's back.

He's standing at the threshold of his door, wearing an untucked, messy plaid shirt and wrinkled jeans. His boots are muddy and sloppy.

As sloppy as my heart right now.

At first, I can't believe he's here. He's back and he's staring at me with a blank face. Although, there's *something* there.

Something that might resemble relief, but I can't be sure.

"You're here," he says like he did the first night I showed up at the bar, his tone abraded with a touch of disbelief.

Finally, I come out of my daze.

My heart starts to beat really loudly. So loudly that it's a wonder the windows don't rattle. It's going louder than I was screaming last night.

When his mouth was on my pussy.

Slowly, I get up on my knees and clutch the pillow to my chest, fist it really. Even tighter than before.

If I don't fist something, I'm going to punch him in the face.

On second thought though, fuck it.

I *am* going to do some damage here. So I launch the pillow in the air. I throw it at him with all my strength and it hits him in the chest.

"Where the hell am I supposed to be?" I scream at him, my hands fisted at my sides.

He hardly bats an eyelash at my throw. All my pillow did was ruffle some of his gorgeous hair – damn him – and fell on the floor with a thud.

Although, my voice does something.

My supposed-to-be angry voice that sounded a little broken and a lot tear-thickened.

That makes him frown and study me. That gets him moving too. He crosses the threshold and comes over to stand by me.

Not only that, he stares down at me and puts his hand on my face. Or tries to before I slap his stupid hand away. "Don't touch me."

"You're crying." He states the obvious in a low, raspy tone.

"Fuck yeah, I'm crying." I push at his chest, tears falling down my cheeks. "You left me a note. You left me a fucking note, Graham. You told me to leave like nothing happened last night. Like I didn't tell you my secrets and you didn't tell me yours. Like you didn't do those things to me. Like you didn't kiss me back."

He clamps his jaw, his hands fisted at his sides. He's silent but his eyes are fraught with all these things that I can't decipher right now.

All the things that I want to know, though.

"It felt like you didn't kiss me back for the kiss I gave you ten months ago," I whisper, all heartsick and sore.

He exhales a tight breath and tries to cup my cheek but I push him away again.

"Let me touch you," he says, huskily.

"No."

"Violet," he warns.

"No." I fist his shirt. "You don't get to touch me after being such an asshole. After making it all seem like a dream."

At this, my tears fall harder. Harder than before, making me hiccup. Making me think that maybe it *was* all a dream.

All of it. His confession. His kisses on my mouth and between my legs.

His whispered *happy birthday, baby.*

God, that still wakes up goosebumps all over my body.

No one has ever wished me a happy birthday before. No one has ever even remembered it. He not only remembered it, he came back early from his date for me that night. He saved that special kiss for me all this time like it was a precious gift.

And it was.

Until he ruined it.

His eyes are piercing, as if looking into my soul, when he says, "It wasn't a dream."

I try to shake him, pulling at him by his shirt, but of course it's useless. He doesn't move. My knuckles dig into his harshly breathing chest and that's it.

He probably doesn't even feel that.

He doesn't feel any of the pain I'm feeling.

"Then how come you told me to leave?" I sniffle.

"I was doing the right thing," he grits out.

"What?"

I'm so confused. What is *that* supposed to mean?

He takes advantage of that. He takes advantage of my confusion and puts his hands on my cheeks. I grab his wrists and try to push him away again but he doesn't let go.

"I can't write poetry for you, Violet," he rasps and my struggles come to a halt.

"What?" I say again but really, I don't understand what he's getting at.

His rough thumbs swipe off my tears slowly, gently as he says, "I don't write poetry. I don't do hearts and flowers and all that stuff, do you understand? I can't. I'm not capable of those things."

I frown up at him, breathing brokenly. "Okay…? So?"

"I don't do them but you deserve them."

"I deserve what?"

At this, he really gets frustrated with me. He grabs my face with an increased force like he wants to stamp it on my brain, whatever he's going to say, and all I can do is hold onto his wrists and watch his impatient, anguished, pained features.

"You deserve someone who gives you his heart out of his chest. Someone who can reach into his own body with his hands and pull it out for you. Pull out that thing that beats only for you."

My eyes pop wide and my own heart causes a ruckus in my chest, more than it already was causing. "I-I do?"

He breathes out angrily. He's angry at me for asking that question.

"Yes," he says sternly. "You deserve that. You deserve someone who takes you out on dates and to movies and someone who holds your hand and walks on the goddamn beach with you or whatever the fuck you want him to do. Paint your toenails and chat with you all night on the couch while eating cheap pizza. You deserve someone who wakes up every morning and gets down on his knees to thank God that you belong to him. And then he does it all over again before he goes to sleep. You deserve someone who lives in awe of you, understand?"

He presses my face and almost shakes me, and I'm left wondering how he does that.

This is the beautiful thing again, isn't it?

This is where he turns all my beliefs upside down.

He thinks I *deserve* things. I deserve hand-holding and walking on the beach. Although I never really liked the beach; too crowded.

But I'd like it if he was the one holding my hand.

The man I love.

The man who's looking at me with so much impatience right now.

"Violet, tell me you understand or I'm going to fucking lose it."

His growl makes me jerk out a nod. "Yeah. Yes. I do."

Breathing out noisily, he nods. He goes so far as to almost close his eyes. "Good. Fantastic. Now, I want you to listen to me and promise me something."

I walk my knees closer to him then. I go to him and touch his heaving chest with mine because touching him with just my hands on his wrists isn't enough.

I want our bodies to touch and keep touching forever and ever.

"Okay," I whisper as I look at him with wonder.

He goes back to wiping my tears off. "I can't do that for you. I'm not going to do that for you."

"You're not?"

"No." He shakes his head and nails me with his gaze. "I'm not going to hold your hand and take you out to the beach. I'm not going to take you out for a movie or dinner, either. I don't even believe in god, let alone going down on my knees for him. I'm not a believer, okay? I never have been and I'm not going to learn now. Not when I'm practically pushing forty. You deserve everything that I can't give you. Everything I'm *incapable* of giving you. So I want you to promise me something."

"Promise you what?"

"That you'll find someone, some dumb college kid, who can give this to you."

"A college kid?"

"Yeah. When you go back to your college, you'll find someone who'll give this all to you. But more than that, you'll find someone who doesn't make you cry."

"Why not?"

"Because it fucks with my head when you cry," he snaps with clenched teeth. "It makes me want to destroy something. I can take anyone's tears but I can't take yours. So promise me you'll find someone who won't make you cry."

"Like you did?"

His features bunch up for a second before he rasps, "Yeah. Someone who doesn't leave you shitty notes like an asshole. Someone who'll give you everything and more."

My chest is shuddering against him. Shuddering and rattling with the furious beats of my heart.

I want him to stop talking. I want him to stop saying these things.

These things that are breaking my heart.

I get what's happening here. I get what he's saying to me as he sounds like a concerned guardian of mine and he's making sure I know what my worth is.

"Are you saying that I should find someone who loves me?"

My question makes him flinch. It makes him draw back.

It's a slight shift but it's plenty. It's plenty to answer my questions.

Although he does reply as his fingers flex on my face, which is dry now; he took away all my tears while he was crushing my heart with his words.

"Yes. That's what I'm saying. You deserve someone who believes in all that shit. Love and unicorns and things like that."

"And you're not that person."

He swallows. "No. I'm not. I never will be."

I stare at him. I study his features. His forehead is lined with a turbulent frown and his jaw is ticking as he lets me look at him.

God, he's beautiful. Even more beautiful because of how open he looks. Cracked open. Vulnerable almost, his eyes dark and melting with feelings, with all the things he wants me to understand about himself.

He's never looked like this before. So angsty, so broken up about the fact that he can't be who I deserve.

But the thing is, I never even thought I deserved something to begin with. I never thought anyone would even see me, let alone love me. And that's why it never even crossed my mind to tell him.

To tell him that I love him.

Not once did I think to tell him that I'm in love with him.

To tell him that I love him enough for the both of us, that I don't want his love. I can survive on my love alone.

I'm hopeless and I'm a romantic. I'm a masochist. I'm addicted to less. I'm addicted to the pain. I'm addicted to *him*.

I can live my whole life on this little piece of him that he's giving me right now. His care. His concern. His anguish. His frustration that I don't understand my own worth.

His confidence that I'm going to college and I'm going to find someone there.

When all of it is a big fat lie.

I'm not going to college; I'm too afraid for it. And even if I was going, I'd never find anyone because I don't *want* anyone else.

I want him. Whatever I can get from him.

"Okay." I swallow and put my hands on his chest. "I promise. I'll find someone. Now your turn."

"My turn at what?"

"I gave you what you wanted. I gave you your promise. What do I get?"

I raise my eyebrows at him, waiting for his answer.

His anguished frown disappears as he senses the shift in the air. The shift that I created with these desires that I can barely keep hidden.

These desires and dreams that I've had since I was sixteen. The dreams that I want him to make true now that I'm eighteen.

He pushes into my chest with his large breath. "What do you want?"

His heart is beating under my palm.

Boom. Boom. Boom.

My own is going at a rhythm complementary to his. A Morse code of some sort.

"I want you to make my dreams come true."

"And what are those dreams?"

"First, I want you to buy me all those dresses you promised," I say with a turned-up chin.

"Yeah?"

"Yes. You can't say it and not do it. And then, I want you to grow me all the roses that I want."

A flicker of something amused and seductive all at the same time passes over his features. "You want roses?"

"Yup. And you have to give them to me."

His fingers creep up and bury themselves in my hair. "Okay. So my baby wants roses. What else?"

My baby hits me in the stomach and a spasm goes through my pussy and I whisper, "And most importantly, I want you to fuck me."

His heart thunders at this request.

It punches his chest and I feel it on my palm.

His heat intensifies and I feel it on my skin. If this is what he'll give me, his body, I'm going to take it.

In fact, I'm going to demand that he give it to me after everything he's put me through.

I deserve it.

That's what I deserve.

His fingers, buried in the mass of my hair, tighten and bundle the strands together. "You want me to fuck you."

"Yes."

"You do know what I just said to you, right? I'm not going to give you more. I'm not going to change my ways for you."

I narrow my eyes at him before I go to the top button of his shirt. "I don't want you to. I'm not a child. I'm eighteen. And ten months. I understand what fucking is."

I pop it out and go for the second one but he stops me with

his hand on mine. "You do, huh?"

Biting my lip, I peek at him through my eyelashes. "Yeah. I don't know where you think I came from, but I am from this world."

"You don't feel like it."

I swallow a lump of emotion at his reverent tone and say, "I am. And I don't want you to be noble or good. I don't want you to do the right thing. I don't want you to write me notes telling me to leave because you should know by now that I'm not going anywhere."

"Yeah?" He pulls my neck back slightly, by the hair and whispers, his face over mine, "So what do you want me to be?"

"I want you to be what you said I make you. I want you to be bad."

Don't all normal girls want to turn bad boys good?

But then, I'm not normal, am I?

I want him to forget his good ways and be bad.

I want him to have me so he can do with me whatever he wants. All as long as he gives me what I want.

Him, however I can get him.

A rush of air escapes him and fans my lips, all rich and delicious. He lets go of my hand on his chest and brings it over to my face. He cups my jaw with his long fingers and says, "You want me to be bad."

I continue unbuttoning his shirt. "Yeah. Because you know what, I think you *are* bad."

"How do you figure that?"

"You tore my dress, remember? And only bad men tear a

girl's clothes off.'"

He tightens his hold on my jaw. "They do, don't they? I am a bad man, then."

"Yup. So you just wasted time being good." I shake my head at him. "Besides, I have a secret."

"You have a secret."

"Yes. I would've let you do it last night."

"Do what?"

"I would've let you put it in."

I'm somewhere down at the middle of his shirt when I say this and his reaction makes my hands stumble. In fact, his reaction makes me gasp and grip his shirt tightly, so tightly that I'm on the verge of tearing *his* clothes off tonight.

At my words, he pulls my head back so suddenly that my neck is all stretched up now. He brings his face so close to mine that his beard is brushing my jaw and chin with every breath I'm taking.

And his eyes.

God, his eyes are all violent and explosive, as explosive as his chest that's crashing into mine with his heavy breaths.

"Put what in?" he growls.

"Your cock."

"Put it where."

"Anywhere."

His furious fingers in my hair curl and uncurl like a time bomb. "Anywhere. What's anywhere, Jailbait?"

"Anywhere means anywhere you want, Strawberry Man. I know what men like, you know. You think I'm so naïve and all but

I'm not. I know they like pussy. But I also know that they some-times like to put it in the ass."

His stomach hollows out. "You want me to put it in your ass?"

"If you want to. I'll let you put it in wherever you want."

He stares at me for a beat, unmoving, unbreathing, before a gust of breath escapes him and he actually looks up at the ceiling. "You're trying to kill me, aren't you? You want me to die. That's what you want. That's why you're offering me your tight ass when I haven't even fingered your pretty pussy yet."

I would've laughed at his conclusions if my pussy wasn't spasming at the mention of her name. If I wasn't creaming my panties like a lusty slut.

"You could have last night. You could've fingered me and fucked me and done anything you wanted to me."

"I could've, couldn't I?" he says, while he shoots me a pen-etrating stare.

"Yeah. It's yours. I've been saving it for you, anyway."

I witness his pupils dilating, then. I've never seen it before and it's glorious. So, so glorious. Like dark ink spreading through water. Night falling in the sky.

"Saving what for me?" he rumbles even though I know he knows the answer.

He wants to hear it from my mouth.

"My virginity," I whisper. "I've been saving my virginity for you, Mr. Edwards."

I don't know why I said it that way but now that I have, I don't wanna take it back. I love that I can call him Graham now, but I also want the right to call him Mr. Edwards.

I want the right to all his names.

They're mine.

The current that goes through him, the aggression and possession in his hold prove that it is, indeed, mine.

"You have, haven't you?"

I go to nod or say something but he grabs it, in the next moment.

He grabs the very thing we've been talking about. The hand on my jaw goes down and he clutches it, gropes my entire pussy in his rough hand. He fists the silky material of my pajama bottoms and squeezes.

I whimper out his name. "Graham..."

"You've been keeping her all nice and tight for me, haven't you? You knew I'd come for this. You knew I'd come for this tight pussy. You knew that, didn't you?"

"Yeah. Yes, I knew."

He gives it another squeeze as he drops his forehead on mine. "Yeah, you did. You knew I was dying for her. You knew I wanted her so you kept her safe. She's mine, isn't she?"

"Y-yes. She is. She is. She..."

I trail off when he rubs the heel of his palm on my clit, making me jerk and moan.

"She what?"

"I... She's been waiting for you too."

Graham presses an open-mouthed kiss over the column of my throat, while still rubbing his palm on my clit, bringing me closer and closer to an orgasm. "Yeah, I bet she has. I bet she's going to grip me real tight. So tight that I won't be able to get out. Yeah?"

I clutch his shoulders and cock my head to the side so he can keep giving me sucking kisses all over my throat.

"You gonna grip me hard, Violet? You're gonna keep me here, huh?"

To emphasize *here*, he massages my entire core again and I can feel that I've practically drenched my pajamas. I can feel the wetness on my thighs. I can feel him rubbing that wetness back into my pussy and I'm almost there. Almost.

And then, he edges me over with these erotic, filthy words that he rasps just below my ear while he licks me there, rubs his jaw and beard over my soft skin.

"Your mommy should've tied you to the bed, Jailbait. Barred your windows. Hidden you from the world. It was only a matter of time before you ended up on the wrong side of a bad man's cock."

"Yes. Oh God, Graham… Oh fuck…"

I babble and come at the heel of his words and because of that maddening hand of his between my thighs.

I'm still twisting and juddering in his arms when he gives me a hard kiss. I'm so limp that all I can do is offer him my mouth for it. All I can do is breathe and sigh while he takes my t-shirt off. Then he goes for my bottoms before lying me down on the bed gently.

I watch him with panting breaths as he reaches back and pulls off his shirt in one go.

With his eyes on me, he toes off his muddy, manly boots and puts them aside. Then off come his jeans.

And he is as naked as me as he advances on me and I know he's going to make my dreams come true.

15

Random things that pop into
my head: Graham has
big hands and big feet.
Does that mean that the other
things he has are big too?

~The Diary of a Blooming Violet, Age 18 years and 10 months

As he climbs on the bed like last night, my immediate thought is that it *did* not look *this* big yesterday in the bathroom, his cock.

It wasn't this big at all.

Because man, it's big.

It is.

It's enormous.

It's either that or my eyes have suddenly acquired magnifying glasses, and everything looks bigger now.

It's more than enormous. It's thick, as thick as my wrist and curved. There's a ridge on the top, so angry and red, so swollen. Was it this angry yesterday?

And glistening with pre-cum.

That drop gets bigger and bigger until it sluices down his length and he has to grip it at the root and pull.

I feel that pull in my own core.

I feel it in my stomach, making everything tight and achy and I have to press my hand there. I have to press it on my stomach but that's not enough so I move it down and clutch my fluttering, rivering core.

I grab my wet pussy like he was not a minute ago. But I don't like how small my hands are or how smooth and without any force. "Were you thinking about me yesterday? In the shower?"

His eyes follow my shameless movements. "Were you thinking about me the other night when you were playing with your pretty cunt?"

"You knew that?"

"These walls are thin, Jailbait."

Then, he kneels between my legs that I automatically open for him, all blushing and flushed over the fact that he knew.

"I just wanted to thank you," I whisper.

"For what?"

"For calling me beautiful."

An emotion moves over his face. "You are. You're fucking breathtaking."

"Okay."

"Say it."

My pussy gushes at his command and I feel it on my fingers. "I'm fucking breathtaking."

"Good."

I squirm under his scrutiny and look away from him.

Stupidly, my eyes go to his naked heavy thighs, shadowed with coarse hair, the hair that suddenly looks much, much darker than it did a second ago. It looks rougher too, denser as he looms over me.

God, one day I wanna come on those thighs. I don't know why but I'm obsessed with them.

Obsessed with him.

"You want it bad, don't you, baby?" he whispers, his hand still on his cock, tugging at it, pulling in slow, tight movements. "You want this?"

My pussy clenches under my palm. "Yeah. I want it."

Smirking, he shakes his head once.

I writhe on the bed as he lets go of his cock and reaches for something by the bedside drawer. He opens it without breaking our gaze and fishes something out.

It's a condom.

With his eyes on me, he tears off the corner of the condom packet with his teeth. I fist the sheets and stare at the view of his sharp, biting teeth that I want on my skin.

His shaft stands upright, pressed against his tight abdomen, touching his belly button when he goes back for it and rolls the latex over it.

I'm watching it all with heaving breaths. Watching him prepare himself for me and my legs widen even more.

Then, the most wonderful and glorious thing happens to me.

Graham, the man I love, covers me with his large, *large*

body.

He comes down on his elbows and fits himself between my thighs.

It's such a novel sensation, silk sheets at my back and his coarse, hot and hairy body on my chest.

God.

I never want to move from this position. I want to live here, between his muscular, heated body and his soft sheets.

He brushes my hair off my face, rakes his fingers through it. I bite my lip and clutch his sides, while rubbing my heels on his calves.

He kisses my forehead. "Well, then I'll give it to you. I'll give you my cock. I'm going to fuck you and make all your dreams come true, baby."

He twists his hips then so I can feel it. I can feel the weight of his shaft on my stomach. The thing that's going to make all my dreams come true.

I arch my back and rub against it and he goes in for a kiss.

He kisses my mouth, my jaw, the column of my throat, and maneuvers himself down until he's at my breasts.

Growling, he kneads one mound in his big hands and sucks a nipple into his mouth before letting it go with a pop. Like my nipples are his lollipop.

"Fuck," he groans. "Your tits taste as sweet as your pussy."

I moan at his declaration and when he goes in for the other nipple, I fist his hair and practically feed it to him, my tit.

But he's not in the mood to linger. He sucks and laves and plumps up my breast before letting it go and rising up on his hands.

He looks at my breasts with hooded eyes. "Yeah, red's definitely my favorite color."

I follow his gaze and find that my nipples are all red and dewy from his mouth, all hard and achy. I wanna offer them to him again, offer my tits for him to suck on and play with, but then I feel the head of his cock over my clit and I moan.

A second later, I feel it again and I realize he's rocking. He's watching me with a clamped jaw and sweat-dampened forehead as he's moving his cock up and down my pussy.

He's rubbing his shaft in the center of my core, right between my folds.

My hands go to his bunching biceps as I arch up into his see-sawing.

I even look down.

I look at the flex and release of his abs, his beautiful fucking abs, and where we're joined but not really.

His shaft is going up and down, looking so dark against my pale, flushed skin. The head of it hits my clit at every up-swing and the root of it grinds against me on every down-swing.

The more he does it, the wetter his shaft looks.

And I know it's me.

I'm doing this to him. My pussy is juicing up and she's slathering my wetness all over his latex-covered length.

Oh God. Oh God, I'm making him as wet and creamy as me.

Something about that is so embarrassing and slutty and erotic that my eyes fall shut and I begin to push back.

I dig my nails in his biceps, making him groan and making

myself whimper.

But more than that, I make myself move and rock and twist against his length. I'm sliding back and forth on his cock, humping against it when suddenly, my eyes pop wide open.

Because holy shit, he's inside of me.

Just like that.

He's just pushed himself in on a groan and a grimace, his eyes still on me but so much foggier now. So much brighter and covered in a sheen that wasn't there before. Not when I closed my eyes a few seconds ago.

Just that look of his, all panting and drugged, makes me come.

Gosh, it's such a virgin thing to do but I can't help it.

My hips hunker down at that one inch of his cock that stretches me like a rubber band and I spasm around him. I flood the head of his shaft with my cum. I scratch his biceps, throw my head back and clench my eyes shut again as I climax around him, gasping out his name.

For some reason, I thought it would be over after this.

I don't know why but I really thought that *we're done now*.

But we aren't because he keeps moving.

Still propped up on his hands by my shoulders, he keeps rocking that one inch in and out, until he goes in more. More and more, all while he watches me with his hot gaze.

Even though my eyes are closed, I know he's watching.

His stare is like a burning lamp and I open my eyes. "I totally came."

He takes in my flushed face and rubs his thumb over my

cheek. There's a kind of worship in his look. Like I'm this magical thing he's marveling over and it makes my eyes sting.

But I control it.

I don't wanna cry when all my dreams have come true.

When he's inside of me. When he's at the center of my being.

"You did," he replies in a sex-drenched voice.

I touch his beard, burying my fingers in it. "You're all the way inside of me now."

It's true. He is.

Somewhere in his rocking and gentle movements, he's gotten all the way in.

He turns his head to press a kiss on my palm. "Does it hurt?"

"No. It feels… full."

I try to wiggle around his length that seems to be breathing inside of me in little pulses and he grabs my hip, stopping me. He checks my face to make sure I'm okay. "You sure it doesn't hurt?"

I nod, smiling. "Yeah. It feels awesome."

He exhales a sharp breath and I feel his stomach and chest moving with it. "Good."

"Do you think I'm bleeding?"

He jerks slightly, his fingers digging into my flesh. Not a lot but enough that I feel the movement ricocheting in my swollen cunt.

"Jesus Christ, virgins," he mutters to himself like he forgot about the bleeding part, panic laced in those words. To me, he grits out, his eyes concerned, "I hope to fuck that you're not."

I wind my arms around his neck and shake my head. "No, no. Don't hope that."

"What?"

"I like that. I wanna bleed." He shudders over me; I feel the muscles of his shoulders quaking. "Because I'm... I'm a woman now. You made me one. I'm all grown up."

His cock lurches inside me as he curses, and comes down on his elbows, as if he doesn't wanna be away from me. As if he wants our skin to touch and slip against each other.

I sigh when the coarse hair on his chest rubs against my swollen nipples.

He presses his sweaty forehead over mine, rolling his hips a little and shifting his cock inside of me. "Stop talking."

I kiss his jaw for that. "You know what else?"

"Stop talking, Violet."

I lick the sweat up from his stubbled throat. "I've got another secret."

He gives me a look that can only mean that I'm torturing him. That I'm inflicting pain on him with my whispered words.

"What?" he clips.

And I smile. I flick my tongue over his beard and rock against him. Slowly, lazily, like we're boats in that lake behind the cabin, bobbing, swaying on the water.

"I thought you wouldn't fit because I can't even fit a tampon in me without hurting."

His lust-slitted eyes widen slightly in alarm and I have to bite my lip to stop from chuckling.

Then, he gives me almost his entire weight. His abdomen

rests on my fluttering tummy and his chest is set against my breasts. He frames my face with his hands. "Why didn't you tell me?"

"Because I knew you wouldn't put your big, bad cock in me and I wanted you to. You needed a little pushing being bad, Mr. Edwards."

I feel his breath rushing out and he can't help but rock against me, as well. Tiny, short pushes of his cock inside me. Sensations explode all over my body, making everything misty and slippery, and I smile, humming.

He chuckles darkly then, taking his first long stroke. He almost completely goes out before pushing back in.

"You should've told me, Violet. You know why?"

"Why?"

I watch him push himself up and over my body. He plants his hands on either side of my head again and I think I have another mini-orgasm just by looking at all the rounded and curved shapes of his muscles covered in sweat.

"Because I've got a secret too."

Then, he curls his abs and rolls his hips in a way that it feels like his cock is lurching up and caressing the upper wall of my pussy. It's hitting something that's only found in the secret recess of my sloppy channel and he's going right after it.

"Graham," I gasp, my eyes wide and my nails clawing at his chest.

"You wanna know my secret?"

"Uh-huh."

"I'm an asshole for you, Jailbait. In fact, I'm the biggest asshole on this planet for my baby. For her slutty cunt and I would've fucked her with my big, bad cock, anyway."

Then, he goes for it.

He fucks me with his big, bad cock and all I can do is revel in it.

Revel in his dirty, perfect words.

All I can do is juice up even more, become even messier and sloppier as he strokes in and out of my slutty cunt.

Cunt that's gripping him so tightly that his stabs are short and stubby. They have to be. My pussy won't let him go. She won't let him out so he makes do with short, hard pumps.

And fast. Oh my God, they're fast.

They're jiggling me up and down, shaking my tits, producing sounds that I never even dreamed of. Wet and smacking sounds. Sounds of my pussy sloshing and running over and his cock shoving into it, pushing into it again and again.

I feel my juices spreading all over my thighs, all over his thighs too. A thick stream of it is running down between the cheeks of my ass and smearing over that dark hole of mine. And that is so shameful, so erotic that my spine bows.

Clutching his biceps, I arch and arch, taking it all, soaking up the sounds, filling my lungs with the tangy smell of our sex. I take it all and I moan.

Yeah, I moan at his every stab, his every ram and his every pound.

I'm moaning as loud as last night, rattling the windows, alerting everyone in the world that I'm being fucked by him.

By the man I love.

And he loves my screams so much that he comes back down

again. He roams his hands on the outside of my body, tracing my sweaty, jiggling curves before settling them on my thighs. He raises them up and hooks them around his waist tightly, making me hold onto him as he rides my cunt.

He rides it and rides it to the point where I think I'll come again.

I'll come for the third time just because he's beating into me so good.

So, so good.

But more than that, it's him.

It's the look he's giving me, like he can't get enough. It's his husky, thick breaths that echo in the room, echo in my soul.

It's the way he's grabbing onto my face with both hands and the way he's so tightly locked around my body.

And it's his words again.

His growly, sand-papery, panting words. "Pussy so tight you can't put a tampon in, huh? How come you're taking me so good now? How come your pussy is eating me up, Jailbait?"

His slurred words make me so full, as full as his cock is making me, as full and tightly wound as if his meaty fist is pressing down on my stomach.

"Graham, I'm gonna... I'm gonna come..."

As soon as I tell him, it happens.

I jerk against him and my eyes clench shut. They shut so tight that I feel like I'll never get them open again.

I'll never catch my breath again either. My heart will never stop hammering. My pussy will never stop clenching over his length.

And he'll never stop telling me things in his savage, broken voice. So savage that it doesn't even sound human. They sound like they belong to a beast.

"Fuck, *fuck*. Tight fucking pussy," he says as I writhe around on his cock. "God, so greedy. So goddamn greedy. You're gonna make me come…"

And then, he comes as well.

He comes with a large shove and stumbling, stuttering strokes that I feel in my teeth. He groans and I open my eyes to catch him arching up, his neck strained and his Adam's apple jutting out. His chest is so tight that I feel like his bones will bust through as he jerks inside of me, his cock pulsing.

He's so beautiful like this. So breathtaking and wonderful.

So perfect that my heart swells.

It floats inside my body with unadulterated happiness.

This is what it feels like, I think. When your dreams come true. When something you've wanted for so long is finally yours.

He is mine.

This man is mine.

At least, some part of him is. At least, until the summer ends and I go back to where I came from. Not college, no. Not to a guy who'll love me.

But to that town that has never seen me. The town that's never looked at me or paid attention to me until I kissed the man I love.

The town where I was always lonely.

Finally, he rides his climax to the end and looks down at me, breaking my strangely morose thoughts. His messy hair falls on his forehead and his eyes look relieved.

Gosh, I've never seen so much relief in someone.

It's leaking out of him like sweat. Drops and drops of it that fall on my skin as he comes down at me.

I meet him in the middle.

I wrap my arms around his neck and lift myself up so I can go hug him, while he's still twitching inside my fluttering pussy.

I kiss his cheek and whisper, "Thank you for making all my dreams come true, Mr. Edwards."

His answer is to kiss me and despite everything, I smile into it.

I smile because I'm eighteen and his.

***

I wake up a few hours later only to find him gone.

His side of the bed is warm, so I guess he's just left it. With a wary heart, I climb out of bed and wear his discarded plaid shirt, going out of the room.

The back door of the cabin is open and I walk up to it.

And there he is.

Under the moonlight, working on his roses.

His shoulders are bent and he's clipping the dead leaves, holding them in his hands so gently, so reverently. Like he held me a few hours ago.

Tears fall down my cheeks. I shouldn't cry, I know. It fucks with his head and I don't wanna do that.

But look at him, he's keeping his promise to me. He's working on the roses.

While all I've done is lie to him ever since I got here.

All I've let him think is that I'm this normal college-going girl who's vacationing. When nothing could be further from the truth.

I'm not normal. I've never been.

I'm a liar.

16

I'm lying.
I'm a liar.
I lie.

-The Diary of a Blooming Violet, Age 18 years and 10 months

"I'm lying to him."

I say this into the phone as soon as Willow picks up the call.

"What?"

I'm sitting on the couch and it's morning. Graham has already gone to work and I'm holding what he left me on my pillow.

A rose.

Fresh and full and velvety. Peace, lemony yellow petals with pale pink edges.

So now I'm crying, sobbing almost because I'm a liar and he's giving me roses for it.

"I've been lying to him ever since I came here and I don't

know what to do," I say, wiping my nose with the back of my hand.

"Oh, Vi. What happened? Why are you crying?"

I sniffle, trying to control it; it's ridiculous the amount of tears I'm shedding as I hold his gift to my chest. But it's just so sad. It's so sad that he keeps being so wonderful to me and I can't even tell him the truth.

Everything about my life is so sad right now because I'm a liar.

"He thinks I go to college, Willow. He thinks I'm vacationing." I bring my knees up to my chest and smell his shirt that I put on last night. "And I'm letting him think that. I'm letting him think that I'm this normal girl whose whole life is ahead of her. When I can hardly get out of my house. If a random stranger even looks at me, I go crazy. I start to hyperventilate. I'm so... weak. And defective and a loser, and he thinks I'm going to college and I'm going to meet someone and I –"

"Whoa, whoa, whoa, okay. Stop," Willow cuts me off and I go silent, sniffling again.

Then she sighs and says, "First of all, you're not a loser. You're not weak or defective. You have an illness. You're struggling, Vi. You've been struggling ever since you got out of Heartstone. Like the rest of us, and that's okay. But you're struggling more because you keep insisting everything is fine. You keep denying it. You keep pretending."

I keep pretending.

She's right and I'm too emotional right now to admit it.

Yeah, I pretend.

I pretend that everything is okay. I pretend that I'm handling things my way.

I pretend that it's okay for me to use crutches and slip in notes to strangers and hide when someone knocks at the door.

I've been pretending ever since I got out of Heartstone and doing that in front of everyone and even to myself was easy.

Pretending to him isn't.

Not when he looks at me in that special, protective way of his. Not when he looks at me like he'll kill and destroy everything and everyone who hurts me.

"He said I was beautiful," I rest my forehead on my knees and whisper.

"Really? He did?"

I've been texting on and off with the girls. I told them about what Brian said and how Graham kissed me the other day. But I haven't shared any intimate details with them.

I didn't want to.

They were mine.

I guess, I'm a true loner. It's hard for me to share things. But I can share this with Willow. Maybe because we have things in common. Things like eighteenth birthdays when our worlds kinda blew up. Plus she's in love like me.

"Yeah. He said I deserve things. He said I deserve someone to hold my hand and walk with me on the beach. He said I'm made of moon and magic."

Willow sighs; it sounds happy and dreamy. "Oh, Vi, that's wonderful. Ah, I'm so happy. Why are you crying?"

I frown. "Because didn't you just listen to what I said? I'm lying to him. He doesn't know about... about my illness and everything else."

He doesn't know that I pretend.

He doesn't know that I do it because it's so easy to deny things. It's so easy to deny because the alternative is dealing with my doomsday brain.

It's so hard to do that. It's so hard to fight anxiety. To distinguish between rational and irrational thoughts when every single insecurity of yours is heightened.

Not pretty. Not worthy. A slut.

I know I shouldn't believe these things – especially after everything he's said to me, and there are moments when I do believe him.

I do.

But sometimes it's so hard. Like right now.

And I'm so weak.

He doesn't know that.

He doesn't know that I drown in insecurities and anxious thoughts every day. And the only way to survive is to pretend everything is fine.

"Then tell him."

"What?"

"Yeah. If you're lying to him and that's giving you so much grief, just tell him the truth."

I lift my head from my knees and stare at the wall opposite the couch. "You're kidding, right?"

"Nope."

"I can't tell him."

"And why not?"

"Because..." I grip the phone tightly, almost shrieking.

I mean, I know it's the obvious solution. If I hate lying so much, I should tell the truth. But I can't.

I can't tell the truth.

"Because why?"

"Because look at my life, Willow. Look at it. I'm alone. I've always been alone. I've always been lonely. No one cares about me. My dad doesn't even acknowledge my existence. My sister has a bone to pick with me about everything. My *mother* wanted me dead. Even before I was born. She wanted to abort me because I'm the result of an affair and she didn't wanna ruin her reputation."

She gasps. "I didn't... I had no idea."

"Yeah." I swallow. "She never cared about me. I've always been a burden to her. A headache. Well, except now. She texts me now. Asks after my health. The yoga thingy. I guess she's only doing it to ease her conscience. I don't know. But it's sure as hell not because she cares about me. And I've always accepted that, you know. I've always accepted that she won't love me or care for me or treat me like I matter and that's okay. I can take that. I have taken that for years. I'm used to it. But I can't... What if..."

I trail off, my heart hammering inside my chest. All these panicky things coming to the surface. All these fears that were easy to keep inside up until now. But they won't stay in anymore. My doomsday brain won't let me.

"What if what?"

"I love him, Willow. I'm in love with him. God, I love him so much and no one has cared for me like he does. Not one person. And he *looks* at me. He's been looking at me since I was sixteen.

I've always been visible to him, Willow. Always. Me. The girl no one sees. What if I tell him and he stops? What if I tell him and he thinks the same thing that *I'm* thinking? What if he thinks I'm defective too?"

Gosh, if he thought that, I'd die.

I'd literally die.

I'm clutching his rose to my chest right now. The rose he left me on the pillow because I told him I wanted it.

And it's not even a dead rose, no. It's not something discarded or dying. He plucked it out fresh and alive and rosy.

Just for me.

I've got it in my hands and I'm crumpling it with my fingers like I imagine my heart would crumple in on itself, if he thought that. If he thought that I was defective too, like everyone else in my life.

I wouldn't be able to live. I wouldn't be able to move on from that.

"Vi, he won't think that. He can't. Because you aren't defective. There's nothing wrong with you. Not *one* thing. And you'll know that if you tell him."

Tears stream down my cheeks. "Why wouldn't he? Everyone else does. I can't, okay. I'm just so scared."

I can hear her tears too. She's crying for me and I could just hug her for being my friend. "Listen, Vi. Listen very carefully, okay? I know it's scary. I know that. I know it's easy to deny and pretend. I did it too, remember? So I know. And you love him. That's scary too. I get that." She pauses before saying, "But now you have to decide if you trust him or not."

"Of course I trust him."

"Enough to tell him about yourself?"

My heart jumps to my throat and all the words I was going to say get trapped there, just off my tongue, unable to get out.

"You have to decide, Vi. You have to decide if the man that you love, the man for whom you drove thousands of miles, the man for whom you were ready to take anything because he was hurting, you have to decide if you trust him or not. If you trust him enough to tell him this scary thing about yourself. You have to decide that, Vi."

I have to decide if I trust him or not. The man I love.

Do I *trust* him?

The thought flashes in and out of my mind all day, long after I've ended my conversation with Willow, long after I've dried my tears.

It comes and goes and it's bobbing on the surface still when he gets back from work.

I hear the crunch of gravel outside and I realize he's here.

I was in the kitchen, finishing some things up, and I rush to the door. I throw it open and run out to the top of the porch stairs. The ones he fixed the other day. It smells of new wood and polish.

But I'm not focusing on that.

I'm focusing on him.

Graham.

He sees me as soon as he climbs out of his truck. Without breaking our stare, he shuts the door behind him. And as soon as I hear the bang of that, I take off.

My sneakers slap against the stone pathway as I run to him and he does the same. He strides over to me and we meet in the middle.

Panting, I watch him.

His eyes are bright, brighter than anything I've ever seen and he's watching me back with breaths as heavy as mine.

He's looking at me. *Looking.*

"You left me a rose this morning," I tell him in a breathless sort of way.

"I did."

His raspy voice gets me right in the gut, right in that quickening that seems to have started the moment I laid my eyes on him, and I bite my lip for a second.

"Because you promised me."

"Yeah. I can't just say something and not do it."

He repeats my casually thrown out words from last night and I swallow. I swallow my heart down because it's trying to get out of my body. It's trying to fly out to him.

"I want you to know that no one has ever given me a rose before you," I say, batting away the wayward strands of my hair. "So that's another thing no one has ever done for me. I want you to know that."

Watching me intently, he takes a step toward me. "People are fucking morons, aren't they? Although…"

"Although what?"

"Although, I'm not sure how good of a gift it is for someone like you."

"Someone like me?"

He nods slowly, still watching me with a singular focus. "Someone who blushes like a rose and looks gorgeous as fuck doing it."

A wave of emotion rolls through me. A wave, an avalanche of it. It rolls through my entire body before settling deep in my stomach. Deep in my soul.

Deep in between my thighs, and I clench them.

I clench them so hard, as hard as my heart is clenching right now.

Because the way he said it… feels like love. The way he's watching me feels like love too.

I know it's a lie. I know that. He told me that he can't love me. That he never will.

So he'll always be this broken dream of mine. This unfulfilled wish. My unrequited love.

But in this moment, he's looking at me like he does. Like he *does* love me.

I'd kill for that look. Kill and steal and lie.

Yeah, I'd lie for that look because if this is the only thing I'll have from him – a look – then how can I lose that?

"I missed you," I whisper, taking a step toward him.

"You did."

"Yes. So I spent the day baking all sorts of things for you. Everything with cinnamon. I know you like that."

"I do." Then he offers me something, something that was in his hand before but I didn't see it. "Here."

I see it now. A bag of lollipops. I take it from his hand. "You bought me lollipops?"

He nods again but this one is tighter than before, kinda bashful. "You were running low."

I hug it to my chest, hug it and squeeze it before tearing the pack open and fishing one out. I give it a long suck before saying, "Is this your way of saying that you missed me too?"

He watches me swirl the candy in my mouth. "No."

I frown, taking the lollipop out. "No?"

Then he closes the last inch between us and grabs me at the waist. He squeezes all the air out of me as he digs his fingers in, as if making sure that I'm really alive and he can finally touch me.

Lifting me up, he puts me on his boots and growls, "This is."

By *this*, he means his kiss.

Because he's kissing me now.

I let go of all the lollipops and the bag falls to the ground. But it's okay. I'll pick it up later. Right now, I need to kiss him back.

I wind my arms around him and do just that. I kiss him back while he kisses my candy-coated mouth before boosting me up with a hand on my ass, and carrying me up to the house while I hang onto him like a spider monkey.

A few seconds later, he breaks the kiss and I find myself on his bed again.

I lean up on my elbows and he bends down at the waist to get closer to my half-lying form. I watch with panting breaths when his hands come to the buttons of his shirt that I'm wearing.

Oh yeah, I'm still wearing it.

In fact, I took a shower and put it back on so I could smell him. I could feel the lingering warmth of his body on mine.

And now, he has his hands on it and I know what he's going to do before he even does it.

I feel it with every banging beat of my heart.

He's going to tear it off. It's in his eyes, his blazing, intense eyes, and he does.

He fists the fabric and pulls. He pulls and pulls until the veins on his wrists stand taut and his face goes tight with the force. So much force that I reach up and caress his harshly hinged jaw.

As soon as I do it, the shirt gives and the buttons pop out.

My spine arches at that, thrusting my breasts out.

He has to look at them then. He has to stare at my jiggling tits as he does the same with the rest of the buttons, tearing his own shirt open.

God, he's such a bad man, isn't he?

Once he's done, he spreads the flaps apart, exposing me to his eyes. Exposing my tiny, blushing body that he can't stop staring at.

Then he bends even further down and takes a nipple in his mouth, giving it a long suck like I gave my lollipop, making me arch up some more and fist the sheets.

He doesn't stop with the suck though. He takes it in his rough hand, gropes it and plumps it up, sticking the nipple in his mouth even more.

As if he loves this, this rough, delicious treatment of my breast, he groans. He grunts and rubs his beard over the tender flesh.

"Graham," I gasp.

"Fucking love your tits, baby. Love how they bounce for

me."

And he proves it. He proves *how much* he loves it by making them bounce. By kneading them in his big hands and making them jiggle, rubbing the nipples with his open palm, making me lose all my sense and thoughts.

He even grabs me around my waist and tugs me forward on the bed, so they jiggle some more. They dance and shake for him, my tits.

By the time he's done playing with them, I'm writhing on the bed. My panties are all drenched and sticky and he comes back up to my mouth for another kiss.

This one's short though.

He ends it quickly, like he's got other plans for me, and moves away.

I sit there, half-slumped and completely aroused and panting. Like last night, he goes for his shirt in an impatient way. He undoes a few buttons and reaches back to snag it off his body in one go, baring his brawny chest and rumpling up his gorgeous hair.

Gosh, he needs a haircut, my Strawberry Man. But I'm not going to tell him that. Because he looks sexy as fuck.

He leaves his jeans on when he gets on the bed and I have to say I'm a little disappointed. But he makes up for it by showing off his huge hard-on inside his pants.

It's tenting his jeans, actually, pressing against the zipper. I can even imagine it – the angry, glorious crown of it, pushing against the confines of his pants, maybe leaking pre-cum. Leaking it so much that he'll get a wet, dark spot there.

Oh God, I so want that.

I want that wet spot on his jeans. I want that as much as I want him to take it out, his big, bad cock, and fuck me with it.

My man has the same thought, I think. Because all the while I was staring at his cock, he's been staring at my panty-covered pussy, his face all tight and clenched up. Even though I'm covered like him, I bet he can see the same thing as me.

He can see how swollen my pussy is and how my lips press against the fabric. How he can make out my seam and how there's a giant wet spot there.

With his chin still dipped, he lifts his eyes up to me. He puts a finger on my right knee, moving it in circles, making my skin break out in goosebumps.

"Does it hurt?" he rasps, and I know he's asking about my pussy.

I flex my inner muscles and shake my head. "No."

"No?"

He goes on and on with his light circles and I wiggle my hips. "No. You took care of it last night, anyway."

He hums, like he's thinking about it right now, picturing caring for her, my pussy.

Before going to sleep last night and before he got up to work on the roses, he cared for me. He brought in a hot, wet towel and pressed it against my core, taking away all the soreness. Turns out I did bleed, but only a little. There was a smudge of it on my thighs and at the base of his cock and he cleaned that spot up too.

He looked a little horrified at that but I distracted him by kissing all over his beard and his chest.

I notice the moment he gets back to the present and out

of last night's memory. His finger stops making circles and instead moves up my thigh. It moves and slides up and up until his hand is a band around my upper thigh.

His thumb is so long and big that it grazes the edge of my panties, the curved edge of my pussy, making me jerk.

"Is she hungry?" he asks, making circles with his thumb there now, touching me over the sticky fabric.

"Uh-huh."

"She wants something?"

I nod enthusiastically, spreading my legs like a whore and inching close to him. Inching toward his cock.

A slow lopsided smile spreads through his lips and he comes down to kiss me. A soft, soft, feathery kiss made a little sting-y when he rubs his beard on my cheek.

It makes me moan, his affectionate, erotic gesture, and I reach up to play with his beard, my favorite thing in the whole world.

"I'll feed her, then. I'll take care of her like I did last night."

"Yes," I whisper.

Moving away, he takes my panties off. They get stuck in my sneakers that I'm still wearing but he maneuvers them and takes them off easily. He doesn't let me take off my sneakers though.

He tells me to keep them on with a shake of his head and this shiny glint in his eyes that pulses through my bared core.

Now, he can see it all.

His eyes drop to my core and he takes me in. He takes in my puffy pussy. I take her in too. She's all colored with arousal, deep pink, almost red, and I get so horny from that, so fucking horny and slutty that I reach down and rub my folds.

I'm sprawled on the bed, still wearing his shirt and sneakers, my knees folded up now, and I'm rubbing my sloppy cunt in front of him, waiting and dying and writhing in lust.

"Feed her, Mr. Edwards," I whisper, peeking at him through my eyelashes.

His features are dark and harsh with arousal but even so, he shakes his head at me. He chuckles out a rusty bark of a laugh before knocking the breath out of me by his next words.

"So you like lollipops, huh," he rumbles, producing the one I was sucking on.

I don't even know when he got it and where he even had it up until now, but I really don't care.

I can't care.

Because as soon as he said it and made me almost mindless, he popped it in his mouth.

Oh God, he has my lollipop in his mouth, that magenta-colored candy that he closes his lips around and takes a long, slow suck of, his cheeks hollowing out.

I have to open my mouth to drag in a breath because holy shit, he looks so sexy doing that. He looks so sexy and masculine while sucking on my candy and I can't even think coherently.

Then he pops it out, his eyes dark with desire and something else, something delicious and dangerous and I have to ask, "W-what are you going to do?"

"Give her a treat," he says in a low-pitched voice.

So low-pitched that I go boneless. More boneless and crazy than before.

"Treat?"

Instead of answering me with words, he grabs my thighs again and pulls me down on the bed. I've been propped up on my elbows up until now but he makes me lie on my back. Then, he comes down at me, his bulk becoming my sky, putting a hand by the side of my head.

Looking me in the eyes, he says, "Yeah, a treat."

And then, he gives it.

He gives it in a way that makes me clutch the sheets and jerk up on the bed. It makes me arch up and shake my tits.

Because he just slapped my clit with my lollipop.

"I'm going to give her something to eat," he rumbles, tapping the candy over my clit again, and I almost go to pieces.

I almost break apart at the shameless thing he's doing.

"You'd like that, wouldn't you? If I gave your cunt something to eat?"

He's asking me?

How can he ask me anything when he's stealing my ability to think, let alone talk? All I do is make some babbling noises as he circles my tight clit, swirls the candy through my drenched folds like I swirl it with my tongue.

"Answer me, Violet. Would you like that? Do you want me to feed your cunt, baby?"

I fist and pull at the sheet so tightly that it snaps out of my hold and I have to go and clutch his sides and dig my nails into his hot flesh.

"Yes," I answer him on a whimper, my eyes blinking and fluttering closed.

"Yeah? You sure?"

His cajoling, teasing tone makes me rub my sneakers up and down the bed, makes me so much more restless and heavy and empty and all the things at the same time.

"Yeah. Yes, I want... I want it."

"Okay. I'll give her something to eat. I'll give her your candy," he whispers, his face saturated with lust before he gives it to her.

He gives my candy to my cunt.

He sticks my lollipop, the one I've been sucking on, the one candy that I've loved as long as I can remember, inside my pussy and everything splinters.

Everything explodes in my stomach. All the sensations and currents and sparks.

I scream.

I think.

I'm not sure. I may also have drawn blood from his skin with the way I'm clutching onto him, and I realize that he hasn't even done anything.

All he's done is stick my lollipop inside my pussy and I've lost my mind.

God knows what I'll do when he does something.

Something like fucks me with it.

Which he does a second later.

He begins to fuck me with my candy and I don't know how to handle it. I don't know how to take that.

So I chant his name. I chant it like a prayer because only he can save me. My Graham.

He can save me from feeling this much, from feeling this full, from falling in love with him deeper and deeper with his every stroke.

But then, he speaks and I realize nothing and no one can save me. I'm as good as dead and gone in his love.

Because Jesus, his words and his voice. Dirty and erotic and so amazing.

"You were right, Jailbait. You were so fucking right," he says in my ear and I realize he's all the way down now.

He's lying on his side, half covering me with his body as he pumps the lollipop in and out of my core.

He runs his open mouth along the column of my throat as he keeps whispering, "Your pussy was hungry, baby. She was so goddamn hungry. She's eating up your candy, sucking it up like a good little kitty. Can you feel that? Can you feel your cunt sucking up her treat?"

Delirious, I turn my face to look at him as I rock into his drives. "Uh-huh, I feel it."

"Yeah, you can. You can feel it. You can feel your kitty lapping it up."

I rock and rock and this heavy but empty feeling in my stomach grows and spreads through my limbs. It spreads and spreads until I have to ask him. I have to open my mouth and form words, which seems like such a big task but I do it.

"God, Graham. Please make me come. Please, please, I wanna come. Please, God."

I need his cock.

I don't want candy. I want him. My cunt wants him.

In the next second, he gives me that too.

He rips the lollipop out of my channel. His heat disappears from my side for a few seconds before coming back and shifting over my body and I open my foggy eyes.

He's leaning over me like last night, bracing himself on the forearms. "Open your mouth."

I have no power left in me to do anything else but open it.

"Stick out your tongue."

I do that too and he puts the lollipop into my mouth. "Suck it."

I close my lips around it and suck it for him. I do it because there's no not-doing it. I'm so horny for him, so hungry, as hungry as my core and so I suck on the lollipop he was feeding my pussy and moan like the whore I am.

I eat it like my good little kitty. I eat what he gives me and God, I taste so good. I'm tangy and salty and so fucking juicy.

"Tastes good, doesn't it?" he asks, as if reading my thoughts.

Still sucking, I nod.

"It's your pussy, baby. It tastes better than the candy, doesn't it?"

I nod again, devouring it.

"Are you a convert now, Violet? Do you like your cunt better than your candy?"

"Uh-huh."

"Yeah, you do. Why wouldn't you? Your pussy is the sweetest thing I've ever tasted. Sweetest and horniest and sluttiest. And you know what else?"

I shake my head, eating my candy like a greedy girl.

But then, I stop sucking. I stop swirling my tongue over it, chasing my own taste, and bite down on it, instead.

Because he enters me in one push.

I don't even know when he snapped the condom on – probably when I was still delirious from his candy fucking – and now, he gets all the way inside of me in one easy stroke, taking away all my breaths and all the emptiness that I was feeling.

Then he throws my thighs over his arms and pushes them back into my body.

My pussy feels even tighter like this. With my legs thrown over my ears and my sneakers up in the air. The laces are undone and flutter around us, swaying in and out of my vision and somehow, it makes me even hornier.

"Your pussy tastes like she's mine," he finally finishes his thought from before and I moan around my lollipop.

He draws his shaft back and out before shoving it inside again, punctuating it with his dirty words. "I want her on tap, your cunt. I want your tight, teenage cunt on tap, baby."

Another drive of his cock, followed by another moan of mine at how good he stretches me.

"And I want to fill her with lollipops. I want to fuck her with them. And then, I want you to suck on that pussy-flavored candy while I fuck you with my cock and blow my load all over you."

At this, I moan the loudest. I even pop the pussy-flavored candy out of my mouth to tell him, "Yes, you can have her. You can have all of her. All of me. I'm your slut. Your whore. Your everything. I'm yours, Graham."

His expression shifts.

It becomes even fiercer and sharper. More than even last night when he took my virginity. In fact, it's the sharpest and most ruthless I've ever seen and I know what it is.

Or what it looks like.

It looks like love.

This dream-maker, dream-causer, dream-weaver of a thing that I want to grab with both my hands. I want to grab that look and never let go. Never lose it. Never do anything to jeopardize it.

I never want him to stop looking at me like that. Like he's in love with me.

A second later, he pops the candy out of my mouth and throws it away before kissing the fuck out of me.

Before fusing our bodies together and slamming his cock into me. Pounding and ramming and beating up my horny channel as he fucks me. Plows into me like a beast.

It's even more intense than last night. The way he's riding my pussy.

His strokes are harder and more powerful. More possessive. Like his need for me only increased after he had one taste of me.

Like he wants me even more now. Like he needs me more.

He needs me so much that he can't control himself.

He slams into me over and over, slapping our flesh together, smacking my ass with his pelvis. He drives into me with such ferocity that my legs go all the way back and hit the wall. The headboard hits the wall too.

It's like he's trying to find something inside of me. He's trying to find a thing he wants, a place he wants even, so he can live there.

His hips work double time as he pounds my pussy and searches for this elusive thing.

And it's so good, so fucking wonderful that I grab onto his ass and make him go harder. I make him go deeper than before. I make him stretch me out more, stretch me out so much that I never feel empty.

That I never feel hollow and lonely. That he finds whatever he wants and takes it from me and keeps it for himself. Keeps me for himself, even.

Because unlike him, I feel it for real.

I feel this love for real. This need to be his and his only.

This need for him to look at me like this. Like he's drowning in me.

In fact, he gets his arms out from under my legs so he can clutch my face with them, with his hands like yesterday. But the way he's digging the pads of his fingers in my cheeks and my scalp is so much more intense and dominating than last night.

There's an urgency in him, in the way he's holding me. Like I'm his lifeline. Like I'm the thing he's losing himself in but at the same time, I'm the very thing that's going to save him, as well.

I would think about it more if not for his cock. If not for him fucking me, driving into my body that my tits jiggle, my teeth clatter and my whole soul shakes.

And all the while he's staring at me.

He pushes and pushes into me. Pushes into my snug channel, made snugger because my legs are thrown up by my ears.

But see, they're not as stable as they were before when he

had his strong, sweaty arms under them, keeping them straight and pulling them taut.

So he finds another way.

He stops and pants, "Hold onto your laces."

I'm reluctant to let go of his ass but I know what he means. Even through the lusty fog, I know he's asking me to grab onto my fluttering shoelaces because he wants me tighter.

And I want that too.

I want to be nice and tight for him that I feel every inch of his thick cock.

So I do it.

I hold onto the laces of my sneakers so my pussy is nice and tight for him.

So my pussy grips him and keeps him inside of me as he fucks me and fucks me.

Until that look in his eyes, that fake love blows up. It explodes into this big, huge thing that feels so real and amazing and wonderful and heartbreaking that I come.

I clench around his cock and his drives become rough and haphazard.

He jerks and twitches, his body slipping over mine with the sweat, the friction we've created. And then, he comes too.

He does it still looking at me.

He doesn't close his eyes. He doesn't get lost in his climax alone.

He gets lost in it with me.

The girl he can't love but looks like he does.

The girl who's thinking, *I can't. I can't. I can't.*

I can't lose that look. I can't tell him. I can't tell him the truth.

I love him.

He steals all my thoughts and my chanting when he grunts and almost falls on me, his hips thrusting one last time as his orgasm runs its course.

But he doesn't rest. He doesn't look away from me either.

In fact, he has a frown, a thick one, bisecting his forehead while he pants over me, all sweaty, his fingers still framing my face.

"Graham?" I ask, my legs coming down and grasping him around his waist and my hands coming to rest on his jaw.

"I don't..." He pauses as he gathers his thoughts. "Did I hurt you?"

Frowning, I shake my head. "No."

His cock pulses inside of me and my channel ripples making us both almost close our eyes. But he pushes on. "I'm not like this. I don't... do these things." He swallows, looking at me with both marvel and confusion. "I'm not this rough. This insane... I don't know what happens to me. When it comes to you. You do something..."

He lets his sentence hang and my heart swells and swells. It pushes against my rib cage with so much love for him and his half-made statements.

He appears so lost and so dumfounded and so fucking laid bare as he tries to explain this change in him. The change that I've brought, somehow.

Me.

The girl who barely makes a dent in the universe is making

a dent in him. I'm somehow transforming him and the things he does to me, *with* me, are new to him. As new and wonderful as they are to me.

I wanna cry. I wanna laugh.

But all I do is smile slightly and reach up to kiss his jaw, which he turns into a long, wet, sloppy kiss on the mouth.

When we come up for air, I whisper, "I love it. Whatever you do, however you are, I love it."

I love you…

How can I tell him the truth about me when he thinks I'm doing something to him? Something is changing in him because of me and because of *that*, he looks at me with wonder. He looks at me like I'm special.

How can I tell him?

How can I lose that look?

I can't. I won't.

I'm too hungry. My heart's so hungry. My soul is so hungry.

That I'm ready to eat up his fake love.

That I'm ready to lie for it.

17

Every day he leaves me a rose on
my pillow and I pluck the
petals off, playing:
should I tell him,
should I tell him not...

-The Diary of a Blooming Violet, Age 18 years and 11 months

There's someone here.

A man.

I didn't notice him at first or even hear how he got here, possibly by a vehicle of some kind. I was busy with my little vegetable garden.

Oh, yeah. I have a vegetable garden now. It's a little patch where I'm mainly trying to grow tomatoes and peppers. Because I thought it'd be something new and fun and also because they're the easiest to grow here. Or at least, that's what it said on the internet: my source of all things because I don't talk to people.

I can't.

But a man is here and as soon as I hear his voice, panic

skitters down my spine, a frisson of it.

"Hello?"

I don't turn around. I can't. My knees are stuck on the ground, grinding actually, scraping into the dirt and I'm staring down at the mud with wide, fearful eyes.

"Hi, excuse me?"

He calls out again and I clench my eyes shut, my breathing going stuttered. I can feel his eyes on the back of my neck. I can feel his gaze *prickling*. Itching and scratching.

And that's the only reason, this incessant prickling, that I turn around.

I come to my feet and see him.

The man who's staring at me curiously.

He's so sharp and clear and so in technicolor that I realize I don't have my Audrey Hepburn glasses on. I don't have my cap on either.

In fact, they're nowhere near because I haven't encountered any situations where I might need them in a long, long time.

Possibly in weeks.

I don't go anywhere.

Whatever I need, I order online and hide the boxes as soon as they arrive so Graham doesn't find out that I'm a hermit, or I just tell Graham to bring me things.

I don't even have to tell him, actually. He just anticipates them and brings them for me. Lollipops; dresses that he promised – I'm wearing one even now, white colored with giant red roses; glitter pens for my journal; all the Bukowski that I need, since I started reading again; roses from his garden.

He brings me everything.

It's the best arrangement really. He doesn't do dates and I don't do going out so we're always here.

In this little secluded piece of the world where no one ever visits. Not even the wind or the sun.

But now this man is here and I don't know what to do. I don't know where to look. All I know is that I wanna run up to the cabin and shut the door. I wanna lock all the newly-painted doors and the newly-fitted windows – done by Graham – and dive into our bed, his and mine.

"Hi, uh, I didn't mean to interrupt," he says politely. "I'm actually…"

He trails off while I stare at his polished boots, fisting and unfisting my cotton dress, feeling all kinds of exposed, fidgeting, shifting on my sneakered feet.

"I'm sorry." He laughs awkwardly. "But who are you? I don't… I'm not being rude. I'm Richard. Richard Owens. I'm a friend of Graham's. I've never really seen you here."

At this, I have to look at him.

I have to.

This is Richard.

The man I overheard that day but never saw.

The man who came to Graham's cabin to give him an ultimatum about his job.

He's tall, but not as tall as my Graham, and he has a polished look about him. He's wearing a suit and his hair's slicked back.

He has intimidating shoulders. They're not as broad as Graham's but while Graham's shoulders make me feel safe, this man's make me feel uneasy and fearful.

"I, uh… I'm not…"

Anybody.

But that's not true, is it?

I'm the girl because of whom Graham left his job in Connecticut. The stuff Richard was talking about when he last came to visit.

Oh my God.

He knows who I am. He *knows*.

I mean, not that I am that girl but he knows *about* that girl. The supposed minor Graham allegedly had an affair with.

He frowns. "I've got some papers for Graham. Is he… Is he home yet?"

I swallow and shake my head like a mute person.

Like I can't form words. And that just makes me even more scared and angry at myself. That just flushes my throat even more.

I clear it then, my throat, and try to speak again. "He's not… He's not here. But I can g-give them to him. The papers."

Graham texted me – we finally exchanged numbers when I told him it was weird that we didn't know each other's numbers – and told me that he was running late and that he'd bring pizza with him so I don't have to worry about dinner.

It all sounded very domestic and serene and peaceful to me.

But now, I have a feeling that all the peace is going to go away.

Richard's considering me with curiosity and I can't take his scrutiny. I can't. It crawls on my skin, slithers on it like some slimy animal.

I get this hysterical feeling that the longer he stands here, the closer he's getting to putting all the pieces together.

"Are you… Have you been living here? With him, I mean?"

At this, my breathing hastens, and I shake my head.

I shake it, sending my dull blonde/brown, straight hair to cover some of my face. "N-no. I'm just visiting."

Oh God. Oh God. Oh God.

That gets me more silence and more curiosity and my breath is going haywire.

I need to get out of here.

I need him to get out of here. Before he figures out who I am. Before the panic takes over. Before it roars in my ears and sets my skin on fire and chokes my lungs and I can't breathe.

"I actually have to…" I swallow and try to moisten my desert-dry tongue. "I have to check on something. I-I'll let him know that you stopped by."

I try to take a step to the side so I can get away from him, but he stops me from going anywhere by his next question.

"Is that your car out front? I saw it parked last time when I was here."

I jerk back a little, all afraid and wary and on the verge of panting. "W-why?"

Richard raises his hands up. "I'm sorry. The question might have come out blunt. But the thing is, the car has Connecticut plates and… I'm just… I'm just wondering –"

"Don't," I snap, panic making my voice high and squeaky. "Just leave. Please."

But he moves toward me and I'm right there.

I'm *right there* at losing my shit.

"I'm not going to hurt you," he assures me. "You look like I'm going to hurt you but I'm not. I don't want to cause you any harm. I'm just... I just want to have a conversation, that's all."

He even reaches his hand out and that makes me even more scared.

That hand.

It's not as big as my Graham's but it's threatening, and it looks dark and cold.

I never even had conversations with people *before* I got this doomsday brain. I'm definitely not having one now.

"I have to go. I have to —"

Whatever I was going to say gets swallowed up by... things.

So many things at once.

First of all, there's the screech of a truck coming to a halt followed by thudding footsteps. Then, there's my gasp. It's loud. It's almost a shriek before I jerk away. I practically lunge away.

But most of all, it's Richard.

He is on the ground with a very angry-looking Graham hovering over him.

Graham fists Richard's shirt and literally makes him stand up by just pulling on it and punches Richard on the face.

He does it so hard that Richard shoots back and almost hits the siding of the cabin. The new siding that Graham installed a few days back.

Graham pins him to that wall with his arm on Richard's throat, and here I am hysterically thinking that Graham is really handy with all this construction stuff. It's because over the years when he lived here with his dad, he got really good at repairs.

And now, Graham is pinning Richard to the wall that he repaired. "What the fuck are you saying to her?"

Where did he even come from?

Like one second I was on the verge of losing it and the next, he swooped in to save me.

Richard grabs his elbow, trying to get free. "What the hell... are you doing?"

Graham doesn't budge, however. In fact, he shoves his elbow harder into Richard's throat so that he goes up on his tiptoes.

"What did you say to her, huh?"

"I didn't... say anything."

"Yeah? Why the fuck were you looking at her? Why *the fuck...*" He shoves that arm into Richard's throat again. "Why the fuck does she look so scared?"

"I wasn't..."

Richard's voice is getting fainter and fainter and I think his feet have started to flail a bit. I think he's going to die.

Oh God, Richard is going to die.

Graham is gonna kill him. Graham is gonna kill Richard because I look scared.

Because I'm standing here, clutching my dress, tears streaming down my face, hyperventilating.

Because someone just *talked* to me.

Someone just tried to have a conversation with me and I freaked out and Graham saw that and now our lives as we know them will be over.

Unfisting my dress, I rush over to Graham. He looks like a breathing mountain from behind, his back so broad that it blocks Richard completely. If not for Richard's flapping legs, I wouldn't be able to see him.

I grab Graham's shirt as soon as I reach the pair. "Graham, stop. Please stop. Let him go."

It's like he isn't even listening to me.

I clutch his arm, the one he's using to keep Richard pinned, and try to shake it loose. "Graham, please. He didn't say anything, I swear. Please let him go. Please. *Please*, honey."

I don't know how it slipped out.

Honey.

Like I'm his... what, girlfriend now? His wife or something like that?

I mean, yes, we've been living together for weeks. We sleep together, eat together, watch TV together, cook together too – well, he cooks and I bake. He wakes me up in the middle of the night because he wants me, he needs to be inside of me. And sometimes I wake him up because I want his cock in my mouth. I need to taste him and feel the largeness of him on my tongue.

But that doesn't give me the right to call him honey like it's the most natural thing for me to say. Most natural and sitting at the tip of my tongue, ready to burst out of me.

Although, it *might* be.

It might be the most natural thing in the world for us because as soon as I say it, Graham whips his gaze over to me, all wild and bright, so loud with emotions.

Emotions that wrap me up, cover me, blanket me in them.

I become invisible, I think.

Invisible to the world and visible only to him.

"Let him go," I whisper to him, my honey. "He didn't do anything."

He doesn't.

He still has his arm shoved into Richard's throat and Richard is still flailing.

"Please." I fist the sleeve of his shirt and try to dislodge his arm nonetheless, as he sweeps his gaze over me, over my tear-stained face, my disheveled, wrinkled dress and my messy hair.

Probably to check if I am okay.

When he sees that I am, he does. He lets Richard go and steps away from him.

I never thought I'd smile in front of a stranger again but I am. Smiling, I mean. It's shaky and broken but it's there, and even though I feel Richard's eyes on me, the prickling isn't driving me crazy right now.

Not when I'm looking at Graham and not when he's looking back at me and we're connected like this.

It's not enough of a connection for Graham though because he turns away from Richard – who's currently coughing and straightening his suit jacket from what I can glean from the corners of my eyes – and stalks toward me.

I start moving back.

What is he doing? Shouldn't he try to fix this with Richard? Shouldn't he try to make amends of some kind?

But it looks like Graham doesn't care.

My sneakers roll and crunch on the gravel, squelch the

grass as Graham advances on me with flushed cheekbones and needy eyes.

Needy and flaming with so much heat that it licks at my skin. It licks at my stomach and thighs and I come to a stop.

So he can come at me. So he can grab my face in his big hands.

Because as it turns out, I want Graham close to me too. I want him touching me and if someone is watching, if someone can *see*, I find that I can't bring myself to care.

I'm not naïve though. I know my issues won't go away just because the man I love has his eyes on me but I'll take this reprieve, even for a few seconds.

So when he *does* reach me and grabs my face, I clutch his wrists and close my eyes, sighing.

I shut out the world. I shut out the man standing just a few paces away from us.

I shut it out while I breathe the same air as Graham.

Until Richard chokes out and shatters the illusion, "What the fuck was that? What the fuck are you doing, Graham?"

I can hear Richard's jerky movements, his panting breaths and it makes me flinch and open my eyes.

Graham doesn't turn around or pay him any attention. Instead, he wipes my splotchy tears off with his thumbs.

Although he does bite out to Richard, "Get out of here, Richard."

"Are you serious? Are you fucking serious right now? You attacked me and you want me to go away?"

My grip on Graham's wrists increases and I look at him

fearfully. It was a bad thing that Graham did for me. Bad and potentially problem-inducing and I can't bear the thought that because of me he could be in trouble.

And not only that, Graham is touching me in front of him. It could be dangerous, right? He could even get fired because Richard knows about the scandal. Richard knows what happened back in Connecticut and I'm pretty sure he might've put two and two together by now. He could take away my Graham's job. He could, because Graham attacked him and there's this girl here, from Graham's past, because of whom he left his old job.

But Graham shakes his head once, at me. As if he could read my anxious thoughts. He even jerks me closer to him, making me go flush against his hard and heated body.

Like some kind of a claiming, in front of another man. In front of the world. Like he doesn't care if there could be problems.

And it gets my heart racing.

Racing, racing, racing.

"Stop," he murmurs to me. To Richard, he growls, "Richard, go away, all right? We'll talk later."

My heart is racing so much that I take a step even closer. I go up on his boots and I smell him. I tuck my nose in the triangle of his throat and hide my face, dragging his scent into my lungs. And he completes his claiming of me by wrapping his arms around my trembling body.

Oh God.

He's picking me over everything.

Me.

"Jesus Christ," Richard snaps, moving around now; I can

hear the muck crushing under his boots. "What the fuck are you doing, man? What's going on? She's the girl from Connecticut, isn't she? Is she even... fuck. Is she even legal? Do you know how much trouble you could get in, shacking up with a teenage girl like this?"

My heart jumps up to my throat and I fist his shirt. I even think of moving away from Graham's body and screaming at Richard. Screaming that I am, in fact, legal. I'm eighteen. Graham isn't doing anything against the law.

But he doesn't let me move.

He plasters me to his body, tightens his hold. He splays his palms over my back and moves them in circles, as if soothing me.

I feel him turning his head to look at Richard. "She's none of your concern, all right? Just leave. I'm asking you to leave. She's scared, okay? Just leave before I do something to you for making her that way."

The vibrations of his possessive words reach through his chest into mine and almost touch my fearful heart, soothing my heartbeats.

There's silence after that.

I'm not sure what Richard is thinking or what's going to happen but I have my eyes closed and I'm hiding away in Graham's arms.

But for the first time in almost a year, I don't wanna hide.

I don't wanna close my eyes and hide my face or wear a cap or sunglasses. In fact, this is the first time I've *ever* felt that it's okay if the world sees me.

It's okay if the world sees me or judges me or finds me lacking because who the fuck cares what they think?

Right?

Who. The fuck. Cares?

Who cares if they think I'm not pretty or not special or not worthy of love or whatever?

I think that I'm pretty. *I* think that I'm special. *I* think that I'm worthy.

Because of him. He's been telling me this and in this moment, I completely believe him. So much so that even my anxiety can't sway me.

This man who has his arms around me and who's choosing to put everything at risk for me.

"This isn't over," Richard says.

Richard's threatening words fill me with so much strength that even Graham's arms can't hold me back. Nothing can hold me or this bright burst of courage and I break our hug. I lean over to look at the angry figure that is Richard.

He's in the process of walking over to the driveway and I stop him. "He's not doing anything wrong. I'm eighteen. I want to be here. I want to be with him. And it's not his fault. Whatever he did. P-people scare me. He –"

Graham fists my hair then. He swallows up whatever I was going to say and forces me to look back at him. "You're not explaining yourself to anyone. You're never explaining, understand? You don't have to."

I'm panting even though I haven't said much. It's not from what I've said though. My breathlessness is from what I was *going* to say.

Only now that I'm staring back at Graham do I realize that

I was going to say: *he doesn't know.*

That's what I was going to say. That Graham doesn't know what I have. He doesn't know that I've got an illness.

I was going to confess and he stopped me from it.

I should be relieved, I know. Strangely, I'm not. I'm restless and I don't understand.

He not only stopped me but right now, he's cupping my cheek. His palm cradles it and his fingers reach up to my hair. Again, he addresses Richard, without looking at him. "Richard. Leave. Now."

I hear Richard scoff but after that I tune him out. I don't care if he leaves.

I don't care if he stays to watch.

To watch me kiss Graham. To watch me claim my man, like my man claimed me.

In fact, I want Richard to watch. I want the whole world to watch when I pick him. When I pick my Graham.

I hike up my thigh until Graham gets the message and he heaves me up in his arms.

I wind my legs around his waist and put my mouth on him.

Not only that, I moan too.

I moan into the kiss that Graham returns with equal fervor. He splays his hand on the back of my head and practically presses my lips on his.

I let him do that and devour my mouth while I open my eyes.

I open them and look directly into the eyes of a stranger in almost a year. I look directly at Richard, who hasn't gone anywhere.

Maybe he was going to but our sudden actions stopped him, Graham's and mine. And now, he's watching us with a frown.

But again, I don't care – I want him to watch – and neither does Graham.

I feel so rebellious in this moment, so wild. So unlike my anxious, shy self.

We kiss and kiss while I'm looking Richard in the eyes, while I'm telling him that my man – my honey – makes it good for me.

He makes it so good, so fucking fantastic that I can't stop moaning. I can't stop writhing in his lap. I can't stop humping his stomach. I can't stop my pussy from going wet and steamy for him and I'm not even wearing panties. I'm probably smearing my wet-ness all over his shirt, making it messy.

Most of all I can't stop acting like a slut.

I'm his slut, I tell Richard.

Who shakes his head like he's so disgusted by it but his eyes are wide and he wipes his mouth with the back of his hand and I know that he's not.

He feels it too.

What we feel, Graham and me. This overwhelming need. This craving.

This thing that's always been between us, right from the beginning. Right from that first look.

The thing that made us outcasts and ashamed and crazy. Maybe even criminals.

But we don't care because we're not doing anything wrong.

We never did.

Finally, Richard realizes what he's doing and gets moving.

He unglues his eyes and his feet and turns around and stalks out of there.

I break the kiss, then.

I pant into Graham's mouth, "I wanna suck your cock."

I want to.

I want to tell him what this means to me. What his support and protection, his claiming means to me. What it means to have no anxious thoughts in my head even for a few moments.

It means that I want to love him. I want to care for him. I want to make him feel special and I know he loves fucking my mouth.

He loves it when I take him in and suck on his crown like candy.

In fact, he goes crazy when I do that.

He changes.

He becomes a beast and I want that. I want to change him like he just transformed me. From a shy and anxious girl to this person who looked into a stranger's eyes and kissed the man she loved.

I claimed him. I stood up for him and this thing between us when I thought I'd never be able to, not ever.

I didn't let my anxiety win for once and I want to love him for that.

"Please, honey."

18

He's salt and musk and thick.
I could live off him
for the rest of my life
like I used to live
off my lollipops...

-The Diary of a Blooming Violet, Age 18 years and 11 months

If I thought my words would shock him, then I would be wrong.

They don't shock him at all.

In fact, he watches me with hooded but knowing eyes. "Having him watch made you hot, huh?"

I blush.

Even though I was the one who started it and I'm the one who wants to keep going.

"Yeah. M-maybe. I just… I just want you in my mouth. Please."

So I can love him.

I even squirm in his lap. I wiggle and wriggle until I feel it.

I feel his cock in the crease of my ass, all hard and thick.

It makes him thrust his hips, jerk off his shaft against my butt. But he doesn't give in. Not yet.

He presses his forehead to mine and rasps, "You okay?"

"Uh-huh."

"You were scared."

I was. I was until he came along and saved me so epically. Both from Richard and from my thoughts.

"I'm not now."

I'm so not. Not in this moment.

In this moment, I'm just horny and thankful.

He searches my face. "You sure?"

I fist his hair and rock against him like I can't contain this need inside of me. To be on my knees right now. To take him in my mouth, to taste him, to smell him.

God, I want him all over me.

"I am. You made it okay. You saved me. You put yourself at risk for me." That gives me a pause and my anxiety creeps back in. "D-do you think my saying stuff to him and kissing you made things worse? I was just trying to –"

He scoffs, cutting my words off. "I told you. You're not explaining yourself to anyone."

"But… will he fire you now?"

Maybe my standing up for him did him exactly zero favors. Maybe my claiming could be his downfall.

He presses our foreheads together. "He's not going to fire me. And even if he did, it doesn't matter. There are a million jobs out there, okay? It's not a big deal."

"B-but, I –"

"Shh." He shushes me against my lips. "Look at me, you're not thinking about it. You're not fucking wasting your time, thinking about it."

I swallow and with it, I try to swallow down my fears and anxieties and every bad thought in my head.

And again, they go away for the moment and my desire for him, my love for him comes back to the surface.

"Okay. Okay." I breathe in deep. "I won't."

"Good."

I shift in his arms, rubbing up against his hard cock again, making it jerk. "I wanna suck it."

He shakes his head at me, his lips stretching into this sexy smile of his. "Right here?"

"Uh-uh. By the roses. Where we danced last night."

We did.

We danced in the moonlight. After he woke me up with the slide of his cock inside me, I asked him, *Have you ever danced in the moonlight, Mr. Edwards?*

When he said no, I brought him out here.

I brought him out by the roses – we have a lot of them now, pink and red and lemony yellow with pale pink edges. I put on my kickass playlist, got on his feet and we danced.

He appeared a little unsure and a little awed at first. And it felt like my heart would strangle itself for him, for all the things he'd never done in his life before.

Before me.

So we danced and danced until that unsure look of his

went away and he kissed me, before he brought me back in and fucked me once more.

He chuckles now. "Out there? In broad daylight where anyone can see you."

I know he's smiling but there's this dangerous current in his eyes that tells me he wants it just as much as me. He's greedy for it as much as me.

I'm not sure what it is, this need in me. Maybe I'm still riding the high after what I did in front of Richard.

But I think it's more than that. It's a wildness in me. This recklessness that I've never felt before. Not even on my eighteenth birthday when I kissed him. On that night, I thought no one would see us and so I could do it, steal a kiss like I stole his roses.

But this is different. This is something completely new and originating from somewhere deep inside of me.

Maybe I shouldn't be surprised at the discovery, though.

He changes me, doesn't he? He takes away my shyness and calms down my anxious thoughts. And I change him. I make him bad and turn him into an animal.

So maybe this wildness was always there in me, waiting for him, my beast. Just like his beast was waiting for me, his beauty.

Rocking against his cock that seems to be lurching now, throbbing against the crease of my ass, I whisper, "Yeah. Here. Where anyone can see me. Where anyone can walk in on me and you know what?"

He narrows his lust-filled eyes, his hands going down to my ass and grabbing it. He covers one tight cheek with his big fingers and squeezes. Hard.

"What?" he clips, his voice all tight and rough with desire.

He's changing too, now. Becoming the beast for me already, his pupils blowing up, his breathing getting heavy, his chest expanding.

"I'll still keep you in my mouth. I'll still keep sucking you in the way that you like. The way you taught me. The way where I lick you all over before going back for the crown and sucking on it. Like I was born to suck it. Like all those years while I was sucking on my lollipops, I was just getting a lot of practice so I could suck you when the time came. And I'll keep doing it until you come. Until you spurt in my mouth, or on my face, or on my tits that you love so much. Or…"

He parts my cheeks with such force, God. I can feel the heat of it all over my body. The stretch of it, the amazing sting.

I can feel the heat of his lust in the way he's handling me. Parting my pussy and that dark hole of my ass with his hands and rubbing his cock there, rubbing it right up the crease of my stretched out ass.

"Or?"

"Or you can decorate me. You can decorate your baby. You can come on her throat and you can give her a pearl necklace like you did the other day."

He did. We were in the bathroom and I was sucking him off in the shower, and he came all over me in spurts.

At this, his chest shudders. It shakes and he clamps his jaw.

He's become so tight and rigid that I think he'll never move. He'll never come unstuck, but he does. He walks up to the roses. They cover a lot of ground now, edged by the trees in his backyard.

When we reach our makeshift garden, he manages to growl, "Get my cock out."

And I scramble to do it.

Clumsily, I get down on my feet and keep going. I keep going down until I'm squatting and my hands fumble with the zipper of his jeans.

By now, I'm pretty used to it, to opening it and getting his cock out, and I do it today as well.

I manage to unzip him and unbutton him and shove his jeans down just enough to free him in a matter of seconds, and then his shaft is out, all big and bad and horny.

I take his pre-cum-soaked head into my mouth and give him his first suck of the day. I moan as his taste hits me like a shot of whiskey or rum that I drank on the night I first kissed him. It goes down my throat like honey, thick and smooth.

My honey's honey.

That just makes me go insane, that thought, and I hollow out my cheeks as I vacuum him in. I wrap both my hands at his base because I know one hand won't cut it. I've tried. My Graham is huge. He needs both hands to cover him.

He needs them so I can jack him off as I pull at his crown with my mouth. I pull at it so much that Graham groans.

He throws his head back and he grunts up to the sky.

He never makes a sound when we're having sex.

Oh, he talks to me and makes me insane with his filth but he only lets out an occasional groan or a grunt while he's inside me and pleasure is really choking him.

But he makes noises when I suck his cock. It's like he can't control himself. The Beast is at my mercy.

Even so, he's an animal and he'll grab and grope. Like he's doing right now.

He has his fist in my hair and his feet planted wide. He's jerking. Not a lot but I know it's coming. I know a time will come, when I have him halfway into my mouth and I'll struggle to get him in more. That's when he'll take over.

He'll put his hand under my widened jaw and the other on my head and he'll open up my mouth even more. He'll slide inside, along my tongue that he'll ask me to stick out so I can lick the underside of his shaft.

And then, he'll slowly fuck my mouth.

Until I go so horny that I'll begin to bob my head. That I'll begin to go up and down and fuck him back.

In a second, that time comes and Graham does all of that. He puts his hand under my jaw and the other on my head, all splayed wide, and he slides in.

He stretches my mouth and I peek my tongue out to lick him, while I twist the root of his shaft with both hands. The hands that have gone completely slippery from the pre-cum of his cock that oozes and drips down like my saliva.

He groans when I do that. When I lick him and twist him at the base.

It's so guttural and if I didn't know better, I'd think I'm hurting him. But I'm not. His lust-laden words and the jerks of his hips prove that.

"Fuck, fuck, *fuck*..." he slurs. "Fucking me so good with your cock-sucking lips... Calling me honey... Driving me crazy..."

I preen at that.

I preen and flush with pride and happiness and possession. He is my honey. I called him that. I claimed him in front of someone like he claimed me.

God, that was amazing. I didn't know I had it in me to do something like that.

It fills me with so much lust and all these crashing and swelling emotions that I stretch my neck up so he can go deeper. I jack off his base, all sticky and slippery, and lick him with the flat of my tongue, tasting his musk and salt.

I do all of that so he can come in my throat and fill my stomach.

But he doesn't.

He drives in and out for a couple of seconds more before he rips my mouth away. His cock comes out and it's all red and slippery and throbbing.

I'm panting, confused. My jaw is wet with my saliva and his pre-cum and my lungs are bursting with breaths that I've suddenly gotten back when he released my throat.

"What..."

He bends down and pulls me up by my arms. Then he puts his hands around my waist and hauls me off the ground. As usual, my legs go around his hips but they don't stay there. They inch up and up.

They have to because he doesn't stop when I'm eye-level to him. He keeps going until his mouth is on my tits and my legs are somewhere around his ribs.

My pussy gushes cream at the sheer display of his strength.

He makes me feel so feminine and fragile and tiny when he does things like this.

When I'm situated as I'm supposed to be, he stares up and into my eyes. His hands knead the soft flesh of my waist and I bite my lip, looking down at him.

"Why'd you make me stop?" I whisper.

He kisses the slope of my breast, just above my neckline. "Because I don't want to come on your face or your neck or your tongue. I want to be inside of you when I blow."

He puts a period on his sentence with another kiss on my breast before he reaches up with one hand, while still keeping me all plastered and secure against his torso, and jerks the bodice of my dress down.

He makes my tits bounce, and looking into my eyes, closes his mouth over my tender flesh and sucks. Arching up into his mouth, feeling his teeth digging into my skin, his beard scraping it, I reach back and unzip my dress so the neck goes down easily.

And it does.

It bares my tits and my nipples. Like panties, I'm not wearing a bra either. I don't have to, not here, when it's just him and me. And he latches on to my puffy nipple while I hug him and rub up against his body.

I'm so turned on that it doesn't even register until he's started to move. He's striding toward something but I can barely care when he's got his mouth on my skin and he's laving his tongue like that and slurping in my swollen nipple.

He breaks away from me when we reach where he was trying to go. It was his truck.

We're at his truck, still out in the open and in the driveway, when he lowers me and drops me on the leather seat, through the passenger side door.

I slide back so he can climb inside before closing the door with a bang and going for my waist again. He pulls me over and makes me straddle his lap.

Only then do I get a good look at his face.

At his lust-slashed cheeks, his moist lips, his drugged-up eyes. Bull of a man, my Graham.

He looks so messy and sexy and masculine with his jeans half-undone and that shaft I was sucking on peeking through the waistband.

"You like dancing, yeah?" he rasps.

Squirming, I nod. "Yeah."

He gets his hand under the hem of my dress that he bought me, making the skin of my thighs coarse with goosebumps. He inches the hem up until my pantyless pussy is all bare and exposed. He does it all while staring into my eyes, but when my swollen, pink cunt comes into view, he gazes down.

He lasers his eyes at my core and licks his lips. My clit jerks and tightens at the peek of his tongue, the tongue that's given it so much pleasure over the past few weeks.

Glancing back at me, he commands, "Dance for me, then. Dance where anyone can see you. Where anyone can see that you're on my lap. That you're giving me a lap dance and shaking those tits for me. But here's the twist, baby."

My throat is all dried up and I can't even swallow. All I can do is watch him with wide, excited eyes and hang onto his every word like if I let go and miss them, I'll fall off this huge cliff and die.

"What?"

He leans over me and kisses me on the lips. "My cock is going to be inside you. You're going to dance on my cock but no one will know, will they? Because your pretty dress will hide us. Your pretty dress will hide your pussy while I fuck you like a bad man. It will be our secret."

I bite my lip. I bite *his* lip at this.

I go so completely delirious at the prospect of making our own secret that I bounce in his lap with excitement.

Smiling with this new-found recklessness and wildness, I whisper, "But there's going to be another twist." I caress his beard and place a kiss on his lips. "Instead of my pussy, your cock is going to be in my ass."

He fists my dress, his knuckles dimpling my thighs, while his eyes are going darker than I thought possible. "Is that so?"

Dark, dark, dark. More beastly.

His tone, his gaze, his intentions.

I can feel them running like current in my veins.

"Yeah. Remember what you told me that night?" I don't give him the chance to answer as I continue, "You told me that you can't take my tight ass because you haven't even fingered my pussy yet. You've fingered it now. You've fucked it, made love to it. So you gotta take my ass now."

His hands have let go of my dress and shifted to my butt in the last five seconds. He's grabbed both my bare cheeks and he's flexing his fingers. Pulling at the flesh and releasing, kneading it, massaging it as if getting my back hole ready for dancing.

"You can't back out now," I urge him on and his nostrils flare.

I watch as all semblance of control and civility leaches out of him, making him go bad. Completely and utterly bad.

Badder than ever before, making me wilder than ever before.

"I can't say something and not do it, can I?" he says in an abraded, low voice.

I put my hands on his shoulders and shake my head slowly. "No, you can't. You have to deliver, Mr. Edwards."

He chuckles but it's more a cloud of breath than anything. It only makes his frame shake with lust. It only makes his truck shake with our desire.

"I'll deliver then."

He lifts me up, while he slides down on the seat, sprawling himself even more, widening his thighs and adjusting himself in a way that he can deliver on his promise.

Then he brings me closer to him and I bend down to place a soft kiss on his lips, even though every nerve ending in my body is demanding that I attack him with my mouth.

Attack him for giving me what I want. Always, *always* giving me what I want.

But for now, all I do is watch him prepare himself.

He gets his cock out and licks the center of his palm. My breath hitches when I watch him wrap that palm around his already wet shaft and pump it up and down, making it all juicy and slippery.

That move is so fucking sexy that both my holes clench.

Both of them get needy.

And when he reaches forward and clasps my entire core, I almost black out. He gathers my wetness and practically pours it over his cock. He gets it so wet and slippery that my pussy gushes at the sight, salivating, drooling.

So much so that he lines his cock up against my cunt and runs it up and down my folds. To really get at it. To really slather himself with all my juices and cream.

All the while, all I can do is watch. All I can do is hang onto his shoulders, hovering over his lap and watch his hips go up and down as he lubes his cock for me, hitting my clit in the process, preparing me as well.

But that's not all.

He doesn't seem satisfied with only that much.

So he takes his cock and plunges it in my pussy, making me throw my head back and moan at the sudden invasion.

He bounces that cock inside me, bouncing me in the process. Bouncing me in his lap, filling me so good and so much.

When I moan and claw at his shoulders because I'm dying with arousal, he gets his shaft out. It's slathered in my juices now. Same as my thighs. Same as his jeans.

He asks, "You sure?"

It makes me shiver, the tone in which he says it. All beaten down and thinned out with lust but still dripping with concern.

"Yeah," I manage to whimper.

In fact, I've never been surer of anything other than this. I've never been surer of *anyone* other than him.

The man I'm going to have this secret with. The man who made me discover this wildness in me.

The man who's going to fuck my ass right in front of the world.

And I can't wait. I can't wait to give him this part of me.

He can't either.

Because in the next moment, he brings the wetness of my pussy to my back hole. He lubes it up like he lubed up his cock, as much as he can. Then he goes ahead and grabs both my cheeks to position me.

Grabbing my butt in his wet, sticky hands, he stretches my hole over his throbbing cock.

"Sit on it," he rasps, looking up at me. "Slowly."

And I do.

I can't wait to do it. I can't wait to sit on him even though I know it's going to hurt. It's already stinging, him parting my cheeks and stretching my hole, but I don't care.

So I push down and try to get his crown inside of me.

It's not easy though. Not at all. All I've had back there is either his thumb or his finger in the past days. He wouldn't agree to fucking me there with his cock. He'd either ignore me or distract me with his fantastic skills in bed.

But he's giving me what I want right now. He's just as needy for it.

He's giving it to me and I'm taking it, no matter what.

I'm holding onto this wildness in me and running with it.

Clenching my eyes shut, I push and push and moan with the burn of it, the sting, the pain. But the fact that he's so patient with me, that he plays with my clit to make me relax and that he shushes me when I whimper and shiver, makes it easier.

That and the mighty hold he has on my waist with his one hand, so he can keep me safe and balanced over him, eases the way. It makes me determined.

And I slowly manage to get his head inside of me and the pain of it is so brilliant and sharp and delicious that I fist the collar of his shirt.

He kisses me on the throat and hums over my skin. I can feel his lust pulsing in the air. I can feel the need he's trying to keep in check so I can adjust to his size.

And to open me up, he begins to move. Like he did the night he took my virginity. He fucks me with that one inch of his cock.

He loosens me up, slowly. While he's groaning over my skin, kissing the column of my throat, licking it and keeping me plastered to his body.

It's so good and amazing and so fucking different that I realize something else.

I realize that he's fucking me without a condom. That we're skin to skin for the first time ever.

For the first time ever, I feel every inch of him, every ridge and groove of his thick length as it stretches me like I've never been stretched before.

"Oh God, honey," I breathe out as everything inside of me gets both loose and tight.

So many firsts that all the feelings, all the sensations, new and old are colliding right now. They're colliding and clashing and

I want him all the way inside.

All the way until he's seated to the root and the skirt of my dress is spread all around us, hiding his cock in my ass. Hiding that I just gave up my virgin ass to him in broad daylight.

With a final push of his hips, it happens.

He's been slowly and patiently opening me up and now, he gets all the way inside, making me hiccup and moan.

Now, I'm completely sitting on his lap, his thick, pulsing length throbbing in my ass.

Breathing hard, I look at him, all full and achy in this new way.

With sweat dotting his forehead, he asks, "You okay?"

I nod, biting my lip.

He finally lets go of my waist and reaches up to thumb my cheek. "Tell me if it hurts."

I shake my head. "It doesn't."

"No?"

"No."

"Good." A hard kiss, then, "Cover us with your dress."

That makes me jerk and tremble, and he begins to move. Very, very slowly with short pumps.

They make my pussy wetter, his slow movements, and my hands shake when I pull down my dress and cover us with the hem, making it look like I'm just sitting on his lap.

Yes, my dress is half-unzipped and the straps are somewhere down my arms, my breasts visible and jiggling. But no one knows that he's inside of me.

No one knows that he's taking my tight ass.

It fills me with a rush. It fills me with so much lust and adrenaline that for a second, I think of all the scenarios where he can fuck me like this.

I think of restaurants, movie theatres, a park bench, all the public places where I can sit on his lap with his cock inside of me and no one will know.

Oh, they'll speculate and guess and whatnot and they might think I'm a slut for sitting in his lap like that but I won't care.

I'll look at each and every one of those people in the eye and smile, while keeping this secret. Our secret.

The fantasy is so arousing, the fantasy that I never even thought I had in me, that I begin to move as well. I begin to move against him and his pumps get smoother and longer.

I give him his lap dance in small, halting movements. I bounce in his lap.

I rock and writhe. I even jiggle my tits, shake them for him, feeling the friction of his jeans over my bare thighs, grinding my clit against his pelvis.

God, I could do this all day. I could do this all the time, for the rest of my life, dance for him like this while he's pumping into me from below.

While we watch each other.

While his hands are cradling my face – as always – and mine are clutching his shoulders. While he breathes over my lips and I breathe over his. While my tits rub up against his chest and his strokes become longer and faster.

While his truck is shaking and rocking with us and the windows fog up.

But more than anything, I wanna do this all day and for the rest of my life because I want to make all my secrets with him. Secrets like this one. So dirty and sacred at the same time.

It's us: him and me. The new us that we've created together.

I told him that night when I wore the red dress for him, that I want us to be *us*, just him and me.

This is us.

Wild and savage and filthy and beautiful. Beauty and The Beast.

And I'm right there, right on the edge of coming for him. He probably senses that, sees it on my face and knows it from the way I'm squirming now, restlessly and erratically.

Because he pushes me over the edge with this:

"I'll keep you here, you understand?" he whispers, penetrating my soul with his gaze that surprisingly looks very clear and alert despite his heavy, erotic breathing. "I'll keep you safe, in my lap. I'll hide you in my arms. No one will hurt you, baby. Ever. No one will ever make you feel scared. I won't let them."

At this, my eyes clench shut and I come.

I have to. I have no choice but to let go and let his words, his look of pure possession take over.

It makes me sob, my climax, it's so brutal. It's so all-consuming that I go completely rigid in his arms, so completely frozen and he hugs me then. He brings me to his chest and tucks my face into his neck, as he moves inside of me.

I pant on his skin with an open mouth as I come and come. I even feel my pussy leak all over his jeans. I feel the juices running out from my fluttering hole and seeping into the fabric and his skin, and it makes me come even harder.

It makes my holes clench and that sets him off.

That makes him splatter his cum inside of me, all thick and hot, covering my walls for the very first time. He jerks below me, his hips pumping once and twice, three times before he completely empties and fills my ass up to the brim.

Through all this, he keeps his arms wrapped around me. He keeps me safe in them, hides me away from everything.

Then he whispers, "Happy birthday a day early, baby."

And I die, or at least, tears leak out of me as this pain grips my heart.

He remembered.

He remembered my birthday even when I forgot. It's my birthday tomorrow and I've been busy living the dream that it completely slipped my mind.

But he remembered.

On top of that, he gave me a gift for it. This was a gift, wasn't it? He gave me what I wanted from him. I wanted him to take my ass and he did.

But he gave me another gift too.

He calmed down my anxious thoughts. He claimed me in front of someone, picked me over everything and gave me the strength to look a stranger in the eyes while standing up for him.

Finally, I understand the restlessness that I felt when Graham stopped me from spilling my biggest secret in front of Richard.

That restlessness was because I wanted to tell Graham. I wanted him to know.

Because how could I have not told him yet? How could I have been so selfish? I can't have him fighting the world for scaring me when he doesn't know the truth.

Besides, it doesn't matter if he can't love me. It doesn't matter that he'll never love me. Or that he'll stop looking at me the way he usually does, like I'm his world.

Love isn't about asking someone to love you back.

It's about loving.

It's about finding that thing you love and letting it kill you because you're going to die anyway. And what better way to go than at the hands of someone you love.

That's what Bukowski said, didn't he? Those were the words that pushed me to kiss him that night when I turned eighteen. So it's only symmetric that they push me now.

I'll tell him the truth and maybe he'll kill me. But it's okay.

Because all along he's been telling me what I deserve, and I've finally realized what *he* deserves.

He deserves the truth.

19

In the end the only thing
that matters is that I love him.
I loved him from the first
moment that I saw him and
I'll love him until the moment
I close my eyes.

-The Diary of a Blooming Violet, Age 19

I told him to paint my nails the other day.

We were on the bed, getting ready to sleep. He'd just come out of the bathroom, all bare-chested and wearing those plaid pajamas of his when the inspiration struck me. I was propped up on the pillows, wearing his shirt that I stole from him as soon as he got home from work – no panties – lifted my leg up and wiggled my toes.

"Will you paint my toes, Mr. Edwards?" I asked, swirling a lollipop in my mouth.

He prowled toward me, making all the lust inside me wake up. Not that it ever goes to sleep when he's around but still.

He reached the bed and looked at my lifted leg once before

focusing on my core, which I was accidentally-on-purpose flashing him.

"Do I look like a dumb college kid to you, Jailbait?" he rasped, glancing back at me.

I lowered my leg onto the bed but kept my thighs open for him. "You look like a sexy hunk of a man right now and I want you to paint my toes."

I thought he wouldn't; I was just kidding.

But he grabbed the shiny nail polish bottle from the side table where I'd left it the last time. Then, he climbed on the bed and knelt between my open legs. He clutched my ankle, widened my legs even more so I was open for him and put it on his hard thigh before getting down to work.

He meticulously painted every little toe of mine. Every single one as he bent over me and stroked the tiny little brush just so.

He wouldn't even look at her, my pussy, that he'd spread my legs for, and for some reason that made her wetter, sloppier.

But more than that it filled me with so much love for him that once he was done, I legit attacked him. I pounced on him and kissed his entire face, ruining his work on my toes in the process but whatever.

Then I told him that I wanted to ride his thigh and come all over it and he let me. He let me ride his bare thigh until I came and spread all my juices over him before he fisted my hair and looked me in the eyes. "You've had your fun, Jailbait. My turn now."

I thought he meant he wanted me to suck his cock but he growled, "Sit on my face."

Not only that, he actually made me.

He maneuvered me and positioned me until I was sitting on his face while he ate me out and made me come again, this time on his jaw and beard, while jacking himself off.

Meanwhile, we'd forgotten about that nail polish bottle and in all of our shenanigans, it had spilled, staining the sheet.

I see the stain now as I wake up the morning of my nineteenth birthday. The token from the night when he painted my toes after he said he wouldn't.

His side of the bed is empty and it's cold, meaning he's been gone a long time.

He's probably at work.

He's probably found out by now. About me, I mean. And he'll talk to me about it when he gets back.

Strangely, I don't have any fear in me.

The fear went away yesterday when he saved me from Richard and my own mind so I could forget that I'm ill for a little while.

I didn't even feel anything other than a pounding heart when I set the plan in motion last night after I turned nineteen.

I thought about how to tell him. How best to convey everything that is inside of me, and the answer was simple.

My journals.

I could give them to him and he could read it all for himself. So I left them on the coffee table, the complete stack of them along with a few other things.

Now he can know everything.

He can know that at sixteen, I saw him and fell in love. At eighteen, I kissed him and a scandal broke out that almost broke me and at nineteen, I'm telling him all about it.

I throw off the covers and climb out of the bed.

The floors creak under my feet and that sound somehow brings me to my knees.

The creak of the floor, the wooden slats of the headboard, the unpolished door of his closet. Things that I've come to love.

It's open now, the closet door, and I can see my dresses hanging with his plaid shirts.

I put them in there as a joke, telling him that if he keeps buying me all these dresses, then I'm taking over the closet. His re-action was to flip me over and fuck me doggy style on the bed with his thumb in my ass, while he made me watch our clothes together. Every time my eyes would fall shut, he'd tug on my hair that he'd wrapped around his wrist and tell me to keep watching.

He'd ask me, *Which one's your favorite, baby?*

And when I'd tell him – the one with pink roses on it – he'd ask me why. He'd ask me to describe it to him exactly like he didn't know what it looked like.

They still look pretty, my dresses along with his shirts, hanging there.

Everything about this place looks pretty. I can't believe I thought that this cabin was falling apart. I mean, Graham has done major work over the past weeks and there's still more to be done but I don't even care.

I like this cabin.

I love this cabin.

I love it because this is my home. This has become my home in the past weeks.

My things are everywhere.

On the nightstand and on the floor, and when I walk out of the room, I see my pink bottles of shampoo and conditioner in the bathroom. Even the air smells like me: strawberry.

This is my home.

My home.

I don't know why I keep chanting it over and over in my head. I don't know why it's hitting me only now that this cabin in the middle of the woods is the first place that I've belonged.

But it is.

It hits me even more when I walk down the hallway and I find him there.

My feet come to a halt.

He's here.

I thought he'd be gone. I thought he'd be at work by now. I thought I had time.

I had more *time* to prepare myself.

God, he's here and he'll have all these questions and I thought I was without fear and I *was* up until I saw him but I'm not.

I'm just so, so weak.

So weak that I whisper his name. "Graham."

His back tenses.

He's sitting on the couch, facing away from me. His shoulders seem to be slouching, bent forward, and I realize he's got his elbows propped up on his sprawled thighs and his hands lying limply between them.

But all his muscles bunch up at my whispered call.

I see them rippling under the thin t-shirt he's wearing. He

usually sleeps bare-chested but by the time I wake up – always later than him – he has one of his old t-shirts on along with his plaid pajamas.

He stands now and slowly turns toward me. He looks... lifeless.

So blank and empty, almost.

It makes me weak in the knees. They almost buckle. I didn't think he'd look like that. I thought he'd be... angry.

Yeah, that's what I thought.

I thought he'd be mad at me for lying or maybe he'd be disbelieving or something like that. I didn't think he'd look so defeated.

Yeah, that's kind of how he looks.

Like he's lost all the battles and all the wars and now he has nothing to live for.

"You're home," I whisper uselessly.

"Your bag. This is what you have in there."

His voice is flat. No modulation, no high tone at the end alerting that it's a question. But it is one and he's waiting for me to answer him. Even though he knows already.

Fisting my hands, I nod. "Yes. I-I carry them everywhere."

By them, I mean my old journals. The ones I used to write in before I went to Heartstone and stopped writing altogether. The ones that held my dreams and desires and *him*.

I can see my journals all scattered around on the coffee table, and I know he's read them all.

"And the pills," he continues in that flat tone of his.

At this, my chest heaves with a broken breath. There are

pill bottles everywhere too, alongside my journals. I left them sitting on the side of the stacked journals for him to find.

"Yeah. I-I need them sometimes. When things are bad." He keeps staring at me and so I go on and explain, "I was on a regular medication. B-before. But they took me off and now, I have these. For when things are not good."

I keep my pills right alongside my dreams, all contained in my fat hobo.

I don't know why I do that, why I keep my dreams and my medication together. Maybe it is to remind me of something. Of things I can't do now. I don't know, I just lump them together.

"I haven't had to take them in a while," I tell him before he can say anything else. "I just took one when I was driving out here but other than that I didn't need to."

That, at least, is true.

I took the pill because I was anxious. I was freaking out about the journey and about seeing him, but after I actually saw him, I didn't need it anymore.

After I saw him, something calmed in me even though I thought he hated me in those early days. But I had something to fight for, then.

I had a purpose. A goal. To give him peace, to make things up to him.

Maybe that's why I didn't need them.

"Is that why you put it in the closet."

By it, he means the hobo. The thing I can't do without.

He noticed that?

Of course he noticed that. He notices everything about me.

Of course, he noticed that I hid the hobo in the closet of his other room when I came in weeks and weeks ago to help him detox. I put it in there so he wouldn't find out. So he wouldn't stumble upon it accidentally and rattle its contents.

"Yes."

He's silent after that and I gauge the distance between us like I did the first night I saw him at the bar and we were talking about him touching that queen-like woman. I look at him, standing by his couch and me in the hallway and I try to think how many steps it would be before I can touch him.

How many steps before I can feel his warmth again, breathe the same air as him, feel the beat of his heart beneath my palm.

"What's Heartstone."

He asks the question after what feels like ages. And again, it's not a question because he probably already knows the answer.

I stopped writing in those journals the night they sent me there. That's my last entry, going to a psych ward, and then I stopped. Until I picked it up again the day Brian called me and I found out that Graham was watching me as much as I was watching him.

I breathe out a long, long breath. "A psych ward. It's, uh, it's in upstate New York. Heartstone Psychiatric Hospital."

"You were there."

"Yeah. Yes. I was."

"How long."

"F-for a couple of months. They have this, uh, six-week program but I wasn't making much progress with it so they extended it and I had to stay there for another six weeks."

"When was this."

I swallow and grip the hem of what I'm wearing. I realize it's the plaid shirt of his from yesterday.

I put it on after he fucked me in the truck, wished me a happy birthday and carried me inside. We took a shower together and he washed me up before fucking me again in the shower, slow and lazy like we had all the time in the world. Then, I put on his shirt and we had microwave-heated pizza – the one he bought for us before we got sidetracked.

His soft plaid shirt that still smells like him gives me the strength now that I probably wouldn't have had otherwise. That and this emptiness inside of me after being full of him for so long.

"L-last year. In the summer and a little bit of fall."

In fact, I was the second last of our gang to leave Heart-stone. Willow was the last one; she had some major incident a night before she was supposed to leave.

"Why? Why were you there?"

The first question he's asked me that sounds like a question. That sounds like his voice is changing. His expression is still blank though, still lifeless, but something is going on inside of him and I don't know what it is.

Don't be selfish, Violet.

Tell him. Love him.

Let him kill you, it's okay.

"Because I have Panic Disorder."

Finally, I see a sliver of a movement on his face. I think it's a wince; I can't be sure. It was very tiny and it was over in a flash. Gone before I can really tell what's going on.

But in any case, it's out there now.

I've told him.

He knows.

And now that he does know, I tell him the rest. I tell him even though there's a chance that he might still think I'm defective and weak.

"I..." I swallow and pull at the hem of his shirt. "I've always been kinda shy and away from the world. Well, except when it comes to you. Uh, anyway, I've never liked people. I've never liked their eyes on me. Mostly because they always looked at me like I was this weird girl with the mousy blonde/brown hair and these giant brown eyes that always make me look like I'm startled or something..."

I chuckle nervously. "But it's mostly because I'm not used to it. I'm not... used to being seen. Not really. So when I kissed you... that night and I suddenly became this, this thing that everyone was seeing, I couldn't handle it. I couldn't deal with it. It freaked me out." I wipe my mouth with the back of my hand and go back to fisting his shirt, fraying it with my fingers.

"It would freak me out so much that I, uh, I think I got my first panic attack when I was at the grocery store. Someone saw me and recognized me and started talking to me. And I just couldn't deal with it. I ran out of there and I couldn't breathe. I felt like someone was sitting on my chest and my stomach was churning and... yeah, it was awful. But then it happened again and again until I couldn't get out of the house. Until I only felt safe in my room or when I went out at night.

"And one night, I was sitting up on the roof and I was

drinking because Fiona called me to brag about her and Brian. So I went up to the roof, and I was sitting there and I saw someone on the street. And then, that someone saw me. They saw me up there and they started walking toward the house and I lost it. I don't even know what they wanted but I got so scared anyway. And I didn't wanna come down from the roof but I had to. I-I had to because someone was there and they were walking toward me and I was so angry at people for not leaving me alone. It was my time, you know. It was my time to be out in the world and watch the moon and write in my journal but I couldn't even do that. So I got into my car because I wanted to drive away from there. I got so tired of everything that I wanted to get out of that town. But a few miles down, I skidded off the road and I was going to hit this tree but I didn't."

Finally, I stop to take a breath. I stop to tell myself that it's over. Or at least, it's almost over. So it's more or less a breath of relief.

Although, I'm not out of the woods yet.

Because he hasn't said a word.

He hasn't changed his expression either. He's doing what he was doing the second he turned around and saw me: staring.

He's staring at me but then again, his fists weren't clenched when we started this.

They are now.

They look even more ferocious than mine. My puny ones that I'm using to take apart his shirt.

I'm not sure what they mean, his fists. If it's good news or if he's beginning to think that I'm so weak and pathetic that just because someone was walking toward me, I freaked out like that and almost rammed my car into a tree.

But I stare at those fists and continue, "They took me to a hospital. Sent me for a psych eval and everything. Then, they gave me the option of going to this facility so I could have a structured environment and I took it. Mostly because I wanted to get away. So basically, I've been lying to you. I've been lying to you about everything. There's no... There's no college. There's no vacation. There's nothing. I'm not sure if I'm even going to college. Because people still scare me."

I crawl the toes of my right foot up the calf of my left, feeling exposed and self-conscious and suddenly so shy in front of him. Something that I've never felt before and I hate this feeling.

He's the one person I never wanted to hide from or lie to and I hate that I have done both.

"What happened with Richard? That was kind of a mini-panic attack. I can't look people in the eyes and I can't talk to them because I'm scared. It makes me anxious. I have these things, my therapist, Nelson, calls them crutches. Cap and sunglasses. I wear them when I go out. Which isn't a lot. I don't go out a lot. I mostly just stay home. I order things online and I talk to people through notes."

At this, I have to laugh a little. Billy, my pen pal.

"I do all those things because I don't like being here. In the world. I was fine on the Inside, at Heartstone, but I'm... kind of struggling on the Outside. At Heartstone, everyone was like me. Everyone had problems and no one looked at me like I was different. But then, I got out and I realized everything was still the same.

The people in my town, their judgment and gossip and all of that. They still thought that I was a slut and they still called you names and all the rumors were still alive. So it was just easier to stay home and lock myself up in my room rather than going out and facing my problems. Facing the loud world and all those people. It was easier to just pretend that it was okay for me to use a crutch and never talk to anybody other than a few people I met at Heartstone. It *is* easier to pretend that I'm fine than dealing with the real problem: my doomsday brain. Anxiety is so exhausting, you know and I just didn't wanna be tired anymore. I guess, I was just weak. I liked taking the easy way out. But if you really think about it, I've always been weak, right? Shy and hiding away from the world and being busy with books and music and all that. So it makes sense that I'd be weak now, in the face of my illness.

"And the reason I didn't tell you any of this..." I lick my lips and make sure that I don't look away from him, "is because I thought you'd think I was weak and a coward, as well. I thought you'd think I was defective. You'd think I have this crazy illness and all these stupid phobias and that I'm pathetic. I'm flawed and I don't know, a million other things that I think about myself anyway. So yeah, I've been lying and hiding things and you should probably hate me now."

But I don't want you to...

I don't say that because well, I don't think I can say anything. I've said all I had in me to say.

I've said it all and I can't look at him anymore. So I go back to staring at his clenched fists. I notice that the tendons on his wrist are standing taut now. His veins are almost bursting out of his skin and I'm so afraid to look at the expression on his face.

What if he thinks all of that and more?

But then, he's always saved me, made me feel beautiful and special. He's made me feel like his world.

So I don't know.

I don't know and I'm so afraid that when he begins to move toward me, I clench my eyes shut. I even take a step back. I tighten the muscles in my stomach and curl my toes and if I could, I'd roll myself up in a ball too.

At last, he's going to say all the things I've been dreading, isn't he?

He is. He is. He is.

I know that. I *know*.

"You're defective."

His words – that I knew he was going to say – still knock the breath out of me. They make me pop my eyes open and take him in.

His features are pulled tight and made angular and sharp by his fury. He's looking at me with violence in his eyes. So much violence that I don't know how to return his gaze. But at the same time, I don't want to look away.

I can't.

He's this beautiful, magnificent thing in my life and I love him so much that even when he breaks my heart, my soul, I have to watch him do it. There's no other option.

"You're weak. Pathetic. Flawed. You're a coward."

I flinch, my lips parted, taking in hiccupping breaths.

"Is that what you are?"

I nod.

Because yeah, that's what I am. I'm all kinds of defective and I've been so stupid in thinking even for one second that I'm not.

I've been so stupid in thinking that he'd be the one person who wouldn't think that about me when everyone else has always written me off.

So stupid, Violet. God, you're so stupid.

At my nod, he brings his face closer to me, his chest moving up and down. "Then explain something to me. Explain how you're standing in front of me, telling me all these things about yourself?"

"What?"

My confusion bugs him and his next words are ripped out of his clenched teeth. "How are you still here? How are you here after all the things I've put you through? All the awful, cruel things I've done to you right from the beginning. Why didn't you run away and lock yourself up in a room because it's safe, huh? Because it's so easy to pretend everything is okay. It's so easy to lie, isn't it?"

"I…"

"I've given you every opportunity to leave. In fact, I've gone to great lengths to have you leave. Why didn't you? If you're so pathetic and such a coward, why didn't you leave? Why didn't you take the easy way out of this, Violet? Why the fuck did you give me your journals? Because if you hadn't told me, I never would've found out. Why tell me? Why tell me when I can clearly see the fear on your face? Why tell me when there's a part of you that thinks I'm going to reject you for the truth?"

Why tell him?

Doesn't he already know? Didn't he read it in my journal, the one I started writing in after I came here?

"Because I love you," I tell him with watery eyes, with my sweaty palms groping his shirt that I'm wearing, my curled toes poking holes in his creaking, ancient hardwood floor.

"You do, do you?"

Swallowing, I nod. "Yes."

He narrows his eyes. "Even when I don't? Even when I can't. Even after I told you a million goddamn times that I'm never going to love you, you still love me."

A tear makes its way down my cheek and he follows its journey with a harsh, tormented expression. "Yes," I whisper. "I do."

"Why?"

"Because I always have. Right from the start. Because you make me feel safe. Protected and warm. And because love isn't about asking someone to love you back. It's about... loving. It's about jumping off a cliff with both arms open wide and hoping that those arms become wings and you can fly. But even if you can't and you hit the ground and you die, it's okay. It's okay because very few people get to die in love. Very few people get to die while *doing* what they love. Very few people get to be that shiny and luminous and bright and... and brave, you know? And..."

Brave.

Did I say brave?

I couldn't have. I'm not brave. I never have been. I mean, I'm the girl who hides herself. How can I be...

"Brave, huh. So you're brave?"

His raspy words make me forget my thoughts. Or rather, they complete my thoughts. All these thoughts that are flashing in and out, telling me that holy fucking shit, I'm brave.

I'm *brave*.

Me?

I get so jarred, like someone punched me in the stomach or pushed me off a cliff. The cliff that I was falling off anyway. I've been falling off that cliff ever since I turned sixteen and saw him.

I've been falling off that cliff and I've been dreaming while in flight.

Dreaming about him and loving him and being brave.

Jesus Christ, I'm brave.

"You're so fucking brave, Violet. So fucking magnificent that sometimes I don't know what to do. You're the bravest person I know," he chokes out.

I am... fucking brave.

My mouth falls open and I take a sudden step toward him. I grab his t-shirt and crane my neck up to him. "I am. I'm brave. I'm... I'm *brave*."

I smile up at him.

I smile because God, how did I not know this about myself? How did I not know that falling in love is an act of bravery?

Giving someone your heart, putting it right at their feet, feet that wear big, threatening hiking boots, is called being brave.

I've been brave since I was sixteen, maybe even before that, and I'm only realizing this now, the day I turn nineteen.

Because of him.

Gosh, *everything* is because of him.

"I'm brave," I tell him again, beaming this time.

"You are."

He confirms it but there's no happiness on his face.

It takes me a little time to understand that.

It takes me a few seconds in which I beam and chuckle and marvel over myself, to understand that he's not doing any of those things.

He's simply watching me, flicking his eyes all over my smiling face like he'll never get to see me after this. His features have become blank again, that wretched defeat that I saw on him when I found him on the couch is back.

Again, he looks like he's lost. All the battles and all the wars.

I don't get it.

"Graham? What's the matter?"

He grits his teeth but otherwise remains silent.

Why does he look like this is the last time he'll ever see me?

I mean, I'm not going anywhere. I'm going to be still here. In fact, now that all the secrets are out in the open, I'm his. Completely and irrevocably.

I'm *his*.

Well, of course there's this minor thing that he can't love me and that my mom thinks I'm at yoga camp but I'm not. That could pose a problem, but I'm brave. I can figure things out.

In fact, I can figure things out about my anxiety too.

I can get better. I can work toward it. I wanna work toward it. I wanna work on me.

So all in all, this is a happy moment.

I reach up and cup his hard jaw. "Why do you look like

this? It's a happy occasion, you know. I actually looked a stranger in the eyes yesterday. Can you believe that? I kissed you in front of him and I didn't even have a panic attack. Although, we do need to apologize to him. But oh my God! I'm so badass. And it's my birthday and someone remembers it and you know everything about me and you don't think less of me. In fact, you made *me* realize that I'm brave. So I think you should probably start smiling and not be such a hardass and –"

My words die when I hear a screech outside.

Tires squealing and coming to a stop. A door opening and closing with a bang. Then crunching footsteps across the gravel, leading up to the steps.

I hear the click-clack of heels across the wooden porch and finally, a knock.

Three pounds of someone's fist on the door and a voice.

A voice I never thought I'd hear, at least not here in Colorado. I never thought she'd come here.

She's never cared enough about me to go anywhere.

But then, she cares about this, doesn't she?

My mother cares about me being involved with Mr. Edwards. That's the only thing she's cared about in all the years that I've been alive.

"Violet, open the door," my mother says from the other side. "I know you're in there. Violet, open this door right now. You've got so much to answer for."

Her voice sounds strange to me.

Everything sounds strange right now. Everything *looks* strange right now.

My hand is still on Graham's jaw and he's still staring down at me with that deadened expression.

And in a flash, I understand.

He wasn't looking happy. He wasn't smiling, because he called her.

He called my mother.

As soon as I realize this, my hand falls away. His nostrils flare with a heavy breath and he steps away from me.

Then he turns around and stalks to the door and throws it open.

Meanwhile, I just stand here, frozen on the spot but somehow limp as a rag doll as I watch his broad back. I watch the dance of his muscles as he breathes in and out.

I can't see my mother though. His shoulders hide her but I can hear her voice.

"Where is she?"

"You don't say anything to her. Not one word," he growls.

"You don't get to tell me how to treat my own daughter, got it? You don't —"

"Do you remember what I said to you last night? You say one word to her and you'd be wishing you hadn't."

"I'm not afraid of you. I know the kind of man you are. I've *met* the kind of man you are. And she's been lying to me for you. She's been ruining her life for you."

"It's over now."

This is followed by a few beats of silence when I imagine them staring at each other. When I'm still trying to comprehend what's happening.

He called my mother.

The man I love called the woman who's *never* loved me. Why would he do that? Why would he betray me like this?

Graham's the one to break the thick, tense quiet. "Don't make me regret calling you."

With that, he steps aside and my mom comes into view, all haggard and unkempt like she hasn't slept in days. As soon as she sees me, she rushes over.

She grabs my arm and shakes me. "What the hell were you thinking? Running away like this? Lying to me like this?"

I stare at her concerned face, kind of detached, a lot confused. "I didn't think you'd care."

She draws back, winces. Her eyes drop away from me before coming back, all guilty and fraught with restlessness. "I've never given you much. I've never been there for you. But you're my daughter. And if I know one thing in life, it's men. I know men like him. I know how they take advantage of girls like you. Crazy, naïve girls who ruin everything for them. Do you think he's going to give you anything? Do you think he's going to fall in love with you and you're going to live happily ever after? That's never going to happen, Violet. All he's looking for is a good time. He'll fuck you. He'll break your heart and he'll leave. No matter what he says, no matter how many promises he makes, he's never going to fulfill them. It's not going to happen. Get out of your dreams and wake up. He's playing you. He's making a fool out of you and I'll be damned before anyone makes a fool out of my daughter. No matter how neglectful or unavailable I've been, I'm not going to let you ruin your life for a man like him. Is that clear? You're coming home with me right now."

When she finishes, I want to tell her. I want to tell her that she has it wrong. She has it all wrong.

She thinks he's promised me things, but he hasn't.

He never promised me anything. In fact, he's been very clear about his intentions right from the beginning.

He's not making a fool out of me. *I'm* making a fool out of me because I love him.

I'm so in love with him that he could've fooled me, if he wanted. He could've taken advantage of me but he never did.

Not even before. When he watched me and I watched him.

So, she has it all wrong. I already know he's not going to give me anything but I don't care. I just want to be with him.

But then, I see a movement from the corner of my eyes and I look away from the beautiful but tired face of my mother.

My eyes find him and from the look of it, he's been standing there all through my mother's insults. And all through it, he's been staring at me.

When our eyes clash though, he gets moving.

He takes in a long breath that I can feel even though I'm standing so far away from him.

And then, he begins walking away and something splinters inside my chest.

He's leaving.

He's *leaving* me. He's giving me to my mother like I'm this object, a wayward child who's wandered a little too far from her home, and now she has to go back.

I don't even stop to think or pay attention to my mom's

shouts when I take off after him. My bare feet tap on the wooden porch and steps. They stumble on the gravel as stones and dirt dig into my soles.

"Graham. Graham, stop." I call after him.

He's at his truck now, his back turned away from me.

I reach him, all panting and scared and with a heart that has a crack running at the center of it.

"Why did you call her? Why w-would you…"

He faces me, his hair all messy and stuck up on the sides. He hasn't slept, I realize. Or at least, he's been awake for a while. It shows on his haggard face now.

He probably read my journals as soon as I set them out and he probably called my mom as soon as he finished reading them.

"Because you need to go home."

"I don't… understand. Is this… Is this your way of punishing me? For lying about everything? For lying about college and all those things?"

He studies me a beat, his shoulders rigid and massive.

Actually, everything about him looks massive, more massive than ever. More angular and sharper and more daunting.

Everything about him and his size that would make me feel secure, intimidates me now.

"I called her because she's right."

"About what?"

"About everything. About the fact that I'm taking advantage of you. I'm having my fun when I'm not going to give you anything."

I take a painful step toward him. "But you're not. You're

not taking advantage of me. I know. I already know that you won't give me anything. I know that. You told me that."

That starts up a pulse on his cheek. "But you didn't listen. You didn't heed all the warnings I've been laying out for you. I'm not going to love you, Violet. I can't. I don't know how. So you need to go home now."

I clutch his t-shirt again. I clutch it and pull at it and shake it because I want him to understand.

I want him to get that I don't need those things.

"I don't need your love, Graham. I don't need it. I can live without it, okay? I can. I promise. I won't need your love. I won't even ask for it. I just want you. All I need is you. You make me feel safe, don't you get it? You make me feel protected and warm and special and that's enough for me. I can live with you not loving me. But I can't live without you. I can't. Please."

By the end of it, I'm crying. I'm sobbing and I want him, I *need* him to hear me. I beg him to understand.

When he steps closer to me, I think he does.

His hands reach out and he wipes off my tears and I tighten my fists in his t-shirt. I try to hold onto him, keep him here so he doesn't go anywhere.

So he doesn't leave me.

I watch him through watery eyes as he leans down and kisses me on the forehead.

God.

God.

He gets it, doesn't he?

"Maybe you don't need those things, but you deserve

them," he rasps against my hair. "You deserve them more than anyone in this fucked up, shitty world. Go home, baby."

He moves away then.

My hold on him is so tiny and so unaffecting that he breaks it easily. And by the time I realize what's happened, he's already opening the door of his truck and climbing inside.

"I can't go home," I blurt out to his back. "This is my home. This. Here."

His hand rests on the door as he faces me.

He takes one sweep of my body, my bare feet, the shirt of his that I'm wearing. My splotchy face and rumpled hair, before he comes back to my eyes.

"This is no one's home. Never has been."

That hits me so much and so hard that I don't recover from it until he's already in the truck, backing out of the driveway.

He does it so fast that all I can see for a few seconds is a cloud of dust.

Once it settles though and he's disappeared down that winding trail that cuts through the woods and ends at that rusty mailbox on the side of the road, I take off after him.

I run and run along that dirt path, hoping to chase him down. I call out his name over and over because how can he say that this cabin isn't a home?

How can he say that?

How can he say that when we've been building it together over the past few weeks?

I run and run after him so I can tell him, it's ours.

This is our home.

But he's gone and I don't see him, not even the tail-end of his black truck, and that just takes away all my fight, and I crumple to the ground and fall on the pieces of my broken heart and my dreams.

Part III

Graham

The cabin feels dead.

It feels like it did the first day I moved back in after years and years of being away. During those initial days, everything was covered in a thick film of dust and old memories.

I cleaned it up the best I could before letting it go and drowning in alcohol.

Until she showed up.

Until she fixed everything. Fixed me. Saved me.

I walk in further, my legs taking me to the kitchen without my volition. As if they can't believe she's gone and they need to check it for themselves. The kitchen is usually where she'd be when I came home from work, always baking something, smelling so sweet and looking so soft.

When I find the kitchen empty – expectedly – my feet stumble.

My body and my heart can't understand the fact that she's

gone. They can't believe that I've sent her away.

They can't comprehend this thing that I've done.

This awful, cruel thing.

They don't get how I called her mother. How I hurt her when I've always promised to destroy anything and everything that dares to harm her.

My brain understands it though.

My brain grasps the betrayal.

It understands the fact that I haven't been able to protect her. I haven't been able to keep her safe from the world.

I understood that last night when I was reading her journals. Her thoughts and dreams that she left for me so casually on the coffee table.

Where they sit even now exactly like I left them.

All this time I kept thinking that my ruined relationship with Brian and gossip, that article, were the only casualty and consequence of that kiss.

And I could've stopped it all.

I could've stopped that kiss from happening if I had just stepped away that night and not been greedy to bask in her light. If I could've just walked inside my house and not approached her when I saw her through the windshield of my truck.

She was there, picking the roses, and she looked so... beautiful and fragile and pale with the moonlight illuminating her delicate lines that I had to go to her.

I had to approach her.

My legs wouldn't listen. Like tonight, they had a mind of their own.

I wish they had obeyed me.

I wish I'd stopped myself from going to her like I had done a million times before.

Then none of this would've happened.

She wouldn't have suffered like she did.

Because the biggest casualty of that kiss was the girl that I sent away this morning.

Violet.

Her.

She paid for it; she was fucking crucified for it. For something so pure and innocent. Something that was supposed to be private and for her and her only.

I could've protected her.

I *should've* protected her. Like I should've tried harder to send her away.

Because I've been hurting her. I've been hurting her in the ways I didn't understand until I read her journals.

She's in love with me.

She loves me.

Or maybe I did understand. She said she had a crush on me, didn't she? So maybe I knew about her love but still, I kept her here.

She's *in love* with me.

Jesus Christ.

That's why she came here. That's why she took everything I gave. She took it and smiled and kept coming back for more.

And I was letting her.

I was letting her take less than what she deserves. I was

letting her settle. I was keeping her here because I couldn't let go of her.

Because the thought of letting go of her makes me break out in a sweat.

It makes me panic. It twists and screws and digs the knife in my chest.

I was being selfish. So fucking selfish.

So I did the right thing. The thing I should've done weeks ago.

I let her go.

I let her go so she could live her life. So she could find someone worthy of her.

Someone who knows how to love. Someone who knows how to protect her and make her smile and laugh.

Someone unlike me.

Someone who doesn't get terrified at the thought of love. At the thought of making himself so vulnerable to another human being that he can't think straight.

I leave the kitchen and walk toward her journals, pick one up and open a random page. I sniff it like a junkie and her smell hits me in the gut.

My heart starts banging. Pounding, roaring.

My legs give out and I drop down to the couch.

I take another sniff and again, it hits me like a bullet. It makes me almost groan.

And after that, I can't stop myself.

I can't stop myself from flicking pages and reading her handwriting and smelling her. I rub my fingers on it, on the pages.

Like they are her skin.

Like by touching them, I can touch her. I can touch her warmth, her softness. I can touch her scent.

I can't.

She's gone. She's not here. I sent her away.

I did the most horrible thing I could do to her so she'd hate me. So she'd finally go back. Go back to where she belongs.

Go back home.

This is my home.

Her words echo around the cabin. They echo and crash against the windows and I hear them clearly.

Not that I haven't been hearing them.

I've been driving aimlessly around all day, because I took today off for her birthday, and I've been hearing her voice. I've been playing her words on repeat.

But something about coming back to this old cabin – that doesn't feel like home at all – makes me hear her clearer.

This is her home, she said.

How could it be though when it was never mine? How could she say that?

Her home is Connecticut. Her home is with her parents.

But then, that's not true, is it?

Her parents have never been her home. Her parents never really cared about her. She was lonely back there.

She was lonely and ignored and alone and... strangely unseen.

Until me.

Until I saw her that night, climbing up on the roof. I saw

her and couldn't stop watching her.

And I watched her be ignored and passed over by narrow-minded, unimaginative people. I watched men and boys salivate after her but staying away because she was unconventional. She was in her own world.

I watched that. I watched all of that and I sent her back to it.

I sent her back to those people who hurt her in the first place. Who took away her safety. Who made her feel unsafe in her own skin. Who made her so afraid that she was ready to drive out of there – drunk – putting herself in jeopardy.

That still terrifies me. It makes my breathing stop. She was so unsafe and so unhappy there that she didn't think about anything except getting out of there.

Fucking Christ.

You make me feel safe...

I make her feel safe. She told me that and I just ignored it.

I ignored it and I sent her back.

I sent her back to people who judged her from the beginning, from the *very* beginning for being who she was.

Moon and magic.

Fuck.

Fuck.

But then, what's the other option? Keeping her here? With me?

I don't even know how...

But I can learn, can't I?

I can fucking learn.

I look at her journals with new eyes. These are her dreams. These have been her dreams since she was sixteen and she gave them to me. She didn't trust me. She thought I'd reject her but still, she gave me her dreams.

Because she's brave.

If she can be that brave, then I can learn to be brave too. Can't I?

If she can love a hard man like me, cynical and old and emotionally stunted, then I can learn to be soft for her. I can learn to protect her better.

Yeah, I can learn.

I can fucking learn.

For her.

20

I have faith...

~The Diary of a Blooming Violet, Age 19

They think I'm crazy.

They think I'm in shock.

They think I'll snap out of it sooner or later when I see that the thing I believe in, the thing that I trust is not going to happen.

They even tell me this.

My mother is the first one to say I'm being crazy and unrealistic. She says I'm being a moon-eyed teenager, a dreamer who'll get both her heart and her mind broken.

She even tells me about my father.

My real father, the one who I've never met before. I never thought she'd tell me his story. She guards that secret like her life depends on it and since the only reason I found out was because she was drunk one night and didn't know what she was saying, I never expected her to tell me about him.

But she does.

She sits on the edge of my bed – my old bed in Connecticut – and for the first time ever caresses my hair. She strokes it and I have to blink back tears while I'm lying on my side, with my hands under my cheek.

She tells me that my real father was this charming guy she met at her country club. He lived in New York City and was in town visiting some friends for a while.

"We fell in love," she says soothingly. "Or at least, I did. I even wanted to leave your father for him. For Christopher. We spent lazy afternoons together when your dad wasn't here. I thought he was going to marry me. He said he loved me and I'd never felt that before. Your dad doesn't love me. I don't love him either. Never did, never will. Anyway, I'd never been in love before, you know. So I thought I was finally getting a chance at it. I was finally getting that dream that I didn't even have for myself. I never thought I'd fall in love. But then, his trip ended and he left. And when I found out about you, I tried to contact him. He told me to move on. It was an affair and it was over. I didn't even get a chance to tell him about you before I found out that he had a family of his own."

My tears sluice down to my pillow but hers are still at the edge, filling her pretty eyes with pain.

"So I decided that I'd never tell him. I decided that I hated him. It was easier to pretend that than actually face the fact that I was a bored, easy suburban wife who fell in love with a charming man from out of town. It was easy to pretend to myself that it was an affair like all my other affairs."

So we're a lot alike, then. My mom and I. We both pretended to be okay. We both were living a lie.

And for the first time ever, I feel like my mom's daughter. As painful as it was to hear, this story brought us closer.

"You look like him. You always did. Brown hair with golden strands that look blonde and chocolate brown eyes. It was hard for me to look at you. To look at the reminder of my broken dream. It's not an excuse but I want you to know that. I want you to know why I was an awful mother to you. Because I was in love with your father. Maybe I still am."

She wipes my tears off and it causes this wound in my chest, my soul to gape open. He does that.

He wipes my tears off, even if he's the one to give them to me.

Swallowing, I grab her hand and squeeze, my already broken heart breaking for her a little. "Thanks for telling me."

She blinks back her tears. "You can't be like me, Violet. Do you understand? I won't let you be like me. He's not coming back, Vi. He's not coming back for you. He called me, remember? He told me where you were. He sent you away. You have to give up hope, okay? Give it up. You have to pick up the pieces and move on because if you don't, you'll end up like me."

This isn't the first time that she's said it. Give up hope, I mean.

She told me this five days ago when she suddenly came to Colorado.

After Graham left in his truck and I ran after him, she

found me in the woods. She lifted me up, helped me up to the house, calmed my sobs down. She packed my bags while I just sat there on the couch, wondering what just happened.

When she told me that we were leaving, I refused. I told her that he'd come back and we'd talk and all of this would be over.

Surprisingly, she agreed and we waited.

We sat there for hours, with my journals scattered around us – I didn't let her pack those.

Give up hope, Violet, she said, after a while. *He isn't coming back. I know men like him. He's a predator who's looking for innocent girls like you.*

I asked her then, about the article in the paper and if she was behind it. She said yes.

"And now, you have proof. You've seen it with your own eyes that he's not coming back. He discarded you. So let's go. Don't pin your hopes on him."

To make her happy and to not argue with her anymore, I did leave. But I didn't give up hope.

I haven't. I won't.

I trust him.

As crazy as that sounds after what happened. After he pulled that move on me, called my mother like that.

But the thing is: I didn't before. I didn't trust him, not completely – he was right. I hid things from him and I lied to him because even after everything he did for me, there was a teeny-tiny part of me that thought he'd be like everyone else in my life. I was too scared.

I'm not scared now.

I mean, I am. Of course I am, a little. But I'm choosing to be brave. I'm choosing to be what he made me realize I am.

I even tell Nelson that when I go for our session. We sit on our respective couches and he smiles at me.

I smile back.

Then he inches up his glasses and asks in his friendly, non-threatening voice, "So how was yoga camp?"

There's an amused glint in his eyes and I let out a broken laugh.

Moon and magic.

I hear his words in my ears and the answer slips out. "Magical."

"Was it?"

I nod, picking at the threads on his sofa. "I learned a lot."

"What did you learn?"

I glance up at him. "That I'm in love with a man who ended up sending me away."

He nods at that, gravely. "How do you feel about him now?"

I shrug. "I love him. I know he'll be back."

Nelson pauses. I know that pause. He's deliberating, trying to come up with a way to break bad news to me.

These might be just crutches, Violet. These might be keeping you from dealing with the real issue.

"What if he doesn't?"

I know what he means.

I've been to enough therapists and doctors to know that they don't tell you to *do* things. They ask you questions and give you a chance to realize things on your own.

Oh, and they are realists.

They want you to have realistic expectations. They want you to make goals and wish for things that you can make happen. They want you to have control of your thoughts and your actions. Because they want you to live a healthy life.

I'm all for that. At least, I am now.

I want a healthy life. I want to deal with my issues. I don't want to deny anything like I did before because it was easier.

This isn't denial though, my trust in him.

I'm not denying what happened. I'm not denying that he hurt me. I'm not denying that it hurts to breathe. It hurts to wake up every morning day after day. It hurts that it's almost been a week and he isn't here yet.

It hurts so much that I cry into my pillow every night and beg for him to come to me. I beg for him to come back in my dreams.

So this isn't a case of denial. This is a case of pure faith.

This is trust.

"He'll come," I tell Nelson, calmly.

Nelson puts a finger on his lips. "Okay."

Smiling at his obvious disbelief that he's trying to hide behind his cool mask, I say, "So I want you to teach me how to get rid of my crutches because I learned something else at the *magical* yoga camp."

"What?"

"That I'm brave. And that if I want, I can work on myself. I can learn to live in the Outside world."

And I want to.

I don't want to be shy or anxious or at least, work on not being those things. I've been those things my entire life. Long before, I hid behind my sunglasses and cap, I used my hair and my headphones as my crutches.

I don't want that anymore.

I want to be this new me, the one I discovered while I was with him.

The one who looks people in the eyes and doesn't hide behind her crutches.

The one who's wild and beauty.

Anyway, same thing happens when the girls come to visit. They all tell me to move on, look at me with pity and throw me sad smiles, hug me like someone has died, and I don't want to accept that.

Through it all, I keep smiling.

I keep my trust in him.

I keep it even when Brian comes to visit.

At first, I can't believe it. I can't believe that I'm seeing him. That he's here. He was supposed to be somewhere in California. And he looks it, too.

He looks tan. Not to mention, he looks tall and broad and so unlike my best friend whom I haven't seen in a year.

My *best friend*.

I'm so shocked that I don't move from my spot on the couch. We keep staring at each other, then he throws me a sheepish smile and I can't stop myself.

I spring up from my seat and run to him where he's standing at the door that the housekeeper has just opened.

I give him a tight hug, which he returns, and I can't help but squeal, "Oh my God, what are you doing here?"

But as soon as I ask it, my heart starts pounding. My breaths go haywire. I break the hug and stare at him with wide eyes.

With eyes full of hope.

I don't have to spell it out for him. We were best friends — still are. He knows what I'm asking him.

I'm asking about his dad. About Graham. I'm asking if he's here, if he has finally come back for me.

"You wanna come sit by the pool with me?" he responds instead, and my heart deflates.

He's not here.

Not yet.

I nod, giving him a brave smile. "Yeah."

We go around the house to the pool and sit on the edge, dangling our legs in the water. It feels like old times. The sun shining on us and the neighborhood all calm and quiet with the occasional whoosh of a car driving by.

"He told me to come see you," he says, and I whip my eyes over to him.

Brian's squinting at something in the water.

"He did?"

He nods slowly. "He said you needed me." He swallows and glances at me. "He said you needed a friend right now."

My doomsday brain starts ticking. My anxious thoughts start to consume all my faith and my trust and everything in between.

You know, when you suffer from anxiety, everything is a disaster. Everything is a catastrophe waiting to happen.

You drown in them, in your bad thoughts. You try to swim across sometimes. You try to get to the shore, get to safety where you can distinguish between rational and irrational thoughts. What your gut feeling is and what is fake – a telling from your ill brain.

But sometimes, it's really hard. To swim, I mean. It's exhausting. You wanna give up. It's easy to give up.

And for a second, I want to.

I want to give up again and assume the worst. I want to lie down and let the anxiety take over and assume that Graham sent his son because he isn't going to come himself.

So I close my eyes and take a deep breath. I curl my fingers around the edge of the swimming pool and plant my butt on the cement.

I'm not budging. I'm not giving up and taking the easy road. I've done that enough.

I'm brave.

"Yeah, I needed a friend," I whisper to Brian when I open my eyes. "I was kinda… hurting."

"What happened?" he asks, all concerned.

"He didn't tell you?"

Shoving a hand through his hair, he replies, "No. He called me from Denver. He said he had to do something. But he told me that you were gone and that he needed me to go see you. That's all. I came as soon as I could."

Denver?

"What's he doing in Denver?" I think out loud.

Brian shrugs. "I've got no clue. I've literally got no clue about anything right now."

Despite myself, his exasperation makes me chuckle. "It doesn't matter what happened. I'm here and he's not."

Not yet.

He goes silent for a few moments.

We watch the water together and I try not to cry, I try not to tear up at the pain in my chest when he says, "I should've asked you out."

"What?"

He faces me, his features open and raw, kind of a younger version of Graham's. Although Graham is a master of the blank expression. It's very rare for him to show anything. Well, except the day he sent me away.

That day he looked like he had nothing to live for.

He looked like a man without hope.

Now, Brian sighs next to me and I see his turbulent hazel eyes that remind me of his dad.

"I should've asked you out long before that night. I should've made my move," he says.

I search his features. "Yeah, but it's irrelevant now, right? Even if you did, you would've realized that you didn't like me so it's kinda moot. Isn't it?"

I was about to chuckle, but then he looks away and it hits me.

Oh God.

It fucking hits me, and momentarily, all the heartbreak, all the pain I've been feeling for the past week, gets buried down under this… thing that I've discovered.

"You still… You still like me," I breathe out, horrified.

He clenches his jaw and that is such a perfect mimic of how Graham does it that I feel dazed. Both by what I've discovered and the fact that I love his dad.

I see his dad in every move he makes and it's gotten worse now, after living with Graham for weeks.

Brian's still looking away from me when I ask, "Why did you… Why did you say that you didn't? That it was over."

Finally, he gives me his eyes, pain-riddled. "Because I hurt you. I hurt you in the worst way possible and I wanted to make up for it. I wanted you to be with him. I wanted you to be with someone you loved and I wanted you to do it without the guilt. And I wanted him to be with you. I hurt him a lot, too. I wanted to take care of him for once, like he took care of me."

"Brian, I-I don't… know what to say."

He smiles sadly. "You don't have to say anything. You love my dad and that's okay. And at the end of the day, you're right. Even if I did ask you out, you would've said no because you've always been in love with him. I just…"

Brian completely faces me and says urgently, "Vi, I don't know what happened. Between you and my dad. Why you're here and he's in Denver but Vi… he's not cut out for this. He's not a relationship kind of a guy and I don't want you to –"

I reach out and take his hand to make him stop. "He is cut out for this."

After that, there's no talk of Graham.

Except when Brian tells me not to say anything to him.

Brian says it will hurt his dad and he's done hurting the man who raised him over something that was never his to begin with.

I don't know how everything became so tangled and tragic. I don't know how me loving one man turned into the pain of another guy but I promise Brian. I promise to never tell Graham about it.

So at night when I go up to the roof, I write a wish, a dream I have for Brian. I wish he finds someone, someone who will take away his pain.

I don't want my best friend to hurt. Especially not from a lovesick heart.

I know how that feels.

I know how it aches and makes you cry while you sit on the roof of your house and watch the moon at midnight and wish for the man you love to come back.

You wish for it so much that when it happens, you don't believe it.

And I don't.

When I hear a violent screeching of tires on the road and see someone jump out of a black truck, someone who doesn't even wait to close the door behind him, I don't believe what I'm seeing.

I don't believe that there's a man out on the street. He's tall and broad and his legs are planted wide.

And as soon as he jumped out of his vehicle and took a few steps toward the driveway, he lifted his face and his eyes found me up here.

Like he knew where to look already. He knew where to find me at this time of night.

It would horrify me that a stranger is staring at me like that. It's exactly what happened the night I lost control of my car.

But it's not a stranger.

It's him and it's real.

Because as soon as he found me, he didn't wait for even a second. He started to stride toward me.

21

Some dreams are dreams.
They're flimsy and foggy
and surreal. But some dreams
are more than dreams.
Some dreams are clear, sharp.
Some dreams breathe.
They have a soul. Like him and me.

~The Diary of a Blooming Violet, Age 19

He came back.

Oh my God, he came back.

I don't even stop to think.

I shove away the journal and flashlight from my lap and climb down from the roof so fast – faster than I've ever done before – that I can't catch my breath.

Only when my feet touch the ground do I take a deep breath, a deep, hiccupping breath because I can see him clearly.

I can see his face under the tiny lights of the driveway.

He's breathing hard like me. That's the first thing.

Like, really hard.

The kind of breaths you take when you break the surface

after being underwater for a long time. The very first, sweet breaths of life.

And then, there are his eyes.

Gosh, his dark, *dark* eyes.

They look haggard and tired and in some major need of sleep, they're bright. Brighter than these man-made, artificial lights in the driveway.

Brighter than the moon I've been watching.

"You could've fallen," he says and I decide I was wrong.

His voice is the most extraordinary thing about him right now.

It's barely there. It's so low and thick and whatever is there, whatever sound is left inside his throat, is pure gravel.

It makes my bare toes curl on the heated cement. "I'm used to it."

"You are, aren't you?" He flicks his eyes over my shoulder to the tree for a second before focusing back on me. "That's how I saw you, that first time. It was my first night here and I saw you grabbing hold of that branch and scaling it up to the roof. I'd never seen someone climb a tree so fast. I thought you were an intruder or something but then you sat down and took out your journal and started writing. I realized that you were the girl next door."

Girl next door.

Yeah, that's what I was and he saw me the same day I saw him: on my sixteenth birthday. It's weird that I never asked him this. I never asked him exactly when he saw me.

But now I know.

I know that we saw each other the same day, maybe hours

apart but we've had this obsession for exactly the same amount of time.

Exactly the same, that's what we are.

Before I can form a word, he continues, "I'd look forward to that, you climbing up to the roof every night. In fact, that used to be the highlight of my day. Watching you in moonlight."

That pushes his chest to the extreme. That makes him punch his shirt – is it even buttoned correctly? – with a gusty breath as he shakes his head once. "I've beaten myself up a lot for that. Watching you, I mean."

I swallow, letting his gaze wash over me, letting him look at me as I look at him. As I still try to soak in the fact that he's here.

I know I've been saying this to people all along and I trusted that he'd come but God, it's happening.

And it feels so real and sharp and breathtaking.

Maybe because he's saying things, telling me things.

He never says anything; I'm the one who does the talking, which is a surprise in itself, really. Because I don't talk much with others.

Only with him.

I'm a different me only with him.

"You're here," I whisper when he goes quiet.

"Yeah."

"Why?"

He swallows. "I came for you."

He came for me.

His answer is more potent than anything else about him right now. More drastic and weightier.

I have to close my eyes for a second and just let it sink in.

Again, I knew that but still.

He's here for me.

Not only that, but he's saying the exact words to me that I said to him the first night I found him at the bar.

I came for you.

That's what I said, and now he's saying it back.

When I open my eyes again, I notice that he's come closer. He's taken a few steps toward me and his focus is on my feet.

I wiggle my toes, confused, and look at them myself. They seem perfectly okay to me, bare and small.

"You left behind your nail polish," he says.

And I realize the reason for his focus. My colorless toenails.

"I left behind a lot of things."

"You did," he confirms.

It's true. I did. I did leave behind my journals, the dresses he bought me.

My home.

I left behind my home when he sent me away and I have to hear it from him. I have to hear it from his mouth. All the reasons why he sent me away and all the reasons why he's back now.

"Why?" I ask him again, my hands fisted in the hem of my red pajama bottoms. "Why are you here for me?"

His chest shifts again and so does his jaw. He clenches it for a second before saying, "Because I fucked up."

I raise my chin. "Fucked up what?"

He notices my defiance. He notices how tight I'm holding myself, and I am.

I *am* holding myself tight.

I *am* standing my ground. I *am* gluing my feet to my spot because damn it, I'm mad at him. I'm fucking furious at him.

Yeah, I've been waiting for him. Yeah, I knew he'd come but he hurt me. He hurt me in the worst possible way and I'm not budging until he tells me everything in his own words.

I'm not going to him. Not this time.

He *has* to come to me.

As if to say that he heard me, he takes another step toward me. He closes a little bit of the distance between us and my heart starts pounding.

"My promise to you," he rumbles.

"What promise?" I try to inject some sternness in my tone.

Another breath but this one is short. "That I'd keep you safe. I'd protect you. But I sent you away. I sent you back to the people, to the town who've always hurt you. And I hurt you myself in the process."

My eyes sting with tears.

Bingo.

He hurt me.

He got that right. But that doesn't mean I'm going to let him off the hook that easily.

No. Not after what he did.

I clench all my muscles, all of them, as I ask, "Why? Why did you send me away? And why did you send me away like that?"

"Because I wanted you to hate me. I needed you to hate me. So I did the worst thing that I could think of," he confesses with a penetrating stare.

"You wanted me to hate you."

"Yes. I wanted you to stop loving me and hate me, instead."

"Why?" I ask again, probably for the third time.

"Because I thought I was doing the right thing. I thought I was doing you a favor. I thought I was..."

"You were what?"

My words – as inconsequential as they might be – seem to have hit him somewhere. His gut, maybe. His chest, his heart, I don't know. But they have hit his body and he flinches with the strike.

He ducks his head down and scrubs his face with his palm. He looks even more tired now. More tired than when he arrived here a few minutes ago and my heart squeezes for him. God knows how many sleepless nights he's seen.

I haven't slept either ever since we came back from Colorado.

The strange thing is that I've never been a good sleeper until I slept in his bed, right next to him. And when he wasn't there this past week, I became an insomniac again.

I became a child of the moon again. Lonely and invisible.

And I'm so mad at him, for giving me all the wonderful things and then, taking them away just like that.

So fucking mad that I almost shout, "Tell me, Mr. Edwards. I wanna know why you want me to hate you. Why can't I love you? What's so awful about loving you?"

At last, he lifts his face, all exhausted and sharply angled. "Because we come from different worlds, Violet."

"What?"

He scoffs and looks at the sky for a second before saying in a hoarse tone, "Different worlds. We're from different worlds, you and me." He shakes his head. "My world is lonely. And I've always lived there. In a lonely world. I've always lived in a world where people leave. Where people break promises. Where people are selfish. Where no matter what you do, you always feel like you haven't done enough, that you *can't* do enough. That you're not worthy. At least, not worthy enough for them to stay. That's the world I live in. My mom left when I was five. I don't even remember her. And as tragic as that was, it would've been okay if it was only my mother. But with her, my father left too. Of course, he was there. Physically. But he was never *really* there. He'd drink. He'd talk about my mother. He'd promise me that he'd stop but he'd pick up the bottle again the next day.

"So I got used to that, you understand? I got used to living in a lonely world. I got used to living in a world where people don't mean what they say. I got used to cleaning up after my father. I got used to distracting myself with the first thing that came along: football. You asked me that, remember? If I wanted to be this big football player? The truth is that I never really liked football. I never really liked playing it. I was good at it. It was easy and it took me away from home. It gave me an escape and that was it. I never really cared beyond that because again, I got used to it. I got used to living in a world where I didn't want anything other than that. Other than distractions and going through the motions and just making it to the next day until I could escape the town I was living in.

"And then, my father died; cirrhosis, and that time finally came. I should've been ecstatic. I should've been happy. I mean, yeah it was devastating that my father died but by then, he was so checked out from the world that he was as good as dead for a long time anyway. But instead of being happy and relieved and ecstatic, I was something else. Do you want to know what I was?"

My tears are blurring my vision now. I didn't think I'd start crying so easily, that I'd give up so quickly and my heart would force me to go to him.

But it's happened.

He sounds so lost and sad that I almost want him to stop talking. That I want to wrap my arms around him and tell him that everything will be okay, but I don't.

Because I think he needs this.

He needs to say all these things. So I stand here, glued to my spot as before, not because I want to be away from him but because I want him to get this out.

"What were you?" I whisper.

He swallows again and replies, "Terrified. I was terrified."

Frowning, he pauses to gather all his thoughts. "I was scared that I was going to do the very thing that I wanted to do for the longest time: escape. I even had a scholarship for a college. And I wanted that scholarship. I worked hard for it. I wanted something that would take me away from the cabin, from my dad and when the time came for me to go, I was fucking shaking with fear.

"But then, Brian happened. I was terrified about that too, about taking care of a baby. I didn't know anything about it. I didn't know if I could do it. But I did. In fact, I threw myself into it, into taking care of my kid. I became everything he wanted me to be. Everything he needed and I did it happily like every other parent, I imagine. It was all about him, his homework, his practice, his friends, his school, his needs, his wants. Everything was about him. I became his father and nothing else. Until you. Until I saw you and something happened to me."

My heart skips a beat when he says that.

Something happened to him...

You do something to me...

He said that too, and even then, my heart squeezed for him. Squeezed for that look of confusion I saw on his face.

He's not confused now, just vulnerable and I breathe out, "What happened?"

He brings his hand to his chest, right where his heart is. I imagine him feeling his own heartbeats under his fingers.

I loved doing that. I loved feeling the beats of his heart whenever I slept with my head on his chest. It was soothing to me.

I hope it's soothing to him too.

He needs that, in this moment.

And since I'm standing all the way over here, I want his heart to give him peace until the time comes for me to close the distance and do it myself.

"When I saw you, Violet, it felt like someone stabbed me in the chest," he rasps.

My eyes go wide. "What?"

He chuckles; it's brittle and thin. "Or at least, it felt like it. I saw you up on the roof, with your thick, gorgeous hair and your arms open wide, something got lodged inside my chest, just under my heart and for the longest time, it felt like a knife of some sort. Something that made me... different. It wasn't that, though."

"W-what was it?"

"My soul," he whispers. "It was my soul waking up. The thing that keeps a man alive, came alive in me when I saw you. You woke up my soul, Violet."

"I did?"

He nods. "Yeah. I'd watch you after that. I couldn't help myself and I was angry about that, you know. I was angry about watching a girl half my age. I was angry that something was happening to me. I planted a fucking rose garden – something I hadn't done in years – just to watch that girl. Just to have an excuse to look at her at night. God, I thought I was losing my mind.

"Suddenly, I started to feel things. I started to want things for myself. I started to crave and I was so used to not doing any of those things, I was so used to not wanting anything for myself that I didn't know what to do. I didn't know how to handle it. I didn't know how to handle you. So I kept away from you. I kept away from you for so many reasons until I didn't. Until the night of your eighteenth birthday.

"And then, everything happened and months later, you found me at my lowest. Jesus Christ, I wanted you to go away. You were so young. My son liked you. You made me *feel* things."

He scrubs a hand over his face again. "And I wanted you to leave me alone so badly. So fucking badly but you never listened. You never left. You never went anywhere. Not only that, you saved me. You went and goddamn saved me and finally, I realized something."

At this, he gives me a look that I've never seen from him. He gives me a look of pure and utter vulnerability. A look that tells me that he's undone.

And it becomes so hard to stand here.

So I give in and take a step toward him. "What did you realize?"

"You told me that your sunglasses and your cap are crutches, yeah? You use them to hide from the world. I use crutches too, Violet."

My heart is slamming in my chest now. Slamming and slamming. This was so not what I expected him to say. Not at all.

"You do?"

"Yeah. I hide behind taking care of my son and a boring, dead-end job because it's easier. It's easier to provide for him because I should be doing that anyway, and to work a job that I hate than to face the truth."

"What's the truth?"

"The truth is that I've never really lived. I've gone through the motions. I've survived, yes. But I've never really been alive. I've never really had a dream of my own. I never had the luxury to dream a dream. Maybe if my life was different and I lived in a world that was less lonely and selfish, I would've learned. I would've learned to live, to dream, to want. But I never lived in that world, Violet, and I don't know how to do any of those things. I don't know if I can. So I used crutches. I hid behind things just because it was easier than to face reality. To face the fact that I'm halfway done with my life and I know nothing about dreams and wants and wishes. But I'm going to try."

So far, his expression has been lost. Both like a little boy who forgot the dream he had last night and an old man at the end of his life who never got to fulfill any of the dreams he saw.

Because he was living for everyone else and neglected to live for himself.

But his expression has changed now. Somewhere at the end of it, it became fierce and determined.

His nostrils flare and he fists his hands at his sides, as if strength has finally returned in his body.

"I'm going to try. I'm going to learn, Violet."

"Learn what?"

"Poetry."

"Poetry?"

He nods; it's a jerk of a movement. "I can learn to write poetry. How hard can it be? It's a drunk man writing about his feelings, right? I read a poem once, *Anesthesia* by this guy. Abrams or something?"

"Thomas Abrams?"

"Yeah. Something like that."

As choked up as I am right now, I get an urge to smile but I suppress it; Thomas Abrams is super famous for his poetry and stuff. "He's a pretty big deal actually."

"Who cares? If he can do it, I can do it too." Before I can say anything else, he goes on. "I can paint your nails too. I've done it once, I can do it again. I can hold your hand and walk down the beach with you. Even though my hands are rough and scratched up and I fucking hate the beach – too many people. But I can do all of that. I can learn to do all of that and more, Violet."

"You wanna learn all of that?"

At last, he takes those final steps and stands right where he can touch me. He reaches out and cups my cheek and I don't have the strength to push him away or be this mad but calm girl.

I don't have the strength not to fist his shirt and look up at him as he wipes my tears, which I didn't know that I was shedding.

"Yes. For you. I'll learn all of that. I'll learn to be soft. I'll learn to be gentle and tender. I'll learn to dream when I've got my eyes closed. Because I don't think I can live in my world anymore. I don't like my world, Violet. I want to live in a different world."

"A different world?"

I realize that I'm parroting his words but I don't know what else to do when he's looking at me with such emotions and intensity.

He's stealing all my thoughts and words looking like he just stepped out of a dream.

My dream.

"Yeah. A world where colors are bright and gorgeous. Where you dance in the moonlight. Where you have a vegetable garden right next to a rose garden. A world where the air smells like strawberries and candies. A world where an eighteen-year-old girl sneaks into the backyard of a man she wants, a man she's been watching, a man who's been watching her as well, and steals his roses. A world where she steps on his shoes because she's so tiny that she can't get to his mouth and kisses him. A world where she follows him just because she thinks she's wronged him. A world where she saves him from himself. I want to live in your world, Violet. A world of moon and magic, if you'll let me."

God, he wants to live in my world.

The world I created because I didn't want to live in the

world I was given. And he wants to live there, in my imaginary world.

He wants to live there with me.

Oh *God*, my heart is so full and I need him to stop talking so I can kiss him right now.

"Graham, I –"

"I fucked up, okay?" He cuts me off, instead. "I know that. And I probably succeeded too. You probably hate me." His fingers flex and jerk on my cheek at the thought. "But you don't have to love me, all right. It's okay if you don't."

"But I –"

He cuts me off again, flicking his eyes back and forth between mine. "If you could put all your dreams in the palm of my hand like you did with your journals, if you could be that brave, then I could be too. I could be brave for you. Because you inspire me to be brave, baby."

More tears fall down my cheeks and saturate the pad of his thumbs. "I inspire you to be brave?"

He nods. "Yeah. You do. You inspire me to live, Violet. You inspire me to live in a world where a brave girl saves a dangerous, old beast and shows him to be brave like her."

A broken laugh escapes me.

But he doesn't smile, no. He doesn't break his focus or his intensity. He keeps looking at me, wanting me to understand.

"So you don't have to love me, Violet," he continues with a low tone. "Because I love you enough for the both of us. And I'm gonna learn to show that, all right? I promise you that. I'm going to learn to show my love to you. It might not happen overnight, but I'll keep at it. All I want is for you to trust me. Just trust me."

I dig my knuckles into his hard stomach and I can hear his heartbeats there, deep in his gut, banging against my fists.

Feeling those beats on my hands, I whisper, "I didn't before. I didn't trust you."

Pain slashes through his features. "I know. But I'd never... I'd never think that —"

"I know." I nod. "I know. I guess I always knew. I always knew that I could trust you. I think it was... my doomsday brain. It wouldn't let me tell you. It kept saying that I'm not good enough and... yeah."

He presses his hands on my cheeks. "You're magnificent, Violet, you got that? You're fucking perfect."

More tears well up and river down. "I'm not fine, Graham. Everything is not fine. I have this thing inside of me and I'm so scared. I know I'm brave; I know that. But it scares me that I have to live with it for the rest of my life and —"

He puts his forehead over mine. "Hey, hey, look at me. Look at me. We'll do this. We'll do this together, okay? We'll take it one day at a time. One step at a time. I've got you. I asked around, all right? There's a bunch of doctors in Denver we can go to. I bought books and stuff. I'm —"

"Is that why you were in Denver?"

He studies me a beat and then nods.

"Is that why it took you so long to come? And you sent Brian, instead."

"I wanted to make sure I knew everything. I wanted you to trust me."

I laugh, then.

It's not a loud laugh or anything. In fact, it's laced with tears. But somehow, it's the purest, most joyful laughter I've ever produced.

It's acceptance.

It's what I felt the day I accepted that I loved him since the beginning.

This is what I'm feeling right now. Accepted and loved.

I laugh and I cry and my head drops down to his chest.

God, I love him. He's an idiot but I love him.

He buries his hand in my hair and presses my forehead into his chest even more. I take a second to rub my nose in his shirt, smell his thick, outdoorsy smell. It reminds me of the cabin so much – our rose garden, the bed, the woods surrounding our home.

I have to pull myself away and tell him. I'm getting so impatient now. I need him to take me away.

"I've been so mad at you, you know. You hurt me in the worst possible way. You made me cry and everyone kept saying that you wouldn't come. That you didn't care."

"Baby, I –"

I put a finger on his mouth. "But I knew. I knew you'd come. Do you know how I knew?"

He swallows another lump of emotion and breathes against that finger of mine, shaking his head once.

"You kissed me," I whisper. "That day. When you sent me away. You stepped up to me and you wiped my tears off and you kissed me on the forehead, and you said what you did on my eighteenth birthday. You said, *go home*. Even though you wanted to kiss me that night, you kept pushing me away. You kept denying yourself. You kept doing the right thing. And I knew. I knew you were doing the right thing on my nineteenth birthday too. You just needed to realize that what you thought was the right thing wasn't really the right thing. And I knew you'd realize it. I knew that because I trusted you. I did and I do. I trust you, Graham."

A breath rushes out of his mouth and my finger absorbs it. It travels down my veins and spreads across my body. That breath of relief.

I take off my hand and shake my head at him. "And you're so stupid if you think that you can make me hate you."

I see the full impact of my words register on his body bit by bit.

At first, he frowns but when he realizes what I've said, his eyes sweep across my face to confirm it. His lips part and the biggest impact is how he tightens his hold on me. How his fingers in my hair spasm and jerk before he digs the pads into my scalp.

Finally, he says in a rough but relieved voice, "Thank fuck you're smarter than me."

"Duh."

His lips stretch into a lopsided smile that I absolutely adore, and I step up on his feet. "I wanna go home. I don't like it here."

He shifts a hand down my spine and splays it on my lower back, pressing our bodies together. "Home. Yeah. It didn't feel like home before."

I grab the collar of his shirt and tell him sternly, "It's our home now."

His eyes flare with emotions. "It is."

"Good." Then, "And I think we need new floors."

His chest reverberates with a chuckle. "We do?"

"Yes. We also need a bigger rose garden because I have ideas."

"You have ideas."

I nod slowly, biting my lip and peeking at him through my eyelashes. "Yes."

A current passes between us, or rather we absorb each other's desire since there's hardly any space left between us for anything to pass.

I wind my arms around his neck and he puts his hands under my ass to lift me up. I hang onto him like a spider monkey.

When I'm all adjusted, he grabs the back of my neck and demands, "Tell me about them."

I rub my fingers in his thick beard and kiss his cheek softly. "Only if you kiss me right now."

"Yeah?"

"Uh-huh. And I don't want it here."

"Where do you want it?"

God, his sexy voice always gets me. *Always.*

It makes me wild. The thing I become when I'm with him.

 "In your old backyard where everything started."

He tightens his hold on my neck as his eyes narrow. "You know there are other people living there now, right?"

"Yup. There's this lady with a bunch of cats. And I think her husband keeps staring at me."

I don't know, actually. I caught him staring once but I don't know if he keeps doing that. I just said it because I want my beast now.

I want him to come out in all his possessive glory.

"Does he now?"

His dangerous voice sends a dark thrill down my spine. "Yeah. So you should just claim me, you know. Show him that you're my boyfriend."

"I'm your boyfriend."

I wrinkle my nose. "Yes. You are. That's what the kids my age are calling it these days."

Amusement flickers over his features as he begins to move. "Yeah, I wouldn't know now, would I?"

Laughing, I kiss him while he walks us to the very spot where everything started. There's no rose garden there; it's covered up by a patch of grass and the loungers and things are different.

Everything is different, yet it's still the same.

I still feel the same way about him. I still have the same urgency in me to kiss him. But before he can close his mouth on me, I whisper against his lips, "Graham?"

"Yeah?"

"I hate the beach too."

"You do?"

"Uh-huh. Too many people."

"Yeah, too many people."

"And I don't think I like poetry all that much."

"You don't, huh?"

"Nope. I think I like it better when you talk dirty to me."

A muscle jumps in his cheek and I know it's lust. "I'll keep that in mind, Jailbait."

"You do that, Strawberry Man."

He comes closer to me but I stop him once again. "Oh, one more thing."

"What?"

"I love you."

He puffs out a breath over my lips, his eyes widening a fraction as if he still can't believe it. Still can't believe I love a man like him.

"I love you too, baby," he whispers.

And then, he's kissing me.

On the same spot.

In the same backyard with probably the same people who're sleeping right now around the neighborhood.

Or maybe not.

Maybe they're not sleeping.

Because I think the new owners just turned on their lights. And another one came on in my own house.

Whoops.

I think I woke up everyone with my kiss again.

It's okay.

Because in his arms, I'm wildness and beauty. And in mine, he's my beast.

It's okay because I'm kissing the man of my dreams and he's kissing me back.

21 & His...

Someone is watching me.

It's a girl.

I didn't notice her before. I was staring at my phone, trying to look at the list of things I need from the grocery store before I can go home.

Man, I so want to go home but there's still a ton of stuff left to buy. And I don't plan on getting out in the world for the next couple of weeks, so it has to be now.

Plus, it's a big day tomorrow.

Like, really big. Phone will be ringing off the hook.

First, I'll get calls from all my girls – The Heartstone Sisters – Renn, Penny and Willow, who just had the cutest baby girl ever, Fallon. Ah, I can't wait to babble with that little cutie on FaceTime.

After that, I'm sure Brian will call too.

I haven't seen him since Christmas last year when he came to visit with his new girlfriend. That's still going strong actually, and I couldn't be happier for him.

Then again, that guy dates a lot like he did back in high school. So far none of the girls have stuck around and the wish I made for him the day he came to see me in Connecticut two years ago is still unfulfilled.

But I'm keeping my fingers crossed that this is the real deal. That my best friend finally falls in love after the inadvertent pain we caused each other.

Oh and my mom might call too.

We talk occasionally and over the last two years, we've come closer. I'm still convinced that it was the story about my real dad that helped pave the way. Although, it could also be the fact that she's waiting for the day I'll wake up from my dream and get my heart broken – since I chose to run away from Connecticut again, despite all her warnings to give up hope – so she can pick up the pieces and say *I told you so*.

But the thing is I'm not waking up again.

The thing is I live in a new world now.

A world of dreams. A dreamland.

Anyway, I've got another person in my life, my sister, Fiona. Although I don't think she's calling. We hardly ever talk and *some people* in my life don't like her.

Well, *one person* in my life doesn't like her all that much. He doesn't even like my mother all that much either, but he tolerates her because I tell him to be nice to her.

Which reminds me I have to tell him again because big day tomorrow.

But that's not the point.

The point is that a girl is staring at me.

It's not a very hard stare, honestly.

The girl who's doing it is looking at me for a few seconds before focusing away, toward the fresh vegetables; we're at the produce section.

So the prickling – the thing that happens on my scalp and the back of my neck when someone stares at me for longer than acceptable – isn't very continuous. It comes and goes with her eyes on me like a flash of lightning and maybe that's why I missed it.

But I can feel it now.

I can feel the prickle. I can feel the flush spreading around my throat. I can feel my heart picking up speed and my doomsday brain banging.

Chaos.

That's what anxiety is.

It's mayhem inside your head. It makes you jumpy and restless. It makes you want to hide or run away to a place where there's silence. And peace.

Yeah, it's a peace-stealer, anxiety.

There are many ways to get rid of it and in the past, I've done it by taking the easy way out. By denying that it's there or by using crutches.

But these days, I handle things head on.

It's not easy. So before I can chicken out, I glance up from my phone and look directly at the girl.

And smile.

"Hi," I say.

She appears startled, her eyes going wide and her lips parting a little. That wasn't my intention at all though. I was just trying to get control of the situation, as my therapist, Kate, says.

Get control of the situation, Vi. That's the best way to beat anxiety. Get out of your head and try to do things, pay attention to the surroundings.

"I'm sorry. I didn't mean to startle you," I chuckle slightly. "I just thought you wanted to say something to me."

Although for the life of me I can't imagine what.

My knee-jerk reaction is to assume the worst. Maybe she wants to tell me that my dull blonde/brown hair is a little too dull or my lips are a little too thick. Maybe she wants to comment on how pale I am.

All these thoughts run into my head but still, I smile. I keep smiling at her, waiting for her answer.

"Sorry." She chuckles too, a little bashfully. "I just... I love your dress."

Surprised, I look at it myself. I'm still not a dress or make-up kind of girl but I do wear both sometimes.

I sweep a hand down the skirt and take a deep breath.

See?

She gave me a compliment. It wasn't anything bad that my doomsday brain made me think. Everything is really fine.

"Thank you," I tell the girl, looking up and smiling again. "I love it too."

"I just love the colors."

"You do?"

"Yeah. I love how pink and red go together."

Okay, now this makes me happy.

Like, really, genuinely happy with no hint of anxiety at all. It fills me with warmth and safety, and I look down at my dress again.

It *is* a pretty dress.

Pink in color, like really girly pink – my favorite, with giant red roses on it – his favorite.

The man who bought it for me. For whom, I wear dresses and make-up. Not because he asks me to but because I want to.

"They do, don't they? I love that too," I say, looking back at the girl.

"I know."

And just because I'm bursting with happiness, I tell her, "He bought it for me."

I tip my chin up and point in his direction. The girl turns and looks at what I want her to see.

Him.

My honey.

That's what I like to call him these days. He's got a lot of names though.

Strawberry Man. The Beast. Mr. Edwards.

Graham.

And the best part? I get to call him by every single one of them whenever and wherever.

Right now, I wanna call him honey.

Because of what he's doing – he's in the candy aisle, directly opposite to me, buying me lollipops, and not just one pack of them either. He reaches up and I see him going for at least a couple of them, which he then proceeds to throw in his cart.

Gosh and he looks so sexy doing it too.

His big hands dwarf the colorful packets of candy and his frown as he reads their label is so totally in contrast with the cheerfulness of lollipops.

But that's how he does things, my Graham.

With care and precision, especially if it involves me.

"He loves me in red. But my favorite color is pink. So we compromised," I continue as I watch him buy me candy.

"Oh," the girl says in a surprised sort of way as she looks away from Graham and focuses back on me.

There's a glint in her eyes. It's a glint that I'm familiar with and if I'm being honest, it's a glint I *kinda* have a problem with.

At least, sometimes.

It's a glint that's speculative and that says she's wondering about us. She's wondering if we're together, Graham and me.

Over the past two years, ever since I started going out and mingling with the world – all alongside Graham, we've gotten quite a few glints and looks like this.

First of all, it's the fact that he's huge and he dominates over everyone around him. He's doing that even now. In his plaid shirt and hiking boots, he's the tallest man in the aisle. Tallest and broadest. So when we walk down the street together – him, all giant and me, all tiny – people stop to take another look.

But most importantly, it's the age gap.

I'm twenty and he's thirty-eight, eighteen years older than me. And people notice.

They notice the lines around his eyes that have deepened and increased in number over the course of time I've known him.

They notice the silver hair in his trimmed beard and his sideburns. They notice the maturity on his face and in his demeanor.

They notice all the things about him that make him so freaking irresistible to me.

Often times, people are okay with it. They don't give us a second glance. Other times, they stare and wonder but don't say anything. But occasionally, we'll come across someone who stares and wonders and also says things.

Turns out, this girl falls in the third category.

"Is he... Is he like, your boyfriend?"

Good.

I'm glad.

Surprisingly, I've come to be a fan of facing things head on. I like when people are upfront. It doesn't give my doomsday brain time to make up disastrous scenarios – something Kate pointed out to me in one of our sessions when I told her that I hate it when strangers talk to me.

Besides, stares are still a trigger for me. I can manage things better but still.

Still looking at Graham, I answer, "No. He's not my boy-friend."

As if he knows we're talking about him, he lifts his eyes and looks at me.

He likes to do it from time to time, when I'm away from him. He likes to stop whatever he's doing and look up at me, to make sure I'm okay.

I smile as soon as his gaze hits me.

I can't see the color of his eyes from here but I can guess.

They are most probably a warm green just like his expression: all calm and peaceful.

Then I bite my lip and I know that they must be changing colors right about now.

They must be going darker.

And sure enough, I see the effects of it on his body. His chest pushes out with a breath and a lopsided smirk appears on his lips. He's still too severe to smile but he tries.

At the sight of his sexy smirk, I can't stay away from him.

I don't even say goodbye to the girl who's staring at me with confusion over my 'not my boyfriend' comment, I think.

I push my cart across the space, keeping my eyes on him. Our carts bump together when I reach him and leaving it, I approach the man I love.

The man I live in my dreamland with.

"Hey, Mr. Edwards," I greet him.

"Hey," he rasps and yup, his eyes are dark.

Then he glances over to the girl I was talking to. "You okay?"

I tap the front of his sturdy left boot with my sneaker, playfully. "I am."

He frowns slightly. "She bothering you?"

I shake my head, tapping his boot again. "No."

He looks down and shakes his head at my playful gesture. "You sure?"

I smile at him.

He always thinks people are bothering me. In fact, he hates the stares more than I do. Because he knows how triggering they can be for me.

Two years ago when he came back for me and I chose to go to the cabin with him, I was in a really bad place. But Graham, along with my old therapist, Nelson, found me a new person I could go to: Kate.

She's helped me a lot over the years but in the beginning, it was really hard. I'd get triggered so easily. I was afraid of everything in the Outside world. Going to restaurants, parks, movies, taking a walk, everything.

It's been a long road and Graham has been with me every step of the way. So he knows.

He knows how freaked out I can get, and my man hates that.

He hates it so much that he glares at everyone who tries to look at me. He's even gotten into fights with people a couple of times.

Which might happen in about five seconds if I don't put his aggression to rest.

I step toward him, then.

I put my feet over his and wind my arms around his neck, kissing his beard. "Yeah, I'm sure. In fact, she said that my dress is pretty."

His hands settle on my waist as he bows down to get our faces close together. "It's not."

"It's not?"

He shakes his head slowly, his eyes all dark and beautiful. "You're prettier."

God.

My fingers fist in his shirt as something inside my belly flips and tightens. I still can't believe that he finds me beautiful. That he finds me pretty and breathtaking and all the other things he murmurs when we're in our own world like this and he's being sweet to me.

I mean, I believe him but sometimes it's hard.

I've always been insecure and shy and on top of that, I have a doomsday brain. So it's hard to believe positive things about myself.

It's hard to believe that I'm pretty and I'm loved and I'm accepted the way I am.

I try though.

I try because I'm brave and because I trust him with my whole heart.

"I told her you bought it for me," I say, my one hand coming down to his chest and pressing over the spot where his heart is.

"You did?"

"Yup. I told her your favorite color is red but mine is pink, so you bought me a compromise."

"What'd she say?"

"She asked me if you were my boyfriend."

At this, he massages the flesh of my waist. He does it so forcefully and deliciously that I feel every inch of his hardness pushing into my body. "What'd you say?"

"I told her no."

"You did, huh."

I nod, kind of squirming against him. "Because you're not my boyfriend anymore."

"I'm not? So what do the kids call it these days?" he rumbles, all arrogant-like.

I roll my eyes at him. "I think it's husband."

His heart thunders under my palm. Not only that, his eyes flare and the hold he's got on me tightens.

He's actually gotten more possessive and protective ever since he stopped being my boyfriend and became my husband. You'd think that since I'm legally his now, he'd relax a little. But nope.

Marriage has had the opposite effect on my husband.

Even so, you can't tell by the casual tone he uses. "Ah, okay. Husband it is, then."

I narrow my eyes at him. He can be such an ass.

His smirk turns into a dark chuckle.

"Take me home, Mr. Edwards," I order, raising my chin up.

Fuck grocery shopping. Fuck everything.

I need him.

Besides we've been driving for hours from Denver, trying to reach the cabin for the really big day tomorrow.

Oh yeah, we live in Denver now because I go to college.

I started in the spring of last year, when I was able to withstand crowds, and I'm actually liking it. I don't have a ton of friends but I do have some, and all of them love Bukowski. We even have discussions about him.

Isn't that awesome?

"Let's go home," I tell him again, going up on my tiptoes and kissing him on the lips.

Because I can't wait.

Okay fine, marriage has had an opposite effect on me too. I've become greedier for him, hungrier. Maybe because I know he's mine and I can have him whenever I want.

So I kiss him harder.

I know it's a grocery store aisle and I know people are around but I'm feeling wild. I'm feeling like his beauty.

And I want my beast.

He comes for me. He does. The man who's kissing me back becomes the beast for me. He shoves his tongue in my mouth and grabs the back of my neck. He presses our bodies together and I whimper, urging him on.

My husband has this thing about kissing me in public. He takes his cues from me.

When I have bad days and my anxiety is roaring in my ears, it's hard for me to be his beauty. So he holds my hand and walks with me side by side, like my protector.

But on good days, like today, when I feel confident and happy and a little wild, he changes from my man to my beast. He gathers me in his arms and he kisses the fuck out of me.

Because I want him to.

When we come up for air, he rumbles, "Okay, Mrs. Edwards, I'll take you home."

And that's what he does.

He takes me home. He takes me to the cabin that's been my home ever since I came to find him there a little over two years ago.

In those years, it's changed a lot, the cabin.

Even though we only spend a few weeks here, Graham has

completely renovated it. Moreover, he's done it with his own hands.

It took him two summers – the summer he sent me away before coming back for me, and the summer after that – to renovate the whole place.

But he did it.

He did it all by himself and I know why.

The night he came back for me in Connecticut, he told me he wanted to live in my world. He told me that he was tired of living in a lonely world and he wanted to live in a place where colors were brighter.

Later when he brought me back to the cabin, I told him something else.

I told him that my world had been lonely too. Sure, the colors were bright and dreams were abundant but they didn't have any meaning. They weren't complete. Not until him.

"We should make our own world," I said, kissing him, tangled up in our sheets.

"Yeah?"

"Yup. We should make a place for ourselves. That belongs to just you and me."

"Okay."

I beamed. "And I want a reading nook in that. You have to build me a reading nook where I can read and write in my journal. Oh and also like, a way to get up to the roof so we can watch the moon together."

He grazed his thumb on the corner of my mouth, mapping out my smile. "I'll keep that in mind, Jailbait."

"You do that, Strawberry Man."

And like all his other promises, he kept that one too.

He made me a new world, our world.

This shiny, new cabin, in the middle of the woods, with a reading nook in our bedroom and a ladder that goes up to the roof.

But mostly, we have a huge rose garden, and that's where I find him hours later.

After that kiss at the grocery store, he brought me back home in record time. By then, our desire was so palpable and strong that he fucked me in the truck. He told me to dance on his cock and I did. I writhed and rocked and kissed him, giving him a lap dance while he rode my pussy from below.

When we finally made it inside the cabin, he took my ass in the shower. It was slow and intense like all things with him. Once my beast is satiated for a bit, he goes all lazy and cuddly, and I can't stop playing with his beard.

He fed me after that and ever since then, I've been sleeping. Until I woke up a minute ago to find that his side of the bed is empty and the moon is lit up in the sky like a light bulb.

A bulb that's illuminating the contours of my husband's bent body.

He's got his usual t-shirt on – I stole his plaid shirt after the shower – and his plaid pajamas and he's gathering roses from his garden.

His garden.

Something he told me that he started doing because he could use it as an excuse to watch me.

It's not an excuse anymore though.

It's his dream.

Yeah, this. Roses.

Just like it took me months to calm my anxiety down to a level that I could get out of the house, it took him months to remember his dream.

"Roses," he whispered one night after we'd just made love.

He was over me, all sweaty and hot when he lifted himself up on his elbows and said, "I've been having this... recurring dream. About my mother. I'm about five or something and my father and me, we're picking roses for her. And when I give them to her, she smiles."

My thighs that were still around his hips, tightened and I cupped his jaw. "Really?"

"Yeah. I think..." He swallowed, giving me a vulnerable look that tugged at my heart. "I think it's real. It's a memory and I'm dreaming about it. I think... I want that."

"Roses?"

"Yeah."

I knew that crying would fuck with his head – he'd told me – but I couldn't stop myself. I burst out crying like an idiot and he had to console me for the next ten minutes.

When I got myself under control, I said, "Let's do it then. Let's build the biggest rose garden in our new world."

And we did.

Not only that though, the gardening books that I found stacked in a corner in his closet? Turns out, those are an extension of his dream.

My big, bad husband wants to own a nursery of roses and he's even working toward it. This rose garden is the testament to that. He started expanding it right after he told me about his dream. And ever since last fall, he's been supplying fresh roses to some of the local flower shops.

Since we live in Denver most of the time where he also works as a coach to a high school football team, he has a couple of guys working for him at the garden. They started helping him out as a favor until Graham could pay them.

One of them is my pen pal, Billy. I finally met him and he's hilarious. He told me a lot of stories from the drunk days of Graham's – both funny and tragic – and I swear I'm so glad that those days are behind us.

Anyway, it makes me smile every time I think of my beast working reverently with something so fragile and delicate. Something that's his dream.

Like he's doing right now.

He's clipping thorns from them and cutting off the stems gently, and I know why.

I climb down the steps of the back door and approach him. He hears me, obviously and stands up.

When he faces me, I notice that he has a bunch of roses collected and he's holding them in his big, rough hands.

Hands that I've always loved so much.

"Are they for me?" I ask when I reach him.

Summer breeze – yeah, there's a breeze now and also sunshine in our part of the world – ruffles his dark hair as he takes me in, in his plaid shirt and sneakers.

His eyes roam over my body lazily, waking up goosebumps along the way.

When at last, he comes back to my eyes, he takes one of the flowers from the bundle and traces the side of my cheek with it. I have to curl my toes at that. At his both tender and seductive move.

"Yeah."

"What's the occasion?" I tease.

He reaches the side of my mouth and traces the curve of my lips as he makes me wait for his answer. He studies it, the curve and seam of my mouth for a second before bending down.

"It's my baby's birthday," he whispers, his eyes all penetrating and intense. "Happy twenty-first birthday, Violet."

Gosh, he's always the first to wish me a happy birthday.

These days, there are a lot of people who do and they'll all call me tomorrow, but his wish is the only wish I look forward to the most.

His wish is the only one that makes my heart beat faster.

Smiling, I take the roses from his hands, including the one he was tracing my mouth with. I bury my face in the blooms and smell them, their scent hitting me so strongly that I have to sigh.

"Thank you," I whisper. "But that's not the only occasion, is it?"

His eyes flick back and forth between mine, his tone both rough and teasing. "What's the other occasion?"

I raise my eyebrows at him. "Remember your gift from last year? The one you gave me on my twentieth birthday?"

"Why don't you remind me?"

Smiling, I shake my head at him.

It was his gift to me, see.

Our wedding.

We got married last year on my birthday.

It actually started when we saw a bride and a groom outside of a church that we were passing by back in Denver.

At their sight, I just stopped. I don't know why but the bride was so pretty and glowing in her white dress and the groom couldn't take his eyes off her. And there were so many roses, all pink and red and beautiful.

In that moment, standing there, watching them laugh and kiss, I saw a dream with open eyes.

I daydreamed about Graham and me. I wanted us to be that one day.

I wanted me to wear a white dress and him in a black suit and I wanted to be surrounded by his roses, holding hands and kissing.

Of course, I never said anything to him but who am I kidding? He guessed and a few weeks later, he proposed.

I told him no and I kept telling him that up until the wedding day. Which he decided on and made all the arrangements for on his own; picked out a dress for me too, on his own.

"I'm not going to marry you just because you think that's what I want," I almost shouted at him on the wedding day.

"Good. Because I'm marrying you because that's what I want," he countered.

"But we never even talked about it before I saw that bride and groom."

He exhaled a large breath, giving me a turbulent look. "Don't you get it, yet?"

"Get what?"

"I'm not a dreamer, Violet," he snapped, running a hand through his thick hair. "I told you. I don't have dreams like you. I don't close my eyes and automatically see what I want. I don't automatically want something. I have to learn to want it. It takes time for me to learn to want it. And when I saw you, all choked up and emotional, high on your goddamn teenage hormones while you were staring at them, I got jealous, okay? I got so fucking jealous because you'd never looked like that with me. I got jealous that your eyes were all shiny and bright and stunning because of something that didn't involve me. And that's when it hit me. It hit me that I wanted that, you understand? I wanted that look from you. I wanted to *put* that look in your eyes where your eyes shine so bright that my chest hurts from it, okay?"

I went all silent after that, all speechless but he kept going.

"I want that look from you, Violet. I want it and I'm going to put that look in your eyes whether *you* want it or not, got that? Now come on, I'm running out of patience here. I've heard a thousand goddamn *nos* from you in the past one month and I'm going to lose it now."

Oh Jesus.

What else could I do but walk up to him and tell him that he was an idiot. That he had no reason to be jealous. That the reason I had that look in my eyes was because I was daydreaming about him and me.

When I told him the last part, his nostrils flared and he went for me.

He threw me over his shoulder and brought me back to his rose garden, where a priest was waiting for us along with Richard

– thank God, their friendship is still going strong and didn't get ruined because of that almost panic attack incident, Brian and Billy.

And that's how we got married: him in a black suit and me in shorts and a t-shirt because he didn't give me enough time to wear the white dress he bought me.

It's okay though. I wore the white dress later that night.

In this moment, I step up to him.

I get on his feet and wind my free arm, the one that's not holding the roses he picked out for me, around his neck.

His hands settle on my waist and my body goes flush with his.

And the roses?

They get trapped between us like they did on my eighteenth birthday.

Craning my neck up, I say, "I'm sorry I kept saying no to you."

"A thousand times," he growls, squeezing my waist.

I guess, he's still kinda pissed about that. "I was scared that you were scared."

His eyes go all liquid at that. All liquid and emotional and beautiful. "I was. I am. But you inspire me to be brave, remember?"

I swallow. "Yeah. You inspire me to be brave too."

An emotion ripples through his features and I rise up on my tiptoes to press a soft kiss on his beard. "Happy first wedding anniversary, honey."

"Yeah. It's that."

"Oh, that reminds me. Don't be an ass to my mom tomorrow when she calls, okay? Be nice."

He gives me a blank look but his jaw tics.

Yeah, he does not like my mom and she doesn't like him. She still thinks he'll leave me brokenhearted even though, we're married now and it's been two years since he came back for me and I left Connecticut to be with him. And he hasn't forgiven or forgotten her years of neglect.

But I don't want them fighting over me.

"Come on. It's a big day." I bite my lip and peek up at him through my eyelashes. "It could be your gift to me."

His eyes narrow in a familiar dangerous and delicious way. "I thought my gift to you was reading that crazy Bukowski guy."

"Hey, he's not crazy. He's my favorite writer. Besides, he was the one who made me kiss you that night."

He brings his face closer to mine. "How's that?"

I can't believe I never told him this story. "Well, he said to find that one thing in the world that we love and then let it kill us. I'd already found that one thing in the world that I loved. You know, when I was sixteen. So I figured that at eighteen, I'd steal a kiss from you and let you kill me."

"Yeah?"

"Yup."

He comes even closer to me, closer and closer, until he's blocking the moon and all the light of the world.

Until he's all I see.

"How about I just kiss you back this time?"

Laughing with my whole heart, I go for another kiss on the night of my yet another birthday. The roses are still trapped between us and I'm still standing up on his feet.

The only difference is that these roses are fresh and velvety, instead of dying and rejected, and he's kissing me back.

Oh and we're kissing in our world.

A world we've built on love and dreams.

A world where he's mine and I'm his.

Forever and ever.

***

Graham

People go through lives barely living.

They never go crazy.

They never crave something to the point of pain.

Their chest never hurts at the sight of someone.

They don't write in diaries. They don't collect dreams in their big, fat hobo. They don't create new worlds. They don't stare at the moon and they don't climb up to the roof at midnight. They don't jump in the water with their clothes on and they don't fall in love with someone at first sight.

I could've been one of those people.

I could've lived a dull, ordinary life but she came along and changed everything.

Because of her I tasted the snow last winter. Because of her I read poetry in front of the fire one night.

Because of her I dance with her at midnight to the songs from her kickass playlist. And because of her, instead of running inside when it rains, I stand on my spot and let the drops drench me.

But most of all, because of her, I'm learning to dream. A thing people wonder about.

I'm learning to want and desire and crave.

I'm learning to live.

Because she's a girl made of moon and magic. She's a girl who has streaks of gold in her thick hair, red as fuck lips. And she's a girl who glows in the moonlight.

A girl I've loved since the first time I saw her.

My beauty.

My Violet.

THE END

Acknowledgements

My husband: As always, he's my strength and my reason to do all of this. Thank you for being my very first and true champion.

My parents and my sister: Thank you for being so supportive and enthusiastic about my very unconventional career choice.

Sophia Karlson: Thank you for your time and invaluable suggestions that made this manuscript shine.

Bella Love: Thank you for being my friend right from the start and sticking with me through the good and the bad. And thank you for reading the book and giving me your amazing feedback.

Danielle Sanchez: I'm so glad that we crossed paths earlier this year. You're so innovative and talented, and I'm so happy to have you in my corner.

Melissa Panio-Peterson: Thank you for always being my cheerleader. I adore you and your enthusiasm.

My team: Najla Qamber – my cover designer who made this gorgeous cover; Leanne Rabesa – for always cleaning up manuscripts and keeping track of timelines and seasons; Virginia Tesi Carey – for being so easygoing about things and for a keen eye that catches everything.

My readers: I want to thank all my readers (blogging and non-blogging) for always supporting me and taking the time to read my words. You guys put a smile on my face every day.

Made in United States
North Haven, CT
13 December 2021